The

S.J.A. Turney is an author of Roman and medieval historical fiction, gritty historical fantasy and rollicking Roman children's books. He lives with his family and extended menagerie of pets in rural North Yorkshire.

Also by S.J.A. Turney

Tales of the Empire

Interregnum
Ironroot
Dark Empress
Insurgency
Invasion
Jade Empire
Emperor's Bane

The Ottoman Cycle

The Thief's Tale
The Priest's Tale
The Assassin's Tale
The Pasha's Tale

The Knights Templar

Daughter of War
The Last Emir
City of God
The Winter Knight
The Crescent and the Cross
The Last Crusade

Wolves of Odin

Blood Feud
The Bear of Byzantium

THE **BEAR** OF BYZANTIUM

BYZANTIUM

S.J.A. TURNEY

Welcome to the city of Gold!

[signature]

2/9/2017.

CANELO

First published in the United Kingdom in 2022 by

Canelo
Unit 9, 5th Floor
Cargo Works, 1–2 Hatfields
London, SE1 9PG
United Kingdom

A CIP catalogue record for this book is available from the British Library.

Print ISBN 978 1 80032 130 4
Ebook ISBN 978 1 80032 129 8

Look for more great books at www.canelo.co

Printed and bound in Great Britain by Clays Ltd, Elcograf S.p.A.

I

*In memory of that most erudite and entertaining of all Vikings,
Robert Low.*

I'll see you in Valhalla, my friend.

The Norns did both good and evil, great toil they created for me.

Christian-era runestone of Þórir from Borgund, Norway

A note on pronunciation

Wherever possible within this tale, I have adhered to the Old Norse spellings and pronunciations of Viking names, concepts and words. There is a certain closeness to be gained from speaking these names as they would have been spoken a thousand years ago. For example, I have used Valhöll rather than Valhalla, which is more ubiquitous now, but they refer to the same thing. There is a glossary of Norse terms at the back of the book.

Two letters in particular may be unfamiliar to readers. The letter ð (eth) is pronounced in Old Norse as 'th', as you would pronounce it in 'the' or 'then', but in many cases over the centuries has been anglicised as a 'd'. So, for example, you will find Harald Hardrada's name written in the text as Harðráði (pronounced Har-th-rar-thi) but it can be read as Hardradi for ease. Similarly, Seiðr can be read as seithr or seidr. The letter æ (ash) is pronounced 'a' as in cat, or bat.

Prologue

'One more push and they could break,' Valgarðr bellowed over the din of battle, elbowing a man aside to swing his giant axe. The six-foot haft swung like a deadly pendulum, his hands sliding easily along it to increase the momentum, and the finely etched iron blade slammed down into one of the Bulgar warriors, cleaving through flesh, muscle and bone as if they were butter. As the man fell away and Valgarðr hauled the great weapon back, the commander by his side grunted.

'They'll fight hard before they break, old man,' Harðráði breathed. 'The lake and the royal guard both block their rear, and their king has filled the flanks with solid men too. There is nowhere for this lot to go but through us.'

With that, his own axe – a shorter, bearded one – swung out, slamming against a shield and knocking it aside long enough for the sword in his other hand to slam into the soft leather covering the man's torso, punching through the toughened fabric and into the vital matter inside.

'Then we're fucked,' Valgarðr said in a matter-of-fact tone.

'We are *Varangoi*,' Harðráði replied with a snarl. 'The emperor is on the field, and while he stands, so do we. If you die now, old man, I will hunt you down in the afterlife and kick seven shades of shit out of you.'

His second-in-command laughed raucously and pushed another man aside to make room for his great axe. Above, the grey clouds of morning that had threatened rain finally cleared, and weak sun shone through like a lighthouse in the mist. The Bulgars seethed forward, this rabble at the centre their poorest fare, levies from farms and hard-recruited alley-refuse armed with whatever could be spared. The heavy troops fought on the flanks, where the generals of the Byzantine army pushed their formidable troops to finish the job and quell this revolt once and for all. But Harðráði had his eyes set on one figure. Beyond the rabble in front of them stood the *karls* who formed the guard of the Bulgar usurper king, and there, visible to all in his grisly glory, sat their master on a warhorse, gesturing with a sword as though he could see what was happening around him.

He could not, of course.

Delyan the Upstart had been mutilated a few months past, his nose hacked from his face and his eyes put out with a sharp knife. Yet Harðráði had to give the man his due. There he sat, leading his men in the last battle, his face a contorted mask around a malformed, bloodied hole, hollow black sockets on show as he turned this way and that, yelling orders. Even Harðráði, brave as he was, suspected he might not show such courage in those circumstances. Still, it wouldn't help the royal *draugr* in the long run, for his death would end this, and so he must fall.

'We're being pushed back,' one of his men yelled, before disappearing among the brawl with a cry of pain, a Bulgarian sword rising and falling above him in a spray of blood.

'The emperor has our back,' Valgarðr replied as he swung once again, accidentally catching one of his own men a glancing blow with the butt end of his great axe, and raising a curse with it.

'The emperor is not the one directing the reserves,' noted Harðráði, glancing over his shoulder. There, a good safe distance back from the fighting, a block of steel and leather stood waiting, shoulder to shoulder – the reserves under the command of Romanos Skleros. The Byzantine nobleman led fully half the Varangians as well as a sizeable military force.

Harðráði's contingent were running deeper into trouble by the heartbeat, and the reserves had yet to move, despite the flanks being under very little pressure.

'The reserves will help us. Ari is with him,' Valgarðr replied.

'Ari is a pompous shit,' Harðráði snorted.

'He's a pompous shit, but he's *our* pompous shit.'

Harðráði made a noncommittal noise. If the reserves were going to be committed, they should have been by now. Someone must have given the order to hold back. 'We have to end this ourselves,' he snarled. 'No help is coming.'

'But Ari...?'

'Fuck Ari. On me,' Harðráði shouted, waving the sword above his head. A roar went up from the rest of his men and he grinned, blood framing his teeth from where he'd bitten his tongue earlier, in the excitement. There was no better unit to lead than these men.

Varangians, the Byzantine emperor's personal guard.

He'd been only vaguely aware of their existence six years ago, when he'd come south and signed on among their number, kneeling like a penitent before the ageing empress. He'd been made *akolouthos* immediately, as was appropriate given his status and royal lineage, and within the year had taken command of the Varangians, which was when he had truly come to know their mettle. Six thousand strong, the unit was comprised wholly of men either from the northern Baltic – Norway, Sweden and Denmark – or of *Rus* origin from Kiev. Just as a man might expect, they retained the fierce pride of the Northmen, yet they were more than the sum of their parts, their impressive warrior skills hardened and focused by the Byzantines. For in the empire they had learned to fight not just for personal gain or for reputation, but as part of an organised force. An army.

The Guard fought here, on this field, for the emperor and for their commander, and while any other Byzantine unit might have broken and fled under such pressure, that was not the way of the Varangians. Until the emperor said 'turn', every man here would face down the enemy until he was either victorious or dead.

As the men of the Guard surged forward behind him, Harald Harðráði, son and grandson of kings, commander of the imperial guard, shouted something that would have made the empress blush, and pushed forward. His men followed with a roar, allowing their famous commander to form the sharp point of the wedge. A fresh push.

That was the thing about battle. After a while you fell into a rhythm, and it became almost second nature. Harðráði had once heard a man trying to remember a poem while fighting for his life, just because his mind had detached itself from the carnage, leaving his body to work on instinct. And so, while the Varangians had been fighting with skill and power, still they were not putting every ounce of their concentration into it. Now, with his command, every mind had focused on the job at hand, and with that came a fresh strength and determination.

Bellowing war cries, some to Christ and some to older, less popular gods, the emperor's guard pushed forward into a suddenly startled mass of Bulgarian levies. The sheer strength and power of the Northmen's push broke their will in an instant. There was nowhere for the poor bastards to run, though, and as they tried to flee from this fresh onslaught, they simply met their doom elsewhere, either turning to be cut down by the royal force behind them, or moving to the flanks where they became embroiled instead in another part of the battle.

Still, they melted away to either side from the Varangian push. Harðráði lashed out with his sword, stabbing and hacking, the axe in his other hand chopping and biting, and never did he hold back for fear of striking his own. He was the point of the wedge, the very front of the attack, and any flesh his blades bit into would be that of the enemy.

'The *bastards*,' someone shouted from behind. 'The reserves are *leaving*.'

4

Harald risked a brief glance over his shoulder. He was a tall and imposing figure, and over the heads of his men he could just see the reserves – the remaining half of the Varangians in the field, along with the *excubitor* cavalry – moving to support one of the untroubled flanks. Someone was going to pay for that, Harðráði swore, for leaving them deliberately in the lurch. For now, he had to make sure they won the fight.

Suddenly, he felt the resistance to their push change. The enemy were less of a panicked rabble and more of a wall of steel and leather. The Varangians had forged a path through the levies and come up against the hardened warriors of the king. Briefly, Harðráði caught sight of the nightmare form of Delyan himself, and then the man was lost to view as the Varangian commander was pulled into another fight, harder than ever. The enemy struck and lunged, slashed and chopped, their swords carving bloody chunks from Harðráði's force. The advance of the wedge faltered. They were too few, with no support, facing the core of Delyan's army.

Knowing that the moment they stopped advancing the enemy would gain the upper hand and the battle's flow would change, Harðráði bellowed the cry of his forefathers and pushed on. He felt a sword slash his side and, despite his lamellar armour, he felt a warm, wet response from his flesh, blood leaking out amid the torn linen and scattered bronze scales. He ignored it. His axe slammed into the neck of a man before him, and he pulled, the beard of his axe digging into the man like a fish-hook and yanking him forward where he fell, screaming, beneath Harðráði's trampling feet. The commander's sword slashed, low, slicing a deadly line across a Bulgar's upper thigh, near the groin, where the blood flowed fastest. As the next Bulgar yelled and readied himself, surprised as the warrior in front of him fell, Harðráði struck once more. His head slammed forward, the iron bar of his nose protector smashing into the man's face, splintering bone and ruining him for good.

A second strike almost did for him as a sword came seem-ingly from nowhere and nearly hit him in the throat. At the last moment, the arm bearing the sword was knocked away, and Valgarðr was there, his immense axe cleaving the wielder almost in half. Another Northman was there to his right in another heartbeat. Snarling, Harðráði pushed on. Another Bulgar fell. The Varangian's axe dug deep, drinking blood, his sword drawing lines of red death across figure after figure as he pushed on.

There was King Delyan once more... closer... so *unbearably* close.

He felt another wound, this time on his shoulder, and now when he lifted his axe, the arm felt a little weaker. They had to finish this soon. He knew his force was diminishing rapidly, and if they turned with no support, they would be cut down to a man. A steely determination rose in him once more. He may be a son of the true Church and a servant of the empire, but Harald Sigurdsson, known as the *Harðráði*, the *iron ruler*, was still a child of the North, a descendant of kings, and his ancestors had been Vikings of the hard black mountain coast. He was damned if he was going to end his days here, uncrowned and slain on a Greek field.

His knee connected with the groin of a man who had prepared himself to parry a sword, and, bellowing rage, Harðráði heaved him aside with the hook of his axe and drove his sword into the unprepared warrior behind. Another blow bounced off his already injured shoulder and he saw the watery sunlight flashing from fragments of bronze scales as they were torn away. Then the man responsible was gone, for Valgarðr's great axe was there again, cleaving a path through the enemy. Another man fell, and Harðráði's sword came up spraying blood that spattered across his eyes and made him blink repeatedly.

As his vision cleared, he thanked both Christ and the Holy Mother, for in the fallen warrior's place he could see Delyan, false king of Bulgaria, sitting astride his horse, his unseeing, hideous face turning this way and that as he tried in his way to keep track of the battle. The usurper somehow sensed the danger, perhaps hearing Harðráði's constant stream of curses, for those hollow sockets turned with ponderous slowness to face him.

Delyan sensed his enemy, and his sword came round.

Harðráði gave him no time. His axe slashed out, hacking into the king's leg just above the knee, deep enough to cut into bone. The king screamed as his leg broke and tore, muscle and flesh separating as he fell from the far side of his horse, leaving half the appendage in place.

A strange, shocked silence fell among the Bulgars across the field at the sight of their king vanishing from his horse, but Harðráði knew it couldn't finish there. For the battle to end, the usurper had to die. Valgarðr, appearing from nowhere, suddenly had the horse's reins, half a leg still flapping around in the stirrup, pulling the animal aside to reveal the fallen, grisly, maimed king, struggling in the mud, blind and ruined. Delyan knew his doom stood over him. His hands came up imploringly. His voice, little more than a croak, began to offer everything: gold, lands, titles, even the throne.

Harðráði's sword slammed down into that ruined face, pinning him to the churned, bloody turf.

Delyan the usurper died within heartbeats, and the moan of dismay spread out through the Bulgarian army like the ripples from a stone cast into a still pond.

The Bulgar army broke.

The battle was over.

–

'Don't do anything stupid,' Valgarðr urged, gripping Harðráði's shoulder as he stomped past, his face white with anger. The commander said nothing in reply, simply tore his arm free and marched on, tucking his blood-coated axe in the back of his belt, sword still out and dripping.

Ari Karsten, *primikerios* in the Guard, stood with his hands on his hips watching the aftermath with an air of disconnected satisfaction. Varangians stood in clusters behind him, while the *strategos*, Romanos Skleros, sat astride his horse nearby, dictating to a secretary. The emperor himself sat not far off, looking surprisingly martial and regal for a man so ill he almost hadn't made it across Bulgaria.

Ari turned at the sound of Harðráði's approach, and his expression slid from satisfaction to distaste in a moment. The commander, even in the grip of rage, noted that and filed it away in his memory for the future. The primikerios made no move to get out of the way – a brave decision, given how Harðráði must look, furious and blood-soaked. The commander stormed up to Ari and his free hand came up, grabbing the edge of the chain hood that sat across the man's shoulders and upper chest. Harðráði's fingers knitting in the steel armour, he jerked Ari towards him.

'Explain yourself.'

'Explain what, precisely?' Ari replied with a curling lip.

'You address me by my rank, or sir, and show some fucking deference or I will add you to the line over there,' Harðráði snapped, using his sword to point to the hill overlooking the stinking battlefield. Ari followed the gesture, his distaste growing. All along the hill, like some grisly hedge, scores of Bulgarian officers and nobles, those who had led the army and the revolt it was part of, had been lashed to stakes. Then, kindling and brush had been packed around each base, and the burnings had begun. The screams of those tortured by the flames were only slightly louder than the screams of panic from those strapped tight and awaiting their fate.

'Explain what, precisely, *sir*?' Ari said, tearing his gaze from the horror that Harðráði had visited upon the captured Bulgarians.

'Explain why, when my force was outnumbered, outflanked, and fighting for their lives, the reserves, including fully half my Varangians, went to help the flank where there was no danger whatsoever? You go too far this time, Ari.'

The primikerios pulled himself free of his commander's grip and stepped back, teeth bared. He growled. 'Commander you may be, but I was serving here while you were still stuck to your mother's tit, *sir*. The next time you grab me like that, I will break both your wrists.'

The two men glared at one another for a time, a battle of wills from which neither was about to back down. Finally, Ari looked away, towards the Byzantine officers nearby.

'Your quarrel is with Skleros. In your absence, he was the senior commander present, and his was the order to commit the reserves elsewhere.'

Harðráði maintained his piercing gaze for a few moments before shifting it to the general on his horse. He did not like Skleros, and never had. The man was a courtier, not a soldier. He had as much grasp of military tactics as a three-legged goat, yet his eminence had bought him a position in the army's command, for the emperor favoured him, or so it was said. Harðráði knew otherwise. The emperor trusted Skleros no further than he could safely throw a horse. Skleros was oily enough in his own right, but his family had made a play for power not too long ago, and any emperor wishing to stay safely seated on his throne kept his enemies close. Expediency was the only reason Skleros was here. With one last glare cast like a throwing knife at the insolent Varangian, Harðráði turned and marched on the general.

The man should have managed to look superior, given that he wore ornate armour that harkened back to the days of old Rome, that he sat above Harðráði on horseback, and that a snap of his fingers could see most men peeled and left for dead. In fact, he looked nervous as the commander of the imperial guard stomped towards him, quivering with rage, sword in hand. Skleros recovered himself in time to plaster an imperious and aloof expression over his fear.

'What is it, commander?'

Harðráði threw out his hand angrily, the tip of his sword almost jabbing into the general's side. 'We were hard pressed, and the battle hinged on our success. Why did you commit the reserves elsewhere?'

Skleros' lip wrinkled. 'You were in no danger. Ari confirmed that you had sufficient force to overcome the centre, and there was a danger on the flank, for the emperor was close to the fray. It is my place to protect imperial interests, rather than thieves and Nordic vagabond mercenaries.'

Harðráði's eyes narrowed. 'I've killed men for less than those words.'

'I do not doubt it, yet it is true. All of Byzantium knows of your thievery, Aráltes Harðráði. The treasury has been losing funds steadily since the day you took office.'

'Which happens to be the same time the emperor came to power, along with his criminal brothers and certain other snakes of the court.'

Skleros snorted. 'You deflect the blame onto those who accuse you? I wonder, if we were to count the ships that leave the city every month, full of gold and bound for Kiev, would we find the sum missing from the treasury?'

'The gold I ship north is my own, gained from imperial donatives and battlefield loot, nothing more. Unlike pampered Byzantines, I do not spend every coin I earn on whores, wine and womanish silk garments.' To emphasise his words, his wavering sword point took in the ornate armour and the silk and velvet clothes poking around the edges of it. 'When my command ends, I shall be a king in the North; thrones are easier to win with gold than with steel.'

'Barbarian.'

'A man might also point out that it was the greed and lust for gold of the emperor's brother Constantine that triggered this entire revolt and led to the wars we now fight. And I would be willing to wager that your fingers were dancing in the same pot as Constantine's.'

'You are a mercenary. Gold is the entire reason you came south and the reason you took your commission.'

Harðráði ground his teeth. 'My loyalty is to the emperor himself. I find it a shame that he seems incapable of identifying the thieves and criminals within his own court and family who weaken his position day by day. Constantine has become a very rich man off the confiscation of other men's estates, after all.'

'Your loyalty is not to the emperor,' Skleros spat. 'All know that it was the empress to whom you knelt, and she to whom you owe your position.'

'Slide off that fucking horse, and I will wipe that smug smirk from your face, Skleros.'

The clearing of a throat attracted their attention, and both faces turned to the new arrival. They had been so caught up in their argument that they had not noticed the emperor and his entourage plodding calmly in their direction. As the master of the civilised world halted his mount, an unreadable expression on his face, Harðráði swiftly ran through everything he'd just said, realising now that he'd said it all within earshot of the emperor. He winced inwardly as he remembered some of his words. And, damn the man, Skleros had been careful to keep his accusations and comments clear of imperial blame.

'It is not seemly that two of my most senior commanders bicker and quarrel like fishwives in front of the army,' the emperor said. Harðráði looked up at him and shivered. Michael the Paphlagonian, emperor of Byzantium, was dying, and everyone could see it. He was pale as porcelain and his flesh had sunk into his bones, giving him the appearance of the walking dead. Still, his voice was imperious and confident, and here, near the end, Harðráði could see a hint of why the empress had chosen him for a husband.

As both Skleros and Harðráði bowed their heads in the imperial presence, the emperor's eyebrow arched. 'There is work yet to do, both here and at home.' He shared a look with Skleros that Harðráði really did not like, and straightened in his saddle. 'Araltes, whom they call Harðráði, you have ever been a faithful and strong commander of my Guard, but your tongue is often barbed and unchecked, and you lack sufficient finesse for court life. I think that perhaps it might be a good idea if you were absent from court for a time. We are entreated by Prince Demetrios of Georgia. He is engaged in a dangerous civil war with his half-brother, Bagrat, who threatens imperial interests in that important land. Your talent for winning wars might be better served destroying Bagrat and his faction than causing friction within the imperial court. Who knows, perhaps the treasury might even heal itself in your absence.'

Harðráði felt the anger wash over him afresh, but he had been in Constantinople long enough to know when to hold his temper. Fighting down the rage that threatened to erupt, he simply bowed his head, noting as he did the smug satisfaction on Skleros' face.

'The Guard will be in safe hands with Valgarðr,' he replied carefully, 'and I shall win your war and return within the year.'

'I think it would be better to take that great axe-wielding maniac with you,' Skleros said, earning a nod of approval from the emperor. 'Your third-in-command, Ari Karsten, will be perfectly adequate to command in your absence. He is more familiar with court etiquette with his long service, after all.'

Before Harðráði could erupt once more, he felt a hand on his shoulder and looked around to see Valgarðr, a warning on his face. With a bow to the emperor, he turned and walked away, the old Varangian with his enormous axe stumping alongside.

'Who gives a shit about some civil war in a provincial back-water,' Harðráði snarled. 'This is shuffling us out of the way so that they can continue their theft and corruption and further work to blacken my name.'

Valgarðr nodded. 'Then we should work to win this war as quickly as possible and get back to the city. Who knows, we might make allies among the Georgians through this, and that could work to your advantage in the long run.'

Harðráði just nodded, his gaze rising to the scores of burning Bulgarians on the hill, then back to Ari, who had been summoned to the imperial presence. 'One day, he and I will come to blows,' Harðráði hissed, 'and then he will wish his fate had been as simple as theirs.'

Part One

ᚠᛟᛚᚠᛖᛗᛋ ᛟᚠ ᛟᛝᛁᛏ

The Golden City

Chapter 1

'Slow now, lads,' Ulfr called, 'and bring us to port a touch. Mind those rocks.'

Gunnhild watched the town slide towards them with a mix of intrigue and ennui. All these Byzantine ports seemed to be the same: a cluster of brick structures around a heart of white marble, poor folk gathered around a rich elite. A port filled with trade ships and fishermen overseen by stuffy, over-dressed officials with endless papers. Occasional fights, gleaming imperial soldiers watching, too important to involve themselves in petty brawling. In some ways they were like ports all over the world, she mused, though like everything Byzantine, over the centuries an administration had evolved to control and record every breath the city took. It was cloying, to say the least.

'A bear,' she muttered, looking down at the bones, which had clearly formed an ursine shape on the deck. As Halfdan plodded towards her across the boards, she quickly swept the scattered items up and dropped them back into her pouch. Secrets were only secrets if you kept them, and the power was not to be explained to others. Besides, the visions had been varied and confused lately.

'What have you seen?' Halfdan asked quietly.

She looked up, then rose from her crouch, gathering up her staff as she did so. Halfdan was smiling. She liked him. Not in *that* way, of course. She was not made for hearth and bed, but for spear and song. But still, she liked him more than most, and he was a good man, which made what was to come all the more troubling.

'Our road continues on beyond Amastris, but some threads of the weaving change here. They fold into another tale, I think.'

A bear.

'We will lose men?' he said, with a touch of anxiety. 'Will we find new ones? We have thirty-eight aboard now, and we cannot easily crew the *Sea Wolf* with fewer.'

Why did he always expect detail and such certainty? That was not how it worked. 'It is... complicated,' she said. 'The weaving changes, but I do not think we need fear this place. I do not see danger here.'

Bears are not dangerous?

She pushed down the voice in her heart.

Halfdan nodded. 'We must restrain Bjorn this time. That last place cost us dearly in reparations.'

Gunnhild looked across the ship to where the big albino was busy rowing with one hand so that he could drink with the other, and gave a weary smile. 'You might as well try to hold back the tide, Halfdan.'

He laughed. He had an easy laugh. Gods, but he was a glowing coal in her cold heart some days.

Gunnhild felt *un*-easy, and only part of that was the uncertainty they faced every day. Given they had been fighting on opposite sides at Sasireti so recently, it had been decided that it would be better not to bump into the Varangians until they reached *Miklagarðr* itself. Consequently, the crew had been following Harðráði and his Varangians carefully back from Georgia, using the same ports and often just one day behind the famous commander.

Part of it, too, was her castings. All the way around the south coast she had been trying to divine what was to come. It was more difficult without a specific answer to seek. When she had been following the weaving of Yngvar the past few years, a goal had been part of her questions. Now, she simply looked into an open future and tried to see what she could. She had been disconcerted by what she had found, though. The strand of her weaving would separate from those of Halfdan and the others. Her threads came adrift, and she could not see far enough to tell whether they could be brought back into the pattern. That made her shiver: to be so far from all that was familiar, and to be separated from the others.

Another part of it, for certain, was the fear of losing the *Seiðr*. She had been taught the ways by the old *völva*, but not fully so. She had some sight and some skills, but she had been torn from the old woman's side before she could learn all. And the compound that helped bring the sight remained a mystery, its ingredients and composition unknown to her still. Her fingers went to the precious pouch containing the meagre remaining supply. When that was done, so too was her sight. She couldn't tell Halfdan of that worry, though, for the compound was as much part of the secret as the skill of bones, or the cadence of the world-song. It was the goddess's gift to give, not Gunnhild's.

Many worries. Much uneasiness.

She continued to fret at these things like a child at a frayed tunic hem while Halfdan, satisfied, turned his attention to the port of Amastris that slid towards them. The town's citadel occupied a headland — more of an island, really — connected to the mainland by a wide spit upon which most of the urban mass sat, a harbour at each side. As with every stop on their journey, they had learned of Amastris at the previous port the night before, and so they had a tavern already in mind for the night. Most of the crew would stay aboard, of course, for there was treasure on the ship to be guarded these days, but half a dozen of them would head into the city and learn what they could in preparation for the next day's sail. Four more sunsets would see them in the great city...

...where Gunnhild's threads would come loose.

She was still picking at the scab of her fate when the ship bumped against the dock and men ran out ropes and secured the *Sea Wolf* to shore. She chewed her lip as Halfdan, Leif and Ketil negotiated with the port officials, filling in the endless forms, paying the fees and slipping the ubiquitous backhander to the pompous fat man. She huffed as the crew settled and her friends stepped down to the dock, and only returned to the present world when Halfdan called for her.

'Are you coming?'

With a nod, she hopped from the ship and joined them on the jetty, striding along as they made their way up into the city. As they navigated the winding streets she occasionally felt odd sensations, as she had done in all these towns. The places were Byzantine, and so to a man their populations, followed the nailed god, but just a few centuries ago they had had their own old gods, and the temples of those powers were still here, either shattered and ignored, repurposed into Christian churches, or sometimes surviving as fragments of colonnades in the sides of houses. And while the Byzantines treated them as little more than shells or quarries, Gunnhild could feel the Seiðr still wreathing those ancient stones.

She tore her gaze from one such ruin as they rounded a corner to see the inn that was their destination. Like most of its kind, it was warm and welcoming in a stuffy, overly organised way, and its nature was broadcast by the sign above the door, which usually showed grapes in some form or other. She felt a shiver of Seiðr as her gaze fell upon this sign. A painted bear gripped the bunch of grapes above some Greek name she did not recognise. Her eyes shot to Halfdan, striding along unconcerned, but she could say nothing. She had nothing yet to say.

Halfdan was the first to enter. It had become the unwritten rule. He was their *jarl*, and it was his place to lead. Bjorn would come last, for he could hold off any pursuit. But the second was always Gunnhild, out of respect, not for her sex, of course, but for her power. That was why she was the second to see what awaited them and to understand at least part of her visions.

A dozen Northmen in impressive bronze and steel armour, with colourful tunics and well-groomed hair and beards, stood around the bar, one greybeard leaning with crossed arms on an axe almost as tall as he was. In the centre of the room sat a table, and at that table sat a man. He was tall, and dressed much the same as those around him, yet he exuded an aura of power that hit Gunnhild like a wall. His fair, golden hair and beard were braided, his eyes ice blue, and he sat with an easy confidence as though he had been here since the world was made, and the inn had been built around him for his convenience.

He was a bear. He was *the* bear, she was sure.

And she was equally sure that this was Harðráði, whom they had been following all the way from Georgia.

The Sea Wolves' hands went immediately to the weapons at their belts, but stopped there as the big man with the axe shook his head meaningfully, and the creak of bowstrings drew their attention to Northmen in the corners, arrow tips trained on the newcomers. These men might look at ease, but one wrong move and arrows would fly.

The big blond Varangian pushed out his foot, sliding a chair back opposite him, clearly an invitation. He was not smiling, though, and the invitation was not one expected to be declined. Halfdan looked around the others, shrugged, strode over and dropped into the seat opposite. The rest of them followed, protectively, keeping close by, their eyes on those straining archers. Bjorn took up a place facing the old man with the giant axe, his face grave, Leif close by. Ketil and Ulfr moved to the far side of the table and stood, arms folded, like sentinels. Gunnhild, as was expected, moved to Halfdan's shoulder.

Harðráði's gaze slipped from Halfdan to her, and she saw a curiosity in it, and something else, something a little unsettling. The Varangian suddenly smiled and gestured to another seat. She shook her head and stayed where she was, raising a shrug from the golden Varangian. His smile vanished again as his gaze returned to Halfdan. There was an odd silence, broken suddenly by Harðráði.

'You have been following us.' The statement was made in the Norse tongue, and it had been so long since they had heard a stranger speak their own language that it took moments for them all to adjust their thinking out of the now-common Greek.

Halfdan said nothing. Silence returned until the Varangian continued.

'I was prepared to believe that you were sailing in our wake for simple safety, given that no pirate of this black sea would be foolish enough to attack a squadron of imperial *dromon* bearing the flag of the Guard. But now we are closing on Constantinople, and so I am forced to conclude that there is something more to this. You seem confident and competent, but you are in my world now, *Gotlander*, and you are out of your depth. Speak, for my archers' arms are tiring.'

After a short pause, Halfdan reached across and took one of the half dozen glasses from the table, taking the jar of wine in front of Harðráði and pouring himself a drink. It was a statement, an assertion of strength and defiance, and Gunnhild could not have hoped for better. He was becoming a fine jarl. Harðráði's eyebrow rose at the bold move, and Halfdan took a swig of the heady, rich wine, and then placed the glass back down in front of him.

'I am growing to like this drink as time goes on,' he answered in fluent Greek, with something of an eastern accent. Harðráði's arched brow rose a little higher. 'I am not quite as out of my depth as you might imagine,' Halfdan added with a smile.

The Varangian's eyebrow peaked again. 'You are audacious, young Gotlander. My God, but you are. You are so outspoken, foolhardy and insolent, you remind me of... me.' His eyes, momentarily sparkling, hardened again. 'You have not answered my question, and I grow tired of repeating myself, young hero. Why are you following us?'

'We are bound for Miklagarðr. Given that we have been a day behind you throughout, I am intrigued how you became aware of us.'

'You are in the empire now, boy. Nothing remains secret here. Your presence has been broadcast by the signal stations along the coast for a week. Had you been a fleet I would have confronted you sooner, but one ship... I became interested.'

The sound of someone in discomfort drew their attention to the archers, who were throwing meaningful looks at their commander. Harðráði nodded to them, and the arrows were lowered, the strings relaxed, though Gunnhild could still sense the danger in the room. These men could turn deadly very fast.

'And what do you seek in the capital?'

Halfdan looked about him. 'We are of a mind to join your guard.'

Harðráði gave a snort. 'Joining the emperor's finest regiment is not a thing a man simply drifts into because he feels it is a good choice,' the man said, but Gunnhild's attention shifted to the old man with the axe, whose gaze had fallen sharply on Harðráði. The expression of ironic mirth on the old man's face suggested that the commander himself had done much the same thing in his time. Harðráði leaned forward and steepled his fingers on the table. 'A man pays a dividend in gold for entry into the Guard. Acceptance is a thing of honour that must be paid for. And even then a man must be right for the role and acceptable to the commander. Some candidates come from the North with heavy purses and still wait years for their chance, only to be told they are not right. Your audacity is impressive, but audacity is not what we seek.'

Out of the corner of her eye she saw Halfdan twitch. Even from behind she knew he was narrowing his eyes and that he was restraining some acidic comment. Time to save him from himself.

'You lost men at Sasireti,' she said, taking a step forward and addressing Harðráði herself. 'Good men, clearly. I have no idea how many Varangians fell in those woods, but I would be willing to wager that *our* thirty-seven good men would fit easily into the hole they left in your ranks.'

'Sasireti,' Harðráði mused with no sign of surprise.

'It was a bloody affair,' she said, 'and a confused mess, but I am sure that even then you recognised the mettle of your cousins who fought for Bagrat – these men.'

Harðráði unfolded his hands, took a sip of wine and then leaned back, looking now at Gunnhild. 'I had assumed your crew was part of that army, of course. Our kind are not so common down here that we bump into one another on a daily basis. I saw what you did to the Alani. Brave. Stupid, perhaps, but still brave. In fact, if you hadn't turned on your own king, it is possible that the battle could have gone very differently. It is even possible it was your actions that won us Sasireti, and for that, I have to admit my gratitude.'

'Yet with the battle won you departed immediately,' Halfdan put in. 'We all know that a battle is only part of a war, and the king survived. Did you not wish to follow through the aftermath and be sure of your victory?'

Harðráði shrugged. 'Demetrios begged for imperial intervention. We won him his important battle. If he and his pet noblemen cannot secure their victory with Bagrat and his army broken and scattered then he does not deserve the throne and God will decide Georgia's future. I was sent to do a job, and that job is done. Now, Constantinople awaits, and I have unfinished business there.'

Gunnhild placed her palms on the table. 'You will take these men into your Guard, Harald Sigurdsson. I can see your thoughts. You have already made your decision, so stop playing with words and speak plainly.'

Harðráði's eyebrow shot up again as he shifted his attention back to her.

'God, but you are an impressive woman. Are you his?'

Gunnhild frowned. She could feel a flush rising, and that irritated her immensely. Forcing ice cold into her expression, she straightened and folded her arms. 'I am no man's. I am a daughter of Freyja, and Halfdan Loki-born is my jarl. Direct your lust elsewhere, Harðráði.'

The Varangian laughed. 'Pagans, too. I should have realised from the wolves on your jarl's shield. You do well to hide your pendants and idols here. Paganism is not well-liked. If you wish to join the ranks of the Guard, you will need to be careful. You will be expected to kiss the cross and to take your place at all appropriate ceremonies and services. Oh, I don't give two shits what you do in private, and I know damn well that there are a few in our ranks who wear their hammer pendants beneath their tunics, but adherence is expected. The emperor likes to believe his Guard are watched over by the Lord just as much as he is. *When* he is.'

Gunnhild could feel Bjorn's distaste even from where she was standing as Halfdan adjusted his sleeve to make sure his Loki markings were covered. The big man did not like the nailed god, for sure. If there was going to be trouble with this it would come from him. Leif was a follower anyway, Ketil habitually changed his outward faith for expediency, and both Ulfr and Halfdan were bright and flexible enough to appreciate the need. Bjorn, less so. As the big man turned, his mouth opening, Gunnhild shot him a look that silenced him. The albino took on an injured expression and turned back to the greybeard in front of him.

'Your faith is only part of it,' Harðráði added. 'With service you will take an oath of loyalty, and unlike these fickle and ophidian Byzantines, we are men of the North, and we take our oaths seriously. If you join us, I will expect your unflinching loyalty to the emperor, and also to me.'

Halfdan nodded. 'An oath to *two* men is an oath destined to be tested. I do not give my oath lightly, but when I do, I stand by it. My oath has brought me all the way from Uppsala to this place, after all. As for the price you require...'

Harðráði shook his head. 'In your cases, I waive the fee. Currently, for a number of reasons, I am more concerned with loyalty than gold. I will take you and your men, each one, into the Guard, to serve in the first *allagion* under Valgarðr over there.' With this he indicated the old man with the great axe. 'Valgarðr is my second, and I trust no one more. Instead of gold, you buy your commissions with a promise of loyalty.'

Gunnhild frowned now. 'Loyalty should be expected. What are you not telling us, Harðráði? What presses upon you that you seek such assurance?'

Once again, the Varangian shifted his gaze from Halfdan to Gunnhild.

'Byzantium is a seething lake of trouble,' Harðráði said, 'with a thousand currents pulling a man in many directions. Loyalties are bought and sold each day, and a man's friend at sunrise can be his enemy by sunset. It is a fascinating place, but the dangers are a thousand-fold, and even within the Guard there are those who would turn upon their own, were it not for the inviolable oath. I have unfinished business, and I need men upon whom I can rely.'

'Count us among them,' Halfdan said confidently, earning a subtle glance of warning from Gunnhild.

'Good. You will travel the rest of the way with us. The rest of my fleet lies at anchor a mile up the coast. Valgarðr will join you on your ship, along with a few of our men, and he will go through everything in detail, from the barracks to the pay. For now, I am tired from a day's hard sailing, and I wish only the comforts of a cup or five of good wine, a soft bed and a softer woman.' His eyes slid back to Gunnhild once more, and she returned the gaze with a look that confirmed flatly she would not be that woman.

Harðráði laughed, and the room began to move, Varangians relaxing and finding seats, the crew of the *Sea Wolf* gathering together, and as they did so, Leif came to a halt in front of Gunnhild.

'You have not said what *you* will do,' the small Rus noted quietly.

Halfdan, overhearing, blinked, understanding filling his face. 'Yes, I doubt the Guard take women. Foolish. I should have thought of this before. I am so used to you as part of the crew that it simply did not occur to me.'

Gunnhild gave them an easy smile, easier than she *felt*, at least.

'My path is not the same as yours, Halfdan. As any of yours, in fact. My thread comes loose from the weave in the great city, and I have my own fate to follow.'

A look of worry filled the young jarl now. 'No. There will be a way. I can persuade Harðráði. Even if it needs gold. Even if we must play man and wife to make it work. I saw the way he looked at you. He will accommodate...'

'No.' She had seen it. Her thread departed, and nothing she could do would prevent that. 'No, Freyja has her own path for me, and I must tread it. When we reach Miklagarðr, we will separate.'

'And how long until your thread returns?' He must have seen the doubt she felt, for he frowned. 'Your thread *does* return?'

'I cannot say. I cannot see that far. I should not even have seen that much, but caught it while I scried for you. For now I must go my own way, and you must go yours. I am in no immediate danger, though. My thread might diverge from yours, but it goes on.'

Harðráði called to Halfdan then, and the young jarl cast one last worried look at Gunnhild before turning back to the Varangian commander.

–

The room was dim and cold, the shutters closed with only weak moonlight between the cracks illuminating the gloom. The noise of the two groups of Northmen down in the inn below was little more than a rumble and hum of life through the thick floor.

Gunnhild sang under her breath, quietly, the old song lifting her, rising out of this place. The pouch with her precious compound back on her belt, safe, just a light dusting on her tongue all she had needed. The song carried her higher and higher, through the clouds as though she were one of Odin's ravens. She looked down on the wide earth below, her fingers nimbly undoing the string of the other pouch. Out came a handful of bones and coins, silver and beads. She cast them down upon the world, feeling the will of Freyja all across the prickled skin of her hands, like gossamer gloves, guiding the casting, helping her.

She looked at the fallen collection and then closed her eyes, remembering their shape, letting it fit into new patterns behind her eyelids. She was in a pond. Fish swam around her, tiny dull things, bouncing off her, nibbling at her, oblivious as larger fish came closer and began to eat the smaller ones. Gunnhild felt the casting changing. Larger fish now, eating those carnivores, then larger still until finally only one powerful fish remained, looking to her as though for guidance.

Byzantium is a seething lake of trouble... Harðráði... the golden bear...

She awoke with a start, eyes snapping open, a cold shudder racing through her as she plummeted back through the clouds into the world below and was suddenly in the dark room, bones and beads scattered around her. Her head began to thump painfully. It always did after she used the compound, after she sang the song and saw the world of Seiðr.

The great city would be the pond, its people the fish. Gunnhild would somehow be at its centre. It grieved her that she had seen nothing of Halfdan there, and yet it was somehow a relief that she had also seen nothing more of the bear that was Harald Harðráði, for the way he'd looked at her made her distinctly uncomfortable, and the way his analogy of the lake had leaked into her vision was altogether too strange.

Of one thing she was sure: the great city of Miklagarðr, which men called Constantinople, awaited her as much as it did Halfdan.

Chapter 2

'What do you see?' Halfdan said, eyes flicking back and forth between the collection of scattered items on the deck and the great city sliding towards them. A year of watching Gunnhild and her strange Seiðr ways had done nothing to clarify what was actually happening when she walked with her goddess.

'I see a young jarl crowding me and getting in the way. It is hard to concentrate when you stand over me,' Gunnhild replied irritably. Halfdan sighed. She had been getting steadily more irritable and secretive all the way along the coast, and seemed increasingly reticent when it came to consulting the Seiðr. It was as though her imminent separation had already begun, in spirit at least.

Of all things new, that was the one Halfdan truly dreaded. Enemies, hardships, the unknown, all could be taken in his stride, but these five people had been with him since they had left the cold north lands. They were his armour, his shield, his axe and his wisdom, his strength and his perception. On a silent night alone, he sometimes contemplated whether he was anything without them by his side. He would miss Gunnhild's guidance and her confidence as much as he would have missed Bjorn's power or Ulfr's skill, Ketil's speed or Leif's intellect. He had prayed nightly to the Allfather that what was to come was but temporary and that the spear-maiden would come back to them soon.

'The city is a snake pit,' Gunnhild said, giving him nothing he didn't already know.

'More?'

She darted an irritated look at him. 'In this place, you and yours can become rich, and either famous or infamous, but with one wrong move you could just as easily be dead, poor and forgotten. You must be as a fallen leaf in a mountain stream. You must allow yourself to float free if you wish to survive the white waters. Do not tie yourself to anyone.'

She rose, turning and jabbing a finger at him. 'Remember this above all else, Halfdan Loki-born. Do not bind yourself to man or woman in this place, for everyone here is dangerous, even Harðráði.' She threw a glance at the Varangian second-in-command who stood nearby, talking to his men. '*Especially* Harðráði,' she corrected. 'You will hide your *Mjǫllnir* pendants here to conceal your true beliefs, but even as you do, you must also hide your thoughts, your motives and your intentions. You must dance their dance.'

Halfdan frowned. Snake pits, white streams, and now dances. Gunnhild was mixing metaphors at a dizzying pace, something she did when she was nervous, and so not very often. 'I will be careful,' he said calmly.

'Use your Loki cunning. Rely upon the others. With the will of Freyja I will return to you all and you will have survived until then. Just remember what I said. Give oaths if you must, but be prepared to break them. If you tie yourself to anyone here, you may never leave the city.'

'I've got it, Gunnhild. Really.'

She gave him one last calculating look, as though she still expected him to march straight into trouble, then nodded and gathered up her bones and debris. Halfdan looked ahead, sizing up their destination. Truly, nothing he had ever seen could match this. Constantinople – he concentrated to get his tongue around the Greek name – was the queen of all cities, greater by far than Uppsala or Kiev or Kutaisi. A vast metropolis of copper domes shining in the sunlight, golden crosses rising above red roofs. Palaces, gardens, terraces, great curved arcades, columns and city walls that could surely hold off gods and giants if needed, and which ran around the coast directly above the water.

The inlet for which they sailed seemed to be guarded from both sides by twin fortresses, the city walls to the south and some second smaller city across the water to the north, and between them, a marvel that Halfdan could never have predicted. Almost half a mile of water separated the two shores, each set with a massive, powerful tower, and across that expanse was stretched a single, titanic chain-linked boom. Even from a distance, Halfdan could see how thick the chain was, each link two feet of hard iron, every seven links hooked into a huge tree bole that kept the whole thing afloat at the water's surface. A massive affair, it must surely stop most ships, or at least entangle them while they could be destroyed from the walls. He stared as the small fleet closed on the chain.

At some unheard command, a small boat set sail from the city side towards the centre of the chain. Whatever they did there, the chain was suddenly halved, and the side nearest the city began to move, hauled in by some massive machine in one of the towers, the iron links and great logs slowly moving towards the walls and opening the inlet to shipping.

The crew boggled at this amazing thing as they sailed past and made for a massive harbour filled with ships of many shapes and sizes.

'Civilisation at last,' Leif said with a grin as they slid towards one of the many jetties.

'Civilisation means they make wine,' Bjorn sagely advised the others, earning a roll of the eyes from the small Rus.

'They'd better make a lot of it if you intend to stay for a time,' Ketil said drily.

Halfdan smiled for a moment, then his expression became serious again as he took in the faces around him. Gunnhild had picked up her kitbag, preparing to leave them. Beyond her, Valgarðr was consulting with his men, and beyond him, across the water in the next ship, the golden figure of Harðráði stood with one foot on the rail, ready to leap ashore. The man truly was larger than life, a hero torn from the ancient tales. Gunnhild had warned him more than once that Harðráði might not be all he seemed, and yet there was a magnetism to the man even Halfdan felt himself drawn to.

He looked back to Gunnhild, and then across to her accustomed place on the deck. Every crew member of the *Sea Wolf* had an oar place, except Ulfr. Even Halfdan rowed his share, and so had Gunnhild, no matter how often Bjorn had told her that women were not made for such work. There was a tiny spark of hope to be found at her empty seat. As with all dragon ships, there were no permanent benches for the rowers, for each man sat on his own wooden chest, which contained his personal effects and, most importantly, his share of treasures. Gunnhild's remained there, in place on the ship, as she prepared to depart. She had told him to keep it safe, for it had not been emptied. Halfdan could not imagine that, if she were leaving for good, she would have left her treasures there. She would have to return for them, surely?

His wandering thoughts were drawn back in as the ship bumped against the timber jetty and Ulfr began the work of securing the vessel to its cleats, directing men with ropes. Ahead, Harðráði and his Varangians were jumping ashore as ship after ship began to dock. Some stuffy official came scurrying forward to bother the commander with endless forms and bureaucracy, the golden-haired Varangian simply brushing the man aside and leaving him for another to deal with.

As soon as the *Sea Wolf* was settled, Gunnhild was the first to drop to the slippery timbers. She hefted her bag over her shoulder and turned, casting one brief look back at them. Halfdan felt the uncertainty wash over him once more, yet he read much in that look. One tiny glance, and yet it said 'Be strong. Lead. Trust no one. Be cunning.' He thought he saw 'We will meet again' there, too. *Hoped* he did.

Then she was gone, elbowing her way through the disembarking Varangians and off into the port. Briefly he saw her once more, approaching a heavy gate in the city wall, where a fat man in a mustard-coloured tunic intercepted her with an armful of documents, two guards at his shoulder. Whatever Gunnhild said to the man, it made Halfdan smile, for the man bowed deeply and backed away in a hurry, leaving her to enter the city freely and without any kind of bureaucracy.

He straightened and took a deep breath. He would see her again soon. This city was huge, but no city would be large enough to hide Gunnhild for long.

'She is magnificent,' a voice said, and his head turned to find Harðráði standing beside him. The Norseman sighed. 'If only she were a princess, but a king must have an appropriate consort.'

'I think you would find her troublesome, anyway,' Halfdan said, quite earnestly.

Harðráði laughed then. 'No doubt. But nothing worthwhile comes without a challenge, as you will learn in this place. Come, and bring your men. I will direct you to your barracks before I present myself to the emperor and empress.'

Leaving one of his men to deal with the paperwork, Harðráði gestured towards the gate. Halfdan frowned and pointed back to his ship. 'We have all our wealth aboard. We cannot abandon the *Sea Wolf*. A guard must be set.'

The Varangian chuckled. 'You have much to learn about how things work in Byzantium. Your goods will be perfectly safe. We have signed your vessel in with the register of Varangian ships. No man will go aboard without your permission. In the empire, a well-written document is more binding and inviolable than any rope or shield wall.'

'Thieves exist everywhere,' Halfdan countered, 'even here.'

'Every man in Constantinople is a thief, young jarl, but in this place even thieves are guided by the rules. The more important the thief, the stricter the rules. And this harbour is watched and controlled by the city garrison. I remember a few years ago a man got curious and took something from one of our ships. The sight of him hanging from hooks on the sea wall will have put off an entire generation of would-be thieves. Your goods are safe. And if you are still unsure, then once we have you settled in, you can come back and bring everything to your barracks. For now, come.'

With that the commander marched off. The crowds of the harbour seemed to melt out of his way, and Valgarðr moved to the man's side, his immense axe over his shoulder like a spear. The rest of the contingent began to disembark now and to gather, ready to move off. Halfdan chewed his lip, looking at the man ahead and then back at his ship, where the rest of the crew were vacillating, uncertain of what to do next. He remembered Gunnhild's words, though. He would keep a tight rein on his trust here, no matter what Harðráði said.

'Ulfr, stay aboard with the men until we've seen what awaits us. Then we'll be back to get the rest and bring our goods ashore.'

The stocky *Svear* nodded his understanding and began to order the others around as Ketil, Bjorn and Leif dropped to the jetty and joined their jarl.

'What now?' the big albino muttered.

'We catch up with Harðráði before we get lost among this lot. Come on.'

They hurried through the gathering crowd, bearing down on the golden figure. As they fell into step with Harðráði and his small gathering of favoured karls, the man turned with a sly smile and a raised eyebrow. 'You left your men anyway.'

'For now. You show me, I'll show them.'

Harðráði gave a low chuckle and marched off into the gateway. Where soldiers had been darting out to interrogate or check the various folk moving into the city, they uniformly stepped out of the way of the commander, and within moments they were through the tower and into the city proper. Halfdan continued to marvel as they entered a vertiginous street. The city was the most highly decorated thing he'd ever seen. Even the brick walls were constructed with an eye for art, patterns built into them, and containing carved, shaped blocks bearing crosses in circles, eagles and many other designs. A few buildings seemed to be partially or fully sheathed in white marble, and copper and gold gleamed all around. The street rose like a mountainside towards a collection of even grander buildings at the summit.

'This must be what Ásgarðr looks like,' he breathed.

'For the sake of my afterlife, I hope this isn't what Ásgarðr *smells* like,' Ketil grumbled, wrinkling his nose.

'Heady, isn't it,' Leif said with a smile. 'I would say the city's general aroma is a mix of dung, fish, spices and perfumes. Every breath gives you a new and unique experience.'

'Smells like a whore's arse,' Bjorn said, and Halfdan laughed to note from his big friend's beaming face that this did not appear to be a negative thing.

At the crest of the hill, the brick buildings seemed to be fewer and the marble edifices more numerous and much grander. Buildings the size of entire villages rose high and gleaming into the blue sky, the roads paved with neat uniform blocks surprisingly devoid of shit. The city was a mass of crowds in colourful dress, though all stayed carefully out of the way of the armoured soldiers as they stomped towards another gate in a great marble structure with a domed chapel atop. A man in the garb of a Christian monk stood at the side of the street, bellowing out prophecy and tales of damnation as citizens walked past, largely ignoring him. Every empty space seemed to be filled with street vendors of some sort, selling things that sizzled and smelled enticing. More enticing than the lower streets, anyway.

Varangians stood on guard at the gate, and bowed their heads as Harðráði led his men inside. Halfdan paused once again as he emerged into the complex on the far side. 'Palace' was a word that hardly did this place justice. He had seen the palace of the grand prince in Kiev, and that of the queen in Kutaisi, but this was no mere building. The Great Palace's walls encircled an area a quarter of a mile wide, stretching right down to the sea walls, and more than half a mile long, the whole filling much of the headland. Within were terraces and gardens, orchards and entire fields where horsemen raced around, whooping. Churches rose here and there in white and bronze glory, and huge palaces and bathhouses abounded, linked by corridors and colonnades. Halfdan was rather relieved when Harðráði directed them to a large building just to the right of the gate, confirming that this was the quarters of the Guard. He mused how easily he'd have got lost in this place had the barracks been placed somewhere less accessible.

Two men stood guard even at the entrance to the barracks, and their reactions immediately struck Halfdan as odd. Where elsewhere in the city each man they'd come across had immediately deferred to Harðráði, these two hesitated and shared a look, almost as if surprised, even dismayed, to see their commander, and only bowed their heads at the last moment. Something was definitely a little off there.

Inside, the building was spacious and well-lit, and they stopped near the entrance. Harðráði turned to face them.

'These are the barracks of the excubitores, which house both our unit's palace contingent, and that of a lesser bodyguard within the city's main garrison. Torsten here,' he gestured to a man seated at a desk covered in documents, occupying an alcove near the door, 'will direct you to rooms where you can stow your gear for now. It will take some time for all the documentation to be produced to admit you to the Guard, but everything should be ready by this evening, and then you will take the oath before myself and Valgarðr. We have, however, several hours between now and then, and I must find my room, make myself presentable and visit the imperial court to report to the emperor on our success. You may have until sunset to yourselves to gather your crew and your goods and bring them to the barracks, and to perhaps spend some time familiarising yourself with at least some of the city. Knowing your surroundings will be of great importance in your time here.'

Halfdan nodded, and Harðráði gave him a smile. 'Welcome to the greatest city in the world.'

With that, he turned and marched off along one of the corridors, several of his men still at his shoulder.

Valgarðr watched him go, then turned to them. 'The commander has much on his mind at the moment, and so forgets about small things. You will not have eaten since dawn, and I suspect you will need to do so soon. Until you have been given insignia and documentation, the mess halls here will be closed to you. Also, until then, I strongly recommend not wandering the palace grounds. There are places guards are expected to keep clear of, and places only for women. Until you are given a full tour, limit your movements here to the gate and barracks. You will retain much of your own gear, but there are certain adjustments you will need to make. You will be issued with a brightly coloured tunic and a coat of leather, you will receive a tall axe like mine, though many choose not to wield them, and you will be given a holy cross on a chain for your neck. I suggest, Halfdan-jarl, that you make better efforts at tucking away your Thor-hammer and wear the cross in its place. It will open doors that your pagan symbols would close. All of this, of course, comes once the paperwork is completed and your oath taken.'

He tapped his chin, then nodded. 'Ah yes, that's where I was. Food. I will speak to the men on duty and you will be permitted to enter and leave the grounds through the main gate for now, without your insignia. If you have coin, there are many places to eat in the city. I suggest you locate a good quality tavern and miss out on the street vendors. Some are very good, but some are little more than diarrhoea factories, and until you know what you're looking for, you would be better off avoiding them all. Taverns have to be better quality because they are still there the next day to be accused of giving a man the shits.'

Bjorn shrugged. 'I have an iron gut. I could eat the three-week corpse of a scabby mule and not get the shits.'

'On the contrary,' Leif said airily. 'I sit beside you at the oars, and from the smell I would say suffering from the shits is your daily fare.'

The little Rus, grinning, ducked out of the way of the big albino's hand, and Ketil stepped between them. 'Our rooms here will have locks?'

Valgarðr nodded. 'Your personal goods will be quite safe for the next few hours. You will find that timekeeping is simple here. There are many churches in the city, and their bells ring at specific intervals. The greatest of the churches is the Hagia Sophia, just beside the palace. If you limit your exploration to the part of the city where you can still see its dome, or at least see the great curved top of the circus, then you will still be close to the palace and the harbour. It is very easy to get lost in Constantinople and from here you can walk more than two miles without leaving the urban centre. Stay within sight of this area and watch the sky and listen for the bells. When the sky begins to darken and the churches ring the evening in, return to these barracks. I will have the gate guards notified so that your entire crew will be given admittance.' He smiled. 'Make the most of this afternoon. Tomorrow you learn the Varangian routine, a seemingly endless round of patrolling, attending services and ceremonies and being glared at by supercilious nobles.'

'Thank you,' Halfdan said, and the old Varangian nodded and turned, leaving the building.

Torsten, a young man with deep red hair and a neatly clipped beard, looked up. 'Just the four of you for now? How many more are coming?'

'Thirty-three.'

The man sucked his teeth. 'I will attempt to move a few rooms around once I have a tally of how many men are missing from the army that we sent to Georgia, and try to put you all together for convenience. Each room in the barracks accommodates four men and their gear. We have a few spare rooms here for visitors, so for now I will give over the nearest to the four of you while I organise more permanent quarters.'

With that, he rose and crossed to one of the doors nearby, pulling it open. He then removed the key from the lock and handed it to Halfdan. 'For now, you can stow gear here and use it for a rest or for changing if you wish. I will take the key back when you are moved, later. Enjoy the city.'

With that, the young man returned to his desk and his work, and the four of them looked into the room. Assuming this was what each chamber in the place looked like, it would be perfectly serviceable. Four bunks, four chests, a tall cupboard and a small table with four chairs.

Bjorn flopped into one of the beds.

'I could get used to this. I'll try not to keep you all awake as I work through the city's women.'

'You really think they'll let you bring whores through the gates of the palace?' Leif snorted.

'If not, then I'll have to find some very accommodating wenches in the palace, won't I? And one of you will have to move a chest so I can fit a wine barrel in, too.'

Halfdan laughed quietly. 'Dump your things. Valgarðr was right. I'm hungry, and this city is a maze. Let's go find the best taverns to be found and eat and drink our fill.'

Dropping their bags, they emerged into the corridor once more, where Halfdan locked their room and dropped the key into his pouch. Blinking in the warm afternoon light, they left the building and stepped out onto the gravel path, only to find themselves face to face with another, unfamiliar, group of Varangians. One of the men, in ornate armour, narrowed his eyes, as he turned to share unspoken thoughts with one of his companions, revealing two bearded axes crossed in the back of his belt.

'These ones I do not know,' the man muttered to his friend. 'You said Harðráði brought strays and waifs back with him?'

39

The man beside him, a giant with a milky eye and a harelip, nodded. 'Some mercenary bunch he picked up in Georgia, or so I hear.'

The leader nodded, looking Halfdan and his companions up and down. 'Vermin. I shall put an official complaint in to the emperor.'

Halfdan gave the man a smile that he knew contained not an ounce of mirth or warmth, the sort of smile a fox might give a lame chicken. 'I realise,' he said, 'that there is etiquette and a system of ranks within the Guard. Deference would be due an officer of your clear status. Fortunately, I'm not yet in the Guard, so fuck off.'

Maintaining his empty smile, he walked around the group, making for the gate through which they'd entered. Ketil followed him, then Leif, each of them casting their own nasty smile at the man. Bjorn stepped rather closer than the rest as he passed, treading heavily on the foot of the big, white-eyed Varangian. The brute let out a furious roar and turned, his fist swinging.

Bjorn was ready for him, having initiated the whole thing, and his great hand caught the swinging fist and closed on it, holding it back. The two men strained, White-eye pushing for a punch, Bjorn heaving to hold it back, veins standing out on their faces.

'Enough,' snapped the officer. 'Stand down, the pair of you.'

White-eye held the grip for a moment, and finally stepped away, pulling back his fist. Bjorn grinned. 'Look for me,' he said, wagging a finger at his opponent. 'Look for me, and I'll show you how a *real* man fights.'

'Bjorn,' called Halfdan, and led his men towards the gate. Once they were away from the other group, and the Varangians had marched on into the barracks, Halfdan spoke in low tones. 'Harðráði said he had unfinished business in the city, and we may just have met some of it. Bjorn, I feel the same as you, but hold off on things like that until we know what we're dealing with. We can't afford to punch out the wrong person here. Let's get a brief meal and then work our way down to the harbour. I want the rest of the crew up here for safety in numbers.'

Once again, as they passed beneath the arch and out into the city, Halfdan wished Gunnhild was still here, with her wise words. He would miss her counsel in the coming days.

Chapter 3

'Meat pie, miss?'

Gunnhild shook her head and walked on through the streets of the great city. Every thoroughfare was crowded with life, from citizens out about their business to sellers with their trays or carts, occasional soldiers moving among them like pike in a stream of minnows, from beggars calling out for alms to arrogant nobles with escorts of hard-looking men and miserable servants, and all the sectors of life in such a place. And yet somehow Gunnhild's path was never hindered by such human currents and eddies. She walked with the power and authority of Freyja, and the world moved around her.

In truth she hardly saw any of it anyway. In her head, she was still picking over her last few castings. Halfdan had pressured her this afternoon, perhaps because it would be the last time he knew he would have the chance, and she had tried to divine something useful for him, but in the end what she had told him, warning him of the dangers of tying himself to anyone here, had come from her own wisdom, and not from the Seiðr. She had told him nothing of what she had seen, for what she saw disconcerted her. Constantinople had been laid before her through the cadence of the song and the dust and the power of the goddess, and the city had been as a *'tafl* board. At the centre had stood the king, as in all games, but *this* king was golden, and his karls moved about the board trying to help him escape while the Greeks blocked every exit. She had known then that the king had been Harðráði and not Halfdan, and that if the young jarl had been on that board at all, he had been one of the man's desperate pieces. That in seeking truths for Halfdan she could not help but find Harðráði instead worried her, though that was not the most worrying thing.

She remembered too her previous castings. That night at Amastris, she had broken the cardinal rule. She had looked with intent upon her own destiny, something only the most confident or desperate völva would do. It was one thing to find yourself shown in someone else's future, and it had surprised and worried her to discover that her thread departed from the others when trying to seek help for Halfdan, but it was another to see your own destiny laid out. There was a tale of a völva who had seen her own grisly end and had gone to any length possible to avoid it, only to bring that very end about by her actions. Destiny was inescapable. Gunnhild had been relieved to be shown only something constructive, in the form of the pond of Constantinople with its ever-bigger fish eating one another, and, emboldened by the success, she had peeked once more into her own weaving during the night before the final leg of her journey, looking further forward. It had been a relief in a way that her future was clouded and unreadable, but what she had seen before that had startled her. Her own thread, distinct from the others, had begun a new weaving, alongside a thread of gold.

Harðráði.

She was bound to him in some way, more than Halfdan could be. Would that she could heed her own advice and avoid tying herself to others here, but it seemed the *Norns* in their wisdom had woven the two of them together. There had been altogether too many different divinings now. The bear, the pond, the 'tafl board, and others too, and yet they were all connected somehow. She felt sure they would in time come clear and perhaps explain each other.

Another street slipped past.

'Repent,' bellowed a mendicant standing on a mounting block in front of one of the innumerable Christian churches. 'Repent and save your soul.'

43

She frowned, suspicious. He seemed to be peering directly at her, then looked away hurriedly as she locked her gaze upon him. Her eyes then strayed back to her surroundings. She did not know precisely what she was looking for, and was wandering with her instinct as her sole guide, but she felt she would know when she found it.

She was in a lesser street now, and something made her skin prickle. Seiðr was at work somewhere. She could feel the cold glow of it nearby, and turned into an alley, her boots clacking on the flagstones, her staff tapping as she walked, bearing neither jewel nor spearhead now.

'Oh, you're pretty,' a voice said from somewhere behind her, and she could sense the leer on the face of the speaker without even seeing him. Another figure coalesced from the shadows of the alley ahead, and folded his arms. 'Now, Isaac, don't let your loins lead you. This is not about flesh.' He gave Gunnhild an unpleasant smile. 'This is not a safe neighbourhood for a lone woman, especially one newly arrived and innocent. For a small fee, we could ensure your safety.'

A snigger from behind. Gunnhild sighed inwardly.

'Ten bronze folles apiece would be fair, I'd say,' Smiler added. 'To be sure that no unhappy accident befalls you today.'

Gunnhild gave a little flick of her staff, and a corroded, filthy coin lying in the dust at her feet leapt through the air towards the thief.

'Take it and be grateful,' she said quietly.

'Is that any way to speak to your saviours?' The man smiled as the near-worthless coin bounced off his leg.

'Begone,' she said and began to walk forward once more.

The man reached down to his side and patted a stout ash club hanging from his belt. 'Perhaps you'd like to rethink?'

Gunnhild closed her eyes. She could hear the footsteps of the man behind her. He had closed, trying to pad quietly up to her while she was kept distracted by the speaker. He was directly behind her, now, perhaps two paces back. In the darkness behind her eyelids she heard him step forward once more, short strides, a small man. As her staff lifted from the flagged street, she gripped it with both hands and swung low, jabbing the length of seasoned wood back and up. She heard it connect, heard a crunch, a squeak of pain bitten down upon, heard the thief fold up and collapse to the ground clutching his manhood.

The man before her had the grace to look momentarily taken aback, but recovered quickly, the club sliding free of his belt.

'You shouldn't have done that.'

'Walk away,' she said quietly.

His grip changed on the club, and his foot inched forward just a fraction as he shifted his balance, ready to leap. She continued to walk confidently, her own grip on the staff changing. The man was fast, but he was also hopelessly predictable. As he jumped, swinging his club, she stepped neatly to the side and brought her staff around in a wide sweep. She heard his arm break and saw the club fall away as the man barrelled on, forward and down, ending in a heap not far from his squirming friend.

'Learn from your mistakes,' she said quietly and, turning her back on the pair, walked on.

She could feel the Seiðr now, somewhere nearby. She turned two more corners, half expecting would-be thieves around each, and found herself in a new street, a steep one. At the northern end, down at the bottom of the hill, she could see the inlet where they had landed, filled with fishing boats, the urban mass bounded down there by a large city wall of white stone and brick, heavy towers at regular intervals. At the top, in the other direction, she could see some grand building with a huge dome. This was a street of locals only, though. Two taverns, a few shops and a number of houses, no hopeful hawkers here trying to attract custom, no soldiers or priests or traders, just the ordinary poor folk of the city.

There.

A building much like the others. These places were common and humble. No decorative or noble marble façades, but timber

45

houses with the odd plain brick frontage here and there among them. One house in particular was drawing her, though. It looked much like the others in most respects, but the plain door sat in a frame made of old columns, beneath a lintel carved with a floral design. Reused stones of an ancient place, still in situ. Once, those columns had been numerous and had supported something grander, Gunnhild believed.

Stepping across to the building, she knocked on the door. There was a spat of muffled cursing, and a lot of shuffling, and finally the door crept open, a suspicious face appearing in the gap, an old man with more hair on his chin by far than on his scalp.

'What?' His eyes widened a little. Whatever he'd been expecting, it was not Gunnhild.

'I need to see in your house.'

The man's face folded into surprise and irritation in equal quantities. 'Piss off, girl.'

'No. Show me.' Her free hand dipped into her cloak and came out with a gold coin, some Byzantine currency called a solidus she had acquired in Amastris. The man's eyes widened further. She'd be willing to bet he'd only held gold once or twice in his life. She flicked the coin into the air with her thumb and the man, despite his age, darted forth and caught it with speed and ease, peering into its glorious design.

'It's yours for a look in your house.'

Still staring at the coin, the man withdrew and the door was opened wider.

She stepped inside, and the prickling of her skin grew to an almost unbearable level. She could feel the Seiðr wreathing the walls of this place like the home of her old völva in Hedeby. This was it. This would do. This was where the fish would come to gather, her place in the pond.

'What is this?'

The old man, still examining the coin with amazement, shrugged. 'My house.'

She looked around. It needed a clean and a tidy, for sure. The room was maybe thirty feet long and fifteen wide, all one open space, with a cooking area off to the rear and the living space near the front. No back door, but a set of rickety-looking stairs led up to a second floor. The sleeping space, she presumed. It was not grand, for all its size, but it was not the form of the man's house for which she looked. It was the form into which the house *had been built* that interested her. There were three and a half more columns visible along one wall, and she felt sure there were others hidden among the timbers. It had been a place of power once.

'What was this place, before it was a house?'

The man frowned. He looked about to argue, but a stray beam of sunlight through a window caught the coin in his hand and threw a beam of gold into his eyes, which swiftly overcame any further reluctance.

'It was a temple, once. Tyche, I think. Come.'

He shuffled through to the back of the room, and then pointed down. Gunnhild's gaze dropped behind the table in the corner of the room. A badly damaged statue, discoloured and chipped, lay on its side, a strange crown on her head, a broken arm still holding a fragment of something. The goddess, whoever she was, had once been a power before the nailed god's priests had torn down her temple. No wonder the Seiðr still infused this place.

She turned to the old man.

'I need your house.'

The man's frown returned. 'Now listen...'

'I am listening. And I am hearing. I need this place, at least for a time. No other will do.'

'This is my home.'

Without taking her eyes from that statue, Gunnhild rested her staff against the table and reached down. She had seven pouches at her belt, some on show, some hidden in the folds of her cloak, but one hung lower than the others, dragged down by a heavy weight. With some effort she untied it from the belt and lifted it, holding it out while she peered at the broken form on the floor. The man, still suspicious, reached out and grasped the pouch. As she let go he almost dropped it, surprised by the weight. Fumbling, he recovered himself and, frowning, undid the string, struggling to hold it in one hand. His eyes bulged as he looked inside. With short, jagged breaths, he tipped the contents onto the table. A single piece of gold of impressive dimensions – Gunnhild's share of Yngvar's gold cross from the far edge of the world. It still showed the jagged marks where Bjorn had managed to cut the thing up with the help of a blacksmith. Gunnhild had no idea of values in this strange world, but she was willing to bet that the single piece of gold on the man's table would buy half this street, let alone this one hovel. The man boggled in astonishment.

'Where did you…? How…? This is…'

'It is yours. It was mine, a prize for a task completed. Now it is yours. I need your house, and in return you are a rich man. Is this not fair?'

'I…' the man stared at the gold, looked around his house, then found his eyes drawn inevitably back to the chunk of gleaming metal. 'I will need time to gather my things. I can use my brother's house for a time, while I…' His voice trailed off in the gleaming light of the gold. 'I need… I…'

Gunnhild nodded. 'You will find help. I do not need your things. If you could leave me a bowl, a spoon and your cooking pot, that will be sufficient.'

The man stared at her and at the gold, his gaze darting back and forth.

Gunnhild nodded her satisfaction. This would do.

–

She watched the man depart with his brother, dragging the small handcart containing his meagre possessions. He had obligingly offered to stay and help her tidy the place and remove anything else she didn't want, but she had shaken her head. She would do what needed to be done.

As the old man and his brother disappeared up the street, she stood for a time in the doorway. Locals had begun to gather around in a small cluster as their neighbour emptied his house of all his worldly goods and handed a key to Gunnhild. Over time, the crowd had grown until it resembled a *skald*'s audience, waiting for the tale of gods and heroes to begin. There was an air of curiosity and of anticipation. No one had seen the gold, of course. The old man had made sure that was hidden and had said nothing of why he was moving. Even his brother had not seen that precious bundle.

Pondering her next moves, she checked her belt purse. She still had a few gold coins from Amastris, as well as sundry bronzes. Enough to tide her over and buy what she needed for now. Harðráði would somehow come back into her life, she was sure, but until then, she needed to live. She looked out at the gathered faces.

'Does anyone know a good, cheap carpenter?'

'There's one two streets over, next to the old stables,' someone replied helpfully.

'And a trader in herbs? I will need many such things, some of them quite rare.'

'There's a market,' another of the crowd said, 'up near the Church of the Holy Apostles. Top of the hill.'

'Thank you.'

She looked around, nodding to herself.

'Who are you?' someone asked. '*What* are you?'

'My name is Gunnhild and I am völva,' she replied, which was not precisely true, though she was at least partially trained, and these people would hardly know the difference.

'Völva?' another queried, trying to twist his tongue around the unfamiliar word.

'I advise. I explain. Sometimes I predict, depending upon the will of the goddess.'

'Goddess?' another asked, suspicion in his tone.

'Do you mean the *Theotokos*?' a woman asked hopefully. 'Maria, the Mother of God?'

A murmur passed across the crowd, and Gunnhild had to force herself not to smile as many of them made a cross shape over their torso with their hand.

'If that name pleases you,' Gunnhild replied calmly. Here was a school of little fish. Somewhere, there would be a bigger fish waiting.

'She is a witch,' someone said. 'Listen to her. I'll not have a witch in my street.'

'She's not a witch,' another called. 'She is guided by the Theotokos. She does God's work.'

'Bollocks.'

'Don't talk to me like that, Heraclius.'

The crowd broke out into a noisy squabble as arguments ensued, and Gunnhild stood patiently in a doorway. One woman in the crowd had stopped arguing and was looking at her with narrowed eyes. 'You are either a witch or a charlatan,' she said, her voice almost lost in the din. 'The Theotokos does not work through Varangian trollops.'

Gunnhild remained still and calm. 'I care not what you think, woman. My path is laid out before me, while yours ends. Before I leave this house, you will be but dust in the wind.'

The woman, on the cusp of an outburst, suddenly stopped, her face in a deep frown, her mouth still open. 'What do you mean?' she said finally.

Gunnhild took a step towards her, and the noise of the crowd died away as all eyes turned to the two of them. As she stepped close to the woman, Gunnhild produced from her pouch something small and gleaming. In a flash she stabbed out with it. The woman recoiled a little, but her arms remained folded. She looked uncertain now, worried even.

'You felt nothing, did you?' Gunnhild said quietly.

'What?' The woman looked down. A bead of blood had risen on her forearm where Gunnhild had stabbed her with the pin. She flashed a look at those around her, guilt suddenly flooding her face.

'You know, don't you?' Gunnhild said, quietly, a hint of sympathy in her voice.

'What have you done?' another woman demanded. 'Is this the devil's work?'

'The woman has the misshaping disease. She has suspected it for some time. She cannot feel pain.' And then to the sick woman once more: 'The disease is taking you and you have hidden it from everyone. You have lesions.'

The woman nodded, her expression frightened, cold.

'Leprosy,' a man said in realisation, his voice little more than a panicked whisper. The crowd pulled away from the woman, a wide space opening up around her.

The woman's eyes took on a flicker of hope. 'You... you work miracles? You are a tool of the Theotokos?'

'There is nothing I can do for you,' Gunnhild said flatly. 'You are too far gone. The disease can be held away in the earliest days, but not after it has ravaged a body this long. It is impressive that you have managed to hide it so, but you will be dead before winter ends.'

The woman let out a hopeless groan.

'You have family, though,' Gunnhild said.

'Yes,' the woman replied miserably.

'Bring them to see me.'

Two young boys edged forward where they had been sitting on the edge of a fountain at the periphery of the action. They approached slowly, nervously. Reaching out, Gunnhild motioned to them. The boys recoiled, but their mother urged them forward, and they continued timidly. Taking one of their arms in a light grip, Gunnhild turned it over, lifted it, looked into the armpit, examined the neck, looked into his eyes, closed her own for a long moment, and then stepped back.

'They are yet untouched by your illness. They can be saved.' With that, she reached into her pouch and produced a small jar.

It sloshed with blue-black liquid, and she opened it and dipped the needle she still held into the liquid.

'This will hurt, but stay still,' she commanded.

The boy looked terrified now, and the moment the inky needle jabbed into his arm, he pulled it away with a shriek.

'Hold him,' Gunnhild said.

'This is sorcery,' someone breathed.

'It's just a tattoo,' a man countered, dismissively.

'This is saving the boy's life,' Gunnhild said, and a big man, a blacksmith from his shape, was there now, holding the boy still, his arm out. As the boy wailed and cried she worked, the arm held firm in a powerful grip, tattooing a small pentacle in the flesh. It had to be a tattoo, for this needed more than a charcoal drawing. If he were to be protected when the *alfar* brought fresh disease to the household, he must bear the mark undamaged. Once the boy was done and sat on the floor, whimpering, Gunnhild started on his brother. The sick mother watched with tears in her eyes, and when the boys, all done, ran to embrace her, she recoiled, shooing them away.

'No. I cannot. You must not touch me.'

Gunnhild straightened, putting away her ink and wiping the needle before replacing it in the pouch. 'They will be protected, but this place is not for them. You have no husband.'

'No. He died in the Bulgar wars.'

'But you have other relatives? Ones outside the city.'

She nodded. 'I've cousins out in the Theme of Thessalonike, by the sea.'

'Your boys should go there. I assure you they will live, and in such a place they will thrive.'

A hush of awe settled across the crowd. The two boys, still crying, huddled together, their mother pale and wan. The woman shuffled her feet. 'I do not know how to thank you.'

'You need not. This I did for your children.'

'She is a worker of miracles,' someone said in awed tones. 'God works through her.'

'She's a witch,' someone snapped irritably at the back, followed by the sounds of a scuffle. A clamour arose again, and the crowd flooded forward, circumventing the leprous woman to gather in front of Gunnhild, all speaking at once.

'My husband has a fancy woman...'

'I have to take a journey, but I have been told the winter seas...'

'Do you protect from stomach illnesses?'

'If I can find the coin, do you...'

The voices rose and fell like waves, folding in on themselves, weaving into an aural tapestry. Gunnhild let them call and beg, enquire and demand, closing her eyes. She would have to make a list. The old völva in Hedeby had not survived on the casting of bones and the singing of old songs. Christians had little need of such things. But a völva knew more than the casting, and it was in the nature of ordinary people everywhere to seek knowledge and advice, to look for concoctions and compounds to dull pain, to ease aches, to make the bearing of children more likely and, in darker moments, to seek poisons. She would have plenty of work, if this crowd was anything to go by, and as she tended to the minnows in this pond, sooner or later the larger fish would take note.

'I have yet even to unpack my bag,' she said loudly, cutting through the clamour. 'I need to shop, unpack, stock my shelves and put this house into some form of order. Give me this night, and when the sun rises tomorrow, bring me your questions and your problems and I will do for you what I can.'

Tyche, she mused, turning back and entering the house, closing the door to the din of the crowd. An ancient place of worship. She would have to find out who this Tyche was.

Chapter 4

'I fail to see how we're going to become rich like this,' Ketil grumbled, shifting the weight of his axe to his other shoulder and gazing out across the water that danced and glittered like a sea of silver. '*Stinking* rich,' he corrected himself, sniffing. 'Unless someone knows a merchant who buys shit for a good price.'

'I like it,' Bjorn said in a genuine tone. 'Horseshit always smells good to me.'

'Given the smells that follow you round, it does have the edge.'

Bjorn just sighed. 'I know what you mean, though. Where's the armfuls of silver? Where's the riches of this great rich city? I hate to think I've given my oath for the opportunity to walk the walls next to piles of dung forevermore.'

'Patience,' Halfdan said, leaning on the parapet of the sea walls, watching the ships drift past, using the current of the channel to pull them from one sea to another. 'It's only been a week and a half. We can't expect to roll in coin so soon. We struggled for months for our last haul.'

A chorus of nods greeted this wisdom, and once again Halfdan felt keenly the absence of Gunnhild and her words of support. As they fell into an aggrieved silence, filled only with the cries of gulls, the crash of waves and the low humming of Leif chanting a Christ-ditty from his Rus homeland, Halfdan wracked his brain, trying to think of a solution.

They had seen precious little of the Varangian commander since their arrival in the city. Harðráði had arranged everything well enough, but had then gone to report to the emperor and empress and had promptly more or less vanished from sight. No one had spoken of what happened at that meeting, but when the commander had returned, he'd borne a face like thunder and had taken Valgarðr and marched off to some palace on the far side of the city.

That first evening, he'd been there, if distracted. The papers had seemed endless, each crewman with his own small tower of documents, each filled in with precision in small, neat Greek letters, each signed, stamped, sealed and counter-signed, stamped and sealed. Every man had been required to read them, or at least to nod sagely while they were read to them, and then to make their own mark, most of which were simple 'X's.

They had received their uniform, such as it was, an eye-watering tunic of bright red and blue patterns, woven with gold thread. Bjorn had noisily mused on whether it was possible to pull gold out of the clothes, but numerous attempts as they had worked on their paperwork had just left him with a slightly shabby tunic. Their armour and weapons they would retain, and they would be free to wear what they wished on ordinary duties, but for any service or ceremony, or when attending the imperial court or any public event, they were to have everything buffed up to gleaming and to wear the colourful tunics.

They had then taken the oath, repeating the words after some rodential priest with a nasal voice. As they had offered their loyalty, their faith and even their lives to the protection of the emperor, the living embodiment of the will of God, Harðráði had seemed only half-there, conversing in low tones over their own words with his second, earning repeated glares from the priest, all of which he obligingly ignored.

Halfdan had felt the importance of what he was offering, as, he knew, did every last man from the *Sea Wolf*. 'Give oaths if you must, but be prepared to break them,' Gunnhild had advised him before she departed, but she should have known better. A Northman took his word seriously. An oath was binding, and a man had to live by it. Otherwise what value was the oath in the first place? And now he and his men had given oaths not only of loyalty to the emperor, but also of obedience to their superiors in the Guard. Even as they repeated the words, Halfdan found himself wondering what that meant for men who already held an oath of obedience and loyalty to him, their jarl.

Fortunately, that did not seem to be an issue. Once the ceremony was over, the paperwork complete, and Harðráði had gone, Valgarðr had appointed Halfdan to the position of Pentecontarch, a low rank that put him in command of the Sea Wolf crew directly. The evening had ended then in wine and ribald laughter, and at one point a chastened promise from Bjorn that he would never again show his bare buttocks to a lady of the palace through the barrack windows. Valgarðr had remained with them for the evening, after the commander had gone.

Harðráði had shown up from time to time since then, but always busy and at speed. Only his second-in-command had taken a moment to pass on such tidings as he could. The emperor was extremely ill, apparently, and the empress concerned, and with their distraction the emperor's brothers had all but taken over the day-to-day administration of the city. Harðráði was seemingly not popular with them, and so had been ordered to the least accessible posting in the city, where he languished angrily, the acidic Ari Karsten commanding the Guard in the heart of the city in his stead. Until the empress took a stronger hand and the grasping relations of the ailing emperor could be winkled out of their positions, Harðráði was more or less impotent.

Whatever it was that had set this Ari against Halfdan and his men seemed to be rooted in a longstanding feud with Harðráði, for the moment the commander was out of the way, Karsten had begun to reassign the Guard, shifting anyone with a real allegiance to their commander into peripheral positions and assigning his own favoured men to the more important duties.

'He's trying to have our contracts nullified,' Leif had told them at one point, 'but Guard numbers are low enough that he was refused permission, lest the emperor be left unprotected.'

And that was how the five of them had drawn the duty of guarding the wall at the waterline, beside the middens fed from the polo fields and the imperial stables. The duty was innocuous enough, but the aroma that clung to the area made it one of the least desirable postings in the city, and it was far enough from anyone of any importance that there was little chance of excitement or gain.

For a moment, Halfdan wondered where the rest of the *Sea Wolf*'s crew were now. *So much for the authority of a Pentecontarch, eh?* With the commander absent, and Ari Karsten in charge, the man had carefully split the crew into handfuls and scattered them around the city, so that they could not count on one another. Halfdan had been white with rage when the orders arrived for his men's reposting. With Bjorn at his shoulder he had marched to Ari's office and smashed the door open without knocking.

'How dare you assign my men.'

Karsten had given him a cold glare. 'The Guard is thin. I have shifted duties to cover everything. Begone.'

'I am their Pentecontarch. They are my men to command.'

'And you are *mine* to command,' Ari snarled, rising behind his desk. 'And my command is that your men be spread across the city, keeping their pagan rot to themselves. Yes, I have seen your ungodly signs, no matter how hard you hide them. Lord, but I can even now see the mark on your arm.'

'I demand...' Halfdan had begun, angrily, but Ari waved a hand at him.

'Nothing. You demand nothing. Have you forgotten your oath already? Or are you some *Pecheneg* animal who holds no value in an oath?'

Halfdan found himself speechless, while vibrating with the need to argue. He couldn't. The man was right. He had taken the oath. They all had. And unless he wanted to go against everything he believed in and be branded an oath-breaker, he had to accept Karsten's orders.

He had left the office then, still furious, but impotent, with Bjorn murmuring in his ear all the way a score of ways Ari might meet with an accident and their true commander be returned. So they had settled into the dung duty as the *Sea Wolf* crew was dispersed around the city, every man throwing him a look of helpless anger, each of which drove into his heart like a nail.

'Harðráði should challenge him for command,' Halfdan had said, the second day of their stinking exile.

'That's not how it works here,' Leif had replied. 'This isn't a dragon ship, but the imperial military. The moment the law is behind him, Harðráði can deal with Ari, but if he makes a move without the say of the emperor, his own life could be forfeit.'

'These laws are stupid.'

'And yet the empire has ruled these seas for two millennia, so it works.'

Halfdan had fallen silent then, partially because he didn't want to admit he had no idea what a millennia was, and so they had slouched on with their tedious duty. For a tempting moment he actually began to consider Bjorn's offer of a 'mysterious accident' before brushing it aside as unworthy. At least their accommodation was comfortable and private, and as long as they remained in the Guard, their monthly pay would be healthy, if they managed a month, given that some of them were already talking about backing out and leaving despite their oaths.

Bells began to clang and clatter across the city and, with the regularity and precision that seemed to be endemic to imperial life, their replacements appeared from the nearby tower doorway and began to stroll along the wall.

Halfdan and the others pattered down the steps of the next tower along and made their way through the great gardens and between the grand structures of the palace, heading for the barracks. There, they paused only long enough to deposit the heavier armour, shrugging out of plated or chain coats and leaving shields against walls and then, locking the door, strode out through the palace gate and into the city.

Two streets from the gate, they felt the weight of the day's ennui lifted as they approached the tavern that had become their regular haunt. It had taken a few days to find a place where armed Northmen were welcome, but which was not full of guards they did not know, for such men could well now be in Ari's purse. This tavern was far from the best, a little dingy and peeling, its drinks cheaper and of lower quality than many. All in all, Bjorn's type of place.

The surprise as they pushed their way into the dim interior to find themselves face to face with Harðráði was palpable. The man had a tired and hunted look, and the fact that he had four very capable-looking, fully armed Varangians at his back suggested that the look was no affectation.

'Back in Amastris, I asked for your loyalty,' he said, with no preamble.

'And you have it still,' Halfdan replied, the other four nodding their agreement. Whatever worries they might have had about tying themselves to the man, with Ari Karsten as the alternative, Harðráði could count on them all.

'I thought so. If you had sold out to criminal purses, you'd not be guarding the shit wall every day. That is heart-warming for me. I have something I need doing, but unfriendly eyes are everywhere in the city these days, and I am under constant observation.'

Halfdan's eyes narrowed. 'If you are being watched and you have come here, then we are now being watched too.'

'There were two pairs of eyes on me. Imperial spies work in pairs to decrease the likelihood of treachery. I sent Valgarðr off halfway here, so they will have split up. When we leave, the spy will follow me, and you will be free.'

'This city is like a great game of 'tafl,' Ulfr grunted.

'You have no idea, friend.'

'Luckily,' Ketil said, with a meaningful look at Halfdan, 'our young jarl here is a master at the game.'

'What is it you need? Hopefully not an army, for my crew have been split up and sent across the city,' Halfdan said, bitterly.

Harðráði shook his head. 'Ari continues to work to undermine me with imperial support, and you are new and unknown to him. For now, your men are probably safer not being near you or me.' He retrieved a leather scroll case from his side and held it out. As Halfdan took it, he threw a questioning look at the commander.

'Port authorisation. There is a ship in the Neorion harbour by the name of the *Grey Raven*, which is bound for Kiev. This is clearance for the port authorities to allow the vessel to depart, as well as orders for the sea chain to be withdrawn, allowing it out into the open waters.'

Halfdan's brow creased. 'Why would such a thing need to be done in secret?'

Harðráði gave a sly smile. 'When your enemies are as insidious as mine, it is often best to keep everything from them, be it something small or something critical. That way they can never be sure what's important. Keeps them guessing. *Grey Raven* is shipping a few things back to allies in Kiev. All you need to do is give this to the ship's captain, a man named Åse. Can't miss him. He's probably the only one-armed Northman in the harbour.'

Halfdan let out a low chuckle, but Leif scratched his head. 'Are you starting to move out? Shipping things back to Kiev as the emperor looks like he's replacing you?'

'Clever,' Harðráði said with a nod. 'But not quite. I've been shipping everything I can spare to Kiev for some time. All my battle loot and imperial pay. I have a throne to retake from a powerful enemy, and silver talks better than honour in some circles. My time here *is* coming to an end, but I will not leave the city in the hands of Ari Karsten, and I owe him a gutting before I depart. For now, though, with the emperor as he is, I must bide my time. Do this for me, and be certain that when the next donative comes and Ari falls, you will not be forgotten.'

As Halfdan nodded and Harðráði and his men turned with a last appraising look and left the building, Bjorn cleared his throat. 'What's a donative? It sounds like some sort of cake.'

Leif explained to the big man as Ketil shuffled closer to Halfdan. 'Be careful,' the Icelander advised. 'It seems natural to trust Harðráði, and for certain Ari is a troublesome piece of shit, but we seem to be in the middle of a war that's been going on for some time. The more we become involved, the more there will be to lose.'

'Agreed. But we are here for silver and for glory, Ketil, and Harðráði is our path to both.'

'Be careful where we tread on that path, then. I fear there will be pit-traps and landslides awaiting us.'

'Then let's go see how it starts.'

With Leif still explaining the imperial tradition of paying military bonuses to a frustrated Bjorn, the five of them waited just long enough to be comfortable, peeked out to make sure there was no sign of Harðráði and his men, and then slipped from the tavern. The Neorion harbour lay close, at the bottom of the hill, and as they clumped down the street, Halfdan kept his gaze on the ship-filled port ahead, while his companions continually turned this way and that, always watching for unfriendly eyes in every shadow. Even suspicious Ketil was confident they had not been followed as they reached the Neorion Gate and, with their identification, slipped through without question. The port was thriving as always, with a ship at almost every jetty. Out across the water they could see the chain closing the Horn Bay inlet. The defence was deployed in times of danger, and in general throughout the winter when shipping was less common and the majority of traffic came into the harbours on the far side of the city. Only during the true sailing season was the chain habitually left open.

One of the port officials stood on the corner nearby, directing a group of brightly dressed *Serks*. It had not taken Halfdan and his friends long in the city to learn that absolutely everything in Constantinople required an official with a title and that if you wanted to know anything, you had to ask the person whose responsibility that information was. The five of them crossed to the man and waited for the Serks to depart before approaching him.

'Hello. We're looking for a ship called *Grey Raven*.'

The man sucked his teeth for a moment, then turned and pointed along the dock. 'Varangian vessel. Jetty seventeen.'

Thanking the man, Halfdan and his friends hurried along to the appropriate position. There were a small number of good northern dragon boats in the harbour, either Rus traders or those belonging to the Varangians, and they could see the *Sea Wolf*, quiet and unmanned, wallowing at the very edge of the harbour not far away. *Grey Raven* was being loaded by sweating, swearing men, while a one-armed giant stood in the prow and harangued his crew. The five visitors came to a halt nearby and waited patiently as four men growled and groaned, lifting a heavy-looking chest from the dockside. Half a dozen armed Varangians stood protectively around them, and Halfdan's suspicions were confirmed when one of the lifters lost his grip for a moment, the chest lurched and tipped, the lid clacked open and closed and a score of gold coins scattered to the dock with a tinkle.

The armed men tensed, ready for trouble as the chest was righted, but the activity was no more of an attention-draw than anything else in the harbour and the tinkle of gold was lost in the din of mercantile action. Ketil reached down and gathered up two of the three coins that had rolled close. Halfdan swept up another.

'Our Harðráði is a rich man, it would seem,' Leif mused.

'Spoils of war,' Ketil said quietly, holding out the gold for all to see. 'Bagrat's head. Plunder from Georgia.'

'Not all of it,' Halfdan added in a near-whisper, showing them a Byzantine coin.

The one-armed man, the load back under control, was looking at them now, eyes narrowed. 'A sensible man would hand them back,' he said.

'Our thoughts precisely,' Halfdan said, face straight and expressionless as he took the two coins from Ketil and approached the captain. 'You would be Åse,' he said as he proffered the coins. One-arm took them, brow still folded into a frown. 'This is from Harðráði,' Halfdan added, withdrawing the documents and handing them over.

The frown disappeared and the big captain gave them a nod. 'Good. Tell the commander that we'll be across the *Svarthaf* by sunset tomorrow. His cargo is safe. Here.' The big man handed him a leather wallet with a seal, large enough only for a small document. Halfdan took it with a shrug, and the captain gave him a salute and then dropped into his ship to direct matters.

Halfdan stood watching for a while, but when it became clear that nothing further was expected of them, the five men turned and walked back along the quayside towards the gate.

'Did you see how many chests they were carrying?' Ketil said quietly as they emerged once more into the city streets.

'No.'

'I lost count, but if they were all full of coins, our friend has enough in that one ship to buy a small army.'

'Thrones cost money,' Bjorn said airily.

'What would you know, you big oaf.'

'You're all young. You won't remember Erik Segersäll and his rise to the throne.'

Ketil stopped in the street and turned to the big albino. 'Nor do you, you big fool. Your father would still have been sucking his mother's tit when Segersäll was on the throne.'

Bjorn took on an injured expression. 'I may have the face of a handsome young dove, but I'm older than you think.'

'You've got a face like a ruptured piglet that's been run over by a cart. Twice.'

'Now listen…'

As the two men squared up to one another, Halfdan's attention was suddenly elsewhere. They had been walking up one of the narrower, lesser streets parallel to the main one from the harbour, but like all streets in the imperial capital, it had been busy in its own way. Ordinary people going about their ordinary business. Halfdan had been paying enough attention to the big albino's boasting that he'd not immediately noticed the civic life ebbing around them until suddenly he looked around and discovered that they were alone.

'Lads…'

'The nearest you got to a throne before you met us was when you were crouched down, squeezing one out,' Ketil snorted, batting away a big pair of hands that were reaching for his neck.

'We might have trouble,' Halfdan said loudly, trying to cut through the argument. Now, Leif and Ulfr were looking about them, frowning.

'I'll show you royal when I crown you myself with a fucking hammer,' snapped Bjorn, managing to get a hand on Ketil's throat.

'Odin,' bellowed Halfdan, starting to lose his temper, and the sudden cry, so out of place in this 'civilised' Christian city, cut through the argument with enough shock to stop the two men mid-brawl. Bjorn's fingers loosened on his comrade's windpipe, and Ketil dropped his hand from where he'd been about to squeeze the huge albino's groin. Both men looked about now and realised that something had changed.

Men appeared from two alleyways, both ahead and behind, half a dozen big, well-armoured Varangians, though none had a weapon out. Valgarðr had warned them about that on their first day. It was one of the things drilled into the Guard. Only bring out your blade if you intend to use it. Too many Varangians had met a short, sharp fate at the hands of imperial justice for getting angry and dealing with a personal problem the way they would have done back in the North. That sort of peremptory justice wasn't acceptable in Byzantium. Probably it didn't involve enough paperwork for the Byzantines. Even *holmgang* was illegal, according to Valgarðr, which seemed madness.

So it came as no surprise that everyone's weapons remained sheathed, but it was equally no comfort, for sheathed weapons did not necessarily mean peaceful intent. Indeed, Halfdan could see men cracking their knuckles and loosening up, spoiling for a fight.

'Stand down,' said a thin one with greying hair and beard.

'Piss off,' replied Bjorn, finally letting go of Ketil's neck entirely and making a gesture that would bring tears to a nun's eyes.

Halfdan noted the increasing number of their opponents. They were currently facing two men apiece. Not impossible odds, but these were not low draftees in a foreign army, but hard-bred men of the North in imperial service. It would be nasty, and it could get worse yet. Still, Bjorn had spoken for them all, now, and the expressions of all around had hardened. Yet perhaps they could still be talked down. They might just be troublemakers with no real agenda.

'We don't want trouble,' he said, waving his hands in a calming gesture, 'and believe me, neither do you.'

Greybeard pointed. 'Hand that over and you can go about your business... for now.'

It took Halfdan a moment to notice that he still had the captain's leather wallet in his hand as he gestured, and that it was this to which the old Varangian was pointing.

'That's not going to happen,' he replied, keeping his voice level. 'But we're still willing to walk away.'

'You can hand it over, or you can have it taken off you,' the old man growled.

Halfdan glanced at Bjorn and Ketil, still standing uncomfortably close together. They both gave him the slightest of nods. With an exaggerated sigh, he held out the leather wallet. Greybeard stepped forward off a kerb, reaching out for it, and at the last moment, when Halfdan judged the man was near enough, he too took a step forth and swung the leather wallet, giving the man a stinging slap on the cheek with it. The man roared in anger as Halfdan stepped swiftly back, tucking the wallet away, but before the other Varangians could move, Ketil and Bjorn had leapt. The big albino had one man in each hand within a moment, and the muscles in his shoulders and upper arms moved like mountains colliding as he brought the two attackers together, their heads meeting with a crack. Ketil was on a third in a heartbeat, his arms locking around the man's neck and pulling him down to waist height, choking him.

Leif leapt. His fingers went to the weapon at his belt, but ever-steady Ulfr was there, his hand preventing the axe being pulled free. They needed to stay on the right side of the law, even here and now. As those two leapt into action and the enemy Varangians moved to retaliate, Halfdan stood facing Greybeard.

'Call your men off and walk away. Ari Karsten outranks me, but you do not. I owe you nothing.'

'You stinking mercenary piece of shit,' the old man snapped. 'Watch how you speak to your betters. Pagans here come and go, but more often than not in a wooden box.'

The threat was not lost on Halfdan. 'Last chance.'

The man simply growled, and so the young jarl, plans formulating, took an aggressive step forward, the old Varangian stepping nimbly back as he sized up his opponent. Without changing his expression, Halfdan took another strong pace forward and, still undecided how to react, the old man stepped back again. This time, however, his heel struck the kerb from which he had first stepped, and he fell, sprawling backwards and collapsing to the dirty stone flags. Another two quick paces forward, and Halfdan's boot was resting on the old warrior's ribs.

'Call your men off. I press down, you die.'

'You press down,' another voice said, 'and this place becomes an execution ground.'

Halfdan looked around, sharply. Bjorn and Ketil continued to fight, unaware of any change. Leif and Ulfr were backing away towards their jarl. Ari Karsten stood a little further up the street, and another half dozen Varangians loomed close by. Each of them held a bow of the sort Halfdan had seen in the hands of Pechenegs and other tribes in the Caucasus, small and curvy. Each had an arrow nocked, and all had a target in sight.

'Stand your men down and pass me that wallet,' the officer said in tones that brooked no argument.

'It's not mine to give.'

Ari's lip twitched just a little. 'You know me, Gotlander. You might think you're a gift to the Empire, but you're just another wide-eyed farm boy fallen under Harðráði's spell. I am one of the most powerful men in the Guard, and with your friend having fallen from the emperor's grace and his old ally alongside him, neither can stand against me. I have the emperor's ear, and near-complete control of the Varangoi. You disobey a direct order from me, your superior, and I can have you hung on hooks from the sea walls by sunset. I would rather not. I need a full Guard, and perhaps you might yet be saved. But first, I need that document.'

Halfdan looked at his friends, but found in their faces only defeat. Even Bjorn and Ketil had now stepped away from their opponents. Halfdan would have to explain later and take the brunt of what would come himself. With a deep breath, he stepped away from the fallen man and handed the wallet to Ari, who took it without a word, his archers still aiming. The officer, eyes always on Halfdan, grasped the wallet and broke the seal, pulling the thongs and opening it, sliding out the paper within. As the document fell into his hand, he simply dropped the wallet on the ground and lifted the paper, unfolding it. Halfdan tensed.

He watched the man's expression and was surprised when a look of fury replaced the one of quiet triumph on Ari's face. With a roar, Ari screwed up the piece of paper into a ball and threw it to the ground alongside the wallet. With a single gesture, he turned and stomped away up the street. His archers lowered their bows and followed, then the men who'd jumped them, and finally the old man from the pavement, wiping the dust from himself as he rose and stalked away, one last glare at Halfdan making it clear that some new feud had been born.

No one moved until they had all gone, and then, finally, the others gathered around Halfdan.

'What was the note?' Ulfr asked.

'I don't know,' Bjorn answered, 'but he looked like someone had shat in his mouth.'

Halfdan, frowning, crouched and picked up the paper, unfolding it and peering at it. He sighed and held it out to Leif. 'I can speak their tongue well enough these days, but their written letters still all look strange to me.'

The small Rus took the note and read the contents. As he did so, a smile glowed across his cheeks. He laughed out loud.

'What does it say?' Ketil urged.

'It says "Better luck next time, Karsten".'

The five of them looked at one another for a moment and then simultaneously burst out laughing. Ari might think he had the edge, but Harðráði was still the clever one.

Chapter 5

'I've got wet feet,' grumbled Anna, for the twentieth time that morning.

'It is not a *thrall's* place to complain,' Gunnhild snapped irritably.

'If I remember, Gunilla, a thrall is a slave,' Anna replied in an infuriatingly superior tone. Moreover, though nobody in the city seemed to be able to grasp her name's pronunciation, when Anna mispronounced it, it seemed more annoying on her tongue than any other. 'I am not a slave,' Anna continued, 'but a free servant. Slavery is not really practised in the empire any more.'

'Save me the lecture. I'm already regretting buying you.'

'*Hiring* me,' the young woman corrected her, earning a glare of daggers. Gunnhild's stoic composure had been almost legendary among the crew of the *Sea Wolf*. If Halfdan could see her now, he would laugh his head off.

'Be careful with that basket. There is a week's takings worth of goods inside. If you slip on the slush and drop it, you will be hunchbacked and grey before I pay you again.'

She could feel the disapproving look even as she stalked ahead.

Autumn had slid into winter with little warning. One evening she had closed up her business to a street of laughing citizens and a chilly, if bright and dry autumn day. The next morning she had opened her door to a light dusting of snow. Anna, her new servant, had proclaimed the world frozen and dead. Gunnhild, who had grown up on the streets of Hedeby, and knew what a *real* winter felt like, had disagreed, which had set off yet another argument. Since then, the snow had come and gone a few times, but the weather had stayed cold, and the streets had never truly cleared of slush.

The complaints of the young woman behind her rattled on in a quiet tone. Gunnhild – Gunilla as she seemed to be to the Byzantines – would have got rid of the irritating Anna some time ago, but the problem was the girl was so good that her habits had to be overlooked. She seemed to know every shopkeeper and market stall in the city, knew who could get things at short notice, knew who to avoid, and even knew the Greek names for components Gunnhild had only ever seen on the Baltic coast. Simply, she was too useful to let go, and so her complaints had to be borne with stoicism... a stoicism that was becoming more forced by the day.

The two women sloshed and stomped up the street. In the old days, Hedeby could be knee-deep in snow, but then Hedeby was flat and coastal. How a foot of slush could settle on a slope as steep as the ones in Constantinople was beyond all reason.

As they plodded their way through the city, the bells of the myriad churches began to toll unexpectedly. Gunnhild frowned. It had not been long enough since the last clanging for a new prayer call, and her eyes rose to the nearest church, then slid back down to the street. The atmosphere in the streets had changed in a heartbeat, as though rather than the pealing of bells, the citizens had heard words of doom ringing out. Folk had stopped what they were doing in the middle of the street and were standing with mouths hanging open and faces paling. Others had emerged from their houses with expressions of shock. Gunnhild's frown deepened and as she turned she saw Anna's face had followed suit.

'What is it?'

'That peal... that is not part of a service.'

'I had assumed. So what is it?'

'The emperor... the emperor has died.'

'Is that all?'

Anna stared at her as though she had slipped into gibberish. 'The *emperor* has died.'

Gunnhild shrugged. 'Kings die. New kings rule. It is the way of things. There will be another emperor.'

Anna seemed to be trying to get her mind around such a calm acceptance, and so Gunnhild simply walked on, leaving the servant to slosh on up the street in her wake. The same scene played out in each thoroughfare as they made their way back home.

Despite this strange obsession with the emperor's passing, as they rounded the last corner, a crowd had still gathered outside Gunnhild's door. Her sudden celebrity was becoming a problem. After a shaky start she had set up, opening her door to anyone with enough coin, administering poultices, unguents and tonics for everything from the shits to infertility. She had read what she could in people's faces and advised and predicted, though her diminishing supply of compound had made her unwilling to attempt true seeing for anyone. Still, her ordinary innate abilities had earned her no small fame among the people of this region of the city, and never a day passed without a queue in the street.

The statue of Tyche, still chipped and damaged, but cleaned and repaired as far as possible, now stood outside the house, by the side of the door. Anna had directed her to a scholar whose knowledge of old gods was good, despite the cross he wore, and the more Gunnhild learned of this faded spirit, the more she liked her. Tyche was a goddess of fortune tied to the destiny of this great city, and the concept rang very familiar to Gunnhild. Despite the goddess's strange dress and armfuls of junk, she was clearly a *hamingja*, a spirit of protective fortune, such as followed all souls in the North. As such, and as a symbol of luck for both herself and the city she now inhabited, Gunnhild had brought the statue into public view. She had wondered whether the pagan symbol would turn away her more devoutly

Christian customers, but with Tyche's close connection with the city, people seemed to be readily able to look past her pagan origins and accept her as their own, a little as they had done with Gunnhild herself.

In fact, she was becoming uncomfortably popular, and had gone so far as to buy a ram's skull and set up an old-fashioned post outside her door, opposite the statue, in the hope of driving away the more difficult customers. Still, she was too busy for her own good.

The clamour began as she approached the door, and Gunnhild took the basket from Anna and pointed at them. 'Sort this,' she said, and then unlocked her door and disappeared inside. The old house-temple had changed in the weeks she had been here. It looked a lot more like a völva's house now, or at least one loosely crossed with an apothecary. Indeed, the set of shelves she'd had built by a local carpenter held such a quantity and array of spices, herbs, animal parts, plant extracts, poisons and more that the whole thing probably represented a treasure in its own right.

Crossing to her table, she swept last night's experiment aside and threw away the failed compound, for she had begun nightly attempts to replicate the essential mixture in her treasured pouch. Thus far she had failed, which came as no surprise. Only *völvur* knew how to make it, and the secret was guarded carefully. She was certain that henbane and two different fungi were among the ingredients, but had no more clue than that.

Sighing, she tidied around, restocking with their haul from the market, and she quickly wolfed down a little cheese and flatbread before crossing to the door and peering through the crack. She stepped back sharply to avoid a broken nose as Anna suddenly swung the door in.

'What? Another emperor died?'

'A noblewoman is coming.'

'Here? How do you know?'

'Because she is being carried in a litter and has an entourage. And where else would she be going in this street? To buy a copper pot or get drunk in a tavern?'

Gunnhild simply nodded. There was logic to that. A woman of import would not even deign to walk this common street without good reason. She looked past Anna to where the crowd outside had all turned away, looking up the hill.

'Make things ready here,' she said, and stepped outside, adjusting her pelt cloak.

The gathering had stopped jostling and were now watching the approach of the noblewoman. Men in coats of bronze plates with spears led the way, then a haughty-looking man with a staff and a long robe. Half a dozen servants plodded alongside a rich-looking litter with damask drapes carried by men with powerful shoulders. More mercenaries followed up, protecting the entourage.

As the litter came to a halt nearby, the curtain was drawn back by one of the servants and a woman appeared in the opening. Her dress was rich and ostentatious, even for this city, her hair ornamentally piled in curls and wreaths and all held down with a gilded cap, her makeup applied carefully, if rather heavily. She was on the plump side, and yet more than a little handsome. Gunnhild knew men who would fall over themselves for such a woman. There was, however, something in her expression that Gunnhild already didn't entirely trust.

'Who was first?' she asked the crowd.

'That would be me,' purred the woman in the litter.

'You are the *last*. I asked for the *first*.'

The crowd remained silent, and Gunnhild gave them a look of disapproval. Fear of such a woman was entirely appropriate in this place, and yet it still annoyed Gunnhild that none of these people would stand up for the fact that they had precedence.

'I do not consult in order of social rank,' she said, flashing a look at the woman in the vehicle. 'All women are equal in my eyes.'

73

The noblewoman regarded her carefully, her eyes boring deep. She seemed to decide that arguing was going to get her nowhere, which at least made her wise in some way. With a single nod, she turned to the man with the staff. 'Pay this rabble to leave.'

Gunnhild began to marshal her arguments, but they melted away as she realised that the gathered crowd's attitude seemed to have changed. Fear and respect had become basic greed, and Gunnhild would have to accept this, since everyone else seemed to. The lackey found a purse of coins from somewhere and passed a handful to each of several other servants, who began to give two coins to each of those queuing, accompanied with the words 'Come back tomorrow.'

Today was clearly going to be a day to test the patience. Gunnhild waited until the crowd began to melt away. 'My livelihood relies upon such minnows,' she said to the woman, meaningfully. 'The shark who drives them off had better make an equal payment.'

A big fish. The first of the big fish.

The woman in the litter gave her a negligent wave. 'Payment is a paltry thing.'

Her litter-bearers carefully lowered the vehicle, while a servant produced a step from somewhere. The woman emerged from her silken chamber slowly, with the sort of grace that only comes with decades of practise. Her red leather slippers were as yet unmarked by the snow, and her silver-threaded blue dress was edged with gilt embroidery at hem and cuffs, her belt seemingly formed of solid gold, studded with gems. Indeed, gold and gems seemed to drip from the woman. No wonder she needed so many armed guards in a city street.

With her haughty look still in place, the noblewoman stepped carefully through the slushy street towards Gunnhild's door. The guards moved in a choreographed manner to keep her from danger, but as she neared the door, she waved them away, and only two maids and the man with the staff moved to follow her. Gunnhild looked through her door. Anna was in a deep bow, ready for the visitor. Eyes narrowing, Gunnhild stepped back to allow the woman entry, but gestured at the others.

'You enter alone.'

The noblewoman shook her head. 'Unacceptable. Unseemly.'

'Unvisited,' Gunnhild replied, and stepped across to block the door. 'I am not a performer of plays. My work is not for an audience.'

The noblewoman seemed to size her up again for a long moment, and finally nodded. 'It is not customary, but I shall indulge you.' She turned and waved the servants away. The man with the staff looked extremely unhappy, but backed off regardless. Once more, Gunnhild stepped aside and allowed the woman in. Following her, she shut the door, leaving the entourage in the street.

The noblewoman sniffed and looked around. 'I had expected more. There is a smell of… I cannot put my finger on it, but it is not pleasant.'

'I have many pungent ingredients,' Gunnhild said flatly. 'I am not in the business of perfumes.'

'Oh I know your business,' the woman said, crossing to a seat, examining it with distaste, and then sinking into it carefully. 'My name is Verina Maniakes. You have heard of me? Or of my husband, perhaps?'

Gunnhild shook her head. 'I am recently arrived.' She seated herself opposite the woman.

'Good. Perhaps it would be better, then, if I had not given you my name at all. Still, I may rely upon your discretion? I hear only good things about you, through the network of my informers.'

'I am not in the habit of gossiping about my work.'

'And your servant?'

'She talks far too much, but not about our business.'

The woman seemed to relax slightly. 'Gunilla, if I might call you by name?' Gunnhild gritted her teeth, but nodded. 'Gunilla, I am the wife of Georgios Maniakes, the pre-eminent general in the empire. Our family moves in the highest of court circles.'

'Your problem must be of some concern to bring you here,' Gunnhild said quietly. 'You must have trusted physicians and magicians at court.'

Maniakes simply looked at her, then steepled her fingers. 'I believe I am with child.'

'Congratulations.'

'Hardly. My husband has fallen foul of the endless conspiring and accusations of the imperial court and has languished in "imperial care" in the *Noumera* prison for many months.'

'More months than your pregnancy,' Gunnhild presumed.

'Hence my problem and my unwillingness to consult imperial physicians. I seek confirmation of my suspicions, and if they are correct, some way to halt the unwanted.'

Gunnhild sat back and folded her arms. 'I can only help if you have not left it too long. If the child has formed, you will need to seek a surgeon.'

Verina Maniakes shook her head. 'As soon as I suspected, I sought out a solution. My enquiries led me to you.'

Taking a breath, Gunnhild rose. 'I do not know how the empire views such things, but I will need to probe your midriff.'

The noblewoman gave an odd smile and lifted her arms. Gunnhild worked her way around the voluminous dress, feeling for the woman's belly and sides. This was not something she had done often, and certainly not since leaving the side of the old völva in Hedeby, but she knew the principles, and certainly what could be done. After a few moments, she sat back once more. 'Your pregnancy is still new enough, but is surely there. I can arrange an abortive of savin and rue. The mixture can be graced with flavours to make it more palatable, but the more the bitter taste is nullified, the less effective it can be. Undiluted, with daily ingestion, your problem should be flushed within a week.'

Maniakes nodded, her lip wrinkling in distaste. 'I will endure any bitterness other than the one caused by my poor judgement. Mix your herbs, Gunilla, and I will pay you well for them. More than enough to pay for your missed day of customers.'

Gunnhild crossed to her shelves of herbs and began to locate the various ones she would need, while Anna fetched her mortar and pestle and lit the fire, putting a pot of water on to boil. 'I would recommend,' she said, 'taking the drink twice daily, each time more than an hour before you eat, so that it has sufficient time to sink into your body before you soak it up with bread. If there is any unforeseen problem, you will need to visit me, and I will examine you. I would recommend, in fact, that even when your problem has passed, you come to me again so that I can be sure that all continues to be well.'

'And so that your purse remains well-stocked,' Maniakes added, but then slid into a smile. 'Coin is no issue. Indeed, perhaps it would be best if I put you on some sort of wage, and you signed your talents over to me for the duration,' she mused.

Gunnhild shook her head. 'I have other people to see. But I shall make you a priority on any return visit. For now I should get to work.'

For the following half hour Verina Maniakes prattled about life in courtly circles and the value of having trustworthy persons upon whom to rely in private circumstances, while Gunnhild mixed and chopped, pounded and ground, and then she and Anna boiled up the result into a potion of dull green-brown, which they then decanted into a bottle.

'This,' she said, as she passed it to the noblewoman, 'contains sufficient doses for one week, twice daily. I leave you to measure out dosage appropriately.'

As the woman took the medicine and rose to her feet, she fished out a pouch from the wide golden belt. 'How much, dear Gunilla.'

'Six of your imperial gold coins.'

She half expected the noblewoman to argue, for that was a vastly inflated price compared to what she would have charged any woman from the street, and easily covered what she would make in a day and more, but Maniakes simply smiled and produced twelve, dropping them to the table. 'A little extra for your ongoing discretion.'

Gunnhild gave her a professional bow of the head as Anna rushed over and pulled the door open. Outside, the entourage had gathered close, ready to escort Maniakes home. The noblewoman climbed into her litter, and gave Gunnhild an indulgent wave. 'Thank you for your time, Gunilla.'

As the bearers turned carefully, ready to carry the litter back up the street, there was a surprised shout from the hill above. Gunnhild turned to look, and raised an eyebrow at the sight of another litter, which had rounded a corner with its own sizeable escort, and was making its way down. She leaned back in the door. 'Clear things away fast, Anna, and boil another kettle. The small fish are done swarming, and the sharks smell blood.'

Anna, bafflement at this creasing her face, hurried about the business as Gunnhild stood in the street and watched the second litter approach. As it neared, a green curtain was pulled aside and a thin, elegant noblewoman wreathed in green silk and gold leaned from the window.

'I am surprised the Maniakes whore can lift her nethers from her bed long enough to travel the city,' she snorted in a derisive tone.

Verina Maniakes's face folded into a grimace of hatred. 'These words are ironic from the mouth of such an infamous trollop,' she snapped, then turned and waved to Gunnhild. 'Watch this woman. If you have any sense, you will close your door and let her wallow in the street.'

'It is you who spends your time in the street,' the newcomer shouted meaningfully. As Maniakes began to move, the guards of both entourages met and began to shove one another.

Gunnhild was beginning to worry that this might break out into open fighting, but fortunately it appeared that each noblewoman had a fount of wisdom among their retinues, and within moments, under the guidance of those men, the two parties separated, Maniakes disappearing off up the hill even as the new woman's litter came to a halt outside, the pair still slinging insults even as they departed.

Gunnhild said little as the thin woman alighted from her vehicle and was escorted to the door. A brief exchange, and the woman agreed to leave her people outside as the previous noblewoman had done.

'You should have nothing to do with the Maniakes whore,' the newcomer advised as she sank into the seat so recently vacated. 'She is little more than a loose woman married to a traitor. Her husband will languish in prison until he dies, while she works her way through the baser men of court.'

'And you are?'

'This,' Anna said, 'is the Sklerina. Maria Sklerina.'

'Oh,' Gunnhild replied, clearly indicating that this meant nothing to her.

Sklerina's eyebrow arched. 'Sorcerers are rare in this city, especially female ones.'

'I am no sorcerer.'

'That is not my understanding. You have the talent to see what will be?'

Gunnhild shrugged. 'If the goddess is willing and the weaving is clear I can sometimes tell of the fate of a man... or a woman.'

'You will know by now that the emperor has passed, of course?'

'All the bells. Yes. Though if you came in response to them, your men must have run.'

'It has only just become public knowledge, but the court knew in the early hours, some time ago. My business is with succession. The emperor's nephew has already been adopted as his heir, but the empress retains much power and she will not spend long alone before she seeks a new husband. The Church will allow her a third marriage. A new emperor will thus be crowned soon, but the empress's new husband will be terribly close to the throne. I seek to discover what you can see of this.'

Gunnhild frowned. 'This will cost greatly.'

'I will pay any sum within the bounds of reason.'

'Then sit, and do not interrupt.'

She turned and nodded at Anna, who fetched her prized accoutrements from the chest at the room's rear. Passing them over with a frown of disapproval, the servant padded off up the stairs to keep herself busy. Anna was comfortable with the apothecary side of their work, but when Seiðr became involved, her Christian values tended to drive her away, which suited Gunnhild just fine.

Slowly, she began to sing the ancient song as she took a seat among the pelts and cushions. At one point as she dipped into a low chant, her eyes opened to see Sklerina watching her with fascination, and she then found her pouch with eyes closed once more and dusted some of the precious compound upon her lips. With a slight sway, she sang the song, ever stronger, the ancient ways of Freyja carrying her higher and higher as her lips tingled and the taste of the bitter mixture infused her.

She felt it all change, felt the mundane world fall away and the heady mists of *Fólkvangr* enfold her, felt the goddess pulsing in her veins. Saw that an old woman stood alone, tall and powerful, a statue in gold robes. Two other women coalesced from the shadows beside her. They were barely formed and indistinct, and yet somehow she knew them for Maniakes and Sklerina. As she watched, one of the two shadow women seemed to age, crumble and fade before her eyes, while the other shattered into many pieces, as though torn apart by forces unseen, leaving the old woman alone once more. Gunnhild tried to open her eyes, for this seemed enough, but something kept them tightly sealed. She railed against her own body's inability to obey her will, and then suddenly three new shapes were there, padding out of the mist to stand beside the old woman.

A bear. A wolf. A boar.

Her eyes snapped open. Gunnhild realised she was shaking. Sklerina was watching her carefully, her expression a mix of concern and delight. She smiled in a strangely predatory way as Gunnhild gradually steadied herself and shook her head to clear it.

'Magic is more fascinating than I could ever have imagined,' Sklerina said. 'What was that you tasted?'

'It is a compound that brings me closer to Freyja. The bear shirts, the *berserkir*, use the same mix to bring them close to Odin in battle.'

She pulled herself up short. She would never normally have said such a thing, though she was still a little shaken and groggy, and it had slipped out. The names of gods did not sit well in the world of Christians. Indeed, the berserkir were a thing of the past, for who in this world of the nailed god would place their life in the hands of Odin on a battlefield? Still, Sklerina seemed unfazed, simply nodding her understanding.

'My lover covets the crown,' she said suddenly, 'almost as much as he covets me. It is my belief that he will be emperor.'

Gunnhild paused and looked at the woman carefully. *Two shadowy ladies with the old woman, one of whom crumbled, the other shattered.* She could lie, tell Sklerina what she wanted to hear, and even the truth was relatively vague, as she did not know which of the shadow women had been which. Yet somehow, she felt the truth needed to be spoken here.

'The empress is old?'

Sklerina, brow creasing, nodded.

Gunnhild sighed. 'I cannot say whether your man will be emperor. The goddess does not always answer that which I seek, but often she shows me instead what I *need* to know. What I *can* tell you is that being close to the empress will do you no good in the end. Neither you, nor Verina Maniakes. If you cleave to such a destiny, only destruction will await you.'

The noblewoman frowned and her hands, clasped throughout, now rubbed together almost nervously. 'My brother said you would be a charlatan. That you would tell me what I wanted to hear and take my money. He does not believe in magic, unless it be an aspect of the Devil's temptation. But you are not a charlatan, are you? What my sources were saying is true. You really *can* see things.'

'I am sorry I have nothing better to tell you. But sometimes the tapestry of fate can be rewoven. Sometimes the warp and weft can be changed. Your lover and your brother might both seek power, for it is the way with most men, but I urge you to do what you can to turn them from such a path. That way lies only pain for all of you.'

Could the tapestry be changed? Where had that notion come from? Certainly the old völva in Hedeby had told her no such thing...

Sklerina nodded slowly. 'I thank you for your candour.' She found a small purse and opened it, picking around the coins within and then, with a careless smile, dropped the whole purse on the table. 'Your renown is well-founded, Mistress Gunilla. I shall ponder upon your words, and I shall visit you again, if I may?'

Gunnhild, still shaken, nodded silently and stayed in her seat as the noblewoman rose and turned, making for the door. She tried to rise then, but her legs felt too shaky. Without looking back, Maria Sklerina opened her door, closing it behind her and returning to her entourage.

Gunnhild sat there for some time, watching the closed door, composing herself, listening to the muffled sounds of Anna cleaning upstairs. The old empress and the two women of the dream did not worry her. In fact, though it had never happened before, even her inability to pull herself out of the dream did not panic her, though it was something she had no wish to encounter again.

What *had* worried her was the three animals walking with the old empress. The wolf could only be Halfdan, and she had long since come to terms with the bear being Harðráði, both of those animals being associated with Odin. But the boar was different. The boar was important. The boar Hildisvíni was the animal of Freyja. And there was only one child of Freyja in this strange southern land.

She had wondered if she would return to the crew of the *Sea Wolf* eventually, though she had known already that her thread would weave for a time with that of Harðráði. Now, though, it seemed that a new tapestry was being made, woven of four threads.

The bells for the emperor's passing were still tolling outside, the clanging dulled by distance and walls. One thing seemed certain: the coming days were going to be interesting.

Part Two

ᚠᛟᛚᛔᛖᛋ ᛟᚠ ᛟᚹᛁᛏ

Imperial Lions

Chapter 6

'I don't understand the oath,' grumbled Bjorn, as he shrugged into his chain shirt, which had been adjusted by the imperial armoury to account for a little extra bulk he had put on since arriving in the city.

'It's straightforward,' Leif said.

'No it isn't, little one. We take an oath to defend the emperor, but the emperor's died. We didn't take an oath to the empress at all, but Harðráði seems to want more loyalty to her than to this new pretty boy.'

'If you remember the words of your oath, you vowed allegiance to the emperor and to the *throne* of Byzantium. That covers a multitude of sins. When there is no emperor, it covers whatever incumbent temporarily occupies the throne, and when there is a question of precedence as there sometimes is with an empress, it automatically encompasses her within our remit.'

'I understood about a quarter of those words,' grumbled Bjorn.

'You swear allegiance to the throne, no matter whose arse occupies it,' translated Ketil.

'Ah. Why couldn't you say that in the first place?' the big man grunted at Leif, who rolled his eyes in response.

'I heard,' Halfdan put in, 'that the empress is of an old royal family. The people treat her like an emperor herself, while the last emperor, and this next one too, are really nobodies. Some even say that when Harðráði came to the city, it was the empress Zoe he bent the knee to, not the emperor.'

'Certainly he seemed happier with the idea of her in charge.'

At this they all nodded sagely. With the death of the old emperor, Harðráði had been summoned to the palace, and within an hour was back in his prime position, and yet despite that, the commander had been sour faced when they'd met him. Not only had the ailing emperor adopted as his successor a nephew that Harðráði despised, but though the empress had managed to return him to his position of command, the new emperor-to-be had refused to allow Harðráði to take any issue up with Ari, who remained a powerful second-in-command.

'*She* sets me free while *he* ties my hands and stands a vulture on my shoulder,' the commander had snarled.

Halfdan had taken the opportunity one afternoon when the commander was taking a breather to raise the question of his men.

'The *Sea Wolf.*'

'Your crew.'

'Yes. I am their Pentecontarch, and yet they remain in small groups scattered throughout the city, courtesy of Ari's commands. I owe it to my men to gather them once more. To protect them if I must.'

Harðráði had nodded slowly. 'I will see what I can do, young jarl. Their division must plague you.'

'I do what I can, visiting them, and assuring them that this is only temporary.'

'And it is,' the commander assured him. 'I have much that Ari has done which needs to be undone, but the new emperor will be of no aid to me, and it will take time to bring everything back into line. The entire deployment of the Guard needs to be changed, and your men will come back to you then, but you must give me time. There is so much to do, and there are so many obstacles in the way of everything these days.'

Halfdan had left it at that. At least now with the commander back, things would change. This new emperor was young. Harðráði seemed to place no value upon the handsome young man, but the empress was no fool, so surely she had chosen well, and the young emperor might perhaps be made to understand what was best for his people. Within hours, the crown would be upon his head, though from what they had heard he had already been at work with the imperial administration all morning, making decrees that would be ratified and announced immediately following the coronation.

'Which axe?' Bjorn asked with unaccustomed seriousness.

'What?'

Halfdan turned from picking up his helmet to find the big albino standing with an axe in each hand. One was his own, a solid warrior's blade with no decoration, but well-used and with an edge that could cut a whisper in half, while the other was one of the long-handled axes that they had been given as part of their uniform.

'Why?' Ketil snorted, 'are you expecting trouble? It's a coronation, not a war.'

'Tell that to Harðráði,' Bjorn said quietly, bringing about another considered silence.

'Just take one of them,' Halfdan said finally. 'We're not really going to be on show anyway. We're not important enough.'

'We've half an hour,' Ulfr grumbled, 'so hurry up.'

Halfdan slid his sword, the beautiful, short eagle-hilted blade he'd taken from the Alani, into its sheath and gripped it for a moment. Oddly it seemed to be a Byzantine style, for he'd seen swords to match it carved upon statues of emperors and warriors of old around the palace. He sighed, drummed his fingers on the hilt and smiled at the good-natured jibes his friends were throwing at one another.

He couldn't have said what it was that warned him, other than instinct or the Loki cunning that ran through his veins. He turned at the gentle click and rumble, a low, quiet noise that was almost entirely lost beneath the din of men arranging weapons and armour and making improper and eye-watering suggestions about each other's mothers.

He caught sight of the ball rolling, snatched a brief image of a fiery spark, looked up to see Leif laughing at Bjorn, oblivious, his back to the approaching sphere. He was moving in an instant, before truly considering his action, for in the blink of an eye he'd been taken right back to those fights against the Jakulus and his Alani warriors, the fire bombs they had hurled in small pots.

The young jarl threw himself through the air with a yell of warning, hitting the smaller Rus hard in the shoulder and knocking him several feet to his left, where the two men hit the floor of the arming room, rush matting dulling the clatter of steel against the flags.

As the other three turned to look in surprise, the two men rolling to a halt, the clay pot with the hissing fuse rolled straight through the space where Leif had stood and smashed into a rack of spears, where the clay shattered and Greek fire exploded in a molten cloud, droplets raining down in a circle, igniting the mats across the floor and racing up the dry timber weapon racks.

Ketil, who had been the closest of the others, yelped in shock as several flaming droplets hit his leg and ignited his trousers. As the tall Icelander reached down in pain and panic to try and undo his belt, Ulfr, practical as ever, leapt across, drawing his long-bladed fighting knife. With no care for further damage, while Ketil still struggled with his belt, crying out with the pain, Ulfr simply hacked at the material and swiftly cut away the burning patch, using the *sax* blade to flick it across the room. Ketil's leg was black and red in places, blotched and burned, but the damage was limited to his calf thanks to Ulfr's quick thinking, and he was already breathing in relief.

Short-lived relief, as it happened, for as Halfdan and Leif climbed to their feet, it was clear that the fire was not going to fade out on its own. The dry racks and timber mats gave the conflagration sufficient fuel to expand, and the room was going to be filled with sticky flame soon enough.

'Out,' Halfdan bellowed. 'Out now.'

They needed no further urging, and the five men barrelled out of the arming room as the smoke began to drift from the door. The corridor outside was empty, but the din was full as Ketil hobbled around cursing the burns on his leg, while Bjorn, Ulfr and Leif variously complained, raged or swore oaths, staring into the burning room, all overlain with the sounds of armour and weapons clattering and the roar of flames.

Halfdan closed his eyes, blocking the sounds out one by one, peeling the layers back, trying to hear something beneath it all, and then suddenly there it was: the pounding of feet.

With a bellow, he hared off down the corridor, ripping his sword free. As he gained distance from the noise of the fire and his friends, he could hear more clearly, and felt sure he was right. The sound was that of heavy boots on stone, and they were running away. Only one man would be running away right now, and that was the man whose hand had cast the grenade.

By the time he reached the next corner, his friends were catching up, especially Ketil with his ridiculously long stride.

'You have him?' the Icelander asked, close behind as they rounded the corner.

'I hear him. Around the next corner.'

They ran on and despite everything Halfdan found himself slightly irked when Ketil suddenly ran past, outpacing him so easily, even with his leg wounded like that.

'Back here, you fuck,' the Icelander shouted as he reached the corner, axe flailing wildly in his hand as he ran. Halfdan rounded the next corner in time to briefly see a human shape disappear through a door into the cold winter sunlight outside, followed by Ketil a moment later. There was a brief scream and a bellow of rage. Halfdan pounded to that doorway, breath heaving and burning in his lungs, the others slowly catching up, and as he rounded the corner to an icy blast of winter air, the young jarl pulled himself up short to prevent barrelling straight into Ketil's back.

Stepping out beside him, his gaze first fell on the man face down in the snow, for he was clearly the one they had chased, and then, spotting the arrow shaft transfixing the neck, his eyes lifted to see two men with bows across the snow-covered white lawn, one with an arrow still nocked, the other slowly lowering his bow. Ari Karsten stood close by, his expression unreadable.

The others piled through the doorway behind him and came to a halt, staring at the cold, white, charnel tableau.

'What the fuck?' Bjorn spat.

'How lucky we were that the primikerios over there happened to be passing with a couple of archers ready to draw, eh?' Ketil snorted.

'Quite,' Leif said. 'At least they got the bastard.'

'They *sent* the bastard,' hissed Ketil in a tone just loud enough to carry across the lawn to Ari's ears.

'And now we cannot interrogate him,' Halfdan said, folding his arms.

'You five attract far too much trouble,' Ari said calmly from the other side of the garden. 'Svend here will bill you for the arrow in due course. Don't be too long clearing that away,' he added, pointing at the body. 'You need to be in place in the great church before the bells start to toll.' With that, Karsten turned, gesturing to his archers, and walked away.

'Harðráði's right about him,' Bjorn said once he'd left. 'He'd look a lot better with an axe in his neck. With luck I'll get to be the man to do it. This one, I think,' he added, holding up his own axe and throwing away the long-handled one he'd carried from the arming room.

'What do we do with him?' Leif asked, pointing at the body.

'You know this city,' Halfdan said, his voice tight, 'there's an administrator for everything. Someone will be along soon to handle it and produce appropriate documents. We need to get to the church.'

'Ketil needs to be seen by a medic,' Leif noted, pointing at the blistered wounds on the Icelander's lower leg.

'It can wait,' Ketil replied.

'But this is a coronation, and I suspect they will want you in intact trousers. Your legs aren't *that* attractive even normally.'

'Straighten up,' Valgarðr said quietly. 'The new emperor comes.'

They could hear the cheering still outside the great church of the Hagia Sophia, where Michael Kalaphates and the empress Zoe had cast coins in the hundred to the people as part of the great coronation tradition, but all inside was still quiet. Somewhere in the maze of this building, the new emperor was being helped into his coronation robe. All around the main floor of this, the largest temple of any sort that Halfdan could ever imagine, the rich and the powerful of Byzantium stood watching, waiting for their new ruler. Here on the upper galleries were only a few priests and a few members of the Guard, keeping their eye on proceedings. More Varangians would be placed downstairs, of course, but every angle had to be covered on a day like this.

Harðráði would be leading the men guarding the procession, of course, along with Ari. The pair would have to hide their mutual hatred thoroughly on a day like this, which made Halfdan rather glad they were up here out of the way.

'You're here for one reason only,' Valgarðr had told them as he moved them into place. 'To watch for any move against the empress.'

'Not the emperor?' Halfdan had said.

'He's not the emperor yet,' the officer had replied. 'Michael, the Caulker, for that's his grand imperial background, is unlikely to achieve greatness. His father was a moron. Back in Sicily, we won almost the entire island back from the Serks over a two-year war. When we were pulled back, his father lost it all again in two months. Harðráði will never look at the new emperor as anything more than the son of an idiot and, frankly, he's not alone.'

'Why did the empress allow this, then?'

Valgarðr had sighed. 'The empress is a great woman, clever and strong. She's survived decades in a position where the unwary die badly. But she has one unfortunate weakness in that she likes a pretty man, and that weakness keeps coming back to haunt her.'

'Women,' Bjorn grinned. 'Slaves to desire, in my experience.'

'Your experience is mostly of whores, though?' Ketil said archly.

Valgarðr waved a finger. 'Keep that sort of opinion to yourself. I've seen Harðráði break a man's nose for insulting the empress.' A commotion suggested that something was finally happening. 'Watch,' Valgarðr reminded them. 'Be prepared to move if anything happens.'

'Is anything likely to?'

'You don't know Michael Kalaphates and his family. Half of them have been exiled for causing trouble. We cannot rule out an attempt on the empress today, which would leave Michael untethered.'

With that, Valgarðr was off, trotting away to his position by the stairs.

Halfdan leaned on the balcony, waiting once more. They had been in position for over an hour now, despite having been hurried into place. Byzantine service seemed to involve a lot of 'hurry up and wait'. He went back to his boredom carving of earlier, where with a small eating knife from his belt he had scratched his name in the marble balcony. Leif had been horrified, but Halfdan had shrugged and pointed to similar markings across the gallery, singling out one that suggested Ari himself had once been bored in this same place.

Adding the last few marks to the runes, he quickly secreted the knife as a door opened below and the sound of that dreadful, droning and atonal Christ-priest warbling echoed around the massive church, rising to the dome. Around the church, noblemen, priests and Varangians crossed themselves and prayed. In a moment of continued defiance, Halfdan pulled his Mjǫllnir pendant from his tunic and let it hang free, a powerful sign even in this place.

He could see several groups of the *Sea Wolf*'s crew around the upper and lower galleries, split up among other Varangians, and resolved once more to press Harðráði to reunite them. His wandering gaze then picked out the grey-bearded Varangian they had met on the way back from the port, standing close to Ari, and he was startled to realise the old man was staring at him directly. For just a moment, the greybeard drew a finger in a line across his throat, gave an unpleasant smile, and then returned his attention to events around him. Halfdan frowned at the man for a moment, and then his gaze slid to the subject of the service once more.

The emperor was, as Valgarðr had suggested, a remarkably handsome man, and that was clear even from up here, and it came as no surprise how rich and complex were the garments the man wore for this important day. The procession of figures seemed endless, filing into the great church to the sound of that cross-god warbling. The empress somehow managed to seem a thousand times more regal than the emperor, even following obediently at heel. As they moved into predetermined positions, the high priest stood near a raised platform with steps to either side, a decorative golden thing. The emperor approached the steps with a regal gait and began to climb as the chanting reached its zenith. As the new emperor tottered into his place on the platform, his heavy robes making even basic perambulation troublesome, Halfdan's eyes went to the crown hanging above him from a golden chain. The crown itself contained enough gold and jewels to buy a small city, and probably weighed more than most helmets. The emperor was in position beneath it now, swaying slightly as the song faded into hollow echoes around the columns and the priest close by his side began to chant one of his rites.

Halfdan frowned and took a half step forward, leaning on the balcony.

'What are you doing?' hissed Leif. 'You'll get us in trouble.'

'Does the emperor look all right to you?' Halfdan asked, peering at the figure. Michael was shaking now, and he'd assumed that to be a reaction to the weight of the robes if not the weight of the occasion, but now it was clearly something else. Even from this height and distance, Halfdan could see that the man's complexion had gone pale and waxy.

'Is he poisoned?' Ketil breathed.

'I don't know. I can't tell such things.' More than ever he felt keenly the absence of Gunnhild, who would undoubtedly have known.

'He's going,' Bjorn warned them.

And he was. As they watched, the handsome young son of a ship caulker, weighed down by a millennium of ceremonial attire, folded up like a portable loom and collapsed in a heap on the podium, hidden to ground level behind a golden panel covered in crosses and images, where he proceeded to shake, watched only from above and those close by.

Halfdan's eyes went from figure to figure around that room in an instant, and all he saw in every quarter was suspicion and blame. The empress Zoe's eyes shot to Harðráði, whose own gaze was levelled at Ari, who in turn glared back, narrow-eyed, at him. Every figure in that room was watching someone else like a hawk, waiting for some sign of guilt. It took only a moment for Halfdan to take it all in and come to the conclusion that while every one of them was suspicious, and probably horribly guilty of something, none of them seemed to be guilty of this.

'I don't think this is an attack,' he said to his men. 'Stand down. I think he is ill.'

Harðráði was the first to move, followed by the high priest, his own face white with shock and panic now. The two men crouched over the fallen not-quite-emperor for a long moment as the empress finally joined them, and then two priests and three more Varangians, including Ari. In other circumstances it might have looked humorous, since the platform was small and narrow, as were the stairs up at each end, and so most of them appeared to be queuing.

Halfdan realised he was holding his breath and allowed it to whisper out between tight lips.

Finally, Harðráði rose from the gathering.

'Calm, everyone. The emperor is well, just a little sickly.' There was a pause, and Halfdan wondered how many people in the room had missed that little jibe. 'He has suffered with the spinning sickness. Vertigo,' he added. '*Skotomatikoi*. Someone fetch oils and hartshorn to revive him while he can still lift the crown.'

Surely no one had missed that last one.

Halfdan continued to watch as oils and potions were brought forth and the emperor brought back from his stupor. As he was helped to his feet, Halfdan watched the empress, and noted the wrinkle of her lip. Could vertigo be induced, he wondered? Because the one person at whom no one had looked with suspicion was the empress, and in Halfdan's mind she had the most to lose right now.

The emperor returned upright, the crowd relaxed once more and the ceremony picked up where it left off, but now Halfdan was watching only one person. His gaze stayed upon the ageing and imperious figure of the empress Zoe Porphyrogenita, and he noted her own eyes occasionally meet the glance of a handsome-looking man in the crowd of nobles.

Something clicked into place. This Michael Kalaphates would have to cling tightly to his crown, for his aunt had eyes on a new lover.

Chapter 7

'I am not a poisoner.'

The Sklerina regarded Gunnhild with an unreadable expression, leaning forward and folding her arms. 'It is not for my own benefit alone, Gunilla, but also for the good of the empire. The empress's gaze strays often to my Constantine, and while I dread to think of sharing his affections with another, she is the empress. An Alani princess, however, is little more than a foreign dog with ideas above her station, and I will no longer countenance how he sighs when he sees her.'

'Find yourself a better man,' Gunnhild said.

'Would that it were so easy, Gunilla, but the heart wants what it wants, and Constantine Monomachos is my heart's desire. The empress could take his body, and I would live with that because he would gain almost unprecedented power, and I know that his heart would still be mine. But give me your untraceable gut-burning poisons for the Alani witch. You will harm no one.'

'Other than an Alani princess.'

'No one *important*.'

Gunnhild rose from the chair. 'I know the noblewomen of this city, Maria Sklerina. I understand that you have spent a life of gilded luxury and you are not used to being refused. Learn. I will not give you poison for a woman I do not know, all because of a man.'

Sklerina's lips pressed tight as she too rose.

There was a taut silence, until finally the noblewoman broke it. 'This is your final word?'

'It is. I will advise you, I will try to determine what the future holds, and I will give you potions and poultices as you require, but I will not supply you with poison.'

'Then I shall source it elsewhere.'

'That is your business.'

With a frosty glare, Sklerina turned and marched to the door, tearing it open to allow a billow of icy wind inside, and rejoined her entourage.

'It might have been more prudent to give her the poison,' Anna said as she carried away the glasses from the table. 'She will get it elsewhere, and I have yet to see you place such value on a stranger's life.'

Gunnhild bit down on the angry retort she harboured, that it was none of Anna's business, and forced a calm tone. 'I care not whether this Alani princess lives or dies, Anna. But the Sklerina woman is making rash decisions with little or no forethought for where it will lead her. She is enamoured with this Constantine Monomachos and is driven to murder by it. The worry is that when she finds out how easy it is to kill, the Alani will not be her last victim. There is something about Maria Sklerina that I do not trust, and I will not supply weapons to a potential monster.'

Anna simply grunted as she cleaned the glasses. Gunnhild found herself grumbling that the noblewoman had exited without bothering to close the door even in the middle of winter, and stomped across to it, though she slowed as she approached, for the sound of angry voices filtered in over the general noise of the city. She caught the word 'whore' more than once, and the pinched, elegant tones of the voices made their owners plain. Verina Maniakes was on the way. Over the past month, Gunnhild had seen both women every two or three days, as well as a variety of other important ladies of the city, and it was inevitable that these two enemies would meet at her threshold again at some point. Gunnhild reached out for the door, ready to close it on the pair of them – bigger fish or no bigger fish, the two women gave her a headache – but she stopped in the process, the door still ajar.

She knew the sound that suddenly intruded upon the argument quite well, and in a matter of moments the crunch of marching boots drove both women outside to silence.

'Cease this quarrelling,' called a strong voice with a distinctive northern inflection.

'Akolouthos,' purred one of the women, 'mayhap you have come to arrest this witch?'

'Silence, daughter of heifers,' snapped the other.

'Silence, *both* of you,' bellowed the man. 'I am here on imperial business. Lady Maniakes, Lady Sklerina, begone.'

With that, and a profusion of irate blusterings from the two women, a single pair of boot steps marched over to the door, which remained ajar.

A heavy hand rapped on the timber, causing the door to swing inwards, even in Gunnhild's grip. As it opened, the figure in the cold morning outside came into view, and somewhere behind her Gunnhild heard Anna mutter something about 'fairhair' in a quivering, girlish voice. What was the matter with women in this city?

But as her gaze met that of Harðráði, she fought down an odd and unexpected fluttering in her own chest. The man was, it had to be said, ridiculously handsome, and carried about him a magnetism that was undeniable.

'You?' Harðráði said, a smile slipping across his face. '*You* are the renowned Maria Gunilla?'

'To some,' Gunnhild replied, keeping her voice under tight control. 'What are you doing here, Harald Sigurdsson?' Her gaze slipped past him to the gathered unit of Varangians, standing in the snow. Were it not for the brick and marble backdrop, they could so easily have been in Hedeby. She smiled inwardly, but kept it there. The last thing Harðráði needed was a boost to his ego.

Imperial business, he'd said.

'You have made something of a name for yourself,' the commander of the Varangian Guard smiled. 'Your deeds are the talk of the ladies in the Great Palace. Indeed, I fear you have already supplanted a number of very important physicians and astrologers.'

'Which self-important lady wants me now, Harðráði?'

'The most important of all.'

Gunnhild's eyebrow rose slightly and Harðráði nodded. 'Her Imperial Majesty the Dowager Empress, Zoe Porphyrogenita, daughter of Constantine the Eighth, requests your presence in the palace.'

'Requests?'

'The sort of request you don't turn down.' He turned to his men. 'Gather the lady's things. Be very respectful and careful. No prying, no damage. Everything here collected with the utmost care.'

'You will leave my things where they are.'

'No,' Harðráði replied quietly, 'they won't. This is an imperial order. Your maid can join us, too. Think of this as a promotion, Gunnhild.'

She narrowed her eyes dangerously, and the commander folded his arms and leaned casually on the door frame as though addressing an old friend. 'Besides,' he said with an infuriating smile, peeking back out into the street, 'I fear you need saving from those harpies like Phineas of old.'

What that meant, what a harpy was, and who this Phineas could be all completely escaped Gunnhild, though his meaning was clear enough, and she set her expression in one of grim resignation. In truth, there was no reason to fight this. She had seen how her thread was woven with that of Harðráði, and had not Freyja herself given her the image of ever larger fish in a feeding frenzy? Surely the empress was the greatest fish of all. And above it all, there still lurked in the back of her mind an image of the wolf, the bear and the boar alongside the old woman. The weaving of the Norns was in this. How Harðráði might fit with the weaving, given that he was a child of the Christ God, she could not yet see, but everything was seemingly tying together the way it should.

And she could not help but admit that it would be nice to move on from supplying sleeping draughts to tired shopkeepers and listening to the tortured politics of the noblewomen in this city.

'The goddess drives this, you know?'

Harðráði simply shrugged, which surprised her. 'The ways of God, or even of *gods*, are not mine to question. Sklerina is a dangerous woman, Gunnhild. You will be well rid of her. Oh, she in herself is not so bad, but her lover is ambitious and her brother even more so, and between them they cannot muster up the morals of a snake. And as for Maniakes? Her husband is a bastard on a monumental scale. I almost broke his nose in Sicily, and though he languishes safely in prison right now, men are not contained for long in the Noumera. They either die or get pardoned, and Maniakes has enough luck to survive. You will be safer from these dangerous women in the palace.'

'What makes you think I am not more dangerous than both of them?' Gunnhild replied, and Harðráði stopped, his brow creasing.

'I do not doubt it for a moment,' he said, but the smile was back. 'Come.'

'My things.'

'Believe me, my men will take every care. The empress awaits.'

Gunnhild frowned and turned to Anna. 'Stay with them. Watch them carefully, and when they are done, lock up and follow on.'

Even the outspoken and difficult Anna had the sense not to argue in the presence of the Varangian commander on an imperial errand, and simply nodded.

'All right, Harald Sigurdsson, take me to meet your mistress.'

He reached for her staff, which leaned against a wall, and tossed it to her. She caught it and as they stepped out into the snowy air, her escort drew a deep breath. 'Here everyone calls me Harðráði or sometimes "Fairhair," or even "The Bulgar Burner." Sigurdsson is not a name I have heard much since I left Kiev.'

'Sometimes it is as important to remember where you came from as where you are bound. A thread has two ends.'

Harðráði chuckled. 'Halfdan Loki-born vaunts your wisdom. He has missed you deeply, I think. I understand why.'

'Halfdan is still young, but he has the makings of a great jarl.'

'And what about me, Gunnhild? Will I make a great king?'

She shivered. Somehow she really did not want to read too far into this man's future. The more she thought about him, the more troubled she felt. But some men were great and you could see it in their very being without the need for the intervention of Freyja.

'I do not doubt you will wear a proud crown, Sigurdsson. And I think great deeds are in your weaving, but I warn you now: bright threads are often cut short.'

Harðráði shrugged. 'A man can grow old or grow famous. Few men do both.'

Something about the way he said it sent a thrill shivering up her spine, and as she turned to look at him, she could not help a small smile tugging at the corner of her mouth. She silently reprimanded herself for such weakness as Harðráði returned the smile, having seen hers and filed it away for later consideration.

Behind them, a dozen Varangians stomped through the white, the rest remaining at the house to gather her things. The people of Constantinople melted out of their way, as was generally the case when the imperial guard made their way through the streets. There was just something about a braid-bearded Northman with a great axe that drew the attention in this place.

They walked in silence now, and Gunnhild kept her attention directly ahead, though she could feel Harðráði's eyes on her as they walked. It both irritated and oddly excited her, which irritated her even more. Perhaps she missed the steady influence of Halfdan more than she would like to admit. Certainly it came as something of a relief when they passed the strange collection of columned and gilded buildings at the top of the city's First Hill and approached the gate of the Great Palace. She had been past the place a few times, largely driven by curiosity, but no one went through the gate except by the invitation of the emperor or empress.

The men on the gate were also Northmen, and there was no attempt to check documentation as their commander marched in beneath the grand, overly decorated arch with an unknown woman and a small detachment of Varangians. There was something curious about the gate, and her gaze played across it as they walked. A grand, three-arched edifice of white stone and gold, mosaics and friezes, it was topped by a small chapel of the nailed god with a cross above. As they walked beneath the arch and her gaze slipped upwards, a great image of tiny mosaic pieces showed a gleaming army of soldiers fighting a ragged and disorganised enemy. The soldiers appeared to be bearing standards and banners of various animals, with not a single cross in sight, while their enemy looked a lot like Northmen. An old image, this, that harkened back to the days before the Christ was all-pervading. That it announced the entrance to the palace of a Christian emperor and beneath a cross struck her as odd. The Byzantines were Christian for certain, and yet their respect for their pre-Christ forebears seemed to remain and even grow over time.

She appreciated the over-organised, regimented beauty of the palace and its gardens as she was led through colonnades, past sculpted shrubbery, along marble corridors with mosaic floors, looked down upon by elegant half-naked statues of ancient heroes. She had a feeling that some of these were those same gods and goddesses who had led the empire to its great strength long before the nailed god's prevalence. Again, an odd dichotomy.

Finally, they were led into a grand palatial building and their escort moved away, leaving them instead in the care of an army of servants and administrators. A man in rich and complex robes bowed his head to Harðráði and gestured ahead, leading them on. As they walked, Harðráði spoke in little more than a whisper.

'In the palace more than anywhere in the empire, etiquette is critical. There is a form for everything. Fortunately, this is a private audience in the women's palace, and so much of the ceremony we would suffer in an official meeting is nullified. From my experience with the empress, she is well aware of how trying such ceremony can be, and has been known to brush aside formalities, though only with those she trusts and never within sight of those she does not. So unless she tells you otherwise, you follow the form of all such meetings.'

'Which is?'

'Incredibly complicated. This is the women's court, the *Gynaikonitis*. Here you will find only the empress and her court, not the emperor and his cronies, for which you should be truly grateful. Those not of noble blood are expected to prostrate themselves in the presence of the empress. You should not look her in the eye unless invited. You speak only in response. You will find a line of black tiles on the floor, and that is the closest you must come to the empress herself. There are many other rules, but that should see you through an initial meeting.'

Gunnhild felt her lip curl. So much abasement. That wouldn't happen, for a start.

They were finally shown to an impressive antechamber, the door to the next room open and divided from them only by a heavy red velvet curtain. A conversation was in progress on the far side, and as they came to a halt at a eunuch's gesture, Gunnhild listened carefully.

'...telling me it's true?'

'It is, Majesty. The emperor's uncle was recalled from his estates yesterday and even now returns to his house in the city, a free man.'

'Then, my dear Psellus, I fear it is time to change the locks on the treasury.'

There was a light chuckle. 'Very droll, Majesty. In all seriousness, however, the emperor does not credit his uncle with the missing gold. He believes... *others* to be responsible.'

'Yes, I know, Michael. Indeed, I suspect the ears of those very "others" are probably burning in my waiting room. Very well. Return to the emperor's side, and know that I am grateful as always for your care and service.'

'It is my honour to serve the great scion of the house of Macedonia, Majesty.'

There were a number of scrapes and shuffles, and the curtain was twitched aside to reveal a thin and studious-looking man with an armful of documents. He stopped for a moment and gave Harðráði a strange look, which made the Varangian grin.

'She sounds in high spirits, Psellus.'

'You heard all that?'

'Enough. Same old accusations that are slung at me every few months. They never hit home, and this will be no different.'

'Be careful, Akolouthos Harðráði. The palace is becoming a pool of sharks, and even your vaunted mettle might not see you through the coming storm.'

'Your concern is touching, Psellus, but I will be fine.'

The bureaucrat gave a snort and hurried off with his papers. Harðráði took a deep breath and, as that same eunuch gestured to him, paced forward. The curtain was pulled aside and Gunnhild stepped into the imperial presence. The room beyond the drapes was quite simply the grandest chamber Gunnhild had ever seen, its floor of ancient mosaics with scenes of incredible creatures and its walls of colonnaded marble lit with high, wide windows below a vaulted roof from which hung great bronze chandeliers and enclosed incense burners. The recesses of the room were hidden with rich curtains. None of this, nor the few ladies in the room, interested Gunnhild, though.

The empress looked like the old woman in her casting, with a few small differences. She was not as thin as Gunnhild had expected, but carried that extra weight well, in a shape that would attract men, even at her age, especially since she seemed to have retained a youthful and smooth look to her skin, which was much paler than most Byzantines Gunnhild had met. Her hair was still golden, though shot through with grey, and it took her only a moment to realise that the gold was an affectation, covering the true monochrome of the empress's coiffure. She was of advanced years, but she actually looked surprisingly young, and when she shifted in her seat at this new arrival, her movement was languid and easy. Her expression was serious, and Gunnhild formed the immediate impression that the empress did not smile often or easily.

Harðráði took a step to the black line and sank to a knee. Gunnhild stood precisely where she was. The Varangian shot her a warning glance, but Gunnhild ignored it entirely and remained still, gripping a staff that any self-respecting body-guard should have taken off her. There were no guards here, and the only men Gunnhild could see she was prepared to wager were eunuchs. They and a few indolent-looking noblewomen were the chamber's only occupants.

The empress fixed her with a calculating look.

'You are not at all what I expected.'

'Likewise, Empress of Byzantium,' Gunnhild replied.

The jaws of the gathered populace dropped in shock at such insolence, and Harðráði was urging her to caution with his eyes from his kneeling position.

'Get up, Fairhair,' the empress said, waving a hand negligently. 'It looks ridiculous with you on your knees while she stands there as though she owns the place.'

Harðráði rose and bowed his head. 'This is the spear-maiden and völva Gunnhild of Hedeby, whom your people call Maria Gunilla, Majesty.'

'Thank you, Fairhair. You may leave.'

'Majesty, I…'

'*Go*, Harald.'

Harðráði threw a last warning look to Gunnhild, then bowed his head again and backed out through the curtain.

'Now we are all women in here,' the empress said, confirming Gunnhild's suspicion about the eunuchs. 'I have heard conflicting reports of you from my spies. The cackling crones who fill the palace variously label you a witch and a servant of the Devil, or say that you are some sort of prophetess sent by the Theotokos. Some say you are here to save the empire, others that your witchcraft tears apart our noble families. The time has come for me to form my own opinion. What say you?'

'I do not recognise your Christ's devil, though I have met plenty of devils in my time, and have seen more than a few in this city. I walk with the will of Freyja and if it is her desire, she makes things known to me that ordinary folk cannot see. That is all. I am no destroyer, nor am I a saviour.'

'But you have power, they say.'

'I have knowledge. To the witless they are the same thing.'

At this the empress gave a laugh. 'Even powerful and knowledgeable women do not address me in such a familiar tone in this place. Perhaps some of the ladies in this room do, but that is because we have known one another for decades and there is a trust among us. You, I do not know.'

'Likewise.'

Again the empress laughed.

'And,' Gunnhild continued, 'from what I have seen of the Skleroi and the Maniakes family, your nobles need no help from me in tearing themselves apart.'

'How very true. I see wisdom in you, young woman, a wisdom which evades even most women of my age. Come, a test.'

Gunnhild stood silent as a eunuch hurried forth at an imperial nod, carrying a tray full of dishes. Five bowls, she noted, as the man stepped towards her. Another servant carried over a small decorative table and placed it before her, arranging the bowls across its surface. The two then withdrew.

'Which of these would you give me?' the empress said, with a languid sweep of her arm.

Gunnhild looked down at the bowls and their contents, then began to examine them closely. Some she sniffed, one or two she rubbed a little of between her fingertips, and one she touched to the tip of her tongue. She straightened.

'None of them.'

'Oh?' the empress said, one eyebrow rising. 'Why is that?'

Gunnhild pointed at one of the dishes. 'Meadow saffron leaf will be of little use. You just crossed your legs, and the way you did so tells me that gout does not afflict you. You are clearly not having bellyache, so there is no need of a purgative like winter rose.' She moved her finger on. 'Red clover would be helpful for increased fertility, but at your age, Empress, I doubt this is of great concern. As for the wolfsbane and the hemlock, I see in your eyes no urgent desire to explore the next life.'

Servants appeared and took away the bowls and the table. The empress chewed her lip in thought. 'If I asked you for one piece of advice, knowing me as little as you do, what would it be?'

'Cast adrift your consorts and heirs and rule in your own name, Zoe of the house of Macedonia.'

'You sound like Harðráði. He has said as much many times.'

'Harðráði is not a wise man, but neither is he a fool.'

'Harald Fairhair is a *good* man. I have known him many years and he has served me well despite my husband's interference. He is a bear, loud to growl, strong as can be, but protective and noble.'

Gunnhild shivered for a moment. *The bear.*

'What shall I do with you, Maria Gunilla?'

'For a start, as long as I remain with you, you could use my proper name.'

'Gunnhild of Hedeby? It is a name of strange and jagged syllables on my tongue. You are presumptuous. You assume that you are of that much value to me?'

'You have had all my goods and my thrall packed up and brought with me. You intend to keep me around. It is, I suspect, my place to walk alongside you, just as it is that of Harðráði. And there is no presumption in this. Christians believe in fate just as much as those of us who walk with old gods. It is the weaving of the Norns, the tapestry of fate, that we walk a path together. I have simply made my way here and answered your call. I could no more ignore it than you could have avoided making that call.'

'You are an intriguing figure, Gunnhild. And by God, yes, I think you will be of value to me.' Her arm swept around the room. 'There are women here who advise me and whom I have known for longer than you have lived, and each has experience and knowledge of the workings of my empire, but one thing we sometimes lack is objectivity. The perspective of an outsider.'

At the crook of the imperial finger, Gunnhild stepped across that black line and into the imperial entourage. She sighed with satisfaction. Things were falling into place. The wolf, the boar, the bear. All of them were coming together in the palace.

Chapter 8

'I still don't understand why Ari Karsten would take the risk of trying to kill us. The daft bastard nearly burned the barracks down.'

Halfdan said nothing in reply to Bjorn as they stomped back towards the barracks, though the same question had been plaguing him since the day of the coronation. At least with Harðráði back in favour, Ari had been hampered once again, although still nothing had happened to reunite the crew.

'I think we are a dangerous unknown element,' Leif replied.

'Bjorn is *certainly* a dangerous unknown element,' Ketil added, glancing sidelong at the big albino.

'Piss off, leggy.'

'No,' Leif said, waving his hands, 'I'm serious. I've been doing some research on our friend Ari. It seems he was in line to become Akolouthos of the Guard. He's served longer than almost anyone in the city, and the emperor Michael the Paphlagonian...'

'The what?'

'Doesn't matter. Michael the fourth. The emperor had promised Ari the command position, but then along comes this dashing young prince from the North, bends his knee before the empress Zoe, and she manages to persuade the emperor that Ari would be a mistake and has Harðráði made akolouthos immediately. They've hated each other ever since, and while the empress favours our friend, the emperor had always supported Ari.'

'But it's a different emperor now.'

'But he's still the same family, the nephew of the last one, and he still favours Ari. It's only the empress's support that keeps Harðráði in place. And while our friend might seem the natural choice for a leader, there are few in the Guard who will defy the emperor's will in his favour, since we take an oath specifically not to.'

'I see what you mean,' Ketil nodded. 'Ari can rely automatically on the support of the Guard, but we're new, and we're Harðráði's men through and through. We're the stumbling block.'

Leif nodded. 'Ari tried to remove us by having our contracts nullified. When he failed, he's gone a different way. But I think we need to be careful now.'

'And not just us,' Halfdan put in, pointing across the lawns.

There, beneath a colonnade, the empress was strolling along with her usual huge entourage, four Varangians following at a discreet distance, but by her side was the figure of Gunnhild, her staff clacking on the flagstones and echoing along the covered walkway as she walked.

'I thought Harðráði must be joking when he said she was the empress's companion,' Ulfr said.

'It seems that like Harðráði, she's tied to Zoe. Maybe she can change this new emperor? Maybe she can steer him to a favourable wind.'

They walked on, though Halfdan kept looking back until the small gathering had disappeared into the next garden. Gunnhild had been in the palace for almost a month now, according to Harðráði, but this was the first time Halfdan had actually seen her, for she spent all her time in the women's palace, and that was not a place Varangians were expected to spend time. Halfdan had considered simply going anyway, but Valgarðr had warned him away. Only a year or two back, one of the Guard had taken a shine to an imperial maid and had been caught looking for her in the women's palace without authorisation. He'd been flogged and dismissed from the Guard the same day.

And so, despite her constant proximity, still Halfdan had not had a chance to exchange two words with her.

'Hello, sounds like trouble.'

At Ketil's words, they paused and listened. Voices were raised in anger ahead in the barracks, punctuated with the sound of crashes and bangs.

'That's Harðráði's voice.'

They made their way towards the barrack doorway and paused as they came close, for a chair came hurtling from the opening, smashing against the door jamb and rattling across the path and the grass in several pieces. Gingerly approaching the doorway, Halfdan peered around the corner, ducking back as a cup smashed against it, then looking out once more.

The entrance hall of the barracks, where Torsten's desk sat in an alcove, was a scene of chaos, broken furniture and spilled food. The desk was leaning precariously, one leg cut through halfway up, the chair gone, though Halfdan now knew where. Torsten's various records were scattered across the floor, and a gouge out of the wall just above desk level was a worrying sign. The officer who kept the records was standing back against a wall not far away, his face pale, as were a number of guardsmen Halfdan knew and liked.

Harðráði was enraged, standing in the corridor and gripping an axe. Valgarðr stood nearby, raising and lowering his hands, trying to talk the commander down. Halfdan stared. He'd never seen Harðráði so worked up, so out of control.

'Back,' shouted Valgarðr, looking at him past the commander.

Harðráði turned, seeing them now, and his eyes narrowed. 'Where have you been?' he snapped suspiciously.

'Patrolling,' Halfdan said in a careful tone.

The commander glared for a while, and suddenly Valgarðr was there, gripping him by the shoulders, turning him. 'You're taking out your frustrations on the wrong people. Everyone here's a friend,' he said.

'Except that bastard,' Harðráði replied, pointing at Torsten. 'He was just assigning quarters. It's his job.'

'What's happened?' Halfdan asked as he and his friends stepped into the doorway, the immediate danger having seemingly receded.

'I am to be confined to the Blachernae, pending investigation. Me!'

Halfdan looked past him at Valgarðr, whose eyes spoke volumes. 'The emperor is having the commander investigated over a sum of around five thousand pounds of gold missing from the imperial treasury. Until the matter is resolved, the commander and his close supporters are being reassigned to the Blachernae Palace at the far end of the city.'

Halfdan felt his spirits sink. He'd never been to the Blachernae, but it was as far from Gunnhild as it was possible to get in Constantinople. 'Has the empress not argued against this?'

Harðráði's eyes began to blaze again. 'Zoe Porphyrogenita is a good woman, but she has the worst taste in men. She agreed to adopt that oily shit Michael Kalaphates and made no attempt to stop them putting a crown on his head, and now he undermines her, removes her supporters from the court and he's all but replaced her. She's powerless, and she let it happen, although she had the power to stop it. Michael the Caulker, dung-headed emperor of Byzantium, listens to insidious villains like his uncle Constantine and that unctuous bastard Romanos Skleros. Between the pair of them, they have the idiot emperor convinced I steal from the treasury.'

'You *do* steal from the treasury,' Valgarðr said quietly, risking increased wrath and raising a surprised look from Halfdan.

'Of course I do,' the commander snapped, 'but only as much as *anyone* does, as much as is expected from a man in my position. Not five thousand pounds, for the love of God. How would I manage such a thing? *Why* would I do such a thing? I'm making plenty for my needs by legitimate means. There will be no trail for this sum that leads to me.'

'But reasonable suspicion will be enough to keep you out of the way,' Valgarðr said. 'And that removes the empress's only remaining ally in court. With us shut away in the Blachernae, Michael is unopposed in his rule.'

'And he'll gradually find a way to remove the empress altogether,' Halfdan realised.

'Quite.'

'And Ari...'

Again, the fire rose in Harðráði's eyes. 'And Ari takes control of the Guard again, of course. Ari gets the Great Palace.'

'Worse,' Valgarðr added. 'The emperor has brought in new blood from Rus lands.'

'And you know where *their* loyalty will lie,' snarled Harðráði.

'He must have been arranging it with the emperor since the day his fat, greasy arse hit the throne,' the old man added. 'The new Guard arrived in the harbour an hour ago. Ari's been in on this with the villains for weeks.'

'If they have nothing on you, perhaps the empress can persuade them to bring you back?' Halfdan pressed.

'No,' Harðráði grunted. 'They've tried all this before and I got exiled to a war in Georgia just to get me out of the way. They've searched my quarters so often the dust never settles. They've been through every ship's manifest and port record for everything I've been involved in – you've seen that for yourself. They never find anything, but it doesn't matter now. At least the old emperor listened to Zoe. This one is arrogant and ignorant and seems to think he cannot be opposed. And I'm bound by my oath. I will do as he says and wallow in the Blachernae until the worst happens.'

'The worst?'

'They find a way to manufacture the evidence they cannot find,' Valgarðr said quietly.

'And then?'

'And then it will be down to politics. By rights, if they can produce sufficient evidence, they can execute him, but

Harðráði here is no ordinary mercenary. He's of royal blood in the North and a close personal friend of Jarisleif of Kiev. It could put the emperor in a difficult position if he does something to Harðráði without sufficient cause. Likely we will be kicked out of the city and sent away. Exile is a common punishment in the city.'

'The empress will be powerless without us,' Halfdan breathed.

'There are still allies in the city, and Zoe is a thousand times more popular with the people than the shits she reigns with,' the commander said. 'I will continue to attempt to influence anyone I can and find a way out of this mess. The Patriarch of the Church favours the empress, and there are still nobles who would support her. Sadly, Dalassenos languishes in prison. He could be of aid.'

'And Maniakes,' Valgarðr added.

'That man is an animal. Nothing more.'

'He's an animal, but he's a lion on the battlefield and whether you two get on or not, he's the empress's man and always has been.'

'It matters not. He's in prison too.'

'We need to get to the Blachernae and take up our new posting.' Valgarðr turned to the men in the doorway. 'You'd best gather your things. Anyone tied to the commander here will be coming with us. Collect your gear and make your way to the far palace. I'll have new quarters assigned for you there when you arrive.'

The five of them nodded and edged around the scene of destruction, slouching along the corridors back to their room.

'What do you make of this?' Leif murmured.

'Sounds to me like Harðráði is cornered,' Ketil replied.

'One day I'm going to tear that Ari Karsten in two,' added Bjorn.

'He's dangerous,' Halfdan acknowledged, 'but it's this new emperor at the centre of it all, and his uncle and this Skleros man who seem to be the cause. And taking on the imperial family and one of the most important nobles of the city as well as the deputy commander of the Guard is a little beyond the reach of the five of us.' He growled and slammed his fist on the corridor wall as they walked. 'Gunnhild would know what to do.'

'She is with the empress. Perhaps she'll change things yet.'

'Perhaps.' He sighed. 'What do we know of the Blachernae? I've not been there yet.'

Leif scratched his chin. 'After the Great Palace, it's the largest in the city. It abuts the city's land walls to the west. It's large enough that it has several churches and cisterns and a port.'

'A good enough place for an exile, I suppose,' Ulfr noted.

'At least if they're gathering all Harðráði's men there, we should have the crew back together.'

This raised relieved nods from the others.

A few moments later they were in their room and beginning to collect their things. The conversation had ended now and each man worked in silence, bagging up their worldly goods. From beneath each bed they pulled the locked boxes or tied bags that contained the gold and silver they had brought from Georgia, their prizes.

'If...' began Halfdan, but stopped in an instant at a hammering on the door. He turned to the others, but spoke to the visitor. 'What?'

'Open up, in the name of the Basileos, His Imperial Majesty, Emperor Michael the Fifth.'

'Unless he's with you in person, fuck off,' Halfdan said, earning a grin from Bjorn.

The door opened with a click, and the five of them turned. A small group of Varangians stood in the corridor outside. He recognised among them the old guard he had wiped his boot on near the port, and who now looked upon him as a direct enemy. The greybeard was commanding his men from the rear, but the look of hatred he threw Halfdan warned of potential trouble.

The young jarl focused on the warriors, suspecting they were prepared for a fight. The man at the front was an enormous, barrel-chested brute with a shaved head and a crooked nose.

'Put down your gear,' the old man at the back said with an air of authority.

'Fuck off,' Bjorn replied with a rumble.

Halfdan turned to him. The palace was full of Ari's men now and any fight they started with these few would undoubtedly spill out into something much more dangerous. 'Down, Bjorn. Remember our oath.'

The five of them complied with the command, though Bjorn defiantly kept hold of his favourite axe.

'Step out into the corridor,' Greybeard commanded. 'We are under orders to search your rooms.'

'For what?' Ketil said, an edge of ice in his voice.

'You are suspected of being in collusion with the thief Harðráði in his crimes against the imperial treasury. We are searching for evidence of the same.'

Halfdan stood for a moment, his mind racing. In a matter of heartbeats he replayed the hours of their arrival in the city. They had made their mark on many documents, and all sorts of checks had been made, but he had no recollection of their personal possessions being logged anywhere. With a sinking feeling, he realised that each man here, as well as their crewmen who were based in various places around the city, had a small fortune in gold carved from that great cross of Yngvar's, as well as gold and silver taken in the aftermath of the battle of Sasireti. The empire had no record of them bringing these riches into the city. Why would they? But right now, while there were plenty of explanations for the gold and silver, including the truth, they would be taken to be at least partial evidence against Harðráði, and against each of them too.

'You'll not go through my possessions,' he said quietly, addressing Greybeard, but as he did so, his left hand slid behind his back and pointed down at the small locked box containing his share of the gold. He felt the tension rise in the room and looked around at his friends. Ketil and Leif's expressions made it clear that they had come to the same conclusion, and Ulfr was looking wide-eyed at the bag at his feet. Only Bjorn frowned in confusion, but then his shoulders set and his face slipped into a grimace of defiance. He didn't know what Halfdan was suggesting, but had no intention of submitting anyway.

'This is an order from Ari Karsten, acting Akolouthos of the Guard, carrying the authority of the emperor.'

'Bollocks,' Bjorn spat. 'My stuff is my stuff, and I'll break the first arm that touches it.'

'Don't make me use force,' the old man said with a hint of menace.

Halfdan's mind was racing. Starting a fight here could just pit them against the entire Guard, and, like it or not, the greybeard had the law on his side. 'Step aside and let us leave,' he offered. 'Remember our last meeting.'

The old man's lip twitched at the recollection, and he growled. 'I am required to give you a last warning, pagan filth, but I urge you to refuse anyway. Give me the excuse I need to gut you from cock to chin.'

'Stick it up your arse,' Bjorn said.

'I'll take the one in the silver shirt,' Halfdan said, identifying his chosen target.

'Fat boy, for me,' replied Bjorn.

'Blondie white-beard,' Ketil said.

'Brown trousers,' noted Ulfr.

'I'll bet,' grinned Bjorn.

The big man at the front, effectively blocking the doorway, reached down to his belt and opened a pouch. 'Know what this is, ice-white?' he said, looking at Bjorn with a feral grin.

'Ah, fuck,' Ketil sighed as the two men behind the barrel-chested man pulled the axes from his belt and took them away.

'Is that...' Halfdan began.

'It is. Put the bastard down before he goes mad.'

The big man dipped his fingers into the pouch and lifted them in an age-old sign that had to stand badly with the Christians by his side, licked the fingers and then drew Odin's knot on his forehead in the wet brown paste. As he did so, the other men in the corridor began to back away.

'Last thing I ever expected to see here,' Ketil breathed. 'Everyone ready?'

'Back off,' Bjorn snarled. 'He's mine.'

'Don't be stupid.'

The barrel-chested Varangian had begun to froth at the mouth, his eyes wide. His arms twitched, the muscles dancing within them. His nostrils flared.

With an incoherent bellow, Bjorn ran at the man, casting his axe away onto one of the beds as he leapt into action. Roaring, the big Varangian jumped at him in reply. The two men met just inside the doorway, and Halfdan found himself holding his breath. He came from a village of the old ways, and yet even there the tales of the Bear Shirts and their Odin-granted battle-lust had been stories of old. Certainly he'd never expected to see such a thing with his own eyes.

Bjorn's hands went straight to the big man's throat and it was a testament to just how big their albino friend was that his fingers met around that enormous neck. He squeezed with a cry of fury in the name of Odin, but the big Varangian was unfazed. Even as the albino closed on his neck, his own hands came up and he began to tear at Bjorn like a bear, fingers raking like claws. The two men were locked in a violent embrace, struggling this way and that, turning slowly, their friend's pale hands gripping tight around the throat, which was slowly going purple, and Halfdan felt sudden fear for Bjorn as the enemy's back came round slowly and he could see that the frenzied clawing of the berserkr had pulled the big man's chain shirt down and torn the tunic beneath to shreds. He hadn't stopped there, though, for the big man was clearly trying to tear a hole through Bjorn's chest. Flesh had been pulled away and blood flowed in gouts.

Halfdan tensed. They had to do something.

As he watched, wincing, the maddened giant managed to get his fingers on the glistening white of Bjorn's collarbone and pulled. The albino howled in agony, the first time Halfdan had ever heard such a thing, and his grip on the man's neck faltered.

Halfdan had not seen it coming, hidden behind the fight, and it came as both a shock and a relief when Ketil smashed the chair across the big man's back. The damage was negligible to the berserkr, but the distraction was enough, and his scrabbling fingers released the big man's bone as he turned to Ketil. The Icelander gave a yelp of shock and danced away as the huge man bore down on him, leaping up onto one of the beds and then jumping from there to the next, getting past him.

Halfdan was moving now. As the big man turned, following Ketil, Halfdan gave him a hefty kick behind the knee. He'd done as much in fights before, and a kick like that was enough to knock down even the strongest opponent. His shock as the kick had no impact and the big man turned to him was total. He could see the Odin Knot on the man's forehead now streaking down his face with sweat, and the man's eyes were peculiar, the black of his pupil having grown so wide as to almost overtake any colour. His teeth were bared, but his lips were a mess where he'd apparently bitten into them repeatedly. He hit Halfdan with one punch, and it was enough. It felt like being struck by a charging bull, and Halfdan found himself barrelling away into the wall, where he leaned, wheezing, checking his chest and side for broken bones.

By the time he'd recovered enough to see what was going on, and was content that nothing was actually broken, the others were all on the big man, except for Ketil. Bjorn was behind him now, and trying to stay there, out of reach, while he clasped one hand to his damaged chest and punched repeatedly with the other. Leif was ducking and leaping, making himself a target to distract the big man as Ulfr moved about, staying out of reach and occasionally darting in to deliver a punch. Halfdan staggered away from the wall, ready to take a turn, and suddenly remembered the other Varangians. As he turned to the door, he realised the corridor was now empty. Greybeard and his friends hadn't counted on this debacle, and had put as much distance as possible between them and the disaster, for someone was probably going to die here, and then there would be trouble all round.

As he staggered forward, Ketil suddenly appeared from the far side of the room. He held Bjorn's axe, but by the head end, brandishing it more as a club. As the dance of violence turned once more, the tall Icelander took his chance, his archer's skill coming in to play. With a single jab, he thrust the butt of the axe at the berserkr's head. The heavy haft connected with the big man's temple with a crack.

Halfdan watched in fascination. The man was done, but it took time for him to know it, realisation coming in waves. First his punching, gripping hands started to fall short, flailing harmlessly in the air. Then his legs wobbled, and he staggered, close to falling. His entire body spun a quarter turn to the right, and Halfdan could have laughed at the man's expression of utter confusion that nothing seemed to be working in his body any more. Finally, the eyes glazed and the man went down like a pole-axed cow.

Halfdan stared.

'Would someone like to pull this thing off me?' grumbled Leif, where he lay trapped beneath the monster's tree-trunk legs.

'Where are the others?' asked Ketil as Ulfr and Halfdan helped their small Rus friend out from under the slumbering giant. Bjorn staggered around, swearing and clutching at his bloodied collarbone.

'Did a runner when it looked like their friend was going to die,' Halfdan said, pointing at the door. 'I think it would be an exceptionally good idea if we were halfway to the Blachernae when they came back.'

Ketil nodded. 'And then we can find somewhere to stash our gold where it won't be searched for and presumed to be Harðráði's.'

'*That's* what you were on about,' said Bjorn, enlightenment finally dawning. 'I thought you were telling me to look at his feet.'

'Why would I do that?'

'That's what *I* wondered.'

The five men grabbed their kit, Ketil taking one of Bjorn's bags for him, and padded out of the room. Leif darted ahead as they made their way through the barracks, checking around each corner for trouble and giving them the all-clear nod each time. Finally, with their first sigh of relief, they emerged into the gardens, yet the tension remained as they made their way to the Chalke Gate that would see them out into the city. There was always the possibility a warning had made its way to the men on guard there. Fortunately, the Varangians in the archway barely gave them a glance as they made their way through.

Emerging into the city streets, their attention was drawn by the sound of many marching feet, and they deftly made their way in among a watching crowd near the arcade of the hippodrome, somewhere safely incognito as they observed. A unit of Varangians, perhaps five hundred strong, was marching towards the palace gate, but there was something unusual about them. They did not look like Northmen, for all their equipment and the braids in their hair and beards. Their skin tone was a little too swarthy, their eye shape different.

'They must be Ari's new men,' Ketil hissed.

'But who are they?' Halfdan replied.

'They're steppe-people... *Scythians*,' Leif replied. 'Half-Rus bred with Pecheneg women. Dangerous bastards. Trouble in an armoured shirt.'

Halfdan pointed west. 'Looks to me like we got out just in time. Let's get to the Blachernae before this place goes to shit.'

123

'What about Gunnhild and the empress?' Leif muttered, looking back.

'Gunnhild can take care of herself,' Ketil replied, 'believe me. Let's just hope she can look after the empress too.'

Chapter 9

'Prophecy is clearly a gift of the Divine,' the empress said, her face serious, her hand steady on the wine glass as she poured a second drink.

'Agreed,' Gunnhild nodded.

Zoe Porphyrogenita sighed and passed over the glass. 'How can you say this when you have no belief in the Trinity? Your notion of the Divine is still rooted in idolatry, demons and false prophets, Gunnhild.' She held up both hands defensively. 'I mean no offence, of course.'

'I have been studying your God-text.'

'The Bible?' the empress said in surprise. 'I thought you could not read our language.'

'I cannot read *any* language, other than that of body and spirit – in my homeland we had little need for such things – but your Father Avouris has been showing me the text. He thinks he will make me one of your Christians. He is mistaken, but the exploration is interesting.'

'How so?'

'There is much chaff, I think, in your holy words. Chaff which needs sweeping away, and yet parts of the book are clearly rules for your people. I am having some trouble with "thou shalt not kill," I admit. It seems to be one of your central rules that everyone ignores for convenience.'

The empress chuckled. 'There is some room for interpretation, certainly. That is why priests are so valuable.'

'That same list also tells you that this God, who is one and three at once, said that "thou shalt have no other gods before me."'

'Yes.'

'Then even your own holy book tells you that there are other gods. If there were not, why would he be so jealous as to tell you that he is first among them? I find your whole system very flawed.'

Zoe stared at her, and finally shook her head as if to dislodge a new and nagging thought. 'The words come down to us through translations from ancient times and need to be interpreted correctly.'

'Then you are saying that your holy words cannot be trusted?'

'No,' the empress said, though her brow had creased deeply. 'The Bible is inviolable.'

'Then it tells you there are other gods.'

'No, no, no.'

'Yes.'

'Gunnhild, you are infuriating at times.' The empress laughed in exasperation. 'I think this might be one for you to argue with the patriarch. He has a mind that can untangle such problems. For now, tell me about your Odin again. He seems to be a strange pagan reflection of the Christ, hanging from a tree for the good of the world.'

Gunnhild rolled her eyes. It was one inescapable thing about Christians. They were capable of a very blinkered focus, ignoring anything that didn't fit with their view, while attempting to impose that view on everything they saw. She marshalled her arguments, for the gods were always listening. Huginn and Muninn would be circling the palace on midnight wings, waiting to deliver their findings to Odin, and Gunnhild would not bow before this Christian 'logic'.

Before she could begin, however, the two women became aware of a distant commotion, which swiftly resolved into a clatter of many footsteps out in the vestibule two rooms away.

'The emperor comes.'

'Your voice is filled with nerves,' Gunnhild said. 'Uncertainty does not sound right on your tongue. You are empress in this place.'

Zoe Porphyrogenita looked at her, and for once Gunnhild could see through the imperial shell to the woman who had grown old navigating the dangerous currents of this place. 'Michael Kalaphates is emperor of Byzantium, Gunnhild. There is no mortal man in this world with more power than he.'

Gunnhild shook her head. 'He has a crown. Beside a man with an axe, he is nothing.'

'Would that were so.'

The footsteps were coming closer now, approaching the antechamber, heavy boots that spoke of Varangians, and that lighter tapping of expensive shoes.

'Why did you adopt him? Why did you let your husband do so before he died? You are older than both and with more majesty than either. Yours has always been the power to make and break emperors, I think.'

Zoe looked at her, that nakedness still there, and sighed sadly. 'There are many – Araltes, whom you call Harðráði, among them – who believe that it was fear of my husband's family that led to my decision. They are a den of serpents, after all. My husband was a good man, inside, and I think he showed it in the end, but his entire brood are little more than monsters. It would be perfectly understandable if I had bowed to their pressure and agreed to adopt our nephew.'

'But it was not that, for you are strong. You would not bow to such pressure.'

Truly naked now, her soul laid open, the empress turned eyes full of sorrow and embarrassment upon her. 'I am strong, Gunnhild, in so many ways. I am the strongest of my sex ever to sit upon that throne since dazzling Theodora. But in at least one way I am weak. I am… vain. And I am led by the needs of a woman as much as those of an empire. At times, my heart contradicts my head. Like my first husband, Romanos, my second was a man of extraordinary good looks. A beautiful man. An Adonis, and I am weak before such beauty. I knew my husband would do me no good, but I could not help myself. When, as the life ebbed from my husband, he begged me to adopt his nephew as successor, I looked at young Michael Kalaphates, and all I could see was a perfect, chiselled echo of my husband in his prime. I could do nothing else. My passion, my ardour and my love of beauty led me to accept the unacceptable, and now Michael rules Byzantium while I wither as dowager.'

'So now you are saddled with him. I am intrigued to meet the man.'

It had been over a month now, almost two, since the coronation, and still the empress, and therefore also Gunnhild, remained in the Gynaikonitis, separated from the men's court. On occasion they had made their way about the palace gardens, but there had been no mixing with the emperor and his court. In fact, Gunnhild could see worse than mere separation to come. She had watched Zoe draft laws and arrange proclamations, which was her right as empress, and dispatch them to the administration. The sympathetic clerk Michael Psellus had visited time and again, always with a haunted look, only to inform the empress that the emperor had read through her edicts and had uniformly torn them up and discarded them before they could be enacted. Power was leeching away from the empress like rainwater in the well-drained lawns.

'Be very careful. Say nothing while he is here. He must have heard about you, and if his attention is drawn to you, he might have you cast out, and I would not like that. You have become a pillar of strength among the shrine of my confidantes.'

Gunnhild nodded. She knew she had taken something of a central role in the women's palace since her arrival. Zoe's friends still came and went as always, offering their well-meaning but often flawed advice, but now, always, Gunnhild was there. In her heart she knew it was because for all their friendships, the others would always say what they thought the empress wished to hear, while Gunnhild spoke only the plain truth. At Zoe's urging, she stepped back into the gloom, close to one of the great, heavy red drapes.

A moment later the doors opened without a knock or a request. The servants who habitually occupied the antechamber, ready to follow the forms of etiquette, hurried into the room, a torrent of announcements and titles spilling from their lips, desperately trying to introduce the emperor before he stepped through the door.

The moment Michael Kalaphates walked into the room, Gunnhild could see it. The man was truly handsome. His skin was healthy and well-cared-for, his hair and beard neat and oiled, his features almost perfect.

Almost…

It took a few moments of looking at him to see past the looks. Some people could wear a shell of beauty while being truly ugly within, and Michael Kalaphates was the epitome of that type. His eyes slid this way and that, and the sly, devious nastiness in them corrupted everything they touched. Gunnhild had a prosaic attitude to people. No one was truly a hero, and no one was unerringly wicked, in her opinion. It was important for a völva to apply only Freyja's judgements, and not to hinder the goddess with their own. Yet the moment her gaze fell on Michael Kalaphates, she was startled to discover that she hated him. It was all the more startling because she had never truly hated before. Her hands rose to the pendant at her neck, shaped for the goddess.

Was this how Halfdan had felt with Yngvar?

A few lackeys followed the emperor, as well as a couple of older men who were clearly related, from their features, and who each carried themselves with ophidian menace. The group was escorted by a detachment of Varangians led by the one she had noted as seemingly opposed to Harðráði. Ari, they called him. Ari Karsten. His men were not true Northmen, either, but angry-looking Pecheneg types wearing a Northman's face with difficulty. This, she decided, was a dangerous gathering in many ways.

'Be gone, witch,' the emperor demanded with a sneer.

Gunnhild, eager to avoid causing any further problems for the empress, took a step towards the door.

'Not you,' one of the older relatives snarled. 'He means the crone.' The insult went unchallenged as the older man pointed at the empress.

To her credit, Zoe Porphyrogenita, daughter and grand-daughter of one of the empire's greatest dynasties, simply rose with imperial grace, bowed her head to her adoptive nephew, and swept from the room, two eunuchs racing to follow her. Gunnhild felt traps opening up below her as the empress was ushered from the room by those hard, dark-skinned Varangians, and the emperor looked the woman left alone in the room up and down. She clenched her hands. There was no fear. A daughter of Freyja could not submit to such a debilitating emotion. But there was tension and alertness. She was in a more dangerous place than any battlefield right now, but she was no Greek. She was a daughter of the North, and she would not bend her neck to this man no matter what he threatened. She would sell her life dearly if it came to that.

'Some say you are a heathen witch,' the emperor said quietly as he took a few steps towards her, hands clasped behind his back. His robes were golden and red, stiff and formal, each garment so rich and extravagant that every one could buy and equip a ship of war. The red leather boots clicked on the tile floor. His crown was gold, overly jewelled, and seemed to drip riches down to his shoulders.

Behind him, the two older men – uncles, she suspected – ushered everyone from the room, even Ari, to the Varangian's clear irritation. Within moments, Gunnhild was alone with the emperor and two of his relatives. It occurred to her that if she felt so inclined, she could probably completely alter the succession of Byzantium in this room. A few well-placed blows, and these men looked like typically oily fat courtiers, rather than warriors. Moreover it would give her the greatest of pleasures to watch the life fade from those serpentine eyes. But that was not to be her fate, she felt certain. Instead, she simply watched the emperor, expressionless.

'Others,' Kalaphates went on, 'say that you are a gift from God. The one thing they seem to agree on, though, whether saviour or demon, is that you do have true power. What say you?'

'I see what I am given to see, nothing more.'

'Remember to whom you speak, in your insolence,' spat one of the older men, but the emperor waved him down.

'These Varangoi are hardy and prickly, uncle, but they have value. Do they not give their lives for the emperor, after all?'

'*Some* of them,' grunted the other uncle, grudgingly.

'You have been using your talents for my aunt,' the emperor said, addressing Gunnhild once more. 'That in itself stands against you, since it seems to have done her no good. She is a hindrance that will soon be removed, God willing, and your aid has done nothing to halt her decline. Would that she simply gave up like the old woman she is and conveniently died. But sadly, she seems to be immortal, and even I, the most powerful man in the world, cannot simply have her killed.'

Gunnhild kept her gaze steady. Said nothing. Tried to suppress the hate.

The emperor stopped in front of her – just out of reach, Gunnhild noticed with satisfaction. The man was not quite as confident as he appeared. 'I have a course of action in mind,' he said, 'concerning the difficult obstruction I must overcome. I live in a shadow and must step into the light if I am ever to shine. I have consulted my astrologers, the most learned men to be found across the empire and beyond, from savage Frankia to the deserts of Persia. They have been commanded to speak plain, and they all advise me against my course of action.'

He began to pace back and forth as though struggling with the problem, one hand coming round to the front to tap on his lip.

'However, I have dreamed that this course will finally bring me into that light, and when I woke from my dream, the great bell of the Hagia Sophia was chiming. It appears as though God himself favours my plan. As such, I am forced to consider the possibility that each and every astrologer in the empire is nothing more than a charlatan. In truth, they are often condemned by the Church for their work, and it may be that I am consulting heathens when I should be placing my fate in the hands of the Lord.'

He stopped again, in front of her. 'I cannot deny that you yourself are just such a heathen, and yet it is said not only that you are a wielder of truly occult power, but also that you are no lackey, and that you speak plainly even to the empress. Such is the advice I seek. No obsequious desire to please, but an honest appraisal of my plan.'

He took in the lack of emotion in her face and his brow knitted. 'I am the emperor of Byzantium. At my command cities rise and fall. Not a single citizen in my empire can refuse a command. Yet I offer you this respect. I will not command you, but ask you plain: will you consult your demons and answer my question?'

Gunnhild stood silent for a moment, fighting the urge to tear his throat out, and then finally spoke. 'What you ask is not a small thing. In the common course, I offer simple advice and common sense. If you truly seek the wisdom that comes through Seiðr from the gift of Freyja, I can do such a thing. But if you seek a true answer, I must know precisely what question I am asking. You tell me so little.'

'You know my trouble. You know what I must do to rule unopposed. I must remove the old woman. I cannot *kill* her, for she is empress and sacrosanct, but somehow I must put her aside and remove her influence. This is all you can know. All you *need* to know. Is my course wise?'

Gunnhild stood silent again. She could answer that with common sense: of *course* it was not wise. But perhaps she was being driven by the strange camaraderie she had built up with the empress over the weeks? Sometimes good flesh had to be cut away to find the rot within. Perhaps the weaving of the Norns *called* for the fall of the empress and the rise of this monster. It was not Gunnhild's place to decide, just to reveal. She had to fight down her instincts. Besides, whatever she told him, she had to know the truth herself.

'You must not question or interrupt,' she said, as she moved to a more open area of floor, where the patterned marble was least busy and would allow her a clearer view. She made a show of some flailing of arms and muttering, turning this way and that as though in a frenzy, all theatrics, but which allowed her to slip her hand to the precious pouch in the folds of her cloak, withdraw a little of the powder and touch it to her lips without the process being easily observed by these three men. Some secrets were not to be told.

Coming to a halt, she dipped her hands into the other, larger pouch which contained the bones, the beads and the hacksilver. She began the song, and made no attempt to hide any of this now, knowing that her words, even spoken clearly, meant nothing to these men who knew nothing of the languages of the northern peoples. In fact, the song was so old and archaic that she doubted even Halfdan would follow much of it. This song had been sung before even these Greeks had risen to power.

She could feel the goddess now. She felt the ripples of Freyja's will in her blood, each wave bursting out of her, pushing her higher, out of the room and into the darkness beyond. Into that place where even gods could only look but could not walk, where Yggdrasill grew from its three springs and all the worlds waited.

She was in a room, or something that *felt* like a room. She could see no walls, for the distance disappeared into darkness all around and above her, only a stone floor visible beneath her feet.

She focused, her skin tingling, her pulse speaking in whispers. The empress was there again, an old woman in a long robe at the heart of the room. Each of her hands rested upon the hair of an animal's neck, at her left a wolf, at her right a boar. Gunnhild shivered. Two. Only two.

A darkness was coming. Not a figure coalescing from the shadows at the edge of sight, but shadow itself, moving into the light. A column of turning, twisting darkness. It moved towards the old woman, tendrils reaching out and whipping this way and that, a darkness threatening to engulf all. The wolf snarled. The boar grunted. Neither moved.

But here was something new. A golden light, cutting into the darkness, melting it, casting it aside. The moment the golden bear emerged from the light and savaged the column, even in her trance, Gunnhild felt a shock. The great claws rent the darkness, the massive jaws closing on it, until the column of dark was no more.

She felt her heart tremble for a moment, and her mind exploded.

–

'She is waking.'

Gunnhild opened her eyes. She was lying on the floor of the women's palace audience chamber, where she had been before. Her hand was still gripping the bones tightly, a few beads and fragments having fallen away. Her head hurt. She felt around and found the back sticky, her hand coming away wet. For a moment she felt rage and incredulity that one of these men might have had the temerity to attack her in the middle of a casting, but then she remembered the shock of the golden bear, and realised that she had passed out. The blood was from where her head had struck the floor, a fact confirmed as she struggled upright and looked down at the mess. No one tried to help her, she noted as she swayed.

'What did you see?' the emperor asked in an urgent hiss. 'Tell me.'

She could hardly think, let alone speak. She stumbled a moment, shaking her head.

'Tell me or I will have you flayed,' snarled the emperor, finally betraying his true self. Gunnhild steadied herself, focused upon him, and saw that his serpentine eyes had regained their wickedness, his body all aquiver with tense, expectant hunger.

'Your course will not be easy.'

Torn apart by a bear...

'But is it wise? Will it work?'

To fall, he must be in the light.

'It is wise. You will suffer, but you will find the light you seek.'

Gods, but that light would find *him*. She shivered.

'You heard her. My course is wise,' the emperor said, turning to his uncles.

'If you are wrong in this, it will go badly for all of us,' one reminded him.

'You heard her. The witch speaks the truth, you have both heard as much.'

There were guarded nods from the pair, and with a gesture from the emperor, one of them crossed to the chamber doors and pulled them open. Ari Karsten and his strange Northmen waited outside and from the knowing smile on the Varangian's face, Gunnhild was certain he had heard everything. The emperor turned his viper eyes to them.

'Just as the empress cannot die, this one must also live. If time proves that she has done me the service I believe, she will be showered with gold. The empress and the witch will be confined to the Bucoleon Palace. No ships must be allowed to dock there without my express permission. The doors shall be closed. The palace shall be as a prison for my darling aunt and her witch. She will have no access to court, nor to treasury. She will have food and a priest to witness her confession. I will return to the palace and have the documents drawn up for her abdication of the throne and her retreat to a house of God. Once all is in place, I will send for her and the old crone will be escorted to a nunnery to serve out her days, safely away from the palace.'

As Ari bowed his head, the emperor turned a horrible smile on Gunnhild. 'You will stay with her until then. Once all is well and she serves God in peace, you will have all the gold you can carry and will leave my domain with all haste.'

With that, the most powerful man in the world turned and strode from the room, cackling with glee. The two older men gave Gunnhild one last disapproving look and then followed. Ari Karsten looked hard at her, as though trying to weigh her up. Once the nobles were gone, the Guard's second-in-command took a few steps towards her.

'Is it true what they say? Are you a völva of old?'

Gunnhild watched him carefully. She still felt shaky. Finally, she nodded. Her training might be incomplete, but in this soft, southern world, she was the closest thing to a völva.

'Did you see me in your casting?' he asked, carefully. 'Will I take my rightful place alongside the emperor? Will I rise?'

She had found nothing of this man's path in her casting. He was ambitious, and she could see that with plain eyes. He was unprincipled, she suspected, and dangerous. Whatever his fate might be, he *deserved* a poor one.

'Stand by your emperor,' she found herself saying, 'and you will share his weaving.'

That brought a shiver. It was a guess. But if this man stood by Michael Kalaphates, he would surely share that fate. A small, guilty, part of her wondered whether she was doing this because it needed to be done, or because of Harðráði, the golden bear. She ground her teeth. Thinking of the man always clouded her thoughts. She had to stop fawning over him.

With a deep breath, she collected her staff and followed Ari Karsten and his Varangians from the room.

Chapter 10

'This emperor has too many palaces,' Bjorn grumbled, looking up at their surroundings as he ran the whetstone with skin-crawling strokes along the blade of his axe.

'Stop fondling that thing and stand up,' Harðráði said, waving his own axe as the others sparred in the courtyard, fighting back and forth in the daily training session. Bjorn rose, putting away the stone and stretching. Harðráði had chosen the big albino to train with as the largest specimen available in the Blachernae, and already the pair had almost knocked each other out several times.

Halfdan paused between bouts, sweating and breathing heavily, looking up into the early spring sky. 'I think an emperor measures his worth with jewels and buildings. This one is richer than most, I suspect. I don't know how many he has.'

'Many,' Harðráði replied, 'though only three main ones.'

'And they say Gunnhild is in the Bucoleon Palace with the empress.'

'At least they're safe.'

'For now,' Halfdan said quietly. 'You've all heard the rumours.'

The rumours had come from Psellus, the clerk, conveyed very carefully while officially visiting upon tedious duties. It was said that the emperor was building a case against the empress, accusing her of all sorts of things in order to give him a legal precedent for her removal. She would then be exiled to a church of the nailed god somewhere far from the city, and the emperor would assume total power. Psellus had been worried, for the emperor himself was impetuous, and might have simply sent her away, but his uncles were wily and had kept the empress under lock and key in her palace while they laid the foundations for her exile. Thus it would be nicely legal and there should be no argument from the court when it happened.

'It's bought us time,' Ketil said between blows, as he and Ulfr separated for a moment. 'While he buries himself in books and lawyers, we have time.'

'To do what?' Halfdan replied in exasperation. 'Even Harðráði over there is powerless right now. The emperor has control of the city with his uncles, the Guard are loyal to him and to Ari, and the only people we can rely on are in here with us, also under virtual arrest.'

Ketil nodded glumly. They were still waiting for the rest of the *Sea Wolf*'s crew to be assigned here with them, and the delay was worrying. Also, there didn't seem to be a way out, and from what Valgarðr had said, they were virtually prisoners. Confined to the Blachernae, they could only enter the city with permission, and Ari and the emperor had all the harbours controlled, and the chain across the Horn Bay. Even if they could afford to simply abandon their plan, they couldn't leave the city. Not that they would leave without Gunnhild anyway.

'This time, I'm going to leave you sitting in the dust with a sore arse,' Bjorn said as he lumbered towards the commander, gripping his axe.

'It's not that kind of session,' Harðráði grinned. 'We may be in Greek lands, but we're still men of the North.'

Bjorn's answering smile turned into a roar as he leapt, his blade swooping downwards. Had Harðráði not reacted in time, the training session might well have been cut short as they looked for a new commander. Fortunately the handsome, yellow-haired man lurched to his left, swinging his own axe out at ankle height, almost separating Bjorn's foot from his leg. The huge albino swore as the blade cut through the leather of his boot, narrowly avoiding drawing blood, and the two men ended the manoeuvre facing one another once more, panting. Halfdan watched, impressed, reminding himself how recently Bjorn had suffered an eye-watering wound to the collarbone. The medics always said it was healing well, but they remained exasperated that every time the wound showed real progress, Bjorn would do something stupidly violent and set it back once more.

The rest of the bouts fizzled to inactivity as each man in the courtyard, twenty in all, turned to watch the duel. Everyone else had contented themselves with simple exercise and the practice of landing blows, but the last contest between these two, half an hour ago, had been fascinating enough to draw everyone's attention. Harðráði and Bjorn seemed intent on actually trying to kill one another.

'You're going to buy me new boots,' the big man grumbled, looking down at his damaged leather.

'Trousers, too, with my next blow, and after that I might make you a eunuch.'

'You'd need a bigger axe for that,' grinned Bjorn.

Harðráði leapt. He was so quick that none of them had expected it, least of all Bjorn, who was still winding up for the slinging of more insults before making a move. The big white warrior could do little to counter, given the surprise of the attack, and had to lean precariously back out of the range of the swinging blade. Halfdan was impressed. The result could have been an accident, of course, but given what Harðráði had just said it seemed unlikely. The keen edge of the commander's axe neatly snicked through Bjorn's belt, and as the huge man lurched and staggered back, trying not to fall, his trousers neatly dropped to his ankles. His pouches thudded and clattered to the ground, his prized carved bone beard-comb now missing several teeth, coins spilling from a purse to roll across the dusty ground.

Harðráði laughed and lowered his axe as Bjorn cursed inventively and bent to pull up his trousers. The commander gathered a few of the fallen items, and then paused at one of the pouches and rose, opening it and looking inside, dipping in a couple of fingers and peering at them. As Bjorn tried repeatedly to tie his broken belt together, Harðráði held the pouch out on a flat palm, his brow folded, face serious.

'So…' the commander said quietly in the strange silence, 'do you wear a bear shirt, Bjorn?'

The big man gave up trying to tie the belt, took a brooch and pinned the two ends of leather together before looking up at Harðráði. 'No. I'm no berserkr. I *eat* bears! I love to fight, and Odin's ever at my shoulder, but I like to know what I'm doing, not go battle-mad.'

'Yet you have this.'

'One thing I have learned is that the smallest touch of this stuff, and my wound doesn't bother me at all. But I stop there. Besides, I know how valuable it is. It's treasure as sure as gold.'

Halfdan frowned. He'd seen that pouch on the big bastard they'd fought in the barracks. 'Is that…?'

'Yes,' the commander replied. 'This is the stuff that turns thinking men into froth-mouthed shield-biters. I dread to think what it would do if *this* monster used it.'

Ketil snorted. 'I'm not sure we'd see much difference.'

Bjorn reached out towards the commander, but Harðráði drew his hand back, swiping the pouch out of reach. 'I think it might be better for all concerned if this was out of your hands, my big friend.'

'Quite,' Leif put in. 'The last thing we want is Bjorn not being able to tell friend from foe.'

'That's valuable,' argued the big man.

'I'll see you're compensated,' the commander replied.

The two men separated, massaging aching muscles and preparing for another bout. As Bjorn pushed Leif and his ministrations away with a snort, Harðráði sidled close to Halfdan.

'Gunnhild,' was all he said.

'Yes?'

'I am expected to marry a princess, of course. But I find Gunnhild... intoxicating.'

Halfdan raised one eyebrow as he turned to the commander. 'Gunnhild will be no man's, I think.'

'I'm not so sure. I've seen the way she looks at people. Even you. She saves most of her smiles for you, but even then they are protective, familial. You are her brother in some way.'

Halfdan just nodded.

'Her smiles for me are different,' Harðráði said. 'She tries not to give me them, but I see them anyway, and I have seen smiles like that before. She can say what she likes through the armour of her demeanour, but she feels it too, Halfdan, I swear it.'

'If that is the case, then the Norns will weave you together.'

The commander laughed. 'I am a Christian, Halfdan. I take your meaning, and fate is what fate is, but the Book of Proverbs tells us "The sluggard craves and gets nothing, but the desires of the diligent are fully satisfied." Fate sometimes needs a helping push.'

Halfdan laughed again. 'Don't push too hard. I've seen her push back.'

If Harðráði had some pithy response it was lost as Bjorn, stretching, waved at them, beckoning. 'This time I really am going to put you on your backside.'

'We'll see,' Harðráði replied, crossing to meet him.

The two men stepped forward again, Bjorn slightly hampered by the fact that he kept having to haul on his belt to keep his trousers up. Harðráði swung, but this time the big albino was ready and caught the blow with his own axe, the clang and clatter echoing around the courtyard as the rest of those in training watched the contest with interest, wondering not so much who would win, but more whether they would need to gather up stray limbs afterwards.

It took a few moments through the ringing of steel and the clonk of wood, the swearing and cursing in the name of Christ and of older gods, before anyone heard the hammering.

At a gesture from Valgarðr, the two combatants pulled apart, sweating and heaving down tired breaths.

The hammering continued, heavy blows on timber. Two of the men not busy training were closing on the gate. Unlike the Great Palace on the far side of the city, the Blachernae was not protected by great walls, towers and gates, but more of a minor boundary wall with sporadic gates surrounding a collection of halls and complexes, gardens and courtyards on terraces leading down to the water's edge. As such there was nowhere for guards to stand watch, and the first they knew of the waiting men outside was when the two warriors pulled the gates open in response to the banging.

Every man on the wide gravel yard inside the gate stopped what they were doing and straightened, turning to look, fingers dancing on hafts and hilts, eyes narrowing, teeth clenching. Through the gateway, they could all see a sizeable unit of Varangians, including a number of the new, eastern Rus loyal specifically to Ari and the emperor. As the gates came open, the new arrivals began to stomp inside without waiting to be called, falling into rough lines facing the sweating trainees across the open ground. Halfdan half expected Ari Karsten to step forward, but it seemed he had more important things to do. His lip curled at the sight of that same Greybeard they had come up against twice now. The man stepped to one side, separating himself from the rest. Their arrival boded no good, for each man there was armed for war, even in the city.

'What is the meaning of this, Erik Boneblade?' Harðráði demanded, taking a couple of paces forward, fingers tightening on his axe haft. Halfdan mentally filed away the greybeard's name.

The old warrior mirrored the commander's move, folding his arms. 'Harald Sigurdsson, you are under arrest on the orders of the emperor.'

'On what charge?' Valgarðr asked, stepping forward to join his commander. Everyone in the courtyard managed to shuffle a little further forward, knuckles whitening, spoiling for a fight.

'Theft of imperial property,' the man replied, 'namely five thousand three hundred pounds of gold from the treasury.'

'Preposterous,' snorted Harðráði. 'Such an accusation is plainly ridiculous, and this is the fourth time it has been levelled at me by corrupt and criminal elements within the court. Never once has a single piece of evidence been raised against me. Leave now or I might start to get angry.'

The old man shook his head, and his smile was nasty as he fixed it on the commander.

'On the contrary, there is now evidence. Circumstantial, admittedly, but enough to warrant further investigation, and so I am under orders to escort the commander to prison while further enquiries are made. Stand down, all of you. My orders currently include only the commander, but I am authorised to expand the arrest to include anyone who attempts to stop us in the carrying out of our duties, and there are certain elements here I would love nothing more for.'

Harðráði took a step back now. 'What evidence? There can be no evidence, for I'm innocent.'

'Your pet warriors you brought from Georgia, Sigurdsson. The ones you involve in your criminal activity, and whose oath to the emperor is suspect at best. Large quantities of gold have been located among groups of them throughout the city, and each man has been arrested appropriately.'

'I know nothing about this gold,' Harðráði insisted.

Halfdan moved forward now to stand beside the commander. 'We brought spoils of war from our campaign in Georgia. It has nothing to do with Harðráði or the empire.'

'I wonder how that might be proven,' mused the old man, that unpleasant smile still in place. 'Very hard to do so. I suspect the investigation will take years. Long enough for a man to rot in a cell, I'd say.'

'Get out,' snarled Harðráði, gesturing with his axe at the officer.

'You would defy an imperial order here in the great city itself? Bear in mind that no matter how many good men you have here, we have more, as well as the excubitores and the rest of the city garrison. I advise strongly against starting a war, Sigurdsson, because you will lose. Submit, and it is only your neck at risk and not those of your fellow criminals.'

Harðráði let out a low rumble from deep in his throat, and reached up, rubbing his face with his free hand, which then dropped to his belt and pulled free his gleaming sax blade.

'Harald,' Valgarðr said, reaching out, 'this isn't the way.'

'Back off,' Harðráði snapped at his friend, and then to the Varangians in the gate: 'I give you one more chance to leave. I will not submit to your false justice.'

The old warrior with the long axe beside him stepped a little closer, his face full of concern, but Halfdan's mind was racing now, and he cleared his throat, moving away a little. 'Do as he says, Valgarðr. Back off.'

'What?' the second-in-command frowned across at Halfdan, who gave him a warning look. 'His hands. The pouch. The bear shirt.'

Valgarðr's eyes widened as he realised. Harðráði had not just been rubbing his face. He still had the compound from the pouch on his fingers. At that moment, the Guard commander turned to his men, and Halfdan felt his spirits sink. Harðráði's eyes were wild and dark, drool at the corner of his mouth. The young jarl danced away fast now, Valgarðr doing the same, the two men falling back to the others.

Harðráði was trembling.

'Take him,' the greybeard commanded, pacing back to the gate.

The Varangians stepped forth. Halfdan noted that despite the reticence of the Guard towards bearing naked blades in the city, each man here had drawn one. Whether that was because of this being official duty or perhaps the unfamiliarity of these strange Rus with common custom, Halfdan couldn't say, but a true fight was clearly being offered.

'What do we do?' he asked Valgarðr, watching nervously.

'Nothing.'

'What?'

'If we join in, this becomes a battle and lots of men die, probably including all of us. Harald still falls, but we go with him. We need to survive so we can help him. We stay back.'

'Besides,' added Ketil, appearing at his other shoulder, 'Harðráði is berserk. Best not to be near him. Let's just hope he doesn't get himself killed.'

The commander suddenly let out a strangled cry, which could have been some sort of prayer to the Christ God, though Halfdan suspected he heard the name Odin somewhere in the roar, and leapt forward. The Varangians reacted with surprising bravery, though perhaps these strange men from the edge of Rus lands had not heard the old northern tales of the bear shirts. They brandished their weapons and roared in response as Harðráði broke into a run.

Halfdan found himself silently asking Odin to watch over the man now, and beside him he could hear Valgarðr muttering similar prayers to his own god.

The berserk commander hit the line of Varangians like a runaway cart. Before anyone could land a blow in reply, his axe had smashed deeply into the leg of one man, breaking the bone and almost severing it, while his sax, a foot and a half of straight steel, had plunged deep into the neck of another. What had happened to the rest, Halfdan could not see, but a small part of the line had been pushed back and had fallen in a heap. With panicked and angry shouts, the remaining unengaged men enveloped the ruckus, and the fight was lost to sight. Halfdan trembled, still praying.

For a moment, Harðráði came back into view, his axe raised, blood spraying in every direction, knife whirling. He disappeared again in the press of men, and when he next appeared, his dagger had gone, and instead he held half an arm in his left hand, whacking it in the face of a man as he howled.

'I don't know who I pity more,' Ketil muttered.

'Stupid,' Halfdan grunted. 'He's only going to get himself killed.'

'We could help,' Bjorn suggested, arriving at their shoulders.

'Not a good idea,' Valgarðr said. 'If we fight this, we'll have to fight the whole city, even the whole empire. They've got the law on their side. No, we have to prove him innocent, instead, and get him back.'

'If he lives through his arrest,' Halfdan said, watching nervously. The commander appeared in view again for a moment, and he was gnawing on something as he tried to pull himself out of the press. He was no longer armed, and men were all over him, gripping, pummelling, trying to restrain him. Finally, someone smacked Harðráði round the back of the head with the flat of a sword. It did not immediately have the desired effect, and the commander managed to turn, even being clawed at and beaten by a score of men, and break the man's jaw with a powerful punch. Finally, though, his mind succumbed to the damage, and Harðráði collapsed in a heap, men all over him.

After a few moments, the commander was lifted from the ground by four Varangians, his body shaking wildly, and borne aloft as though part of a jarl's funeral procession. Halfdan watched, alert, making sure that they were not the death shakes, but it seemed that the man lived. Indeed, he seemed remarkably uninjured, barring marks and contusions, considering the fact that at least five bodies were being lifted up, several men limping or clutching wounds. Harðráði's axe and knife were handed to the greybeard, who looked across at the palace garrison, a little disappointed perhaps that they had not joined in and given him the excuse he needed to wipe them out.

'Wait,' the man said to his guards. 'The wounded and a dozen other men, take Harðráði away, along with the dead. The rest of you, our business here is not done.'

Halfdan felt himself tense at the words, and everyone gathered in the training yard moved close together now, prepared for the worst.

'You did not submit to a search of your gear in the Great Palace,' Erik reminded them. 'Your shipmates have proved to be hoarders of stolen gold, criminal allies of the commander. You will submit to that search now, or I will have you detained on suspicion of involvement.'

Bjorn let out a defiant bellow, but Halfdan held out a restraining hand. 'Let them search.'

As they stood there in the dusty sunlight, Greybeard sent his men into the nearby barrack block, while a detachment of his men, limping and groaning, carried Harðráði and several corpses out of the gate, bearing them away across the city. As the enemy commander began to direct his men into other buildings with impunity, Valgarðr turned to Halfdan.

'What do you know of this gold they found?'

'Exactly what I told them. We earned gold and silver in Georgia, fighting for a deluded jarl. This was our share. Nothing to do with the commander or this city at all. It was unfortunate timing. We managed to stop them searching our gear, but we were sent here straight away and I haven't managed to speak to the others.'

'What will they find here?'

'Nothing. Leif assures me of that.'

Valgarðr nodded silently, though Halfdan could feel the disappointment glowing off the man. For months, Harðráði had managed to avoid real trouble by being untouchable, as they'd seen with the impudent note they'd delivered to Ari from the ship captain, and now the very men the commander had brought in to be loyal to his cause had handed the enemy the evidence they needed. It was all very unpleasant, and all very neat. They would find nothing else, of course, but now they had sufficient cause to keep Harðráði locked up until *Ragnarok* while they twiddled their thumbs.

Damn it.

They stood for some time, musing on failure and disaster, as the frantic Varangians hurried this way and that, turning every room in every structure in the palace upside down. In truth, it would take hours for them to even attempt such a complete search of the Blachernae, but they would focus on the areas Halfdan and his men occupied and have to consider that sufficient for now.

Almost an hour passed before the greybeard gathered his men once more and gestured to the gate.

'Just because we found nothing does not mean there was nothing to find. I am watching you all like a hawk.'

'So we are not under arrest?' Valgarðr asked.

'You are still assigned to the Blachernae. That has not changed.'

'But as guards, not prisoners. We are free to go about our business, in the city if we so wish?'

Erik Boneblade chewed his lip irritably, in silence, for some time, and finally gave a single curt nod. Clearly he would have loved to have confined them to barracks, but despite the free spirit of all Northmen, those serving in this city were bound by the same rules as every other citizen of the empire, and the man could not flaunt those rules here, lest he endanger the authority he carried. With a final glare, the old warrior turned and marched away.

'Erik there is making a funeral pyre for himself,' Valgarðr murmured.

Halfdan nodded. 'Once, not long ago, I stood on his chest with my sword at his throat. I'll vow right now before both your god and mine that it'll happen again before the snows come.'

Valgarðr gave him an unpleasant smile. 'I'd say the same about Ari Karsten, but God help the man who gets between him and Harðráði when the time comes.'

The others were gathering now, and not just Halfdan and his friends or the Varangians who'd been training, but all those considered to be Harðráði's men and who'd been reassigned to this peripheral place. Leif was smiling.

'Where did you hide the gold?' Halfdan asked quietly as the gates were shut once more and they were free of listening enemies.

The small Rus's grin widened. 'There's a small church to the Theotokos down near the water. It's already full of imperial treasures. A few extra pounds of gold are lost in the fortune.'

Halfdan laughed. 'Quick thinking.'

'What do you intend to do with this gold?' Valgarðr asked quietly.

'What? I don't know, yet. Each man to his own, I suppose. Why?'

'Because there could be a greater use for it.'

Halfdan folded his arms. 'I'm listening.'

'We are not trapped here, and so let us make use of our time. Harðráði is imprisoned, and so are the empress and your friend. Our time is limited, for once the emperor and his cronies are ready to move, the empress will be taken out of reach, and there will be no hope of freeing the commander then. We need to start moving, to speak to anyone who will ally with us, from the disaffected nobles who don't like this low-born upstart emperor to the Patriarch of the Church who almost refused to crown him. But there will be more we can do. Byzantines are a practical and avaricious people. Gold buys loyalty here much more easily than in the North. I will direct you to powerful figures who will covet your gold, and who might be willing to trade their oath for it.'

Ketil cleared his throat meaningfully. 'I might remind you that that gold is ours, not yours.'

Halfdan gave his friend a sympathetic look. 'But it is our gold that bought Harðráði a prison cell. We owe him.'

Ketil fell into a grumbling silence, yet still he nodded. They all did.

'But what can we do?' Halfdan asked. 'What use is raising a few nobles and a priest? What do you intend?'

Valgarðr fixed him with a steely look. 'Simple. I intend to start a revolution.'

Part Three

ᚹᛟᚴᚠᛚᛖᛋ ᛟᚠ ᛟᛞᛁᚾ

Streets of Blood

Chapter 11

'Hear, citizens of the empire, the words of His Majesty, the Basileus *Autokratōr* Michael the Fifth, son of Michael the Paphlagonian.'

Gunnhild leaned on the ledge of the window and peered out into the open square before the Bucoleon Palace, squinting into the sunlight. This open space was thronged on even the quietest of days, but today, as the spring weather warmed the stone and the air carried a pleasant breeze off the sea, it veritably seethed with humanity. A man in an elaborate uniform stood in a small clear space, the masses held back by six of the new dour-looking Scythian Varangians. The people of the city were silent, straining to hear, and Gunnhild could just make out the very same words being spoken a few streets away.

'This is happening all over the city?'

The empress nodded. 'The Eparch will be reading the edict in the great forum of Constantine at the heart of the city, and copies are being relayed in every street to be sure that no soul misses it. Now quiet, Gunnhild, and listen.'

'...the honour and respect due your emperor, and has proved herself ill-disposed to the rule of your rightful basileus. Still, the emperor is merciful in the eyes of God, and endures the empress's constant betrayals and slights with a stoic calmness.'

'I'll slight *him*,' Zoe spat angrily.

Gunnhild simply listened, half expecting what was coming next already.

'...evidence that has come to light concerning a plot devised by the Porphyrogenita to poison the emperor. Had it not been for the alertness and composure of the emperor's new Scythian Guard, the basileus would have followed his father and the great Romanos into the arms of God, for it now becomes apparent that three generations of emperors have all succumbed to the machinations of the empress and her poisons.'

'If I'd wished to poison the rat, I could have done so many times, though I consider some things beneath me. Now, I begin to regret *not* having done it.'

Gunnhild found herself recalling her first meeting with the empress, and that tray of ingredients. Two of the five had been virulent poisons. Why, she found herself wondering, would the empress have such a thing to hand? She hauled her thoughts back to the present, as the official was still delivering his announcement.

'Because it is an abhorrent thing to contemplate the execution of one of imperial blood and of an ancient and respected line, no matter how criminal or wicked they might have proven themselves, the emperor is minded to clemency, and forgives the empress her many crimes, commuting a clear sentence of death.'

'How generous,' Zoe rumbled.

'Therefore the empress will be shorn of her locks and taken henceforth to the island of Prinkipo, where she will be permitted to take the habit of a daughter of the Church and contemplate her crimes, atoning for them in the island's nunnery to the end of her days. These are the words of Michael the Fifth, Basileus of Constantinople and master of the empire. Hail the emperor.'

There was a strange silence.

'Can they do this?' Gunnhild asked quietly.

'The Guard will be here for me within the hour. My time has apparently come. Gunnhild, while ladies I have known and trusted all my life have fled my side, you have served me faithfully throughout this disaster, and I thank you. As the worst comes to pass, I charge you with this single thing: leave the city.

Take your servant and get away from this place, for Michael will turn the city and the empire into a pit of serpents where every shadow harbours death.'

Gunnhild turned a look on the empress that startled her. 'Let the emperor and his cronies pray for mercy should they decide to come for me. They will regret it. I have seen things, Zoe of Byzantium, and this is not over, however it might look.'

She caught a momentary glimpse of Anna through a doorway, keeping out of the way of the empress, while trying in her unsubtle way to catch what was being said, then the girl was gone again.

A commotion was growing outside now. As both women looked out of the window they could see the discontent among the people in the square. The official was leaving, heading back towards the palace, surrounded by his armed guards, but he was moving fast, and fragments of refuse and rubble were being thrown at them by raised hands in the angry crowd. A piece of roof tile smashed into one of the new Varangians, and his friend had to grab him and steer him away, his head bleeding.

'The city will not take your fall kindly,' Gunnhild noted.

'I have been their faithful empress for generations,' Zoe replied quietly. 'Michael is an upstart, the nephew of another upstart. The city will seethe, but there is nothing they can do. Bakers and wheelwrights are powerless in the face of the Varangians and the city garrison.'

'Do not underestimate the low-born,' Gunnhild warned her. 'An axe is just an axe, but a thousand empty fists can be an unstoppable force.'

'You do not know Byzantium,' the empress said sadly. 'This is a place of order and rules. The city might be angry, but nothing will come of it.'

'You do not know your friends, I think,' Gunnhild replied. 'I sense their hands at work here. Halfdan and Harðráði and others loyal to you. This is not just disaffection, but woven disobedience.'

'Harðráði is more securely imprisoned than I,' Zoe sighed.

A bear, a wolf, a boar.

'This is not over,' Gunnhild said again. 'Whatever might happen, this is not over.'

The empress said nothing, simply looked out of the window. 'See how they come for me already?'

A small group of Varangians was now making its way through the crowd, enduring thrown missiles and clawing hands. Five men. Gunnhild let a slight smile creep across her face. 'Those are not your escort. Those men are allies.'

As Gunnhild waited, the empress moved to her throne. Whether she would be greeting friend or foe, Zoe Porphyrogenita was determined to meet her fate as an empress. Still it seemed strange for Zoe to wait, grand and imperial, with only Gunnhild and a few worried-looking eunuchs in attendance, for all those ladies of the court whose advice Gunnhild had overwhelmed these past months had either disappeared when the tide turned against them, or had been kept away by the emperor's Varangian jailers.

A new commotion broke out below, and Gunnhild peered down from the window. Halfdan was arguing with the guard on the palace gate and in moments the five men were in the palace. As she listened, she heard heavy footsteps approaching the door. Another brief muffled argument with the guards out there, and finally the doors opened and Halfdan walked in, full of purpose, his face grim. Ketil, Bjorn, Leif and Ulfr were at his heel, and each of them was armed for war. Once again, out of the corner of her eye, Gunnhild caught sight of Anna flitting past a doorway, momentarily taking it all in.

'The city is a hornet nest, Majesty,' Halfdan declared, without any preamble, bowing his head sharply to the elegant, grand figure on the throne. 'And someone has kicked it. The whole of Miklagarðr is ready to explode. The emperor has made a critical mistake in levelling his accusations.'

'Halfdan,' Gunnhild said in greeting. She had not realised how much she'd missed the young jarl over these few months.

'Gunnhild,' Halfdan smiled, turning to her. 'It is good to see you well. Not safe, though. A hornet's nest, I tell you. Harðráði might be locked away, but Valgarðr steers things in his absence. We have powers in the city in our purse now. The city is on the edge.'

'You heard the announcements?' the empress asked.

Halfdan nodded, turning to her. 'We are at a critical moment, Majesty. There are men who stand by you, but they themselves are in danger. The emperor has sent men out to arrest all those who have spoken in your favour, including the patriarch of your Christ Church and several senior nobles, all men we have been twisting to our cause for weeks. But arrest may not be the worst they face. Ari Karsten has set his best killers to the task.'

'He was never going to stop at mere arrest,' Gunnhild said quietly. 'The city bucks and heaves. Michael the Caulker can only maintain control if all those who stand against him die. The patriarch will never leave his chambers alive. The emperor would see Harðráði die in his cell. Many others too.'

'You should see the people out there,' Halfdan said. 'They are a pyre of dry tinder awaiting a flame. One more wrong move by the emperor and the fire will start. It may be that the death of the patriarch will be that spark.'

'No,' Zoe said, rising slowly from her throne. 'No, the people will not rise against their emperor for a priest, even one as great as Patriarch Alexios. His death would be futile, and he would be a far greater symbol of reason and resistance alive.'

Gunnhild frowned. 'You plan to sacrifice yourself,' she said.

'I will fight my enslavers when they come and do so in full view. Let the people see me manhandled and desecrated by my nephew the emperor. I will not let them take me alive. Let the people see me killed by Michael. *That* is the spark you seek. *That* will see him fall.'

Gunnhild was shaking her head, and Halfdan caught her look and replied to the empress. 'Your loyal guardsmen have not been idle, Majesty. The patriarch is not the only man of power we have in our grip. We must defend this palace against your captors. We can hold them off and save you.'

'No. My fall will be the spark.'

Gunnhild made an irritated sound and threw her arm out in exasperation. 'What is it with jarls and empresses? Why can you never see the middle road. Why must it always be fighting to the death, or soppy sacrifices? Things can unfold in a more satisfactory way with just a little patience.'

Another door opened into the room suddenly, the one that led to the private imperial apartments, and one of the empress's eunuchs bowed deeply. 'Majesty, a ship comes.'

Turning, Zoe swept from her throne and crossed the great room, passing through that door and along a wide vestibule to where a large decorative window with a balcony looked out over the Propontine Sea. Gunnhild followed her, staff in hand, and Halfdan and the others clattered along, earning fearful looks from the various servants as they passed.

The great, wide balcony overlooked the private dock of the palace, and all could see the huge imperial dromon sliding through the quiet waters to the jetty side, its oars rising and falling in perfect order. The figures aboard were clearly Varangians.

'They come to take me to Prinkipo.'

'Where is this Prinkipo?' Bjorn murmured.

'Around ten miles across the water,' Leif replied.

'That's not out of our reach, then.'

'It doesn't matter,' Halfdan cut in. 'We're not letting them take the empress.'

Gunnhild looked back and forth between Halfdan, the empress, and that great ship. 'No, Halfdan. Listen to me. The middle path is the one we need.'

He looked at her, frowning. 'This is our chance, Gunnhild. We can fight this.'

'No. Our time is yet to come. The empress is correct: she is the spark for your fire, and before the city burns our time will come, but not yet.'

'Why not?'

Gunnhild turned a determined look on the young jarl. Sometimes Halfdan was a little too impetuous, but she had seen it, had she not? She had seen the empress with the three of them, a bear, a wolf and a boar. Never had she stood alongside Halfdan and Harðráði, and she had to believe that the path would yet become clear.

'Do you trust me, Halfdan Loki-born?'

'You know I do.' He looked abashed, offended even.

'Then listen to me. This has to happen. You cannot save the empress now, but her path will not end here.' Gunnhild swallowed down the hope that she was right and forced her expression into one of empowered certainty. 'There are others who need your help now. Save the Patriarch Alexios.'

Halfdan frowned. 'I will not turn my back on an empress to whom I swore an oath just to save a priest of the nailed god.'

Zoe Porphyrogenita turned to him then. 'You swore an oath to the throne like all Varangoi. Heed then my direct order. Do as Gunnhild says. Save the patriarch. Go now.'

Halfdan paused, a worried look sliding across his face as he glanced back and forth between the two women.

'Go,' Gunnhild said again. 'I will see you again soon. Trust me.'

Still the five men paused until Ketil finally grasped Halfdan's shoulder. 'If we are going, we must go now, or we'll miss the chance. Ari's men are likely already on the way.'

Finally, Halfdan nodded helplessly, glancing once at the empress, and the five men turned and pounded along the corridor, racing back for the main door.

'I still see no route but a sacrifice that will ignite your fire,' the empress said to Gunnhild once they were gone. 'If they take me, it will be the end.'

'No,' Gunnhild shook her head. 'No, it will not. If they will take you, that will be enough to enrage your people, without the need for your death. You may never even reach the island before things change. Your thread is not yet broken. Do not cut it yourself.'

Outside the window, the dromon slid against the jetty and even as the sailors secured it, Varangians were leaping ashore and stomping into the palace. Gunnhild recognised Ari Karsten among them. This was an important job, and not one to be left in the hands of an underling. The acting commander of the Guard had come to take control personally.

'I am afraid, Gunnhild,' the empress said, suddenly. 'It is not seemly for an empress to be afraid.'

'You are strong, Zoe of Macedonia. These men who come for you are weak. The empire is yours, not your nephew's, and you can sense as much if you stay still. Listen. Let your very skin feel the change.'

The empress stood silent at the window, the only sounds the muffled entry of Varangians a floor below, the noise of the ship being secured, and the nervous moans of the servants. But Gunnhild could feel it, and she saw the strange realisation dawn on the empress's face too. Every place had an aura, and Gunnhild had always known as much. She could feel when a forest was expectant or calm, when a building harboured ancient Seiðr or was a place of death, when a ship was fated to sink. Since coming to this great city, she had felt the soul of Constantinople as a background rhythm behind everything else. The city had a steady pulse, but that had changed in the past hundred heartbeats. It now felt like a battlefield awaiting the first blow. Like two armies eyeing one another warily. Halfdan had been right. All it needed was a spark.

'You never told me what you saw when Michael demanded your visions,' the empress said without turning from the window.

'He wanted to know whether he should do what he planned.'

'This?' The empress stared at her. 'You told him he *should*?'

'I did. I confirmed that only then would he get to stand in the light, out of your shadow.' Gunnhild, looking out across the city, missed the glare the empress threw at her.

'Then you could have *stopped* this? And yet you advised him to level these accusations?'

Gunnhild turned to her. 'It seems heartless, I know. A betrayal, even. But I did what must be done for Michael to step into a trap of his own making. This has to happen, Zoe of Macedonia. Can you not see? For things to change there must be a catalyst. You are that catalyst, and your adopted son *will* stand in the light, but only long enough for his enemies to find him.'

The accusing glare of the empress lingered for a moment, and Gunnhild straightened. 'Have I yet steered you wrong in all this time, Empress? Have I ever given you reason to believe I would sell my honour and buy your nephew's gratitude with your life?'

'No. No, of all those who have been my friends, only you stood with me.'

'Then remember that, Zoe of Byzantium. I look not at the fine stones and glass fragments that form the mosaic, but at the grand picture it creates. Small things, however unpleasant, must happen for the big things to come to pass.'

There was a moment, then, when the empress wavered. She fixed Gunnhild with a look that was, at best, partially convinced. 'I hope you are right. Come.' Zoe Porphyrogenita turned, striding back along the vestibule to the great arcaded chamber where they had spent the past few hours. As Gunnhild followed, the empress took her place on that throne once more, carefully arranging herself.

'If I am to be your catalyst, the city must see this,' she said, 'and I must greet my fate as an empress. If I falter, I charge you now, be there for me.'

Gunnhild nodded, and now they could hear heavy boots in the next room. At gestures from the empress, the few eunuchs fell into place as a small court, two maids emerging from the empress's bedchamber to bolster the unimpressive numbers. Anna remained out of sight, not part of the empress's court, but Gunnhild would bet she had an eye and an ear on proceedings from somewhere.

The room sat silent as there was the click of a lock and the door swung open once more. Ari Karsten marched in full of purpose, axe swinging in his belt. Not once did he even incline his head in respect. Behind him came an old grey-haired Varangian with hateful eyes, and behind them a gathering of their warriors, all men of the new Scythian corps brought in by the emperor. Varangians with little of the North about them, flat-faced and with an air of unrestrained violence.

'Zoe Porphyrogenita,' the commander said loudly, 'it is my lamentable duty to inform you that you are hereby deposed. Henceforth you will be recognised by no man as empress of Byzantium. For your crimes...'

'*Fictitious* crimes,' the empress interrupted.

A slight tic appeared in the corner of Ari's eye. '*For your crimes,*' he repeated, 'you are hereby sentenced to permanent exile until the day of your death at the nunnery on Prinkipo. You will be tonsured and taken to your new home immediately, by imperial order.'

Gunnhild glanced at the empress and saw a slight tremor where her hands gripped the arms of her chair, knuckles white. What was a tonsure, Gunnhild wondered, to bring such fear?

Slowly, the empress rose from her throne, one of the eunuchs straightening her robes. With the crook of a finger, she beckoned to Gunnhild, who approached with a frown, which only deepened as Zoe reached up and, with some effort, removed the heavy, gilt crown from her head. Her hair remained in place, braided and coiled elaborately, as the empress handed the crown to Gunnhild with a meaningful look. Gunnhild took the thing and immediately wondered how the old woman ever managed to move about with such a weight upon her head every hour of the day.

Without a flinch, the empress then strode from the throne to the wide windows that overlooked the square. As she came to a halt there, Gunnhild heard a roar from the crowd outside at the sight of their empress.

'Step back from there,' Ari said quietly.

'No. You will do what you must, Varangian, but you will do it within sight of my people.'

Gunnhild saw the commander struggling with this for a moment, and the old warrior beside him leaned closer. 'Sir, if you tonsure her in front of the people, think what they will say.'

Ari's head snapped round. 'And if instead she is forcibly dragged from the window by the Guard? Is that any better? This way it is the emperor's order they see, not Varangian cruelty.'

Rolling his shoulders, Ari slipped the straight-bladed sax from his belt and crossed to the empress. 'Stay very still. One slip and this could go very badly for you.'

To the empress's credit, she remained perfectly still, standing at the window in full view of her people as Ari Karsten began his work, sliding the knife in among the oiled tresses of the empress's hair. With a *snick*, a coiled braid came free and fell to the floor. Gunnhild stared. What strange ritual was this? As she watched, coil after coil of hair fell, leaving the empress of Byzantium in a matter of heartbeats with a poorly trimmed head, little more than tufts and sprouts of jagged hair. It was, to say the least, unsightly... and *deliberately* so. Like all Northmen, Ari would be quite capable of neatly trimming or even shaving heads, and yet she stood there like some badly shorn sheep. The roar of the crowd below had become more angry still, and voices were calling the empress's name in desperation. The mood had changed again. The feel of the city. The two armies were on the move, the pace increasing.

'Take her to the ship,' Ari snapped, turning to his men as he wiped the oily sax on his trousers and sheathed it once more.

'Remember what I said,' Gunnhild called as Zoe Porphyrogenita was grasped by burly warriors and hauled away from the window, out of view of her people. 'This is not the end.'

'You are mistaken,' Ari said, turning to her.

'I am völva,' she replied in a menacing hiss. 'You doubt my wisdom?'

He actually recoiled for a moment, as though she had slapped him, but recovered quickly. 'No. I do not doubt you. You said this would happen. That the emperor would come out from under her shadow, and he has. And I shall rise with him.'

Gunnhild caught out of the corner of her eye the look the empress levelled at her, one of uncertainty, tinged with accusation. She ignored it. For now there were more important matters than Zoe's feelings.

Ari reached out a hand. 'The crown,' he insisted.

'Stays with me.'

Ari's eyes narrowed. 'The emperor will demand it.'

'You have the empress's hair for him. He will be content. This stays with me.'

'That is not acceptable.'

Gunnhild tightened her grip on the crown and on the staff upon which she leaned. 'If you intend to take this, you will have to pry it from my hands. You may kiss the cross, Ari Karsten, but is there enough Northman still inside you to understand what that means. Freyja protects her own, Varangian.'

Ari stood silent, but she noted that the tiny tic at the corner of his eye had intensified into a true twitch now. Finally, he shrugged. 'The empress is no more. Her crown is meaningless. Remember the emperor's offer, though, völva. He will see you rewarded for this, but you will then leave the city. Find us at the Great Palace and he will shower you with gold. He may yet want that crown, though.'

With that, the Varangian commander and his men turned and marched from the room. As the empress was roughly dragged away, that look of accusation had only deepened at Ari's fresh revelation. One last glare and she, and the Varangians, were gone.

Gunnhild stood near the throne, listening to their retreating footsteps, surrounded by horrified, sobbing servants. With a snarl, she waved her hand at them and pointed to the vestibule. She had much to decide and much to do, and the wailing of eunuchs was stopping her thinking straight.

As the last of the servants vanished and shut the door behind them, Gunnhild crossed to the window and looked down upon the crowds below. The spark had been lit. She could feel it now. The battlefield was charged, the two armies stomping inexorably towards one another. The empress would likely never reach Prinkipo, she suspected. If she did, she would not stay there long enough to watch another sunrise before she returned. And when she did, Gunnhild would still have her crown.

Halfdan would save the high priest of the nailed god, and the man would join the voice of revolution, for the people of this city listened to priests almost as much as to the emperor. Halfdan was with Gunnhild once more, but she needed Harðráði too, and the man languished in prison. Michael Kalaphates stood finally in the light, and if he were to fall, she needed both the wolf and the bear. Taking a deep breath, she crossed to the inner doors and pulled them open. The servants were gathered there, faces drawn and bleak.

'Who among you has strength and resolve?'

The servants said nothing, trembling.

'Will none of you come with me? The empress will rise again, but I need two of you.'

Finally, a thin, gaunt woman in the dress of a chambermaid stepped out from the cowering eunuchs. 'I will help you. What do you need?'

Gunnhild surveyed the group. A moment later, a familiar figure emerged from behind them. Anna would be perfect.

'Good,' Gunnhild said, tossing the heavy crown to one of the burlier eunuchs. 'Keep this safe,' and then to the two girls: 'Prepare yourselves. We are going to free the Varangian commander from his prison.'

Chapter 12

'You realise Ari's men have a good head start on us,' Ulfr said between gasping breaths as they ran. 'It's quite likely they've already killed him.'

'Then we'll have to settle for vengeance,' Halfdan grunted.

Ketil glanced back over his shoulder, his long legs eating the distance with ease as the rest struggled to keep up. 'If you lot weren't so tiny, we'd be there by now.'

Halfdan looked around as they encountered yet another angry gathering. He'd seen armies in the field, and he'd seen angry punch-ups in villages, but this was something new and astounding to behold. Miklagarðr itself, the great city of Constantinople, was rising entire. He'd been sceptical to say the least when Valgarðr had used the word 'revolution', but he was being forced to rethink with every passing moment. How had it come to this so fast?

Over the past few weeks, the emperor had consolidated his position, gradually pushing the empress further and further from any hint of power or influence until he felt the time was right to sever any connection to her and to cast her adrift. During that time the emperor's control over the city had become all but total. The Guard had changed likewise, Ari and his loyal bastards in control of everything, anyone they couldn't entirely trust either marginalised or sent away, most of the *Sea Wolf*'s crew either arrested for the possession of suspicious gold or still assigned to peripheral duties. The only thing that had stopped death sentences being levelled at them was the ridiculous Byzantine need for everything to follow procedure.

Thus Harðráði remained in prison and Halfdan and his friends continued to patrol walls, until the time came when Ari could claim sufficient cause and authority to do away with them. That time was coming, with the emperor's sudden autocracy, now unhampered by Zoe Porphyrogenita.

But Valgarðr had set something in motion. With what gold they could gather, they had bought the loyalty of men of questionable oath, while other, more noble, men had thrown themselves into the cause of their own free will. The patriarch had been with them from the start. What a priest of the nailed god, half a dozen hedonists, and a bunch of untrustworthy officials could do against an all-powerful emperor with a faithful army and a Guard under Ari's control, Halfdan had not been able to imagine. A bunch of grumbling citizens against the axes of empire.

Only now, heaving their way through the streets, did he understand what could happen. Every public space, every wide street, every forum and market was filled with the ordinary people of the city, and half of them had found stout lengths of wood, farm tools, large knives, any kind of makeshift weapon. Each gathering roared with anger, and through it all two names were audible above everything: Michael the Caulker, emphasising the derogatory nickname, was a name being spoken everywhere with fury and hate, the man denounced as evil and a liar, as a usurper and a false emperor, while the empress was lauded and praised. She was *Porphyrogenita* – born to the purple. She was a true empress from a respected dynasty that had taken Byzantium to greatness, and she had been insulted, humiliated and supplanted by her nephew on plainly false grounds.

Constantinople was no longer on the verge of eruption. It had exploded.

Pushing their way through the crowds in the Mese, the great porticoed main street of the city, they could see the gleaming dome and cross of the Hagia Sophia, the great imperial temple of the nailed god ahead. The irony continued to strike Halfdan, that five men who followed the true path of the old gods were racing to save a Christian priest from other Christians.

'You say the patriarch's house is attached to the church?' Ketil asked as they ran.

Leif heaved in a few breaths. 'I've never been in it, but it's on the south-west corner. The two buildings are connected by a porch, but there is an external door too, leading out into the square.'

'You realise we've got a fight coming, whether they've finished or not.'

'I fucking hope so,' Bjorn said as he pounded alongside them. 'I haven't punched anyone in weeks, and I'm getting bored.'

Their progress was slowed once more as they emerged from the end of the great street into the wide square bounded by the church, the palace and the hippodrome. The entire square was packed with shouting people, arms waving angrily in the air. Across the way, Halfdan could see debris and unmentionable detritus being hurled at the palace gates which were now resolutely shut.

It was not difficult to force their way through the press, for between them Ketil and Bjorn provided enough bulk, muscle and gleaming steel to persuade most people to move aside, and so like a rowing boat in a lake of humanity, they inched their way across the open space towards the patriarch's palace.

Ketil was the first to stop, his view clearer than most, for he stood a head above almost the whole populace. The man dropped down a little, neck and shoulders hunched as he gestured for them to stop.

'We need to find another way in.'

'Why?'

'That has to be the palace we're wanting, right next to the church.'

'Yes.'

'Well there's a dozen of Ari's men at the door, and they're busy beating the shit out of a bunch of ordinary people.'

'Maybe we should help the common folk?' Bjorn said.

Halfdan fixed the big albino with a look. 'Think about it, Bjorn. Varangians attacking the people. We appear. We're Varangians.'

'But we're on the other side.'

'They don't know that, Bjorn.' He nodded to Ketil. 'Steer around it. Let's avoid trouble.'

Led by Leif now, who knew the way better than most, they skirted the edge of the growing fracas and made for the main door to the great imperial church. It struck Halfdan as curious, as they pushed their way inside, that the order and decorum built into the Byzantine mind meant that while the world was utter chaos outside, the city close to burning, the citizens had avoided bringing their anger and destruction into the church, the place remaining serene and spacious. But something was still wrong. It took him a moment to realise that the interior of the Christ-temple was the *precise* opposite of the city outside. It was completely empty. In the course of months of duties, Halfdan had been in the place a number of times now, and it had never been so quiet. There were always a few priests and attendants going about their business.

'Stop,' he said, holding up a hand. 'Listen.'

They did so. For a few moments all they could hear was the muffled din of the people in the city outside, but then they caught it. From somewhere nearby there were shouts of alarm and a series of rhythmic thumps. 'That has to be them.'

Leif pointed towards one of the archways and they ran, boots clacking on the exquisite marble floors as they headed for a wide, open double doorway. The portal led into a vestibule of some sort with a beautiful, brightly painted ceiling showing priests of many sorts, all with beards, the walls and floor of bright colours and rich marbles, a mosaic of some ancient emperor being godly above a window. The sounds of fear and violence became louder now, and they ran on. The vestibule opened into a large hall, two storeys high and as decorative as anywhere in this great complex. The noises were clearer still, the thuds reminiscent of a battering ram, the cries those of men panicking, and the sounds were issuing from another doorway opposite.

Even as the five men emerged into the hall, pausing, looking this way and that, three men suddenly burst from that doorway across the room at a run. One was a priest of the nailed god, his terrified flight somewhat hampered by the ankle-length robes he was trying to hitch up like a woman as he ran. Behind him were two of Ari's Guard, both Scythians that had replaced the heart of the Varangians. Both men had murder in mind, and both carried bloodied weapons.

'Get behind me, little priest,' grinned Bjorn, beckoning to the panicked man while he pulled free his war axe with the other hand and gave it an experimental swing.

'Ketil, help him,' Halfdan shouted as they made for the doorway beyond the Varangians. 'He's still sore and weak at the collarbone.'

'No,' Bjorn snapped angrily. 'I'm fine now, and I get two. You can't have one.'

'Listen, you big oaf,' began Ketil, but Bjorn waved his axe angrily, only slightly wincing at the discomfort he still felt. 'Unless you want to be first, run on, bean-pole.'

With a shrug of acceptance, Ketil pounded along with the others. One of the two Varangians made to swipe at them, but Ulfr neatly caught the sword with his axe blade and turned the blow aside. The man turned to attack again, but that was his fatal mistake. Bjorn, determined to have them both to himself, had settled for simply barging the first man out of the way in order to deal with the second. Halfway across the room, the screaming priest disappeared into the doorway through which they'd entered, while the man who'd been hot on his heels floundered on the floor, picking himself up. The second Varangian pulled back his axe above his head to strike down at the retreating figure of Ulfr. He swung and seemed surprised when the weapon would not move. He turned his head, brow furrowed, to look at his axe, only to come face to face with the enormous, grinning shape of Bjorn Bear-torn, one hand wrapped around the raised axe haft just below the head, the other holding an entirely different axe, held in reverse.

'Thank you,' Bjorn smiled, and smashed the iron poll at the rear of his own favoured weapon into the confused face of the Varangian. The man managed to let out a stifled cry as his face caved in, but no more, and by the time the agony paralysed him, Bjorn was finishing the job, flipping the axe in his hand and swinging again, this time with the blade to the fore. The blow opened up a second mouth below the man's chin, cutting off a sizeable portion of beard in the process, and the enemy warrior devolved into a gurgling and shaking mess as he tottered back and collapsed in a heap.

Bjorn, satisfied, turned to see the other Varangian on his feet now. The man looked at Bjorn, then at his fallen victim, and turned and ran.

'Oh no you don't,' snarled the big albino and ran after him. Bjorn was not gangly and fast like Ketil, though, for all his impressive size, and it was immediately clear that he would not catch up with the runner. The big Northman roared his impotent fury, begging Odin to let him have just one more. He then heard a scrape and looked up, a grin spreading across his face. The fleeing priest was closing the door on his pursuer. The Varangian, letting out a worried squawk, tried to pick up speed, but the door was closing too fast, and Bjorn was on him now. With a moment of resigned bravery, the warrior turned, hefting his sword.

Bjorn laughed. 'Thank you, Odin, and thank *you*, little priest.'

Stretching his muscles and patting irritably at his collarbone, he advanced on the Varangian.

Halfdan saw nothing more as he, Ketil, Leif and Ulfr pounded through the doorway. They were in a second hallway now, this one much shorter, though equally decorative and rich. At the far end, another set of double doors stood closed, and seven Varangians occupied the corridor. Three, one of them an officer, stood by the wall, arguing, while the other four held a long bench or pew, two to each side, repeatedly drawing it back and then hammering it against the doors like a ram. Each blow was having an effect, the doors slowly weakening, as they could see from the dust cascading down and hear from the cracks and ligneous groans with each strike. The doors would not hold up to such punishment for much longer. On the other side, several voices, mostly elderly males by the sound of it, were raised in one of those awful nailed god dirges. A small pile of butchered priests who hadn't made it in time lay just to one side, soaked with blood and missing appendages, but none of them was richly dressed enough to be the patriarch.

Halfdan felt his pulse quicken. It appeared that they had made it.

'Stand down,' the officer snapped, noticing them and identifying their Varangian gear in an instant.

'Fuck off,' replied Ketil, breaking into a run and tearing both axe and sax free of his belt. In his wake, the others followed suit, and the three Varangians stepped across to block the corridor as best they could despite its width. The men with the makeshift ram faltered, ready to defend themselves, but the officer threw a finger out towards them. 'Get that door open.'

'Deal with these three,' Leif said confidently as they ran, and Halfdan turned a frown on his small friend. Much had changed in the little Rus since the day they'd picked him up in Kiev. He'd never been a warrior born, but after almost a year aboard the *Sea Wolf*, he was a warrior *made*, full of self-assuredness and strength. It was a testament to the clever fellow that none of the other three made any move to argue, each picking their best target. Halfdan, at the left, was facing one of the rare Varangians they saw these days who still looked like a Northman, gripping a bearded axe with a wicked hook at the rear. Ketil, in the centre, faced the officer, while at the far side Ulfr would have to deal with one of the new Scythian Rus.

Ketil struck first, of course, for his great gait carried him ahead of his companions. To give the officer his due, he reacted well. His big axe, one of those great-hafted things favoured among the Guard, came out, held vertically, and caught Ketil's swinging weapon just below the head. The man, his lip wrinkling, twisted the long pole, Ketil's axe ripped from his hands as the timber caught beneath the razor-sharp beard. It was of little comfort to the man, though, for Ketil simply let go of his axe, which had been only the first of two strikes. Even as the Varangian twisted the weapon from the Icelander's right hand, his left slammed forward and upwards. The straight blade of his sax, a foot and a half of gleaming death, slammed into the man's throat, the momentum carrying it on upwards. The chisel-tip passed through the lower jaw, tongue, and up through the palate into the Varangian's brain.

The man was transfixed already before Ulfr and Halfdan reached their men. The red-haired, barrel-shaped shipwright feinted a low blow, drawing the man's own axe downwards to parry. At the last moment, Ulfr flipped the axe up so that he had one hand below the head and the other on the butt end of the haft, lifting it sharply and horizontally. The ash pole smashed into the man's jaw, snapping his head back and sending him sprawling.

Halfdan cursed as he attacked, realising that he had the clever one. The man had seen his sword coming, had predicted its trajectory perfectly, and had stepped aside. The young jarl had cause once more to give thanks to Loki, whose sign on his arm ever reminded him that his luck was a gift of the god, for though his blow missed, and he was dangerously overextended, his boot came down quite by chance on the man's foot, hard. There were the cracks of many small bones, and the man hollered and slammed back against the wall.

Even as Halfdan recovered himself, his face flushed at his near disaster, Leif swung into impressive action. The little Rus had

173

not bothered with the hand axe tucked in the back of his belt. Instead, he had a sax in one hand and a smaller but still sharp eating knife in the other. As he passed the fight, heading for the four men with the bench, he threw himself to the floor. His momentum carried him forward in a slide along the polished marble, and he disappeared with some skill beneath the bench. Halfdan could not see for a moment what the small man was doing, but he realised in a heartbeat as the two rear men cried out in agony and collapsed, their ankle tendons cut through with razor-sharp blades.

Halfdan's elation at the athletic manoeuvre turned to fear in a moment. Even as the first two men shrieked, Leif had done the same to the men at the front, four ankles sliced with two knives in little more than two heartbeats, but the move had cost him dearly. The agonised Varangians automatically let go of their battering ram as they howled and dropped away to the side, and the heavy pew slammed down on top of the sliding Rus, crushing him to the ground.

That was all Halfdan had time to see, for his own target, hobbling, was back on him now, an axe cutting this way and that through the air. Halfdan danced back out of the way of each blow, backing across the corridor. He passed Ketil and was faintly annoyed for a moment that the big Icelander did nothing to help, but then he realised that the man was more concerned with Leif and was leaping forward to try and lift the pew from the struggling Rus. Ulfr was still locked in a deadly struggle with his man, though he was clearly getting the best of the fight.

The true Varangian took a step forward, and Halfdan smiled. The man was favouring his good foot, keeping the injured one back out of the way, putting his weight on the healthy one. As Halfdan brought his beautiful, eagle-hilted sword up to turn the blow aside, he stamped down once again, his heavy boot delivering a crushing blow to the man's other foot. The Varangian screamed again, and staggered, unable to put adequate weight on either leg, tottering while trying to keep his attention on the man attacking him. Halfdan had the advantage now, and his sword lanced out once, twice, thrice, turned away with desperate luck the first two times as the man lurched back towards the wall. The third one caught him in the gut. The Varangian wore only a padded *vápntreyja*, an arming shirt meant to sit beneath one of chain, either assuming his task of butchering priests would involve little danger, or perhaps hurrying out of barracks before he could arm fully. Whatever the cause, his lack of a chain shirt was his undoing. The eagle-blade slid deep through the padded cote and disappeared into flesh and organs. The man made a strange gasping noise and looked down in horror. Halfdan was not going to give him another chance. With a great deal of effort, he dragged the sharp blade back and forth twice, opening a huge gaping wound in the man's belly. As the sword came out, so did yard upon yard of the man's gut, much to the Varangian's terror. Halfdan left the man to it as he dropped his axe and tried to push his innards back into the hole.

He turned to find Ulfr looking at him curiously.

'Stop showing off,' the taciturn man said without a hint of humour, and then rushed to help Ketil lift the bench from their friend.

Leif groaned as he rolled free. Halfdan, breathing heavily, looked around to satisfy himself that the four other hobbled men were still out of the fight and then went to help Leif up as Bjorn appeared from the other room carrying a head, the mouth open in a huge O of shock.

'Did you have to?' Leif breathed in distaste, wincing as he clutched his side.

Ketil and the big albino spent a few moments putting the hamstrung men out of their misery and in short order the corridor was filled only with the five of them and a gathering of dead Varangians, crimson smears and pools all around.

'How does that feel?' Bjorn asked, prodding Leif in the side without warning. The Rus let out a blood-curdling howl.

'I suspect there are several broken bones,' Ketil noted.

'One more now, I reckon,' Leif hissed, glaring at Bjorn.

Leaving them to it, Halfdan stepped around the fallen bench and knocked on the door. 'Open up. We are friends, come from the empress.'

There was a brief, muffled discussion on the far side of the door, and finally the sound of a bar being lifted. As it swung open, Halfdan had to force himself not to laugh. The patriarch, heavy robes and ostentatious hat intact, stood in the centre of the large room, but his priests were prepared to defend him. One swung some sort of golden bowl on chains as though it were a weapon, while another held a man-sized candelabra out towards him like a trident. The head of the Byzantine Church took in the scene in the corridor in a trice and gestured for his priests to lower their makeshift weapons.

'You are from Valgarðr?'

Halfdan nodded. 'We heard that an order went out for your arrest.'

'Arrest? Pah!' the patriarch snorted. 'Execution, you mean. But the city is roused, my northern friends.'

Halfdan nodded. 'Every square is packed with angry people.'

'Then the time has come to dethrone the monster and save our empress,' Patriarch Alexios announced, then turned, all business, and threw out his hands to his people. 'Go into the great church and get to work. Send word to every house of God in the city. Ring all the bells. Call all the people to war. The time has come.'

The priests bowed their heads and scuttled off as Alexios stepped out into the blood-soaked corridor. He fretted as he tried to step between the growing pools and lines of blood with his expensive leather slippers, and Halfdan rolled his eyes. After the third failure, the most senior priest in the empire gave up trying and simply paced and slithered through the blood.

'Where are we going?' Halfdan said, turning to follow, the others at his heel.

'To the Great Palace,' Alexios replied. 'The empress is on her way to Prinkipo, and the man who sent her still rules. He must be toppled.'

Halfdan nodded and the small group hurried back through the complex and the great Hagia Sophia, out into the open. Already the bells of the great church were clanging wildly, and two others nearby had taken up the frantic ringing. The city was rising, the priest was right. Halfdan had seen battles, but this was something different. A single man with his guards and garrisons trapped in a palace while a population of millions rose to war. The very thought of such odds, a million being a number he'd never have been able to contemplate at home, sent a shiver up his spine.

As they broke out into the open, accompanied by the roaring of the city, a force was pushing its way across the square in the direction of the palace. Halfdan felt a great sense of relief to spot Valgarðr at its head with a pair of unknown noblemen. Behind them stretched lines of soldiers, both hardened Northmen of the Varangian Guard and swarthy Greeks of the Byzantine garrison, all those still loyal to the empress. Halfdan couldn't help but grin with mad relief to see men of the *Sea Wolf* among them.

Valgarðr spotted Halfdan as the small force joined the head of the army.

'Well met, young Gotlander. You found the patriarch.'

'And you found allies,' the priest replied with a smile.

'This is Kabasilos,' Valgarðr said to Halfdan, indicating one of the noblemen. As his finger moved to the second, Halfdan marvelled, for the other nobleman was perhaps the biggest man he had ever met. A veritable giant to match the Pecheneg they had fought on the Dnieper. 'This is the renowned general Georgios Maniakes,' Valgarðr smiled.

Halfdan looked the giant Byzantine up and down. His fearsome size was only part of the impressiveness. He was clearly a man made for war, and was in his element. It was not hard to see how he and Harðráði might rub one another up the wrong way.

'To the Palace,' Maniakes said loudly, for the benefit of the gathered crowd. 'Let the Caulker fear for *his* life for a change...'

Chapter 13

'This is madness, Mistress Gunilla.'

Gunnhild waved an irritable hand at the chambermaid, which did nothing to silence her worried mutterings. Freyja walked with them, and she could see it clearly, for the sea of humanity parted to make way. The street, all the way to the great square before the palace, was crammed with angry citizens all shouting their support for the exiled empress, yet somehow, without having to speak or gesture, space seemed to open up to allow them passage, one northerner with striking looks and a staff of power, two panicked-looking servant ladies at her back, sliding through the mass with ease.

'Tell me what you know of the place,' she said as they climbed the hill towards the heart of the city.

'It is called the Noumera,' Anna said, a fount of local knowledge as always. 'In the days of the ancients it was a great bathhouse, but it has been a prison for many lifetimes now. There is a unit of the garrison called the Noumeroi who guard the city's prisons, and they are housed there. It is not so much a prison as a fortress with cells. Justina is right. This is madness.'

'I do not know of these bathhouses. How are they made?'

'There are many rooms with baths hot and cold, swimming pools, steam rooms and more, but that was long ago.'

'How were they heated?'

'With underfloor channels from a furnace, but it is said that the cells are now under the floor, so any access will long since have been closed.'

Gunnhild nodded. 'And entrances?'

'I don't know the place, Gunilla. I've only ever seen it from the outside.'

'The doors are *on* the outside. You will have seen them.'

Anna sighed as she struggled to keep up with Gunnhild's purposeful gait. 'I know of a main door facing the Hagia Sophia, opening onto the square. There is a door close to the hippodrome stands also, but I've never seen it opened. We can't just knock and walk in, Gunilla. This is a barracks and a prison.'

Gunnhild stopped so suddenly that the two girls walked into her, and took a deep breath. 'There is not time for the old song, to ask for true sight, but Freyja walks in our steps. The goddess is with us.'

Anna and Justina crossed themselves with nervous expressions, as they always did when Gunnhild spoke of the powers. A small space had opened up around them again. They were standing beside a merchant's store, the open frontage filled with copper and ironware, pans and tools and, Gunnhild noted with a sharp eye, a large bathtub. Under her breath, she muttered a plea to the goddess for guidance. There was no time for proper ceremony. The city was on the edge of open warfare and coming closer with every heartbeat. Reaching into the larger of the pouches at her belt, she withdrew a handful of bones, beads and hacksilver, along with a feather she had picked up recently in the palace gardens for its fascinating scintillating colours. With a nod to Freyja, she cast them to the flagstones in an area with less detritus than most. They fell, scattered, and she peered at them carefully. There was no clear shape to them, though if she were to attempt any interpretation she would see three distinct groupings. Perhaps that referred to the three of them? Other than that, nothing seemed to be of help.

She frowned.

The feather had gone. While the two girls watched her with nervous curiosity, she ignored the three indistinct shapes on the ground, her head snapping this way and that, trying to find the feather among the crowds of shouting and flailing humanity. The feather had seemingly caught an updraught from somewhere, and she found it billowing up above head height, wafting across to the edge of the street. As she watched, the brilliant colours twirled in an eddy and then settled into the large bronze bathtub.

'Where will we find a rope?' she asked, an idea forming.

'What?' Anna asked. Then: 'There is a shop in this street. He sells hardware of all sorts, just a few doors up. He will have rope for sure, at least in short lengths. Why, though?'

'The underground will be sealed, you say, and the doors will open into garrisons of men. There is only one way in, then. We have to use the roof.'

The two girls stared, wide-eyed. 'That's insane. Impossible.'

'No. That is our route. Trust me.'

With that, she scooped up her scattered debris and dropped it back into the pouch. Turning to the store, she selected from a table three of the largest cooking knives on display, tossing a gold coin to the shopkeeper. As he greedily pocketed the overpayment, Gunnhild passed a knife to each of the girls, tucking the third into her belt, carefully so that it would not jab her as she walked, and then paced on up the street. Sure enough, Anna was right. Three shops up the slope, another hardware store included lengths of rope hanging from nails beside the door, in three different thicknesses. As she peered at them, trying to estimate what length they might need, Gunnhild felt an odd change in the crowd around them. From the angry, seething resentment there now rose a sense of anticipation, even excitement. She pulled out a pouch of coins and passed it to Justina. 'Buy thirty feet of rope.'

The servant stared at the pouch, but then turned to the merchant, who was busy trying to make sure in the chaos that no one took his wares without paying. Leaving her to it, Gunnhild observed the crowd. There was a general surge of movement now, though only slowly, due to the press of bodies. 'What is happening?' she demanded of one eager-looking man.

'The emperor is addressing the people in the hippodrome,' the man said, before turning away.

'The palace is attached to the hippodrome,' Anna explained. 'Do we go and listen?'

'No. The important thing now is to release Harðráði.'

She turned to find Justina struggling to hold three long coils of the narrowest rope. Taking one from her, Gunnhild passed it to Anna and then took a second for herself. Three ten-foot lengths should be enough. Hurrying now, they pushed on up the street.

'There,' Anna said, finally, pointing to a large structure of domes, apses and heavy blocks, built of elegant white stone and narrow red bricks. 'That is the Noumera.'

Even as they approached, they could see activity there. The main door of the prison onto the square was currently open, and armed and armoured Greeks were pouring out of it, pushing their way through the crowd, using shields, elbows and fists to shift the tide of humanity. The door would remain closed to the women, however, for as the last men emerged, the heavy portal was slammed shut once more.

'See how Freyja clears our path of obstacles,' she told the two girls. 'The noisy emperor bleats to his people, and his soldiers flock to his side.'

'So many,' Justina said. 'The prison must be empty.'

'A minimal guard,' Gunnhild nodded. 'See the far side, close to the palace gates? There the roof comes to a low level. That is our way in. I would have liked to know where Harðráði is held, but there will be no one out here who knows such a thing.'

'Is this a good time to tell you that I'm not good with heights,' Justina murmured nervously.

'Heights are no worry. It's depths you should be concerned with.'

'That is not a comforting thought,' the chambermaid replied, eyeing the knife in her hand with eyes close to panic.

'Concentrate. This is for your empress.'

With that, she led them on through the crowd, away from the great central square and towards the rear of the huge complex. It might now be a prison, but its upper level was clearly largely unchanged from earlier days. Likely the cells were underground and heavily reinforced, but the main building above was little more than a barrack block for the Noumeroi, and so was not heavily fortified.

'There,' she said, pointing up to a roof.

'What?' Anna asked, peering up after her.

'See the shape? There is a hole at the top.'

The roof of this apsidal extension rose in concentric circles of tile, delicate and clever, but even from here it was clear that the topmost circle of tile was not at the apex. If the roof were solid, she should be able to see the point. She could not, and so there must be a hole.

'It is an oculus,' Justina said. 'There is a similar one in the palace baths. It allows light and air into one of the rooms. And rain on a bad day, of course.'

'You,' Gunnhild said, pointing at a burly man nearby who was listening to a speaker haranguing the crowd. The man turned, frowning, and pointed to himself. 'Yes, you,' she replied. 'Help me up to the roof.' She pointed to the lowest edge of the tiled half-dome.

'What?' he said in surprised confusion.

'Are you loyal to your empress? Do you wish to see the Caulker fall?'

The man's eyes shifted nervously this way and that, as though she were setting a trap for him. 'Y-yes?' he stuttered in a guarded voice.

'Then help me,' she said, leaning her staff against the wall.

Something in her tone goaded the man into action, and he turned and followed her to the wall. She could see how windows had been bricked up when the place had been changed into a prison and barracks, but the way the Byzantines built their world left more hand and footholds than any thief could readily need, and so as she clambered up onto the man's shoulders, her hands found plenty of places to grip. With little difficulty, she hauled herself up and pulled her body over the edge of the decorative cornice onto the lowest slope of the tiles. The man made to leave, but she waved. 'Now them,' she said, pointing at Anna and Justina.

With ease, the big man helped the lightly framed girls up, one at a time, Gunnhild reaching down to grab their hands and helping pull them up onto the roof. Their activity was drawing a small crowd of fascinated watchers from below, but with everything that was going on, church bells ringing all over the city, military units pushing through the crowds, an imperial address in the hippodrome and a riot waiting to spring into action, their audacious plan was largely ignored in the grand scheme of things.

Gunnhild rose to her feet, reaching down to help the others up. Anna rose with a little difficulty. Justina stayed crouched, eyes wide as she looked down into the crowd, the blood drained from her face. 'Look up, not down,' Gunnhild said, hauling the terrified maid to her feet. She wobbled for a moment and then turned and dropped face down on the sloping tiles, as far from the edge as she could manage.

Gunnhild followed suit, shifting the rope coil over her shoulder so that it did not get in the way and checking the knife at her belt to prevent accidental injury. The big man below watched them for a moment, and Gunnhild pointed to her staff. 'Guard that with your life, and I will pay you well.'

With a nod to the two girls, she led the way, crawling up the slope of the roof, which was relatively shallow, towards that circular opening at the top. In moments she reached it with ease, and looked down. The room below appeared to be empty, other than a bunch of barrels and boxes stacked around the edge out of the danger of rain through the oculus. A small circular pool at the centre, a carry-over from the days when this was a bathhouse, would collect that rain, and a single door led off into the rest of the building. Searching around, she found what she was looking for. It took wiggling a tile loose to reveal the hole that must have been part of the roof's original construction technique. Two more tiles followed, the three skittering down the slope and falling among the crowd to shouts of alarm and anger from those they almost struck.

Carefully, she unshouldered the rope and looped it through the hole, tying it in three tight knots and then pulling on it hard. It would hold. She looked down. Twenty feet, she estimated. They'd more rope than they needed.

Turning, she gestured down to Justina. 'Throw your rope away and climb up here.'

'No.'

'Yes. You can't go back anyway. Up is much easier. Anna, help her and then come up and bring your rope.'

Justina fought it for a few moments, but there was little she could do. Up was the only option, and with Anna pushing her, she began to climb, slowly and in near panic. She flinched as Gunnhild finally managed to grasp her hand and pull her up to the oculus. Behind the maid, Anna was climbing now. Justina looked over the edge into the room and made a terrified squeak.

'We're nearly there,' Gunnhild said, in what she hoped was an encouraging tone.

When Anna finally reached the oculus, Gunnhild took the rope and began to tie one end to her own, then tested the strength again, nodding her satisfaction. With a deep breath, she tossed the twin coils into the hole and watched as the whole thing unravelled, swinging this way and that, to finally hang down the centre. Perfect. The rope ended three feet from the small circular pool.

'I will go first. Then Justina. Anna last.'

Before they could argue, she swung herself out into the open, gripping the rope and shimmying down it with ease. She dropped the last few feet and landed with a splash. She could hear Justina and Anna arguing above, but her attention was drawn instead to the sound of footsteps. There was only one door, and the noise was coming from beyond it. With a prayer cast to Freyja, she hurried to the wall and then stepped to the side of that door, waiting, quietly, her hand drawing the knife from her belt.

Just one set of feet, and no sound of conversation. A man alone, then. She braced herself as she heard hands closing on the door and a quiet click. The door swung open in front of Gunnhild, obscuring her from the man responsible. Above, the fevered exchange between the two girls ended with a squawk as Anna, with little sympathy, pushed Justina out over the edge, the latter gripping tight to the rope and calling her companion a number of very unladylike things.

The soldier who'd entered immediately had his attention drawn to the strange display at the rope, and he hurried forward, sword in hand, demanding to know the meaning of this. Calmly, Gunnhild stepped out behind him. Her left arm closed around his chest and arm, while her right, gripping the knife, came round to his throat. The man reacted instantly like the trained soldier he was, arm coming up and attempting to throw off her grip, but with just a single jab, the kitchen knife was at his windpipe drawing a bead of blood. The man fell still in an instant. One wrong move and he was dead, and he knew it. He was armoured in a shirt of tiny stitched bronze scales, and well equipped with undershirts and boots and the like, but his throat lay bare and in danger.

'Drop the sword,' she said quietly, but with a great deal of menace.

The man did so instantly, remaining still and watching as a squeaking maid slid down the rope into the pool, cursing her burned palms. A moment later Anna swung out into the open and began to descend, one hand over the other.

'Where is Harðráði,' she asked.

'You will never—' the man began, but stopped, sweating, as a fresh trickle of blood was brought forth from his neck. 'The cells are empty apart from the akolouthos and two of his men who tried to stop his arrest.'

'Where?' she repeated simply.

'I'll take you to them.'

'Not necessary. Where are they?'

He swallowed, and regretted it as more blood flowed. 'Through that door and then the one to the left. Down the stairs and then left again. Through the barred door.'

'Guards?'

'Few. Everyone was called to the emperor's aid. One man on the door to the cell corridor is all that's between you and the akolouthos.'

Gunnhild nodded, then with an easy stroke drew her razor-sharp knife across the man's throat. His eyes bulged as the blood began to sheet from his neck, bubbles forming and popping in the froth as he tried to speak. She let go, kicking his sword away, and stepped after it, picking it up.

'Why did you do that?' Justina asked in a shocked whisper as the wheezing body collapsed to the floor. 'He answered you.'

'Never leave a live enemy behind you,' Gunnhild said. 'You Greeks are too squeamish.'

Turning, she approached the door, listening, a finger to her lips keeping the other two quiet. There was no sound within the building. Just the din of the outraged city from the hole in the roof. 'It seems he was right that they have all left. When we get to the cells, go ahead of me and bluster liked panicked girls, begging to see your lovers. You should be able to manage that well.'

'What about you?'

'I'll be right behind you.'

Moving swiftly but with care and on light feet the three women crossed the next room and opened the door. Following the dead guard's instructions they descended into the lower level and approached a door, beyond which there would undoubtedly be another guard. As the two servants readied themselves, Gunnhild tucked the knife back in her belt and lifted her pouch of coins free, weighing it in her left hand, the right still gripping the purloined sword. It was still quite full and of a good weight. She stepped to one side of the door and nodded to the others. Anna reached out to the handle and opened it while Gunnhild stood unseen to one side, listening. She could hear the waver of nerves in Justina's voice as the pair hurried through and began to blabber about being allowed to see their husbands. There was a single response, a deep male voice, suspicious, surprised. She heard the sound of a sword being drawn. A moment longer, for him to become embroiled with the inane babble.

Ready, she suddenly ducked into the doorway, throwing the pouch hard the moment the guard came into view. The heavy purse struck the distracted man full in the face, knocking him back with a cry of alarm. Gunnhild was moving in less than a heartbeat, her plan to push her way between the two girls and sink her sword into his unarmoured gut before he could recover. To her surprise as she leapt into the room, before the guard could straighten, shaking his head in confusion, Anna had stepped forward and driven her kitchen knife into his chest. The guard gasped and staggered back again, the handle jutting from between his ribs, blood blossoming into his tunic.

'Don't call me sweetheart,' Anna spat at the dying guard.

'Neatly done,' Gunnhild said with a nod of approval, then looked on down the corridor, which became darker as it disappeared into the gloom, heavy doors dotted along each side.

'Odin,' she shouted along the passageway.

'Gunnhild?' came a surprised voice from some way along.

'Sigurdsson,' she replied, and began to pace off into the darkness. Justina lifted the oil lamp from its alcove near the door and hurried after her, golden flame guttering, casting eerie shadows in this terrible place. The three women followed Harðráði's voice as he expressed his astonishment at hearing them, and arrived outside a cell door. There were no locks, just three heavy bolts on the outside, and she drew them clear and then pulled the door open, stepping back.

Harðráði appeared in the doorway with a grin on his face. He made to step forward and embrace her, but Gunnhild levelled the sword, keeping him at bay.

'You smell like a dead dog. Stay out of reach.'

He laughed, and then moved to the cell doors to each side, sliding the bolts open on each. Two of the commander's faithful Varangians emerged, blinking and rubbing their scalps. 'These are Halldor Snorrason and Ulf Ospaksson,' Harðráði introduced them, 'two of my favourite Icelanders. They made a brave, if foolish, effort to stop Ari's men carting me off and ended up sharing my fate. How did you get here, Gunnhild? Where are the guards?'

'There is much to tell you,' Gunnhild answered. 'The empress has been taken away by ship, though I doubt she will have got far. The emperor thinks he is winning, but the city is rioting at the instigation of your friend Valgarðr, of Halfdan, and of the patriarch. The Caulker is busy making announcements in the hippodrome, though I doubt much will save him now. Most of the Noumeroi have left to run to the emperor's side. We will find little difficulty leaving this place, I think.'

Harðráði laughed out loud. 'You are a wonder. I might not need an army to take the crown of Norway if you were by my side. Why would I want a pretty but vapid princess when there is Gunnhild of Hedeby?'

'Save your flattery and your lust, Sigurdsson. I'm no heifer to be traded in the market.' Yet as she spoke, Gunnhild turned her face aside, fearing that a flush had risen to her cheeks despite the words she pulled on as habitually as armour.

Again, he laughed. 'Your tongue is sharp, Gunnhild, but your eyes say something different. And you have a smile I've seen that I think you save only for me.'

'And you can back off, too,' Justina said meaningfully, pushing away one of the two Icelanders they had released.

'Things move apace,' Harðráði said, shaking off the moment and becoming businesslike once more. 'If what you say is true, the city stands on a knife-edge. We must move swiftly.' With that, he hurried back towards the door, pausing to collect the dead guard's fallen blade. One of the two Icelanders looked hopefully at Gunnhild's sword, and her eyes narrowed. She pulled the kitchen knife from her belt and passed it to him as she gripped the sword all the tighter. Ospaksson laughed as he took the knife.

With Harðráði in the lead, they made their way back up to the top floor. At each door that lay between them and the outside, the Varangian commander paused, listening. Twice he pulled open a door and gutted the man behind it with breathtaking ease, and then finally they swung open a last door into a crowded street.

'We need to go to the palace,' Gunnhild said.

'No. The hippodrome,' Harðráði replied.

'Why?'

'I need to hear what the Caulker is saying, and it will be easier to get into the palace there than through the main gate anyway.'

Gunnhild nodded. 'One moment, then. Wait here.' Leaving the five of them, she ducked around the corner, found the big man who'd helped them up, retrieved her staff and pushed two gold coins into his hand. 'Thank you. Stay safe,' she said, making a warding sign against elves over him, and then hurried back to the others.

'All right. Let's hear the emperor's words.'

Chapter 14

'What is he shouting?' Halfdan bellowed over the noise as they pushed their way into the great sandy arena floor from the starting gates.

The hippodrome was packed with the people of Constantinople, and not just the stands, but the racing circuit too. Every man and woman there seemed determined to have his grievances heard over everyone else, the sound of a hundred thousand angry people creating enough of a din to drown out the announcement itself.

A ripple of surprised and expectant silence began to spread out from them as the gathered populace finally noticed the military pushing their way into the arena, with some of the city's most notable men at its head.

'I can't tell,' Maniakes replied in his deep giant's voice, 'but look. The emperor fears for his safety.'

There was no denying that. The *kathisma*, the imperial viewing box from which generations of rulers had watched the races, and which connected directly to the palace, was occupied by a small well-dressed party, but the crowds were kept well back from it by a mixed force of Varangians and city garrison troops – the *Teicheiotai* and the Noumeroi – occupying the stands in a ring around the raised box. The emperor was little more than a small, gleaming and brightly coloured figure at this distance, but it was clear he was accompanied by important and rich men and senior officers. He was addressing the crowd, judging by his oratorical flailing, but whatever he was saying was lost in the boom of angry voices.

Valgarðr turned and passed word to his men, and in moments the soldiers with them were beginning to forge forward, making a way through the great venue for their commanders. Halfdan and his friends remained with Maniakes and Valgarðr in the hippodrome while another force, led by Kabasilos and the patriarch, had separated outside the arcades and was now addressing the people before the palace gates. The rippled silence continued to spread, and as they neared the heart of the hippodrome, Halfdan's view of the imperial box became gradually clearer. He could see the emperor now, though not in true detail. He could imagine it, though, the cold sweat, the twitch, the nerves.

Even as they finally came to a halt and the noise had dropped to little more than a pervasive murmur, the activity in the kathisma increased. The emperor was announcing something about the empress, and Halfdan was straining to hear when the subject became clear without the need for words.

Zoe Porphyrogenita, Empress of Byzantium, was brought forward into public view. An awed hush descended upon the crowd, and Halfdan's mind raced. He wondered if they saw what he saw, or just the empress they loved. Even from this distance, he could tell that the empress was unusually pale. Her crown was missing, and her head had been covered with a voluminous hat to hide her stubbly shaved pate. She was dressed in rich robes, but Halfdan had seen the empress often enough to recognise that they had not been carefully arranged and dressed by servants, but hastily thrown over her. He could almost smell the salt of the sea upon her.

The emperor had done the only thing he could. With the whole city rising against him, he'd had the empress's ship halted and turned round, bringing her back to the city. He'd had her swiftly dressed as regally as they could manage and then brought her out to appease the mob and prevent any escalation in violence.

Still, despite the odd hush, the emperor's words were hard to make out. Halfdan caught certain words, though, that made the tone of the speech inescapable. Clemency. Restoration. Reconciliation... *Seniority*. Even in a desperate attempt to save himself, Michael Kalaphates would not relinquish his newfound power. He was officially forgiving the empress for the crimes he'd concocted and restoring her to the palace, but the overtone was impossible to ignore. He was still the emperor and she little more than a powerless consort. He would no longer live in her shadow.

'Abdicate!'

The call came from somewhere deep in the crowd, and the reaction was impressive. The entire crowd, including the emperor, fell silent. The echo of the word whispered through the air, and then another voice caught it up.

'Abdicate!'

Then a half dozen voices. Then a torrent of sound, all calling that one word.

Halfdan turned a frown on Valgarðr. 'What does abdicate mean?'

'Abdicate? To relinquish power. They're calling for the emperor to give up the throne.'

Halfdan frowned at the figures in the kathisma. He was no student of the Byzantine court, but still he could not imagine any world in which that man was going to willingly step aside for the empress. Indeed, as the call became a roar, Zoe Porphyrogenita was grabbed by Ari's Varangians and manhandled back out of sight.

'You realise the crowd might just have signed the empress's death warrant,' Valgarðr grunted. 'If she can't be used to buy the people off, she's of no further value to the Caulker.'

With a snarled oath, the emperor threw his cloak around him and turned, stalking off into the hidden recesses of the imperial box, his courtiers and then his guards following. The forces in the stands surrounding the kathisma similarly began to melt away through entrances amid the seating. Halfdan and his companions watched the figures disappear as the crowd in the hippodrome raged, their cries mutating now from calls to abdicate into threats and curses.

'There is nothing for it now but war,' Maniakes said, 'and civil war at that. This will be a long and bloody day, I fear.'

Halfdan frowned again. 'Surely it will be swift? The entire city rises.'

Maniakes shook his head. 'The emperor has several regiments of men in the palace grounds, and they are trained and hardened men. Their mettle was forged on the battlegrounds of Bulgaria and Sicily under my own leadership. They will not fall readily, and the palace is easily defended. There are only three real approaches. Our own troop numbers are small. This will rely heavily upon the stamina of the ordinary people of the city.'

With a gesture to two of his soldiers, the imposing giant stepped forward towards the *spina*, the raised centre of the racing circuit. As the crowd parted to let him through, Maniakes climbed with ease up onto the stone plinth, then further, onto a statue base where he matched the impressive dimensions of some long-gone emperor's likeness in stone. Once more the crowd descended into an expectant hush.

'People of Constantinople,' Maniakes bellowed, his voice every bit a match for his enormous frame, 'the empress is held against her will. The Caulker has shown his colours. Will you stand for this low-born liar over the daughter of an ancient house?'

The answer came in a roar.

'We must take the palace and fell the tyrant,' he added, as soon as the surge of noise abated, sending the din into a crescendo once more.

'Maniakes,' a voice called, and the big man turned and looked past his men towards the gates of the hippodrome. Halfdan followed his gaze and his heart warmed. A space was opening up, and into it strode Gunnhild and Harðráði with a small group of men and women.

'Sigurdsson,' Maniakes acknowledged in tones that confirmed there was no love lost between the two men.

'Your war has begun,' Harðráði shouted, pointing back outside. 'Houses burn and fall, and citizens have gone to find the empress's sister.'

Halfdan blinked. He didn't know she even had a sister.

'The first house to burn was the emperor's uncle's,' someone added from near the gates.

'But the snake escaped to the palace first,' another noted.

'The Great Palace must fall, and tonight,' Maniakes said.

Harðráði nodded. 'Kabasilos is organising an assault on the Chalke Gate. Word is that a rabble approaches from the waterfront, across the polo fields. They need a leader.'

Maniakes's eyes narrowed. 'Be my guest.'

'No. They need a general.' Harðráði's finger shot towards the kathisma. 'That was Ari Karsten and his Scythian animals up there. I have a score to settle, and you will not get in my way this time, Maniakes.'

The air between the pair almost crackled with tension, and Halfdan was worrying that a second battle might open up here between two men on the same side, but to his relief, finally, Maniakes nodded. 'Lead your Varangoi, Sigurdsson. I shall see you in the emperor's consistorium.'

The giant dropped from his perch to the sand, waving a hand to his officer. The garrison soldiers who had accompanied them to the hippodrome surged forward at their general's orders, and Maniakes threw a beckoning arm out to the mob in the area. 'To the Tzykanisterion Gate!' With the cry, he led soldiers and bellowing citizens alike out of the hippodrome. As a large part of the crowd gradually drained away, Harðráði looked at his friends.

'With any luck the great arse will be pulled to pieces on the polo field before he gets anywhere near the palace.' He looked from face to face among the loyal forces on the sandy track. 'Anyone who holds a blade inside the palace is fair game.

No quarter for any man who stands for the Caulker. Kill them all. Be merciless. Any unarmed servants or administrators who surrender, however, should be ignored, and make sure the empress is not harmed.' He gave them a hard look. 'And no one touches Ari Karsten. Any man kills that bastard I'll tear apart myself. Karsten is mine, and mine alone.'

Halfdan nodded. 'And the old one, Erik Boneblade, he's mine.'

'Agreed.'

'How do we do this?' Halfdan said, looking up at the imperial box and the looming shapes of the sprawling palace beyond. Already the citizens of the arena had decided the time was nigh and were charging for the kathisma, but even as they surged across the stands, arrows were whipping out of hidden recesses in the shadowy arcade of the imperial box. Men and women dropped where they ran, crying out, shafts sprouting from their torsos and limbs.

The kathisma, for the emperor's safety, projected out above the stands before it, an overhang that would make it extremely difficult to climb, and to each side a sheer marble wall presented similar difficulties. A dark arch below the kathisma was already filled with rabble waving makeshift weapons and bellowing hate, pushing deeper in.

'It is not easy,' Harðráði admitted. 'With a little effort we might get into the box. The door in the rear leads into a small complex where the emperor can relax before games, wash and cool himself, change his clothes and so on. There are also guard rooms there, and a small audience chamber for meeting the racing teams. The doorway below connects to the whole thing, and there are two more entrances within the stands. All of them will now be locked tight, and they are good solid gates. Even when we get into the kathisma complex, we will likely have to fight our way through it, down the staircases and into the connecting passage. That place is wide enough to field a unit of men, and even beyond that is another defensible gate before we're into the palace. And in half a dozen places there will be positions for enemy archers. A lot of blood will be spilled before the last gate falls.'

'And yet you choose this place over other approaches?' Ketil snorted.

'It is difficult, but still the best. It is closest to the emperor's apartments, where we will find him and the empress, if she still lives. The main Chalke Gate is a much more troublesome proposition. Kabasilos will have his work cut out there, and the approach from the polo field is up a steep slope and furthest from anywhere we all need to be.'

'All right,' Valgarðr said. 'You take the main arch below the kathisma, I'll take a third of the men and cover the northern door in the stands. Ulf Ospaksson can take another third and use the southern approach. Three prongs attacking the kathisma.'

'Four,' Halfdan said.

'What?'

'We'll take the box itself.'

'Don't be stupid.'

'It's a way in, and there are archers in there killing people by the dozen.'

'Including you if you try.'

'I wish I had my shield,' Halfdan admitted, 'but if we can borrow five shields, we can do this.'

'*Six* shields,' corrected Gunnhild, stepping between them.

'I won't let you go,' Harðráði said flatly, though he flinched visibly as Gunnhild turned a look on him.

'It will go badly for you the next time you give me an order, Harold Sigurdsson.' She turned to the gathered Varangians. 'Six shields. For Freyja.'

As the Christian guardsmen looked to their commanders, familiar faces pushed their way through the gathered warriors, men from the *Sea Wolf*, leaving the armies that they had become part of and returning to the side of their jarl. Six shields were held forth, taken from the dead and wounded, and Halfdan gave his crew a welcoming smile. Their numbers were considerably reduced since the day they had arrived, but at least they were together once more.

The six of them each grasped a shield, and the crew of the *Sea Wolf* drew their weapons, loosening up muscles with experimental swings. 'For God and the empress,' Harðráði said, a cry taken up by the men behind them.

Halfdan and his friends made their own, older, silent vows, and with that the loyal Varangians began to move, splitting into groups and hurtling off towards their targets. Halfdan looked around his friends with a feeling of completeness. To have his men back, even if they now numbered but a score, was a relief, but having Gunnhild back among them made things right. His gaze fell upon two serving women, both of whom looked a little nervous. The one called Anna he recognised as having been with Gunnhild these past few months, the other he did not know but she was dressed for palace life.

'This is not your fight,' he said in what he hoped was a sympathetic voice.

'I cannot do this any more,' the better-dressed one said in a cracked voice.

'I can,' said Anna with a determined expression.

Gunnhild turned to them. 'Justina, you have done more than enough. Go and find safety. Anna, are you sure?'

'No. But I'm coming anyway.'

Gunnhild nodded and turned to Halfdan. 'Would you care to tell me how we get up there? I have ropes not far away, but it will take time to retrieve them, and without grapples, ropes are little use for an ascent.'

Halfdan nodded, turning to look at the kathisma. A frontal approach, under the overhang, would protect them from arrows, but there was no way to climb. The sides of the box's balcony, thanks to the incline of the seating stands, were less of a climb, but still difficult. A notion struck him and he smiled as he turned back to the others, the Loki serpent on his arm itching faintly, suggesting that what he had in mind enjoyed the favour of the gods.

'We have a human ladder,' he said. 'We approach under the overhang, move to the side, and there I would reckon the box is between fifteen and twenty feet from the stands, would you agree?' Frowning, the others nodded. 'Bjorn and Ketil between them can do it.'

'What?' Leif said. 'Ketil must be more than seven feet and Bjorn six and a half, but that still finds them short, Halfdan.'

'Add the length of their arms. Bjorn supports Ketil, and the two form a ladder from stands to box. All we need to do is climb them. Once a few are up, it should be easy for the rest.'

'I am not a fucking ladder,' Bjorn said angrily.

'No. Ladders are brighter,' Ketil said with a sidelong look. 'But he's right.'

'You *would* say that. You'll be the one on top.'

'I'd do it the other way round,' Ketil said, 'but I would walk into Greek fire before I'd get that close to your arse.'

'Listen, you gangly cock-pocket...' began Bjorn, but Leif shushed them all.

'It's workable. Whoever gets over the top needs to race straight for the archers.'

'Well volunteered,' Ketil said.

'Ah, no,' Leif smiled. 'I'm a lover, a skald, a scholar and a thinker, but I'm not a suicidal idiot. Besides, I'm wounded. I can't climb. I'll have to be pulled up with the rest.'

Halfdan smiled to see the rather warm look this received from the girl at Gunnhild's side, and he took a deep breath. The crew were with them once more, but he needed to reinstate his position as their commander. 'I am jarl here. I will go first, for the honour of Odin and the *Sea Wolf*.'

'All right. Let's go,' Ketil urged them, for the fight had begun. Ospaksson and his men were disappearing into one of the many arched entrances to the inner tunnels of the stands, and at the far end Valgarðr was doing the same with his men.

Harðráði's contingent were making straight for the arch below the kathisma, and the masses within the hippodrome were joining all of them, flooding towards the various approaches. The early attempt to get to the kathisma had faltered in the face of an impossible climb and enemy arrows, and now the citizens sought other approaches, while archers loyal to the emperor continued to loose missiles from behind the columns into the masses below.

With Halfdan in the lead the Sea Wolves began to run, hurtling towards the imperial box. As they reached one of the various doors that led from the sandy track up into the stands, usually closed during race days, but yanked open by angry citizens, each of them lifted a shield. Soon they would be targeted by archers. Anna had no shield, but as she ran, Gunnhild and Leif flanked her, the two raised boards providing sufficient shelter for the three of them.

Through the door they piled and out into the shallow stands of marble seats. Instinctively, they split into two groups as they reached that great arched tunnel packed with Harðráði's Varangians, providing less of a bulky target for the archers above. As they raced up the steps to either side of the passageway, the arrows started to fall. A cry drew Halfdan's attention, and he looked across the gap to see that one of the crew had been pierced through with a shaft. Close behind the stricken man, Leif was struggling to hold the shield above his head, his broken ribs inhibiting him. In a trice Anna had taken the shield from the small Rus and was holding it above the pair of them as they ran. Ketil, of course, was out front, his lengthy stride easily taking two stepped seats at a time. An arrow thudded into the Icelander's shield, and a second clacked off the marble step close to his ankle, and then he was safe, darting under the overhang of the imperial box, where he stood, barely out of breath, beckoning to them.

Bjorn let out an angry shout as a stray arrow tore a line across his bicep, and he raised his shield a little for better cover, heaping unpleasant curses upon the hidden archers. Behind him another of the Sea Wolves fell with a cry. More arrows clattered and thudded around them, and Bjorn was next under the overhang, then Halfdan, then Ulfr, and finally Gunnhild and Anna, sheltering the wincing, hissing Leif as he held his side. As they moved towards the upper edge, the rest of the crew piled in after them, leaving a third man pinned with arrows to the hippodrome seating.

'Are you sure you should be doing this, little man,' Bjorn asked in the closest thing to sympathy the big albino ever displayed towards his Rus friend.

'Sit this out and never hear the end of it from great stinking bears like you?' Leif snorted. 'Hardly. As Virgil said, fortune favours the brave.'

'As Bjorn Bear-torn said,' the big albino replied, 'stick it up your arse sideways.'

'Ah, it is always good to hear the great philosophers,' the small Rus said, an eyebrow arched at his friend.

'If you're quite finished?' Halfdan asked meaningfully, indicating the gathered warriors, waiting expectantly.

The seven of them stretched once more, sheathing weapons and slinging shields over their back for the climb. Arrows were still whipping out from above and dropping into the stands, aimed at the tail ends of the three forces assaulting the palace entrances.

'Ready?'

Nods.

'Odin keep your back,' Halfdan said, and they moved.

Bjorn ducked out to the side, still too close to the kathisma to be seen from above, and cupped his hands together. Ketil followed and leapt, his foot planting heavily in the stirrup of the albino's hands. The tall Icelander jumped even as the big albino beneath him heaved, and Ketil's reaching fingers brushed the lip of the marble balustrade above. Ketil struggled, fingers slipping, and almost fell back, but then he had it and settled himself, his hands rising again, gripping the lowest section of two small pillars tight. Bjorn called him a few unpleasant names as he shuffled underneath, trying to get comfortable as the Icelander's boot brushed his face and pressed down on sore areas. No other pair of men in the crew, and possibly in the whole of Constantinople, would have the combined height for such a feat.

Halfdan was on the move straight away. If the archers above caught sight of Ketil's hands gripping the balustrade, everything would start to go wrong. With as much care as he could afford, while maintaining good speed, Halfdan grabbed Bjorn's shoulders and started to pull himself up. The albino grumbled irritably, but in moments Halfdan was gripping Ketil, who was cursing and saying something about his fingers. Then the young jarl's own hands were on the marble rail. Their stealthy approach was about to end.

Gritting his teeth and with a prayer to both Odin and Thor, Halfdan heaved, his muscles screaming. With impressive speed, he pulled himself up and over the balustrade, tumbling to the flagged floor of the balcony and suffering countless bruises from the shield on his back. In a move he had been practising often, he swung the shield round, ducking his head through the strap, and bringing it up in front of him even as he ripped the glorious, eagle-hilted sword from his belt.

Arrows began to fly again now. He felt one scrape his shin and heard two thud into the shield. As he raced across the balcony another parted his hair, leading him to lift the shield a little. Another arrow whipped past and raised an angry curse from behind in Ulfr's voice, signalling the arrival of a second warrior.

Halfdan's gaze, around the curved edge of the shield, fell upon one of the archers, busily yanking another arrow from a quiver as he tried to hide behind a column. Halfdan was on him in a moment, the edge of his blade cutting through the bowstring and the man's fingers together before finding a sheath in his flesh. The archer screamed and fell away. Another arrow appeared from somewhere, thudding into Halfdan's shoulder. He felt the thing punch into the chain shirt, bringing numbness and bruising, and, despite the dull pain, he thanked the gods that the chain had stopped it.

Ulfr was beside him now and fumbling for his battle axe. Halfdan looked past him to see another archer lying on his back with a throwing axe jutting from his chest. As the young jarl turned and caught another arrow on his shield, running for the next archer, Gunnhild joined them. Despite everything, as he ran Halfdan found himself wondering how she'd made the climb with her staff. Then she was on one of the archers, the stout timber swinging hard and breaking heads. Ulfr was laying about himself with his axe, and Halfdan was bearing down on the last archer on this side as the man nocked another arrow. On sheer instinct, as the man lifted his bow, drew and released in one swift manoeuvre, Halfdan dropped his shield a little, and with it caught the arrow that had been aimed for his leg. He hit the archer at full force, barging with the shield, knocking the unarmoured man to the ground, where he stabbed with his sword again and again, blood spraying up across him and filling the air with crimson mizzle. Content the man was no more, he took a deep breath and rose, wincing at the pain in his shoulder.

The fight was over, all the archers down. Leif and Anna were struggling into the arches now, as Ketil and Bjorn climbed over the balcony with difficulty, the rest of the crew now at leisure to climb up as best they could without the fear of falling arrows.

'You didn't leave me one?' Bjorn snapped angrily.

Halfdan jerked a thumb at the door that stood at the rear of the kathisma.

'Plenty more behind that,' he said. 'This was just the start.'

Chapter 15

'Ready?'

The others nodded, hefting weapons, shields up against the danger of more hidden archers. With a nod to the two biggest among them, Halfdan gripped his sword and prayed for them all that the door was not as strong as the others down below. Gunnhild prepared. She could feel the Seiðr virtually crackling in the air around her as her foretellings hurtled towards a conclusion.

Bjorn and Ketil took a deep breath and counted together, tightening their grip. On three they ran, each holding an arm and a leg of a dead archer from the colonnade. To give their makeshift battering ram added strength and weight, Ulfr had grudgingly given up his helmet, which they'd screwed onto the unusually large-headed guard's skull until it removed flesh. Leif had been scathing about the idea, but Bjorn had, as usual, ignored his small friend's ribbing.

They hit the door hard, and Gunnhild tensed. The timbers shook and there was a horrible crack, but she wasn't at all sure that the crack came from the door and not the corpse. Certainly the impact did more to pulp the man's head than to open a path. The helmet was driven deep into the broken skull, and Ulfr watched the debacle with a sour face as the mashed head lolled, almost detached.

'Someone's going to owe me a good helmet after this.'

'You missed the lock,' Halfdan said, pointing. 'You hit the door in the middle. You need to hit the lock.'

'You need to stop this foolishness and listen to me,' sighed Leif from the corner, where he was fiddling in a pouch while Anna carefully wound fresh dressings around his middle.

'This is not science or poetry, little man,' Bjorn brushed the comment aside. 'This is a job for brute strength.'

'No. This is a job for me.'

'A wounded midget with a big brain, but small muscles?' Bjorn snorted. 'This is a door, not a book.'

'Just try again,' snapped Halfdan.

The two men took fifteen steps back, out into the open kathisma, gripping their bloody, pulped ram tight, and then counted and ran once more. This time their aim was better, and the corpse smashed into the door close to the jamb, yet with sickening sounds the body fell apart in their hands, leaving no appreciable sign of success.

Gunnhild turned to see that Leif had taken something metallic from his pouch and was fiddling with it as Anna tied off a bandage. The little Rus was clever, and perhaps clever was what they needed here.

'Listen to Leif the Teeth,' she said, drawing the attention of the others, with the exception of Bjorn, who was still concentrating on the door.

'Let me,' the big albino said, ignoring her as he dropped what was left in his hands and pulled his axe from his belt. Stepping close to the door, he motioned the rest of them back and stood to one side, pulling back his weapon as far as he could, axe turned rear-side on. He swung with all his strength and the heavy iron poll at the rear of the blade smashed with perfect accuracy against the lock. The door boomed, but did not move. Bjorn stepped back, shaking his head, his muscles twitching from the reverberation of the blow.

With a sigh and a rolling of eyes, Leif threw a knowing smile at Gunnhild, clasped Anna's hand for a moment, and walked past the quivering Bjorn to the door. He winced and whimpered as he bent, his ribs aching, and selected gleaming shapes from the thing he'd found. Settling upon a specific one, he inserted it into the lock and began to waggle it around, adding a second metal prong. His tongue poked from the corner of his mouth as he worked, and finally, as there was an audible click, he grinned and rose.

'Brains,' he smiled at Bjorn. 'Sometimes heads are for more than storing wine and smashing into doors.'

With that, he turned the handle and gently pushed the heavy door inwards, revealing a dark room, three windows opposite covered with drapes and admitting barely any light.

Exchanging glances, the others swept into the room in an instant, fanning out to be certain of encountering anyone lurking in the gloom, each of them armed and ready, Anna running alongside Leif and holding the shield in front of both of them. Gradually, as the leaders moved to the edges, the remaining men of the *Sea Wolf* flooded in behind them.

Their eyesight had almost adjusted to the dark when Bjorn, helpfully, threw open the central heavy curtain, momentarily blinding them all again. As they cursed at the big albino, he shrugged and pulled back the other two drapes. Light filled the room and confirmed that it was unoccupied. The defenders had clearly drawn their lines further back.

'Why no guards?' Halfdan mused.

Gunnhild closed her eyes, thinking. 'The doors are buying the emperor time to gather his forces somewhere and prepare.'

In addition to the entrance behind them, through which their men were still pouring, there were two lesser doors here, one to each side. These they ignored for now, instead gathering around the windows and peering through them. Below they could hear the roar of the mob and the hammering of timbers, but this place was oddly calm. This room apparently stood above the alleyway that ran between the hippodrome and the palace, and from the windows they could see across the imperial complex.

'Those are the emperor's main rooms,' Gunnhild said, pointing at an impressive collection of buildings, tantalisingly close. They could see the whole palace here, from the Hagia Sophia on the hill to the left, all the way down to the water, the Bucoleon Palace and the Lazarus Gate on the shore, where a ship lay docked, as always, for imperial convenience. Between there and this complex, they could see a mass of people gathered around one of the lesser gates on the slope, close to the polo fields, one of the three groups assaulting the palace.

'But how to get there fast,' Halfdan said. 'On sleepless nights when I've tried to find other crewmen, I've found all sorts of old passages and unused doors in the palace, but they're all inside. None of them lead outside the walls.'

'That's our way in,' Gunnhild said, looking down. The approach below them seemed to filter off to the left into some sort of connecting structure that passed inside the palace grounds. 'It connects this complex to the palace.'

'Which door?' Halfdan said.

Ketil pointed to one side. 'If we need to be to the left we might as well start in that direction.'

'Agreed.'

Gripping weapons and shields once more, they waited as Bjorn approached the door. He tried it and was unsurprised to find it locked, though this one was much thinner than the last, and one hefty blow with the rear of his axe soon changed that, the door, splintered at the lock, swinging inwards. The room beyond was poorly lit by one high window, unlit oil lamps sitting on shelves at strategic points. Ahead, a grand staircase descended into deeper gloom, and off to their left a solid, heavy door strained under a number of blows from the other side.

Halfdan nodded at Bjorn, who bellowed 'Step back,' and crossed to the door. The lock on this one seemed to have been ignored in favour of a solid bar, and the big albino had little difficulty in lifting that out of the way. As the door swung open, they saw Valgarðr at the head of the masses outside. A roar of triumph greeted them as the way became clear, and the attacking citizens, led by Varangians, flooded in. Halfdan and the others gathered together and waited for Bjorn to struggle back to them, then began to push their way down the stairs along with the flood of angry humanity.

Some of the lead elements of the mob had already managed to open another door below, and as the friends reached the bottom of the great staircase, their army of citizens and guardsmen had doubled, a second wave flooding through another entrance. It took only moments for them to spot Harðráði, and the Varangian commander was with them and Valgarðr a heartbeat later.

Gunnhild felt the Norns at work now, the Seiðr all about them as strands of the weaving combined. Her own thread with the gold of Harðráði, and now, for the first true moment, the bear, the boar and the wolf together.

Her eyes narrowed as she looked at her companions.

The bear...

As they pushed their way on, Gunnhild thought back over what Halfdan had told her of Harðráði's capture. She stopped suddenly amid the flow of angry people, her hand finding the commander's collar and pulling him around to face her, his expression one of surprise.

'Gunnhild?'

'Where is the powder of Freyja?' she said sharply. 'Of Odin,' she added.

'What?'

'You still have it? They did not take it from you when you were imprisoned?'

'Oh, you mean Bjorn's pouch?' the man said, understanding. 'Yes, it's here.' He retrieved it from his belt and held it up.

'You are bear enough without this,' she said. Oddly, she seemed to see the man differently for a moment, two Harðráðis superimposed, one a great, golden bear ready for war, the other a smiling, warm man, frowning in concern. She had a horrible feeling she was flushing again and, snatching the pouch, turned her face away.

He frowned. 'I cannot fathom you sometimes.'

'This is dangerous for you,' she said, recovering herself and turning a face of deliberate seriousness on him. 'For *all* warriors. The Allfather's frenzy takes friend and foe alike. It is a gift best kept for Freyja.'

Ignoring his confusion, she tied the pouch to her own belt, a flood of relief washing through her. She had been worrying for months at how little of the precious compound she had left, and here was enough to last her for years. Thanking the goddess, she gripped her staff and shield and strode forward again. The weaving was coming together into the true pattern. Here she was, backed by her friends and an army of warriors and citizens, but before them all she strode, the boar of Freyja, with the bear of Harðráði to one side, the wolf of Halfdan to the other. All they were missing now was the empress.

Despite their pauses they were still near the front of the mob as it spilled out through a beautiful marble hall, bursting open a set of ornate double doors and emerging into a long vestibule, lined with columns and high windows, the floor a mass of complex mosaic designs and images.

In her heart, Gunnhild found herself grateful that they had not been the leaders of the mob at that point, for the masses burst into that great corridor and met death in droves in an instant. The emperor's excubitores had taken up a defensive position here, a shield wall across the vestibule halfway along, bristling with spears and swords, fifteen men deep, and beyond them, archers and even two men with tripod-mounted crossbows stood. It was these missile troops at the rear who had released their cloud of death as the doors opened, a hundred arrows whipping into the mob, folding the front line up and dropping them to the ground, clutching shafts jutting from limbs, torsos and faces. More had slammed into the following ten feet of the wave of humanity, creating a barrier of groaning, writhing flesh that the mob was forced to clamber over to approach. This, in turn, bought time for the archers to reload and loose once more, and another three dozen citizens fell, adding to the rampart of ruined flesh.

The angry army of Byzantine commoners wavered now in the face of such brutality, and in a heartbeat the first group of Varangians was past, pushing through the panicking citizens and running for the excubitores, shields up, roaring battle cries. Harðráði and the others were running with them, in the wake of that first attack.

Though the archers had time to nock and loose once more before the true fighting began, their efficacy was diminished now, for their targets were protected by shields and were hardier, less prone to panic. Here and there a Varangian disappeared with a cry, but many ran on, even those who had been caught glancing blows with arrows.

The archers continued to loose over the top, their arrows almost touching the corridor's ceiling as they then dropped into the sea of humanity flooding towards them, but battle had been joined at the front. Axes, swords and spears chopped, stabbed and slashed, the clonk of embattled shields, the shush and clink of armour joined with the furious cries of battle and the howls of the injured.

The Christians might think their God gave them strength in battle, but their God was distant, and inclined to peace. Gunnhild could feel her gods with them in that very vestibule. Odin, Freyja, Thor, Tyr and even Loki, all part of this surge of battle. Something drew her attention and she looked down to realise that she was standing on one of the mosaic images. It came as no great surprise to see a shape that resembled the statue from her house, and which could only be Tyche, the fortune goddess, looking up at her. She shivered as the Seiðr wreathed the corridor. This was all meant to be.

As the man in front of Gunnhild fell with a cry of agony, blood from his ruptured neck clouding the air, the Greek soldier responsible pulled back his sword and paused, his face registering his surprise at finding himself face to face with the striking Danish girl in her finest cloak and dress. His reticence was his undoing. As he stared, the butt end of Gunnhild's staff slammed forward, breaking his face, shattering his nose, upper jaw and cheekbone. The man gave a gurgling scream and fell. Then she surged forward with the rest, and they were in among the excubitores, the shield wall broken.

There was little room in the press to swing a staff, and so Gunnhild contented herself with using the shield in her other hand to batter and push, occasionally punching out with the fist that was wrapped around the ash staff. Had she the time, she'd have torn the sword from her belt and used that, but there was no opportunity.

They fought with the gods in their blood: the wolf, the bear and the boar, Harðráði beside her with an axe, cleaving and hacking, Halfdan at the other side stabbing and slashing with his Alani sword.

In a welter of blood and thrashing limbs, a spray of crimson and the cries of the brutalised and the dying, Gunnhild and her companions carved their way forward until they had broken the ranks of the excubitores. Behind them and all around them the triumphant bellowing of Varangian and civilian alike confirmed that the three were far from alone and that the assault on the palace was succeeding, the defenders breaking. They were among the archers now, killing with impunity, and the enemy were trying to flee. The doors at the far end of the vestibule, leading into the palace grounds, had been resolutely closed, but now they were open, archers fleeing through them, trying to get away from the brutal assault.

In moments they were through. Gunnhild paused in a well-appointed courtyard with Harðráði and Halfdan heaving in breaths at her side. She turned and counted the faces she knew, then threw her thanks to Freyja, for they might have lost crewmen in that mad and frenzied killing, but not her friends. Bjorn had acquired a new bloody wound, but seemed less than perturbed by it, and Ulfr had lost his shield and was clutching his arm, cursing, but they were all here and all still walking, even Leif and Anna, who had, without Gunnhild realising, somehow become part of their group side by side.

With a roar, the invading force of citizens began to flow through the enormous palace complex like a river in flood, filling every channel, every corridor and open space. Gunnhild watched for a moment as some of them, with Varangians leading, raced to take on other units of soldiers coming to reinforce the failed defences, while others devolved into mindless looting and vandalism, smashing imperial statues and stealing anything that gleamed. It was unavoidable. With any mob there would always be opportunists. It was a price that had to be paid. In some ways it was to be welcomed, a small echo of the days of raiding dragon ships and the word of Odin being carried to new lands in return for plundered silver.

With Valgarðr and the Sea Wolves at their back, Halfdan, Harðráði and Gunnhild turned and began to run towards the emperor's complex at the heart of the palace. They burst through the outer door and into a wide, spacious and bright corridor, where they paused once more as the people of Constantinople ran riot around them.

'What's wrong?' the Varangian commander asked, noting Halfdan's frown.

'Something is missing,' the young jarl said, looking around. 'Where is Ari? Where are the Varangians we should have had to fight our way through?'

Harðráði nodded. 'If the emperor is here, they should be defending this building.'

'What other ways out of the palace are there?' Gunnhild asked.

Harðráði shrugged. 'There are three main gates, each being attacked by our people.'

'And lesser gates?'

'A few. One at the far end of the hippodrome, one up near the old acropolis wall, the Bucoleon, of course, and the private harbour of the Lazarus Gate.'

'Do not waste your time chasing shadows in this place,' Gunnhild said. 'The emperor is gone, and so is Ari. That is why we have not found them.'

Harðráði scratched his head. 'Then we have to chase them down. Find them and bring them to justice. I want Ari. The emperors have protected him from me before, but no longer. Now he pays.'

'No,' Gunnhild said, turning a look on him. 'In time you can deal with your own enemy, but now you must remember your oath. You swore to protect the empress and she is in danger.'

Halfdan nodded. 'The Caulker doesn't need her any more. She's more use to him dead now.'

'Not yet,' Gunnhild replied. 'She is valuable at least as a hostage until he is safe. He will not relinquish her until he is away. And to flee this place, he would be safest by ship.'

'The Lazarus Gate,' Halfdan and Harðráði said at the same time, sharing a look.

Then they were running again, out of the palace complex and across the manicured lawns, past colonnades and pavilions, gradually descending the slope towards the sea walls. In an odd moment, they burst out of an ornate gateway, two score of men at their back, to find General Maniakes and his army coming the other way, having finally broken the gate near the polo fields. The general gave them a strange look as they ran away from the centre of the palace, but none of them felt inclined to explain, and so they ran on. Arriving at another complex, they gave it wide berth, for part of Maniakes's mob were engaged with another of the garrison units there, and on they ran, hurtling towards the inconspicuous Lazarus Gate.

This entrance through the great sea walls was a simple arch protected by a massive oak door, a scattering of functional buildings just inside, but without flanking towers. Only emperors or those on direct imperial business came and went by this gate, for all it led to was a single jetty hemmed in by the walls, where only one ship could dock.

The gate was open, and a small gathering of Varangians could be seen within the arch. Gunnhild squinted. Through the gap, above the warriors, she could just make out a ship putting to sea and already some distance from the jetty.

The emperor had fled.

'No,' Halfdan bellowed as they closed on the Varangians.

The score or more of flat-faced Scythian guardsmen, standing with the empress in the gate arch, turned now to face this new threat, and Gunnhild felt it all coming together. The empress had been stripped of her robes once more, her stubbly bald head and her plain white nun's underrobe sodden and dirty. She was still standing tall, however, even as two Varangians grabbed her. A third brought an axe up and examined the edge.

'The empress,' Gunnhild urged her friends.

'Run,' Halfdan cried, but Harðráði shook his head.

'No time,' the commander replied and turned, dropping his own weapon and tearing the throwing axe from the hand of Leif, who had been running along behind them. The little Rus blinked as the weapon was taken, and Harðráði flipped the axe with the skill of a master, pulled it back and sent it off with a deft flick of his hand. The third Varangian, who had nodded in satisfaction at his blade and had turned, drawing his weapon back to end the life of an empress, was suddenly plucked from the ground as the axe smashed into his shoulder. The blow would not have cut through the chain of his shirt, but had undoubtedly broken his shoulder blade, and his own weapon fell away as he hit the ground with a cry and rolled.

The other Varangians made to finish the job for him, but they were too late. By that time their attackers were on them. Harðráði slammed into one with his shield, sending him sprawling away from the empress, while Halfdan hit the other like a charging bull, smashing him aside and then stabbing and slashing with his sword, cutting the man down. At the centre of the weaving, Gunnhild came to a halt beside the shaking empress. All around her now, her friends were finishing off the execution party, all except Leif who, with Anna's help, was busy trying to pull his throwing axe free of the thrashing man in which it was buried.

As the empress clutched Gunnhild to steady herself, the fight slowly came to an end. Four of the enemy remained, and they had backed into the gateway once more with their arms raised in surrender. Halfdan, rising from the man he'd killed, spotted among them Erik, the old greybeard Varangian officer and, with a snarl of fury, charged towards him. He was halted, mid-run, by Harðráði, who knocked him aside.

'He's mine,' Halfdan snapped, pulling himself back upright.

The commander nodded. 'But not before I find out where Ari Karsten is.'

'And the emperor,' Gunnhild added.

'Michael has fled to the Church,' the empress said in a shaky voice.

'What?'

'He and his accursed uncle seek sanctuary at the Studion monastery.'

'What is *sanctuary*?' Bjorn asked.

'He is protected by the Church,' Leif explained. 'Sanctuary is inviolable.'

'Not by me,' Halfdan growled.

The Varangian commander took a deep breath. 'All right, we can follow the emperor in good time. We know where he's bound, and he'll be going nowhere from there once he's claimed sanctuary, but where is Ari Karsten?' he demanded, turning to the survivors in the gate.

'We don't know,' Erik replied. 'He disappeared long before the emperor settled upon flight.'

Harðráði cursed, throwing his shield to the ground in anger and stamping his foot. 'The bastard. He'll not get away, though. For the first time he's not protected by imperial order, and he knows it, so he runs. But we have Constantinople now. I will have the whole fucking place sealed tighter than a Roman's purse and I'll tear it apart building by building until I have the traitor. Ari cannot leave the city. He can go to ground, but I'll find him. That I promise.'

'What do we do with these four?' Valgarðr asked, pointing at the surrendered Varangians with his great axe.

'Death to them all.'

As the four stared in shock, the empress frowned. 'Have you no Christian mercy about you, Harald Sigurdsson?'

He shook his head. 'These men tried to kill you. Their life is automatically forfeit. They are lucky that this came down to a fight and they can die by the sword. Had I the inclination, hooks and hot coals might have been involved.'

The old officer bent and retrieved his sword. 'I'll not die so easily, Harðráði.'

The commander turned to Halfdan and nodded.

The young jarl stepped forward, an unpleasant and chilling smile creasing his face. Erik Boneblade took a step, his axe raised. Halfdan came to a halt in front of him, his battered shield – still bearing two broken arrow shafts – steady, sword in hand. He waited.

The older man roared and leapt, his axe sweeping round in a deadly arc. It was a fast move, and sudden, but Halfdan was ready. His left arm came out to meet the blow even as he took that last pace forward and his right arm struck.

The axe slammed into his shield, smashing the timbers and reaching as far as the iron boss at the centre. Halfdan knew he was going to pay for that later as he felt the pain of the axe cutting a line along his forearm in its passage, but still, the boards had stopped the killing blow. His sword, however, struck Greybeard between the collarbones, at the base of the neck, angled slightly upwards.

The old man looked down in horror, and with some difficulty, as Halfdan dropped his shield and brought his wounded, bloody arm up. With both hands, he slammed the blade deeper as it cut through muscles and tendons and broke bones, bursting from the back of the man's neck. He held tight as the old man fell away, gurgling, and only just managed to pull the blade free before it went with him.

'Feel better?' Harðráði asked Halfdan drily.

Gunnhild looked around at them. The bear, the boar and the wolf, protecting the empress. In a way, what she had seen was over, for she'd dared look no further, and yet she knew they were not finished. The emperor lived, and Ari lived, and so there would be a reckoning.

Still, for now they had won and Constantinople was theirs. So why was she feeling so jittery?

Part Four

ᛈᛟᛚᚠᛗᛋ ᛟᚠ ᛋᚾᛁᛏ

A Court of Serpents

Chapter 16

'Tell me again why you won't just kill him?'

Harðráði glanced sidelong at Halfdan as they strode across the square, the baying crowd peeling back to create an open passage to the great monastery ahead.

'An emperor of Byzantium rules by divine right. He is appointed by God,' the commander explained.

'And that means he can't be killed?'

'It means that any man who would dare to end his life puts his own soul in immortal peril.'

'Then let *me* kill him. Odin makes no such threats and your nailed Christ is powerless over me.'

'It matters not. This is the way things are done here, Jarl Halfdan. But you will surely play your part if you are still willing to go where we cannot and do what we dare not?'

Halfdan nodded. It seemed there were advantages to be gained by having 'heathens' in the Guard. Behind him, Gunnhild strode, staff clacking on the pavement, and then Bjorn, Ketil and Ulfr, with Leif bringing up the rear, alongside the now-ever-present Anna. Varangians, the real ones and including men from the *Sea Wolf*, reinstated by the empress, formed a line on each side, holding back the crowd.

The city was back under control. Harðráði had his command once more, and all senior officers who had supported Michael Kalaphates had been removed from their positions and exiled, with new, trusted men in their place. The palace was secure and the city locked down until all the last traitorous elements had been rooted out – notably the still missing Ari Karsten.

The empress had been placed back on the throne, the only slight hiccup being that her sister had been forcibly drawn back from a life of religious obscurity and crowned alongside her. Theodora and Zoe now shared rule, and it had swiftly become apparent to Halfdan that the two sisters were far from the best of friends. There, another trouble loomed. But for now, things were being put to rights, and once the cowering emperor had been dealt with, the empresses would be secure.

After taking control of the palace, an allagion of the Guard had raced for the imperial Studion monastery in an attempt to prevent the emperor from reaching sanctuary. They had failed, though only just, and for the best part of a day now Michael Kalaphates and his uncle had languished in that complex, safe from harm but trapped.

Even after everything, the empress Zoe had been reluctant to order her adopted son's arrest, though it seemed her sister Theodora had less compunction. The Guard were sent to deal with them, delivering accusation, sentence and punishment, though without breaking the sanctity of sanctuary. A difficult problem... for a Christian. Harðráði had been almost gleeful when he'd come to Halfdan with a job seemingly made for them and they had accepted the task with similar zeal. Only Gunnhild had been less than willing to step forward. Since the empress's return and their victory, Halfdan's friend had been taciturn and thoughtful.

Something was bothering her, and that, in turn, bothered Halfdan.

The grand door to the monastery's atrium stood open, inviting, and Varangians stood to either side. A small party of imperial administrators waited close by, patiently, and Halfdan recognised the calm, organised figure of Michael Psellus among them. Of course, this was Byzantium. No one could be killed or mutilated without the appropriate paperwork.

Passing into the atrium, Halfdan looked about with interest and approval. He knew he was becoming somewhat blasé on the subject of grand buildings now, given that little more than a year ago he'd never even seen a stone church, but he had to admit that the Studion was one of the more stately and grand buildings of the city. Still, this was no sightseeing tour, and he tore his gaze from the elegant columns and focused on the job at hand. In moments they had crossed the open court and made their way into the great church, which gleamed with marble of many colours, lit by high, impressive windows, so spacious that their footsteps seemed to echo forever.

The braver, or more impetuous, citizens had entered the church before the Varangians had come to take control, and now small groups of silent, glowering people stood to either side, held back by armed guards. At the far end of the colon-naded church stood an ornate altar before an apse, a smattering of priests and attendants standing around and looking more disapproving even than usual for their kind. The emperor and his uncle stood behind the altar, as though it were a battle-mented wall, keeping them safe from harm.

Halfdan and his friends came to a halt in the centre of the great church, Harðráði with them, and Psellus now also. Halfdan tried not to sneer at the sight of the emperor. The man wore only a plain and poor smock, as did his uncle. Gone was the crown, gone the ostentatious clothing, gone the red boots of office, the jewels, the gold, and along with them any sign of grandeur or importance. He looked frightened and powerless. Halfdan searched his soul and found not an ounce of respect or sympathy for the man. At least the man's uncle, a criminal in his own right by all accounts, stood tall and defiant.

Halfdan looked to Harðráði, who in turn nodded to Psellus. The clerk stepped forward, clearing his throat, and looked to the emperor's uncle first. 'Constantine of Paphlagonia, in the name of the Porphyrogenita empresses Zoe and Theodora, you are hereby charged with voluntarily aiding the former emperor Michael Kalaphates in his censure and persecution of the rightful empress of Byzantium.'

223

Now he turned to the emperor himself. 'Michael Kalaphates, you are officially removed from the throne of Byzantium and from the succession of the imperial line. You are charged with treason. There are sundry other charges, but in the face of the first they need not be mentioned, for that alone carries a sentence as heavy as can be pronounced against one of imperial blood.'

The *nobelissimus* Constantine, his uncle, straightened. 'I had not been privy to my nephew's plot against the empress. As you will certainly be aware, I was at my own house and not in the palace until the revolt of the city was already underway.'

The emperor turned bulging eyes of shock on the uncle who was now betraying him in turn, but Constantine was not done. 'I encouraged him in none of his designs. Had I wished to restrain him, my reward would have been calamity. Michael was so headstrong in his ambitions that my family would have fallen to mutilation, fire and sword had I opposed him.'

Psellus nodded, not in agreement, but in confirmation that the charge had been answered, and Halfdan marvelled that anyone could write so quickly, for the clerk had copied the words down into the book he carried as they were spoken. Now the emperor, face drained of colour, turned from his uncle to his accusers. His expression had become one of defeat and acceptance, which surprised Halfdan.

'Truly, God is not unjust,' the shivering man said. 'I am paying the penalty for what I have done. The throne is mine no longer, and now I will seek to make restitution for my evils by devoting my remaining days to the Lord in this place.'

'That is not to be your fate,' Harðráði said quietly, yet for all the softness of his words, they carried an air of menace as they echoed around the walls and columns of the hallowed place.

'What?'

'The empress has ordered that you be made ineligible for the throne, against the possibility of you ever rising against her rightful rule in times to come.'

Halfdan had thought the emperor pale, but now he realised how much colour had remained in the man's face, for all of it drained, leaving a ghostly, horrified visage, the mouth open in a silent O.

'You cannot. I have sought sanctuary here. You dare not defy the Church, Akolouthos. Any man here dares to lay a hand upon me in violence, or even to remove me from the church, will condemn his soul to an eternity of Hell's fires.'

'That will not be a problem for men who see their future sitting in a pagan heaven, drinking with their god and waiting for a final battle,' Harðráði said with an unpleasant smile, and nodded to Halfdan. The young jarl beckoned to the others, and together they began to walk once more, stalking down the nave of the church with purpose, a purpose only they could have in carrying out a task only they could consider. The emperor's uncle had acquired a twitch, but he stood impassive, hands clasped behind him. Michael Kalaphates, however, let out a frightened squeak and turned to the priests.

'You can't let them do this. Sanctuary! I claimed sanctuary!'

The priests were, to give them their due, glaring at Halfdan and his men with disapproval, but they were also wise enough not to stand in the way of the armed bodyguard of the empress. Halfdan looked to the nobelissimus. 'You will not fight this?'

'Would it make any difference?'

'No.'

The uncle nodded and walked quietly forward to stand beside Ulfr and Ketil, each of whom had a bared weapon ready. None of the Christian guards, Halfdan noticed, had drawn their blades inside the church, but such restrictions did not bother the crew of the *Sea Wolf*. Halfdan came to a halt by the altar, opposite the former emperor, while Bjorn rounded the great block and bore down on him. Kalaphates backed away, eyes bulging, flesh almost translucent. The smell of fresh urine wafted through the dry, dusty air. The emperor gave another brief shriek as, in an attempt to get away from Bjorn, he backed into Gunnhild.

'You!' he squawked, turning to face her. 'You lied to me. You said I would stand in the light.'

'I never said for how long.'

Another small, panicked noise emerged from the emperor, and then Bjorn was on him, grasping the pee-soaked smock with distaste and then grabbing the emperor's arms, pulling them tightly together in a massive grip. Bjorn urged Kalaphates forward with a jerk that almost dislocated his shoulders, and the fallen emperor of Byzantium was painfully marched from the altar, down the nave and out of his place of sanctuary. His uncle followed, walking steadily, head held high.

As the gathering turned, allowing the pagans to take the prisoners from their place of sanctuary, Gunnhild slowed close to Halfdan. Her face was troubled again.

'What is it?' he whispered.

She glanced at him momentarily. 'Not now.' And with that she walked off towards the open door. Halfdan followed, then paused as he emerged into the light of the atrium, for all attention seemed to be on the struggling emperor, and no one was looking at the uncle, who had moved close to Harðráði. He whispered a few words, which Halfdan tried to hear over the shrieks of the emperor. All he caught was the word 'gold', and Harðráði's reply that there was not enough gold in the world to buy his freedom. Something in the prisoner's expression suggested that he thought differently.

The citizens had followed them out of the church, though still kept at bay by the Varangians, and as the emperor and his uncle were marched out into the forum beyond the atrium gate, the people of Constantinople made their feelings known with a roar of hate directed at the two men. Things were thrown at them, though this behaviour was soon quashed as the Varangians hauled out those responsible and gave them a thrashing for their efforts.

A small cart hauled by a bored-looking ox had been positioned in the middle of the square, in full view of the people. It had been fitted with a wooden cage, a door in the rear standing open, inviting.

'What is this?' the nobelissimus asked, as his nephew cowered and wailed, held fast in Bjorn's grip.

'The emperor's fall must be seen by all. We go to the Sigma, to the imperial Church of the Theotokos Peribleptos, the most holy and most visible Mother of God, founded by the empress's family. There even God will watch us.'

The uncle simply nodded. He was a cool one, this Constantine.

'Thank you, my friends,' Harðráði said to Halfdan and the others. 'I trust, when the day of reckoning comes for you, and your misplaced faith in idols proves false, that Saint Peter recognises that what you have done today was for the greater good of the world.'

Halfdan gave him an odd smile. 'I have a feeling that your god might not want you, Harald the Bulgar Burner, but be cheerful, for I don't doubt that Odin already has you marked for his hall.'

Harðráði gave a carefree laugh and then turned to the cart as the nobelissimús climbed into the mobile cage, his nephew struggling fruitlessly as Ketil and Bjorn shoved him unceremoniously through the door and locked it behind him. In a few moments the cart began to rumble forward, slowly, up the gently sloping road back towards the heart of the city. Varangians walked alongside, and also formed a vanguard and a rearguard, beyond which the population of the city followed, baying for blood. More citizens were lining the street ahead, and more appeared all the time from side streets as the master of their world for the past four months was led to his fate.

Halfdan still didn't understand all of this. He'd offered to kill the pair himself. What worry did he have about displeasing the nailed god, after all? But still, Harðráði had shaken his head. This was Byzantium and the order had been given. It would be carried out the way it always was.

Because it was the law here…

A blind man could never occupy the throne.

Halfdan had noted that neither could a dead man, but it appeared that even death did not render bureaucracy unnecessary in Byzantium.

They marched on, the creak and rumble of the cart, the constant murmur of the crowds and the clank and jingle of armed and armoured men still not enough together to drown out the wailing of the former emperor in his juddering cage as he begged his god and his captors over and over to save him from this terrible fate.

If Halfdan had still harboured any respect for the man, it was now gone. Kalaphates should be damn grateful that he was just losing his sight. In the young jarl's opinion, death was the clear and obvious fate for the man, and the only question was whether he deserved it fast, or dreadfully slow, like Odin hanging on the tree. Instead, the man was blubbing about mere blinding. Halfdan sneered at the quivering heap, remembering a blacksmith in Visby back on Gotland who'd put out his own eye in imitation of the Allfather in an attempt to gain wisdom.

He was still musing on the feebleness of a man who had held every life of an empire in his hands proving to be such a coward when the cart finally rumbled to a halt. Here the thoroughfare they had been following met one of the larger Mese streets that crossed the whole city. At the junction, a square of sorts had been formed as the buildings dipped back from the line in a Σ shape. The Sigma. A fountain burbled away to itself at one side, and facing that square stood one of the many grand churches of the city. Clearly Harðráði had sent word ahead, for here the crowds were already held back by Varangians, and a wooden platform had been put together in open view before the church. Beside it, half a dozen men in a uniform Halfdan didn't know were tending a large brazier, and a table stood strewn with metal implements. Typical that in this place even something as swift and simple as blinding had to be done with great ritual.

The emperor, who had by now become little more than a whimpering heap, had apparently caught sight of what awaited him, for now he started to shriek once more, clawing and hammering at the wooden cage with bleeding fingers. His uncle watched him with disdain. As the commander and a few of his men moved towards the platform, Halfdan moved to help open the cart, but Gunnhild grasped his arm and held him back. He turned to her with a frown.

'This is Harðráði's part to play,' she said quietly. 'I saw the emperor's end at the golden hand of Harald Sigurdsson… and…' Her voice trailed off as she watched the commander approaching the table of horrors.

'And?'

She turned that troubled look on him again. 'And I think our work here in Miklagarðr is done.'

Halfdan blinked in surprise. 'Done? Why now, Gunnhild?'

There was something worrying still about her expression. She looked unsure, nervous even, which was new to him. 'I have seen…' she began, then started again. 'It is dangerous to become too involved, Halfdan. I warned you against tying yourself to anyone here, but every day binds you tighter to Harðráði, and I fear even I failed to take my own advice with Zoe. But now Miklagarðr is clear. Our enemies are overcome, and you must have taken a sizeable sum in pay over half a year? Every day we stay now, we endanger our future.'

Halfdan's frown deepened. 'Have you seen something new?'

'No. I dare not look now. But mark me, Halfdan. We have done what we could, and both Harðráði and the empress are grateful. If we take whatever reward they are willing to give and leave, we can consider that a victory. If we do not, then beware what the future holds.'

Halfdan shivered, but countered with logic. 'Many of the *Sea Wolf* crew were killed by Ari's men when they found the gold, and those of us who weren't lost all our prizes from Georgia in trying to overthrow the emperor. If we leave now, it will not be as rich men, Gunnhild. We will have *lost* gold, not *gained* it. And I cannot leave anyway until Ari Karsten has paid for what he did. Never leave a live enemy behind you, remember? Are you sure this is not about you and Harðráði?'

She levelled a glare at him that could have cut through a ship's hull, and he shrugged. 'He spoke to me. He more than just desires you, Gunnhild. He is lost to you. He would have no other, I think. And he... I too... suspect the feeling is closer to mutual than you would have us realise.'

Gunnhild's unblinking eyes were making him twitch now. She straightened. 'This is not about the Norwegian lunatic, no matter how I might feel. This is about all our futures. See to Ari's fall and no further, Halfdan. Remember that.'

Any further conversation was made impossible, for the crowd had begun to roar their hunger for blood. Varangians had dragged the emperor and his uncle from the cart and escorted them across to the wooden platform.

'Show some spirit,' the older man spat at Michael as the sobbing wreck was thrown unceremoniously to his knees. Harðráði reached out a hand without looking, and one of the uniformed men by the table carefully handed him a metal rod with a hook at the end, glowing so hot it was almost white, the air shimmering around it. The commander approached the uncle and held the glowing hook before him. He said something very quietly, and the prisoner simply shook his head. Halfdan could sense frustration about Harðráði then, but the commander nodded anyway and passed the hook back to the uniformed man, who returned it to the brazier.

'See how bravely I bear calamity,' the uncle called to the crowd in a loud voice, which cut across the murmuring audience, silencing it.

'Tie him down,' Harðráði said, pointing at the man.

'There is no need,' Constantine replied, as he sank to the boards and lay calmly on his back, arms at his sides. 'If I move you can *nail* me down.'

Harðráði shrugged and reached out once more. The hook was passed to him again, heated back up to glowing white, and the Varangian commander dropped swiftly to a knee beside the prisoner. Two uniformed men joined him, hands out, ready to restrain the victim if needed while nearby the former emperor continued to shake and whimper in the grasp of the guards.

Halfdan nodded his approval and respect at Constantine as Harðráði went to work, slowly and carefully lowering the hook to the left eyeball. There was a sizzling noise they could hear over the now hushed crowd, and then a strange, wet sound, and suddenly the eye was gone, unspeakable liquids streaming down the side of the man's face as the flesh around the empty socket crisped with the heat. The nobelissimus let out only a tightly controlled hiss. The procedure was repeated with his right eye, and the man even had the strength of character then to fight off the soldiers as they tried to help him up. He rose to his feet, turning his ruined face to the crowd as if looking across them.

There was an odd, tense silence, and then a blood-curdling scream as the former emperor was grasped and forced down to the timbers amid the spatters of aqueous matter his uncle had left. There was no stoic acceptance from the second victim, and half a dozen of the soldiers were employed tying him to the boards and even then holding the thrashing figure still. The hook was taken away and dropped into a bucket of water with a stinking hiss, and a second identical implement lifted from the glowing coals and passed to Harðráði.

The commander lowered himself to the former emperor, and Halfdan was close enough to the position, and the crowd silent enough, that he caught Harðráði's whispered words as he knelt.

'Thrash all you want, Caulker. In fact, the more the better.'

And he did. Despite being roped and held down by six men, Michael Kalaphates was fighting to the last, struggling and bucking. Halfdan shook his head. That would only make it worse for the man, and surely he knew that?

It was an appalling sight, worse by far than the neat blinding of the man's uncle. Every flinch and shake sent the steaming hook this way and that, where it burned lines across the victim's face and sloughed crisped flesh away. The hook managed no neat prick of the orb, but instead tore and pierced crudely.

Michael Kalaphates screamed through his fate, and when he was finally hauled to his feet, he was shaking uncontrollably, his white smock soiled with shit and soaked with urine, his face ruined, burned and gouged. Even half his hair had been burned away. Harðráði had not been gentle, but Michael himself had made his own fate far worse.

'Take them to the Elcimon monastery,' the commander announced to his men. 'There they will make their peace with God.'

Halfdan watched the two men being led away by Varangians. Harðráði washed his hands thoroughly in a bowl of warm water and then, shaking them dry, wandered across to the seven of them as the crowd jeered at and booed the former emperor.

'Now only Ari remains, and the city is back on track. You will help me hunt the man?'

Halfdan nodded, though out of the corner of his eye he caught a silent warning glance from Gunnhild.

Chapter 17

'No one seems to know how to begin,' Harðráði huffed. 'We're in the largest and busiest city in the world, and we're looking for one man.'

'Hardly,' Halfdan cut in, leaning across the table. 'Twenty-three of Ari Karsten's new Varangians are unaccounted for. Ari's far from alone.'

'We *think* so,' Valgarðr put in. 'It will be weeks before everybody from the last few days turns up. He could still be alone.'

'Ari will have surrounded himself with steel,' Harðráði countered. 'He knows I'm coming for him.'

Gunnhild watched and listened, her irritation building with every comment. Last night, when the menfolk had retired, she had opened the pouch of Harðráði's powder and had taken a small share of it. She'd felt the Seiðr enfold her, like a cocoon of power, and had looked ahead to see what she could of the pattern. What she had found had done nothing to quiet her nerves. The thread of her life stretched on but soon became entangled in some sort of knot, with both the plain, unassuming thread of Halfdan and the golden line that was Harðráði. Then, unexpectedly, those two separated and raced off into the future alone, and her own line was with one of them, but she just could not tell which.

She had spent an almost sleepless night then, alternately cursing the Norns and apologising to them, cursing her own mentor, the völva of Hedeby, for not finishing the job and teaching her all there was to learn, and simply cursing luck, fate, and, invariably, all things Greek.

She felt a little guilty at being so hard on Halfdan, suggesting that it would be his choices that might land them in trouble, while she was now fairly confident that at least some, if not all, of the troubles that awaited them would be of her creation. For over an hour in the heart of the night she had mostly cursed Harðráði for being so damned enthralling. She had trouble thinking straight around him, and admitting that to herself was even worse. She was *better* than this.

Halfdan had agreed that they needed to finish things with Ari, but that their involvement need go no further, even if they came away poor, acknowledging her wisdom. Still, Gunnhild had a feeling that things would not be so easy.

Back in the present, in that room in the palace this morning, she listened to them murmuring their unanswered questions to one another, and when finally there was a pause, she stepped forward and smacked the table, which was covered in a map of the city, with her staff.

'It is very simple,' she said.

'It is?' Harðráði said in surprise.

'It is. Ari Karsten was on the ship that left the Bucoleon carrying the empress. That was the only ship docked within the entire palace circuit, and you know this.'

'Agreed.'

'He will still have been with the ship when it turned around and put ashore at the private imperial dock. Therefore Ari Karsten was in the palace from the moment the empress returned. We know that he was not on board when the emperor took the ship away again to flee to the Studion. That gives him perhaps an hour.'

Again, Harðráði nodded.

'If he did not flee until the empress returned, then the rising of the city was already in progress. That means,' she said, tapping places on the map with the tip of her staff, 'that there was nowhere for him to escape the palace all the way from the Hagia Sophia right down to the Bucoleon, as we and half the city were busy trying to get in.'

'Yes. Go on.'

'The Bucoleon was still sealed tight and the docks empty from being the empress's prison. In addition, since then the whole palace has been searched, Bucoleon included, and you can be content that he did not hide there or take a ship from its dock.'

'Yes.'

'Already,' she went on, 'early in the riot, the slopes around the polo fields were filled with people storming the palace.' To illustrate her point, she drew a line of impasse around the palace from the Hagia Sophia in the north-west, all the way round to the polo fields in the east. 'The only direction Karsten can reasonably have gone is north, and only in that short time.'

'That gives us a solid start,' Harðráði said with a grin. 'You are a remarkable woman, Gunnhild.'

'Pull your tongue back in, Sigurdsson,' she said drily.

She then sat back as the men in the room ran around issuing orders, arranging a search of the northern walls of the palace. For her part she couldn't care less whether Ari Karsten lived or died – if he fled the city he would be out of their way anyway – but clearly Harðráði was not going to let go of this, and as long as he pursued it, so would Halfdan and the others.

For two hours, as the Varangians searched the northern reaches of the palace grounds, Gunnhild tried to relax herself. She tried to sleep, but it wouldn't come. She tried to meditate, but thoughts continually attacked her. Only when she finally took time in the palace baths did she find any peace and comfort. Indeed, she'd finally relaxed when a maid hurried in and told her that the commander had asked after her. Regretfully dressing – even the maid had seemed shocked to find Gunnhild bathing naked – she made her way back to the room she had so recently left to find the men arguing once more.

'...does not mean just one man.'

'I didn't *say* it was just one man,' Ketil snapped irritably.

As she cleared her throat, the arguments stopped, and each of them turned to her. 'You have found something?'

Halfdan nodded, jabbing a finger down at the map. 'Subtle. A recent mark where a piton was driven into the wall top, probably to hold a rope.'

'He must have had accomplices that remained in the palace,' Leif said, glaring at Ketil. 'Someone had to untie the rope once he'd gone. We don't know how many went over the wall.'

'That wall is lower and easier than others,' Harðráði pointed out. 'It's very old, from the early days of the city, constantly repaired and rebuilt over time but still in poor shape. Ari and whoever he was with must have left to the north, onto the acropolis hill.'

'And he's still in the city,' Valgarðr said. 'He has to be. No ship has left since the riot, all the gates have been sealed and all the walls patrolled, looking specifically for Ari. He has to have gone into hiding. He's too well known in the city to go about unnoticed. He looks like us, like a Northman, and he's been in place long enough that half the city knows him.'

Harðráði nodded. 'So he hides and he waits for us to give up so he can slip away. Sooner or later we have to open the gates and ports to trade once more.'

'But *where* is he hiding?' Halfdan said, scratching his head and looking at the map.

'Think,' Gunnhild said, as though she were trying to explain something simple to a child. Must she walk them through this too? 'Think of what he needs.' The others turned to frown at her and she sighed. 'All men need food and water. Wherever he is, he must have access to both. He needs to stay out of sight or he'll be recognised, so he must be hiding somewhere nobody goes. You can perhaps presume that he has anywhere between a dozen and a score of men with him. He will not have done this alone, and the Scythian Rus have as much to lose now as him, since the rest have been rounded up and imprisoned. So wherever he is, he must hide at least a dozen men. He cannot have gone too far across the city, again in case he is seen and recognised. He seeks a way out, and so likely he is somewhere close to the harbours in order to move as soon as they are opened. Given all that, it cannot be hard to track him down.'

Harðráði's grin was back. He hurried over to her, and she backed away, one eyebrow arched. 'If you hug me, Harald Sigurdsson, I will interfere with your chances of founding a dynasty.'

Smiling still, Harðráði turned to the table and beckoned to Valgarðr. 'What do you think?'

The second-in-command perused the map from every angle, tapping places and shaking his head or making sounds that suggested possibility. Finally he leaned back and folded his arms. 'As far as I can see there are only three possibilities. Over here to the west,' tapping the map with a fingertip, 'is the old palace of Romanos Lekapenos. It's been a ruin for decades, but it's large, has a cistern of water, is close to plenty of markets, has a defensible tower, overlooks the harbours, and there are tales of evil spirits haunting the palace. That's why it's never been torn down, and why only daring adolescents enter.'

His finger slid a little closer to the palace. 'Then there's the Xenia Palace.' For the benefit of the recent arrivals, his explanations continued. 'The Xenia is where foreign dignitaries are accommodated when they visit, if they are not close enough allies to be trusted in the company of the emperor. But the last time it was used was for emissaries of Tsar Semuil of Bulgaria, and that was more than a dozen years ago. It was patrolled for a while, but it's been sealed and largely ignored for at least five years. It fits the bill: close to the harbours, large, empty, water and food available, defensible.'

Finally, his finger slid closer, to the hill just outside the palace wall. 'Then there is the theatre. There has not been a performance held there since the time of the empress's grandfather, and it sits largely derelict other than a few vagrants. It does not have its own cistern, but there are several within a few hundred paces, and the imperial orchards nearby could feed someone for a time if they were desperate.'

Harðráði nodded. 'I agree, old friend. Three sites. The most likely is the Xenia, closest to the docks. I will take an allagion of men and surround the place, searching it out. But we must hit all three at once, for if Ari hears of us searching, he could move.' He pointed at Valgarðr. 'You take an allagion to the Romanos Palace. That is as close as he is likely to get to the city centre, and still overlooks the docks. Halfdan?' He turned to the young jarl. 'My instinct to trust you back in Amastris has paid me well. You have held fast through storms and disasters. Will you lead an allagion of the Guard and search the theatre?'

Halfdan nodded. 'I will. I'll take what's left of the *Sea Wolf* crew and a few others. And when this is over, you will reward us for that service?'

Valgarðr nodded his agreement. 'They have earned *more* than their pay, Harald.'

The commander drummed his fingers on the map. 'I will speak to the empress. She will likely agree a healthy donative.' He gave Halfdan a sly grin. 'But you give me Gunnhild and I will pay you a kingdom's ransom.'

At this, having kept her lips sealed thus far, Gunnhild snorted. 'Even if I were Halfdan's to give, he wouldn't dare.'

–

Halfdan looked around at his men. 'If Ari Karsten is to be found here, he is not to be killed, remember? Any man who finishes him will have to answer to Harðráði, and he'll regret it, I think. Capture, not kill. The rest are fair game, though.'

He turned to Leif. 'You know about these theatres? The closest I've been to one is listening to a good skald by a camp-fire.'

The small Rus nodded. 'I've been to the one at Chersonesus at the mouth of the Dnieper, and I'm told they're all much the same shape. It's a half circle of seats rising as they fan out, facing a straight wall with a stage where the actors tell their story. There will probably be two or three doorways in through the stage at the back, and half a dozen at the bottom of the seating stands. If all entrances are covered there is nowhere for a man to go, as the drop from the top of the seats or the stage will be too far.'

Halfdan nodded. 'Then we don't know how many doors we need to cover. It will not be long before the bells ring,' he added, looking up. The bells would be the combined signal for all three Varangian forces to move in on their targets. 'I want everyone spread out, all over this hill and approaching the theatre from every street. Time's up. Go now, and be ready.'

The various commanders led units of men off through the streets, including Halfdan's good friends. Only Gunnhild remained by his side, along with Leif and Anna and half a dozen hand-picked warriors from the *Sea Wolf*. With a quick glance at Gunnhild for confirmation, Halfdan waved an arm and led his group off. They moved through the streets, here a region of spacious, wealthy houses with large gardens, and after a few moments the unmistakable curved upper arcade of the theatre came into view. Holding up a hand, he signalled everyone to stop.

'This is the right one?' Halfdan murmured as they neared the corner and looked out over the deserted structure. Someone had mentioned in passing that there was more than one theatre in the city.

'It is,' Leif confirmed.

The jarl nodded and they settled to watch the D-shaped building with its high walls. Gunnhild wondered momentarily what these theatre performances were like. It seemed far too big a building for a skald to stand at its heart and regale a crowd with stories. How would they all hear?

Slowly, as they waited, she saw other groups appearing at the entrances of other streets, lurking. They were not obvious, but if you were waiting for them they were easy enough to spot. The clanging of bells from the city's churches came suddenly, and Halfdan gave a signal for them to move even as the other groups left their positions and closed in on the theatre.

With the semi-autonomy of northern warriors rather than the rigid rules of a Greek army, the Varangians moved and flowed, groups joining together or splitting up instinctively to cover every entrance as they converged on the theatre from all sides. Gunnhild ran behind Halfdan, the others at her heel, making for a door much like all the rest. Somewhere in the upper stands, a call of warning went out, and the swarming men surged forward anew at the sound, unmistakable evidence that someone, at least, was hiding here.

Halfdan tore at the door, which was unlocked – yet more confirmation of occupation – and he pulled it open, revealing darkened corridors beneath the stands of seating. Inside, the passages split off all over the place in a confusing warren, and the young jarl turned.

'Three men stay on this door. No one gets out. Everyone else, search as best you can.'

He and Leif, Anna and three Varangians disappeared into the darkness, moving swiftly, but watching every black maw of tunnel as they searched. Gunnhild followed Halfdan, leaving the others to their work. It was not easy keeping track of where they were in these tunnels, especially since occasional archways led up into the stands, and the light repeatedly blinded them to the dim labyrinth. Still she kept on Halfdan. Here and there she could hear the sounds of discovery: surprised shouts, calls of warning, the clang of metal on metal echoing along endless corridors.

Halfdan climbed a set of steps now, then doubled back to another such flight, and then a third, Gunnhild always on his heel. They emerged into an upper corridor, and two of Ari's Scythians burst from some unseen place in the darkness, cursing in their thick Rus accents and swinging weapons.

Halfdan parried the blow of a bearded axe with his shield, a strong swing that knocked him to the side, but he recovered quickly and was on the second man in a trice, eagle-hilted sword jabbing and slashing. The first man, the one with the axe, left them to it, his eyes falling on Gunnhild's shape in the darkness, his advance slowing, careful, wary. Gunnhild was not to be trifled with, and everyone in the Guard would know that by now.

His axe swung this way and that, carving arcs as he advanced. She watched him warily, and saw the change in his eyes as he prepared to attack. The axe suddenly stopped its pendulum swings and came up and around in an arc, swinging from high, down towards Gunnhild. She had anticipated it, though, and had already stepped away as the swing descended, meeting only air, causing the man to fight to maintain his balance. She struck. He was big, and trained in the art of war, but she had a staff, which gave her far greater reach.

The five-foot ash pole smacked into the man's head, just above the temple. He was wearing a helmet with an elaborate eye protector and nose guard, but it only helped so much. The result sounded like a bell and left a dent in the steel. The man spun away, axe flailing, as he staggered in stunned confusion. She gave him no chance to recover from the shock, her staff smacking into his wrist, breaking bones and making him drop the axe. As he cursed and shook his head, backing away, she struck again, her staff giving her adequate reach. The butt end caught the helmet's nose guard and bent it into his face even as it smashed his teeth. He howled, and suddenly Halfdan was there, his sword slamming into the man's neck from behind, just below the helmet. The Varangian jerked and gasped, then slid gracelessly to the floor.

She threw a disgruntled look at her friend. 'I had things under control.'

'You were playing with him,' Halfdan replied, 'wasting time. Come on.'

She glared and watched him go, stepping past the bodies of the two fallen men. Her ears picked out footsteps somewhere, and her head jerked this way and that. There were two nearby bright white exits from the tunnels into the stands, and the two of them were roughly halfway between them. Halfdan was running towards one now, and Gunnhild, working solely on instinct, made for the other. As she approached, she screwed her eyes tight, protecting her sight from the worst of the glare, and so as she emerged into the theatre proper she could see well enough, despite the coloured blotches in her retinas.

They were on some kind of semicircular walkway at the top of the stands, arcs of seats stretching out below them down to the centre. Small groups of men were visible here and there, some searching, others fighting, but her attention was drawn inevitably to the figures nearby.

Halfdan had been faster, closer to his exit, and was already advancing along the walkway, bearing down on Ari Karsten, who was spitting curses, his axe and shield held up, ready. He was prepared for a fight, and Gunnhild could see it now: the man was determined to win or die. He would kill Halfdan or he would fall to that elegant sword, for Karsten had absolutely no intention of being dragged before Harðráði.

It would be down to her. She knew Ari would hear her if she advanced from the tunnel entrance, and would react accordingly. She had to surprise him, and so, without moving along the walkway, she motioned to Halfdan and pointed to her staff before slipping back into the shadows. To his credit, the young jarl clearly saw her but did not react in any way. He did not wish to warn Ari. Halfdan advanced, and Karsten waited.

'I presume gold is of insufficient value to you right now,' Ari Karsten said calmly.

'There is not enough gold in the empire to save the man who killed half my crew for a lie.'

'I will not submit, you realise?'

The young warrior's first attack was furious and swift. He leapt and thrust, swinging his blade, bringing his shield round as the sword swept free, using that as a weapon too, a violent onslaught that forced Ari to step back, and then again, under the sheer force of the attack. But the man was a veteran warrior, and his counter-attack was almost as furious as Halfdan's, and much better controlled. The young jarl was driven back a step, and then another, and Gunnhild watched in frustration. One of these two was going to die if she didn't do something, but Ari still could not know she was behind him if this was to work.

Taking a steadying breath and kissing the rough-carved figure of Freyja on the thong around her neck, she padded quietly out onto the walkway again. Her eyes darted sharply this way and that, watching the two men struggle, but not their eyes, nor their hands. She watched their feet, felt the rhythm like a song of battle, scuffing and thudding, stepping and sliding. In a heartbeat she was joining the rhythm, her own feet playing out that same harsh melody, her rhythm in time with theirs by instinct and the will of the goddess. She stepped in their footsteps, her footfalls masked by theirs, gradually approaching Ari Karsten from behind.

The staff came up. She would get at best one guaranteed blow. As soon as she was in range, she pulled the great length of ash back. Karsten paused in his onslaught, suddenly aware of the threat, seeing the truth in Halfdan's eyes as the younger man looked over his opponent's shoulder.

Ari turned his head as Gunnhild struck.

The clonk of wood on bone was audible, and she was relieved not to hear a crack alongside it. The man's skull was intact as he spun, his eyes rolling up into his head as he dropped to the path, unconscious before impact.

Halfdan grinned.

'What kept you?'

Chapter 18

'Every day in this city adds risk to our future,' Gunnhild said, glaring at Halfdan. 'And not just *your* future, but mine too, and all the others who remain.'

Halfdan sighed. It was all very well for Gunnhild to be so stubborn over what needed to be done, but a jarl had to weigh such things against practical necessity too. He'd thought long and hard about their future. He'd told her that he needed to at least deal with the Ari situation first, and that was ongoing even after his capture, at least until this afternoon, but there was more to think about yet, and Gunnhild simply hadn't considered these things.

Halfdan was still relatively new as a leader. He'd proved successful for the crew in Georgia, but it had been close, and could easily have been a disaster. Now he needed to tie them further to himself, but so far in this great city he had seen half the Wolves of Odin imprisoned and killed by Ari's men during the period of the traitor's ascendance, and the remaining members had either lost their hidden gold during the riots or used all they had won in Georgia to help bring the cursed Michael Kalaphates down and save the empress. Even with their pay as Varangians and the donatives Harðráði had secured, they were still less wealthy than they had been when they arrived.

If they left now, he would have failed them as a jarl, and it would be only a matter of time before someone issued the challenge for leadership. Ketil was bound to him now, but he had once been these men's leader himself, and no true Northman would cleave to a failed jarl for long. Command was only ever one challenge away. Gunnhild clearly didn't look at things on that level. She looked into the heart of gods and planned for futures but, in Halfdan's opinion, without paying attention to the current situation there very well might not *be* a future.

There were other issues, too. Half the crew had gone, thanks to Ari. It would not be practical to sail the *Sea Wolf* away and back up the Dnieper with only half the oars manned. Even if they reached the rapids, they would never be able to portage the ship. And to acquire new crew members, they needed money and fame, while currently they were becoming progressively poorer. In addition to all that, they had signed on to the Varangian Guard for a term of a year. If they left without fulfilling that contract, they would be branded as deserters by the empire, whose reach stretched from the western seas to the Dnieper. And when Halfdan had broached the subject of seeking an early end to the contract, Harðráði had told him flatly that the empress would not consider it, with her position still a little shaky. She wanted every guard she could rely upon in the city.

In short, there was no swift way out, no matter what Gunnhild was urging. Besides, there was something about her manner these days that suggested she was more worried for herself than for the rest of them, which was new and a little odd. Off-putting, to say the least.

'I will continue to request an end to the contracts,' he told her patiently. 'And by sundown, the Ari problem will finally be over, and Harðráði might perhaps add his weight to our demands. But even then, unless you can find me at least twenty new oarsmen we'll not get far.' He felt the irritation at her blinkered refusal to recognise the problem rising. 'Perhaps you can supply me with a ton of gold so we can afford what we need?'

'Watch how you speak to me, Halfdan Loki-born,' she snapped. 'Remember how far you would have come without Freyja's guidance.'

He nodded, fighting down the frustration. In this, she was right, and he should remember it. Still, he could not simply do as she asked.

'I will, as I keep saying, see what I can manage.'

Bjorn leaned around the door. 'If you two can stop arguing for a minute, Harðráði is calling for everyone.'

Halfdan nodded his thanks and straightened. 'Let's see what Harðráði has dreamed up.'

As they left the barracks and began to make their way to where a small unit of Varangians had gathered near the Chalke Gate, Halfdan readied himself. This would not be pleasant, he was sure. Harðráði had been brutal with his enemies in the month and a bit since the restoration of the empress.

For a while it had looked like Ari was on his way down to Hel, for even the day after his capture no one had been able to wake him. The palace physicians had used the word 'coma', which seemed to mean a deep sleep from which a man could not be woken. It appeared that Gunnhild's staff blow had been a harder one than she'd intended. The physicians had pronounced the captive as good as dead, which had sent Harðráði off into a rage, but Gunnhild had persevered. He would live, she said, and so they continued to have him fed and watered as best they could, and he slept on in his filth.

He had woken after two weeks, and had been confused and lost for a time. By the end of the third week, though, he had been almost back to his old self, and Harðráði had begun to plan the man's demise, now that he knew Gunnhild had not cheated him of his revenge. Still, she worked, and with another week of recovery it seemed everything was finally ready.

Harðráði had kept himself busy rooting out the remaining Scythian Varangians and having their heads removed and stuck on spears around the city where the public could spit at them. Indeed, much the same had happened to a number of men in the Greek garrison, and perhaps a tenth of the palace staff too. Executions had become a daily entertainment for the people of Constantinople. The city was back under full imperial control.

Falling in alongside his friends, with what remained of the *Sea Wolf*'s crew gathered around, Halfdan gestured and led the way. The message had been simple: Ari's end would come today, and it would come in the hippodrome. Just a few minutes saw them making their way through the great gates and into the massive racing circuit, and Halfdan was surprised by the silence. Somehow, he'd expected Harðráði to have filled the stands with citizens to watch his revenge. The hippodrome was empty. It seemed that this display was only for the benefit of the Guard whom Ari had so terrorised.

Perhaps three hundred Varangians were gathered in an arc around the end of the hippodrome. Of Harðráði or Ari there was no sign. The *Sea Wolf*'s crew found a space among the watchers and waited. The late spring air was warm and the sky a clear cobalt blue, which made the stands of the hippodrome blinding and the sand of the track a rich gold. They stood for perhaps a quarter of an hour, silent, waiting, as the last few Varangians who had been called arrived and took up position.

Finally, the gates were shut and a second door in the *carceres* opened up. Valgarðr emerged first, leading a small and ominous procession. Behind him came four of the most senior Varangians, between them bearing a wooden board, or stretcher, upon which lay Ari Karsten. The man had been crucified, after a fashion, his wrists and ankles nailed to the board and then bound tight to it with leather straps, more of the same around his thighs, biceps, waist, neck and forehead. For just a moment, Halfdan wondered what weird punishment Harðráði had dreamed up, but then came the others carrying the table, the implements, and very carefully conveying a brazier full of glowing coals.

'Blinding?' Bjorn spat. 'Is that all?'

'I doubt it,' Halfdan said. 'There is more than that. This is just the opening move of the game.'

Harðráði appeared then, in the battle gear of the Guard, no ceremonial akolouthos uniform. He walked in a stately manner, and Halfdan found the man's expression disturbing; a weird mix of aloof disdain and gleeful hunger on display upon his face.

Ari's stretcher, dripping blood from his recent crucifixion, was laid upon the raised spina of the hippodrome at its centre, and everything was put into position. As Harðráði approached his longstanding enemy, Ari tried to turn his head, though he could not because of the leather bindings. His eyes swivelled and for all his snarl of hate, the fear in them was visible.

'Speak your accusations, Harald Sigurdsson,' he sneered, 'and I shall deny them all. I have only ever served the emperor, as our oath demands. It is *you* who is in the wrong, favouring an empress over the man to whom you took your oath. I defy your accusations.'

Harðráði came to a halt. 'I have no accusations to level, Ari Karsten. We are beyond such things, you and I, and you already know that. This is not a trial, nor even an execution. This is righteous vengeance. This is the Lord's work. An eye for an eye, you might say.'

Ari spat angrily. 'You can blind me, Sigurdsson, but you'll not see me flinch or scream. I am not some wilting flower of a boy. I have stood in mud and blood and shit and taken a sword to the gut for the emperor in my time.'

Halfdan could not see Harðráði's face, but he could guess how it looked as he spoke. 'By the end, Ari Karsten, I will hear you scream as no one has screamed since Lucifer fell.'

With that he set to work. Halfdan watched, fascinated, as the glowing hooks were used to take out Ari's eyes. To the man's credit, he did little more than hiss his agony throughout, and as Harðráði stepped back, the blind, gory figure on the board bellowed his defiance and hatred still.

Harðráði gave a nod.

More Varangians appeared. They were carrying lengths of thick wire, armfuls of timber and closed buckets. Halfdan frowned, though his brow unknitted as the men went to work and he realised what they were doing. The wire was left to one side, but the timber and kindling was stacked around the base of one of the three columns that rose from the spina of the hippodrome.

'They're going to burn him,' he murmured.

'Good,' Bjorn said irritably. Leif, reaching down to his almost-healed ribs, nodded his agreement.

Once the pyre was ready, at a gesture from their commander, his four assistants approached the stretcher and unstrapped Ari Karsten. The prisoner began to struggle, trying to fight them off, but his wrists and ankles had been broken when he was nailed to the plank, and more so after he'd been torn from the nails while being lifted from the board. He screamed now, and flailed weakly, but the four men easily picked him up and carried him. At the great pointed column they struggled a little, clambering over timber and bearing Ari to the great monolith. With the aid of the men who'd prepared the pyre, they used the thick wire to bind Ari to the column with bands around his shins, waist, chest and neck. They were made tight enough to hold his arms and legs still and to prevent any real movement.

'What is this now, Sigurdsson?' Ari spat. 'What will you try next?'

'Next there is only one thing, Karsten,' Harðráði said quietly and in a truly menacing tone. As the Varangians began to add small kindling and dry grass and brush now, Harðráði stepped closer. He spoke in a low tone, but still loud enough for all to hear.

'It is a shame you cannot see, Ari, for I am wearing the battle gear I wore on that field against the Bulgars at Ostrovo. The day you took away my reserves and left me to die at the heart of the battle. The day you and the emperor turned on me. The day you arranged my convenient exile to Georgia. The day you accused me of emptying the treasury.'

There was an ominous silence.

'The day,' Harðráði said in a nasty hiss, 'they gave me the name Harald the Bulgar Burner.'

On cue, four more Varangians took the lids from the buckets and splashed pitch around the wood and across the bottom of Ari's legs. Karsten began to writhe in panic, trying to free himself of the wire bindings, but there was no hope.

'This is not God's work,' Ari bellowed in a frightened tone. 'This is all about Sigurdsson's revenge for imagined slights.'

'Think what you like, Ari Karsten. Think fast, though.'

With that, he picked up a long pair of tongs from the collection of metal implements and used them to select a glowing coal from the brazier. The Varangians all melted away from the pyre now, retiring to a safe distance, and Harðráði made sure to walk forward slowly. The silence was almost absolute, and the blind Ari had to be able to hear what Halfdan could: the crunch of boots closing on the pyre, and the hiss of the white-hot coal.

'No,' Ari shouted finally. 'All right, Sigurdsson. You get what you want. I'll confess to my failure on the battlefield, to my attempts to bring you down. Even to the falseness of the theft accusation. Just stop this.'

'I don't need your confessions,' Harðráði replied quietly. 'I know of your guilt. And I know who took the gold from the treasury now, too. I am, and have always been, innocent. And now your time has come. Farewell, Ari Karsten. I shall not see you again, for while you descend to the pit, I shall shine with the Lord.'

There was another moment of silence as the burning coal arced through the air, and then struck the pitch-soaked timbers. The pyre burst into roaring flames in a moment, the fire racing across the wood and up Ari's legs. If Halfdan had thought he was screaming before, it was nothing to what they heard now. Moreover, it made Halfdan tremble, for he knew that sound well. Across Georgia he had heard it where the Greek fire struck flesh and stuck and burned. He closed his eyes and for a moment he was back in that forest at Sasireti, Georgian rabble burning as they fell and staggered through the trees. Still, those men had perhaps deserved more, but Ari Karsten, the man who had butchered half the *Sea Wolf*'s crew for a lie, deserved nothing.

He opened his eyes, and the sight that greeted him was not much better. Ari was still screaming, though he wasn't really Ari any more. Just a lump of charred meat held together with wire, crisping, sloughing and glowing.

'One last warning,' Gunnhild said quietly, close to Halfdan's ear. 'Remember what I said. Don't get yourself tied to anyone in this city, including Harðráði.'

Halfdan nodded, turning to her. 'Advice I could safely give in return, Gunnhild.'

Her eyes narrowed, but this was not the time for another fight, and so Halfdan turned back to the scene, for something new was happening. Ari was beyond conscious thought now, and even the screaming had stopped. Fresh movement had drawn their attention, though, for a new party of Varangians had emerged from the carceres, leading a figure in a long white smock. Halfdan squinted into the sun and realised with surprise that the blind man being led across the sand was Constantine, the former emperor's uncle, blinded a month ago at the Sigma and having languished in a monastery since then. He walked proud still, his plain-sandalled feet crunching on the sand, chin high.

Harðráði turned to him as he approached, and Halfdan was surprised at the hate and anger burning in his expression. Yes, the man had proved to be a villain and, despite his denials, had clearly been part of the emperor's usurpation of Zoe Porphyrogenita, yet Halfdan had not realised that Harðráði had anything *personal* against the man. Still, there was no denying the intimacy of the hatred he could see on the commander's face. For a moment he frowned, and then, with recall, everything fell into place.

That day of the blinding, Constantine had attempted to buy his freedom. Harðráði had told the man that he couldn't possibly have enough gold for such a thing, but the prisoner had clearly thought otherwise. Just now, as fiery death approached, Ari Karsten had confirmed before all present that he would attest to Harðráði's innocence over missing gold. Halfdan wracked his brain, thinking back. *Five thousand pounds of gold*, he recalled. Gold missing from the imperial treasury and for which Harðráði had been investigated. For which several of Halfdan's own men had died. And this blind figure being led forward had been a member of the imperial household all that time, had even been close to the treasury. Close enough to engineer the blocking of the empress from such funding. Close enough, perhaps, to steal five thousand pounds of gold. Ari had stood against Harðráði through personal rivalry according to Valgarðr, but Constantine had *also* stood against him, masking his own theft by laying the blame squarely at Harðráði's feet.

It *was* personal. But the commander couldn't do this, Halfdan knew. Ari Karsten had been the commander's to deal with as he pleased by imperial order, but the empresses had sentenced *this* man, along with his nephew, to blinding and to exile in a monastery. If Harðráði burned him, he would have to answer to an angry mistress over it.

Yet sure enough, Varangians were constructing a second pyre at a similar obelisk further down the spina. More buckets of pitch were being carried, and guardsmen used two long poles to lift the glowing brazier and move it down the track towards the second column. Without needing an order, as Harðráði and his men moved down the hippodrome with the prisoner, the Varangian audience kept pace, moving with the action, paying close attention.

'Is this about the gold?' Ketil muttered, a hint of greed in his voice.

'Gold?' asked Bjorn, suddenly interested.

Halfdan nodded. 'Five thousand pounds of gold. Enough to buy an army or a city. I think that man stole it. So does Harðráði. I suspect our commander's about to clear his name.' Halfdan cast a sidelong look at Gunnhild. 'Even a fraction of that gold would be enough to buy our freedom, make us rich, and replace our missing crew.'

'And every day you spend trying to find it will bring us one day closer to trouble,' she said. 'You have stopped listening to me, Halfdan, and that means you have stopped listening to the gods.'

'Not this again. I've explained it all, Gunnhild. Unless Freyja is going to put in a personal appearance and help row, we cannot leave until we can afford to, until we are officially free to, and until there are enough of us to man the *Sea Wolf.*'

She stopped walking, her glare lingering. Halfdan almost paused, but hardened himself and kept moving. He could see every day that she was struggling, but she was also being bloody-minded and unreasonable, and he was doing everything he could. He would make it all up to her soon. He would stick with Harðráði until this gold was located, and find a way to make some of it his. Then he could hire new men, buy their freedom, and they could leave, at least as wealthy as they arrived, and he would be unchallenged as their jarl.

It would just have to be that way.

His attention was drawn to Constantine, uncle of Michael Kalaphates, as they passed the burning shape that had once been Ari. The blind man sniffed, lip wrinkling.

'Who is your new victim, Bulgar Burner?'

'This was Ari Karsten. He regretted his crimes in the end.'

Halfdan watched uncertainty pass across Constantine's face then, and that doubt only deepened as he was led across a pile of uneven timbers to a column.

'What is this, Sigurdsson?'

'Today is a day for truths and revenge, Constantine. Ari has paid his price. Now you pay yours.'

The prisoner would have stared if he could. 'You can't do this, Sigurdsson. I have endured my sentence. You yourself will be condemned.'

Harðráði snorted. 'For disobeying the empress? I think you underestimate Zoe's care for me. I will receive a smack on the hand at most. You are an *insect* to these people now, Constantine of Paphlagonia, and nothing more. Whatever the empress's given sentence, mine is death by fire. Not for theft from the treasury. That is the empress's charge to level. Mine is for trying to blame me for your crimes. And for that there is no solution. No recompense. You owe me.'

'I offered you gold once, Harðráði. Remember? When you did *this*,' he added, pointing to his empty, ruined eye sockets.

'You offered me a thousand pounds of gold. I told you then it was not enough.'

'It is all I have.'

As the Varangians wound thick wire around the prisoner, pulling him tight to the column, Harðráði laughed. 'No, it isn't. I know it, and so do you, and I imagine every man here – for your death will be watched by half the Guard – also knows it. I say you owe me, and I give you two choices right now: hold your silence over your crime, and burn, or tell me where to find the five thousand pounds of gold you stole.'

'I am not *guilty* of that.'

'Yes you are,' Harðráði replied flatly, and then to his men: 'Burn him.'

Pitch was slopped across the timbers, and Constantine flinched as it slapped over his shins. He sniffed, and panic began to rise, taking control of his expression.

'*Please*, Sigurdsson…'

'Your thievery,' was the calm reply.

As a shimmering, white-gold coal was lifted from the brazier with a hiss, the former emperor's uncle wailed, 'All right! No more. Save me, Harðráði, and it's yours. Send me back to my cloister to live a quiet and peaceful dotage.'

'Five thousand pounds,' Harðráði said, holding a glowing coal that meant death in the metal tongs close to the timbers.

'Five thousand, *three hundred* pounds,' Constantine corrected. 'Plus perhaps a bit more. It was nearly six thousand, but we had to spend some of it. It's yours, just don't do this!'

'Where is it?'

'It was stored beyond the reach of your searches, underwater in the cistern below my house.'

Harðráði gave a nasty smile and, for a moment, Halfdan thought he was going to burn the man anyway. Instead he turned, dropped the coal back into the brazier, and gestured to the men at the pyre. 'Take him down and return him to his monastery. He's paid for his crime with his eyes and with gold. Let that be an end to it.' He then turned and threw out his arms to the crowd of his men. 'You have stood by me for a year, through all these accusations. I have always protested my innocence. Know now that I am vindicated. I am not the criminal, and the real criminal has been caught.'

A cheer went up through the crowd, and as it died away, the commander gestured to Valgarðr. 'Take a message to the empress. Tell her we've found her gold. Tell her who took it and where it is hidden.'

Valgarðr nodded, but paused before moving. 'You know Constantine's house was the first to be demolished in the riot. It is a heap of rubble now. There's weeks of work just getting access to the cistern, and then we'll have to make sure the gold's there, then drain the place to get to it. It's a long job.'

'Best let the empress know straight away, then,' Harðráði grinned, then turned and stretched. 'Today is turning into a good day.'

Chapter 19

Gunnhild felt the pull of the world once more. The song had reached dizzying heights and she'd walked among clouds and looked down upon mountains, soaring with Odin's ravens and walking with the goddess. She had seen many things this time, wondrous to behold and terrifying to endure, and yet as she plummeted into herself once more and her eyes snapped open, the after-image dancing on her retinas was not one she'd expected, and most certainly not what she would have wanted to see. In fact, and not for the first time these past few months, she regretted having looked, having even sung the song. Perhaps it would have been better for everyone if that pouch had never turned up and she'd run out of the goddess's gift.

How could she tell Halfdan? She'd urged him to leave, for she knew that the longer they stayed the more danger there was of something disastrous happening, both to him and to her. Although perhaps *disastrous* was not the word for the weaving that lay before her, if she were to be fair, since many in her place might have seen that vision as a blessing rather than a curse.

Not her.

Not now.

For she had seen again the boar, the bear and the wolf. This time there had been no empress, no Ari to be revenged upon. Just the three of them. A very simple image, and yet so complicated in what it clearly meant. The boar that was Gunnhild had walked on into the future shoulder to shoulder with the bear that she knew to be Harðráði, while the wolf had stalked away alone.

She shivered at the truth that held.

Something was coming to an end.

Damn Harðráði. Damn Halfdan for not listening. Damn the Norns themselves for weaving this.

'What?' she snapped as her eyes refocused to find Anna standing in the doorway, hovering in that uncertain way she did when she knew that Gunnhild was walking with the goddess. Anna did not approve, she knew, yet the girl was loyal for all that and managed to overcome her cross-god disapproval most of the time. Momentarily, she wondered where Leif was, for it was rare now to see the girl without the little Rus almost attached to her.

'The empress is asking for you. The empress *Zoe*,' Anna added helpfully.

'It would only be that empress.' The coldness and suspicion she had seen in Zoe's face that day she had been tonsured and dragged away had swiftly been forgotten since her return. The empress had acknowledged, briefly, but in a heartfelt manner, that Gunnhild had clearly done the right thing by her all along, no matter how it looked. From hovering on the edge of suspicion, events had instead now bound her tighter than ever to the empress of Byzantium, outstripping any noble advisor.

'Take me to her.'

She could have argued. She didn't really want to spend time yet again listening to Zoe Porphyrogenita rattling on about how her sister and co-empress Theodora was a hard-faced cow, how she deliberately got in the way of anything Zoe tried to do. How Theodora was clearly the more junior of the pair, being younger and less experienced at court, having spent most of her adult life in the Church. How this and that problem were all the sister's fault. Indeed, the rift between the pair had been widening all the time in the weeks following the fall of Michael Kalaphates, who still moped in a monastery somewhere with his uncle. Gunnhild was forming the private and unspoken opinion that if Zoe was locked in a room on her own for long enough, she would fall out with herself. She seemed to be a terrible decision maker, something that perhaps explained why she continued to cling to Gunnhild.

There were any number of excuses she could have found to avoid this meeting, but the simple truth was that *any* distraction was welcome right now if it stopped her pondering on the meanings of her latest casting.

Chewing on her lip irritably, she stalked through the palace corridors in the wake of Anna until the maid came to a halt at the doors to the empress's rooms. There she was handed off to one of the eunuchs, who bowed and admitted her without a word.

The empress was sitting rather primly on her throne, as regal as could be, though only her servants and eunuchs were in evidence in the room.

'Ah, Gunnhild,' she said, warmly, 'I'm so grateful to see you, and just in time.'

Gunnhild frowned. *In time for what?* She said nothing, let the empress continue in her own time.

'The situation has become untenable,' Zoe said irritably. 'Theodora gainsays everything I do merely to appear powerful. She has no understanding of how the city and the empire work, and she is throwing sticks between the spokes of my wheels, risking everything we hold dear simply to seem as though she has more of a say in how things are done. I simply cannot let this go on.'

Images of trays of poison ingredients swam through Gunnhild's mind, and she pushed them away. It would be a neat path to sole rule, of course. It seemed unlikely that Zoe would cry over the death of her sister, and she might even find a way to overcome the sanctity of imperial blood that meant she shouldn't kill her according to the rules of their peculiar religion. But the basic fact was that Zoe had been accused of attempted poisoning by Michael all those weeks ago, and if she was discovered to have poisoned Theodora now, it would cast doubt over her innocence back then.

'I have pondered long on the situation and how it can be changed,' Zoe said. 'There are elements in court, among the noble families, even in the Church, who are not comfortable with a woman sitting on the throne alone, and two women sharing it is no better for these people. Byzantium is seen still as a patriarchy, and there is an emperor-shaped hole in the people's world since Michael's blinding.'

Gunnhild felt her spirits sink. She had a feeling she knew where this was going now, and nothing good could come of it.

'If I am to shuffle my sister into the background,' the empress continued, 'then the simplest way to do so is to provide the people with an emperor once more.'

There it was. Another bad decision loomed. Gunnhild kept her mouth resolutely shut.

'If I marry, then my husband will be emperor of Byzantium, and since I am the older sister, Theodora's place in the court will be diminished sufficiently that she will likely abandon the whole thing and return to her nunnery, which is where she is always most comfortable anyway.'

Silence descended, broken finally by the empress as she leaned forward. 'Have you nothing to say, Gunnhild? I asked you to come because you know I value your wisdom.'

'You will not listen to me, Zoe Porphyrogenita.' Gunnhild sighed, her mind wandering briefly to an image of Halfdan arguing. '*No one* listens to me these days.'

The empress frowned now. 'Truly, I will listen. In fact I seek your advice very specifically.'

A deep breath. 'Then my advice, Empress, is to abandon the folly of another husband. Your sister has less claim on the throne than you, and you have enough supporters that any dissenting element can be overruled. Simply impose your will on Theodora — send her back to her nunnery if you will it — but a husband would be a foolish idea.'

'I was not seeking *that* sort of advice.'

'Precisely. You will not listen to me. But I have been told about your first husband. He took a mistress over you. He tried to limit your power, and you dallied with dangerous courtiers. Some even say you poisoned or drowned him. And your second husband? Michael the Paphlagonian? Did he not ignore you entirely and drive you further into the arms of others, and even manage to persuade you to adopt the lunatic Michael Kalaphates? And I hardly need to remind you how that worked out. Empress, I fear you are not destined to be a married woman. Alone you rule well. With a man you are prone to unwise decisions and often shuffled aside.'

The empress's eyes had become flinty. No one else spoke to her like this. Even Gunnhild, influential as she was, was walking a dangerous line being so frank and open, and even insulting. But Gunnhild had worrying matters of her own to deal with, and her patience for Zoe's foolishness was far from limitless.

'The matter has been decided, Gunnhild,' the empress said icily. 'It is the only way, I am convinced. But there are choices to be made. A number of potential suitors have been suggested to me, and I have narrowed that choice to three. I want your considered opinion of the three men between whom I shall choose.'

Gunnhild rubbed her face with tired hands and sighed. 'You are set on this course, Empress?'

'The decision to marry has already been made. Just not to whom. This must be a considered choice. The Church allows only three marriages, and even then a third is frowned upon. The Patriarch Alexios speaks against it, and so only the correct choice will bring everything together.'

'The correct choice is none of them.'

'Gunnhild, if you cannot provide me with advice on a problem I offer, what use are you to me?'

'Then I should go.'

Gunnhild turned and started to leave.

'Wait,' the empress said, an edge of nerves in her voice now. 'No, wait, Gunnhild. I spoke rashly, for I do value your advice, but you must realise that while you understand people and the world and many things in it, you do not understand the *empire*. I do. I know this needs to happen, but for it to work, it needs to be done correctly. I need you to consider my three suitors and counsel me as to which will be the best choice, through your... *rituals*... if necessary.'

Gunnhild paused in the doorway and turned. Perhaps, though clearly the empress was set upon a self-destructive path once again, Gunnhild might at least limit the damage. If she could help avoid putting another Kalaphates on the throne then she should not pass up the chance.

'All right, Empress. Who are these men, and how do I meet them?'

'For convenience, I have arranged for them to be together. Since they are all senior officials in the court, they are each used to attending official business. All three have been summoned on the pretext of their roles in the imperial administration to bear witness to a minor edict. They await in my antechamber and at my call they will be admitted. I would like you to remain at the periphery of the room, observing them. Form your opinion and when they are done, advise me.'

Gunnhild sighed. 'Very well,' she murmured, and shuffled to the side, away to a bench beside an expensive wall hanging, where she sat and folded her arms. The empress busied herself with her staff, arranging everything, and finally the doorman was sent to summon the courtiers. Gunnhild focused on the matter at hand, trying to push away the nagging image from her casting that continued to surface whenever her mind wandered. This was a terrible idea, and she was convinced of it, but there were still grades of terrible, and she could at least make *some* difference.

Her heart sank at the sight of the first figure to stride purposefully through the doorway. For a brief moment, she wondered what the empress could be thinking with this man, then she realised Harðráði was not here as one of the suitors – he was simply escorting them. Still, the commander's presence was of no comfort to Gunnhild at all.

Harðráði bowed to the empress and stepped aside. Half a dozen senior Varangians followed him in, thankfully not including Halfdan, for Gunnhild had enough on her mind right now. As the soldiers took up positions to protect the empress should any visitor prove of evil intent, the three courtiers made their way in.

Gunnhild watched them as they entered. The first of them was an older man with salt-and-pepper hair and a matching beard. He was almost of an age with the empress, and like her had managed to retain his looks. He was stately and imposing. Gunnhild took in what she could. He was impeccably dressed, not quite as ostentatiously as most Byzantine noblemen. Tasteful, though clearly rich and intent on showing as much. The man had been a warrior in his time, for he bore the marks of battle upon his flesh. He walked with confidence. Perhaps a little *too much* confidence in the presence of an empress. He reminded Gunnhild of herself in that regard. That was a warning sign. A man like that was unlikely to bend to Zoe's will.

The second figure followed on the heels of the first. He was strikingly handsome and dressed moderately, more quietly than the first, and in good clothes, but not so rich. His skin was smooth and unmarked, and there was nothing martial about the man. As he glanced around, Gunnhild was surprised to see a glint of what appeared to be benign intelligence in his eyes. She had not expected to approve of any of these three. In fact, the man was everything an empress might hope for, at least at first glance.

Her gaze shifted to the third, and there her spirits sank once more. This man she knew of, and had seen around the court. This man she would stand on a rooftop and scream defiance against if she had to. Constantine Monomachos, the lover of Maria Sklerina, that weasely and dangerous noblewoman who had been one of Gunnhild's first patrons. Monomachos was handsome enough, but there was something about his face that made Gunnhild twitch. Not intelligence, and certainly not wisdom. A rodentlike wiliness was all she could identify. And his clothing was as rich as could be, which spoke little of moderation. He shone with gold and fair dripped with jewels.

It came as no surprise, as the men came to a halt, that all three were extremely handsome. Zoe Porphyrogenita was clever, but she lacked wisdom, and too many of her decisions were made by her passions without bothering to consult her mind. The door shut and the empress was announced by a servant with all her many titles and honorifics. The three men were named, and Gunnhild listened carefully. Constantine Monomachos she knew of. The older one was Constantine Dalassenos, who Gunnhild only knew as a former general who had languished in prison throughout the brief and dreadful reign of Kalaphates. The younger, plainer one was Constantine Artoklines. Why was half this city called Constantine? Even the damned city itself carried the name.

'Handsome bunch, aren't they?' murmured a voice close by, and Gunnhild, startled, turned to find that Harðráði had wandered over unnoticed and stood next to her bench.

'Terrible choice upon terrible choice,' she replied irritably. 'But hush.'

She tried to listen to the torrent of compliments each of the men paid the empress, but in the middle of it, Harðráði interrupted again. 'I have been trying to find time to speak to you, Gunnhild of Hedeby.'

'Will you be quiet?' she hissed.

As the commander fell silent again, she listened to the initial exchanges. It was easy to form an impression of each man from the way they spoke to the empress, from their manner and their stance. Dalassenos considered himself her superior, but for the accident of her being born to the purple. If the crown sat upon his brow, it would not be long before he was sole ruler, and Zoe shuffled off into a nunnery. And the worst thing was that he would achieve it, because he was strong and popular enough to avoid the fate of Kalaphates. Clearly he would be a terrible choice.

Monomachos was oily. The man was playing for her favour, and Gunnhild could see it. She had no idea how the man could know what was truly happening here, but she would be willing to bet that he did. The man was playing the game and playing it well. The only one who seemed to be speaking with respect and wisdom was the younger, more dour one, and Gunnhild would have leapt upon him as a choice for the empress, but for the fact that as the man moved, she spotted a wedding ring upon the man's finger, and he repeatedly caressed it.

'You see, I've been thinking about my future, after I leave the city,' Harðráði said suddenly, cutting across the conversation at the throne.

'Will you shut up?' Gunnhild hissed.

'I don't think I need a princess, you see? I've a golden fish already on my hook, since Jarisleif of Kiev has already set aside his daughter for me, but I find myself fascinated with other, more exotic, prey.'

Gunnhild turned an angry face on the commander and jabbed a finger painfully into his ribs. 'Another word until this is over and I'll break your arm, Sigurdsson.'

He fell silent again, but his smile was even more off-putting than his voice, and she hated the fact that it took her a while to drag her eyes from it. The three courtiers gave their advice on the edict at hand, one haughty but approving, one smarmy and dripping with praise, one honest and straight, and then they signed their names as witnesses to the document.

'You realise she'll choose the prettiest,' Harðráði said in a conspiratorial whisper.

She turned sharply. 'You know?'

Harðráði chuckled. 'Something like the empress looking to marry becomes common knowledge very fast. The court in Constantinople is a pond where gossip is the water. There were seven suitors suggested by some very bright men, some of whom were good choices, some bad, some handsome, some dour. It should hardly surprise you that only the three handsome ones, Adonis reborn in each case, have made it to the empress's side. She is a good woman, our empress, but in one important way she displays an incredible lack of foresight.' He gave Gunnhild another smile that unsettled her further. 'Some of us look deeper, and for us beauty is merely a healthy bonus.'

'Roll your tongue back in, Sigurdsson, before I step on it.'

With that, she rose and moved a few paces away. The meeting was breaking up now, and the three men were being dismissed, seen out of the room by the eunuch. The Varangians followed, Harðráði taking the rear position and throwing one last look at Gunnhild before closing the doors and leaving them alone.

'Well?' the empress said, an air of nerves in her voice.

'I cannot advise you to choose any of these men. If you cannot rule alone, cast your net wider and find another. Perhaps look to the other choices that you discarded?'

The empress looked taken aback, her brow creasing. 'My last husband will be one of these three, Gunnhild. The people must love their emperor. He must almost glow with divine glory.' She had the decency to keep her eyes lowered as she said this last, for Gunnhild knew 'divine glory' was a requirement that had nothing to do with the world beyond Zoe's bedchamber.

'Which *one*, Gunnhild?' the empress said, looking up once more.

With a sigh and then a deep breath, the daughter of Freyja put her hands on her hips. 'You want my wisdom, Porphyrogenita? I cannot recommend any of them, but I *will* tell you *why* I cannot. Constantine Monomachos is a power-hungry fool. He has no substance and lacks even the basic spark of wisdom. He is a ferret in a human body, wrapped in gold leaf and jewels. He will tell you whatever you want to hear until he is in a position where he does not have to any more. And perhaps worse, I know that he is involved with

Maria Sklerina, and that the pair have been trying to engineer this very situation since before I arrived in the city. It would be disastrous to choose such a man.'

She paced back and forth then as she spoke. 'Constantine Dalassenos is too arrogant. He will overshadow you the moment he can claim his own power. He will see himself as emperor and you as little more than a stepping stone that he has to keep around for the look of it. I am not saying that Dalassenos would be a poor choice for the *empire*. Perhaps a strong general is what it needs, and the fact that your previous husband and son kept him safely locked up says much about him. But for you personally, he will be a disaster, for with him on your arm, you will effectively have given up your throne for good.'

She stopped again, right in front of the empress. 'Constantine Artoklines would be an excellent choice. Despite his good looks he is, in fact, a deep man with respect in his heart and wisdom in his head. But I watched him. When he looks at you, he then casts his eyes down and plays with the ring on his finger. He is well aware, just as the others are, of why they were truly here, and throughout this his thoughts were on his wife, especially when he looked at you. You will never have Artoklines' heart.'

The look that passed across the empress's face then made Gunnhild's spirits fall further. What she saw in Zoe's expression made it clear that the man's heart was not her prime concern. She would let another have his heart if she could have the rest.

'You have made your decision.'

'Your advice, Gunnhild, is always appreciated. And though you will not advise me to choose any of them, your summary is most informative, and it does help me make my decision.'

Gunnhild huffed. 'Then I hope you and another woman's husband have a very happy life together.'

The empress's eyes narrowed dangerously. 'I trust you, Gunnhild of Hedeby, and I value you, but sometimes you walk very close to the edge of my patience. I suggest you take a walk in the summer sunshine and shrug off some of this icy hauteur you seem to have acquired.'

Gunnhild needed no further encouragement, and gave a short bow of courtesy to the empress before striding from the room, the eunuch hurrying to open the door for her and close it afterwards. In the gloomy hallway, Gunnhild stood still for a long moment, rubbing her head. She felt tired and empty. Used up. The longer she stayed in this place, the more she felt it. Indeed, she was feeling the presence of Freyja less and less. The castings were becoming more of a strain, the Seiðr harder to locate or summon up. She wondered briefly whether Byzantium was actually snapping the threads that tied her to the goddess.

'The thing is,' Harðráði said from somewhere nearby in the gloom, making Gunnhild jump, 'that you seem to be avoiding me.'

She fought down the butterflies of panic in her stomach. 'Why are you lurking in darkened corridors, Sigurdsson?'

'Because it seems to be the only way I can speak to you.'

'I have no time for prattle.'

'Really? Because the last thing I just heard was the empress commanding you to go for a walk. I have exceptional hearing, and the door is a little thin. Why are you avoiding me, Gunnhild?'

She turned, and mentally brushed aside once again the image of the boar and the bear side by side. She fixed the man with a look, and was reminded once again of how ruggedly handsome Harðráði was. It irked her intensely that this moment gave her more than a little insight into how the empress felt because, for just a moment, she pictured herself at the prow of a dragon ship with Harðráði, the spray of the whale road in their faces, and it felt both right and good.

No.

'I am avoiding you, Sigurdsson, because you insist on pursuing me like a hunter with a stag. I am not made for matrimony, for hearth and home. I am a daughter of Freyja, wedded to the spear.'

'And that is why we would work so well together, Gunnhild. I am being neither presumptuous, nor arrogant, though both of these things are second nature to me, I'll admit. With you, though, I know you feel it too. I *know* it.'

She growled. 'I have things still to do. I have friends to look after, for without me they would have foundered on the rocks long ago. They need me, and I have work. I have no time to go all moon-eyed over a man who will never accept that I will not be his. And I will never take your cross-god, Harðráði. Now stop this childish pursuit, and leave me in peace.'

She turned and walked off, leaving him standing in the shadows, but the last image she had of him as she spun included a smile that said more than anything that this was not over.

Damn the man.

Chapter 20

'This might be our last chance to leave,' Gunnhild said.

Halfdan sighed. He shouldn't have come. In fact, he was visiting her less and less these past few weeks, because every conversation inevitably spiralled into accusations that he was delaying departure for no good reason. He *had* a good reason, and he'd tried to explain it every time, but trying to talk sense into Gunnhild was like trying to cut the sea in half with an axe.

'We are so close, now, Gunnhild,' he said in an exasperated tone.

'So close to *disaster*.'

'So close to being able to leave,' he replied with strained patience. 'I know. It's been weeks, but Constantine's house was in such a state after the riot that it's taken a lot of effort. The workers the city has for that kind of thing are being used all over Constantinople repairing and rebuilding, so they can't help us. Besides, given what's in there, Harðráði doesn't want anyone but the Varangians working on it. We guard the place carefully.'

He sagged. He had once helped raise a house in Visby, as a boy, stripping the timbers and hauling on ropes. He'd seen and marvelled at the work and the huge amount of materials that had gone into a simple town house in Gotland. Helping dig through the remains of Constantine's house, which was more of a palace, had been eye-opening. He'd wondered if perhaps the great black sea beyond the city was the hole left from the quarry when they built the place. The amount of stone, marble, concrete and every imaginable material they hauled away was astounding. They'd even found hollow tiles to allow air to move through them. These Greeks planned everything, even down to what was *inside* the walls. The result was a heap of burned rubble that had taken weeks to clear, and even three days ago, when the last of the detritus was finally removed, it had taken some time to locate the cistern underground beneath it, only to discover that the way into it, too, was blocked with rubble. Further work had then begun.

'The cistern should be opened by sunset tonight,' Halfdan explained. 'It's possible Constantine lied, but I don't think so. Not when he was facing what he was. He buried the stolen gold there, and we're a few feet from reaching it.'

'Even then it is the *empress's* gold, not yours,' she countered.

'Harðráði is confident that we can take one part in ten with her blessing. It's standard, apparently. Donatives. When the Guard do something loyal, above and beyond their oath, the emperors reward them. We will have given the empire back so much gold, a reward would be expected. By tomorrow we will all be wealthy enough to crew the *Sea Wolf*, and we'll be able to end our contracts and leave. One day, Gunnhild. We're *one day* away.'

'One day might be one day too long.'

'Nothing will change enough to stop us in one day.'

'You don't know that, Halfdan.'

He sighed. 'Have you consulted Freyja? Have you seen the future?'

She flinched at the suggestion, and once again Halfdan considered that there was something personal at stake here, far beyond the safety of the crew, something she was hiding, perhaps even refusing to face herself. She straightened. 'No. Nor do I have to. I have eyes and ears, and the wisdom to use them. The court shifts once more like the surface of the sea, and we move from good sailing weather towards another storm.'

'Is he that bad?'

It was a naïve question, and he knew it. The new emperor would be terrible.

It had been a turbulent few weeks in the empress's life. She had settled upon the mild and sensible Constantine Artoklines, much to the relief of all those in the know. Unfortunately, Artoklines and his wife had been far closer than the empress had realised. When the Guard had come to escort him to the palace for an official betrothal, they had found him dead, poison having eaten out his gut, bloody froth around his mouth, his unseeing eyes wide with agony. Whether he had taken the poison himself to avoid his imperial fate, or whether his wife had refused to let him go, no one seemed sure. Whatever the case, the result was the same: Artoklines was no more, and the throne was still open.

Halfdan had wondered who would be selected to step into his red shoes of office, though it would clearly be one of the other Constantines, Dalassenos or Monomachos. When he'd mused on the question openly, Gunnhild had spat the answer. 'Dalassenos would be good for the empire, but she will never accept him, for he sees her as inferior. So that means she will choose the pretty boy with the weasel mind.'

'If he's not bright, she might be able to keep control,' he'd said, only to be snorted at in derision.

Now that dismissive sound was back in her voice. 'Monomachos is the property of Maria Sklerina,' she said, 'and she is closely tied to her brother, Romanos Skleros. Between them they are wilier than a pit of snakes. Monomachos will be terrible for both the empress and the empire, and now it seems inevitable. I've tried to persuade her to look elsewhere, but she will not.'

'Still, this new emperor will have no reason to turn on us,' Halfdan said. He'd never even met the man, nor the woman or her brother. Why would they be trouble for the Wolves?

'Don't be so stupid, Halfdan,' Gunnhild snapped. 'Monomachos will do whatever the Sklerina asks, and she will do whatever is best for her brother. Skleros hates Harðráði, almost as much as he hates Maniakes. And with the giant general now off in Italy with the army, your commander is running out of powerful allies.'

'They were never allies.'

'They may not like one another, but they were on the same side. Skleros is not. Harðráði continues to be the empress's man, and that will be a problem for the new emperor. He will not let you and your friends stand in the way of power. Mark my words, the ship of empire is headed for white-water rapids and dangerous rocks, and none of us who are close to the empress will come away unscathed. I warned you about this from the start. Avoid becoming bound to anyone, I said. It will be dangerous. Now you are bound to both Harðráði and the empress, and it has made you a target for a man who is about to become master of the world.'

Halfdan took a deep breath. 'Perhaps you should have listened to your own advice, Gunnhild, since you're as tied to Zoe Porphyrogenita as the rest of us.'

'I know,' she said, the anger subsiding into a tone of regret. 'I know. But I did what I *had* to do. What the Norns had woven for me. I think it was necessary in order to save you all when the troubles began under the Caulker, but I think it should have ended there. That is why I kept appealing to you. That was the time to sever our mooring lines and sail away, before the real trouble struck. Now it's here, in the shape of Constantine Monomachos.'

'What would you have me do, Gunnhild?' he said, exasperated. 'I've explained it time and again. Without the gold, there is no way out. We're almost there.'

The crunching of boots on gravel reminded the pair that they were far from privacy here in the gardens, even in parts rarely frequented, and a glance between the neatly planted line of cypresses revealed a small party of Northmen kitted out for duty, marching from one archway to another. As they watched the oblivious column of Varangians, the familiar figure of Harðráði appeared at their rear, walking alongside the clerk Michael Psellus, deep in conversation.

On some sort of preternatural instinct, the Varangian commander looked up in their direction, piercing icy eyes beneath a quizzical brow. His sharp gaze picked out Gunnhild and Halfdan. The smile that he threw their way was loaded with meaning and questions, and Halfdan knew immediately that it had not been meant for him. He turned to find Gunnhild rolling her eyes.

They waited until Harðráði and his men had marched on out of sight, the latter with a lingering look at Gunnhild, and then the young jarl turned a grin on her.

'He turns into a moon-struck boy around you.'

'He is a fool.' She sighed. 'I keep finding him outside my door. I had a poem shoved under it once, Halfdan. A *poem*! There was no name on it, but I had no trouble working out who it was from. He has his eyes on me and he will not leave me alone.'

Halfdan shrugged. 'There are worse men you could find yourself with. Harðráði is a good man, and one day he will be king of Norway. Of that I'm sure.'

Again there was something strained, uncertain and hidden about Gunnhild, and it took her a moment to reply. 'He will be more than that. Much more. But I... I cannot be his. We need to leave this place, Halfdan, before he imprisons me as his personal prize.'

Halfdan gave a light laugh, but it slid away as he realised she was serious. 'The Norns have woven us a path together, Gunnhild – you and the Wolves. All the way from Hedeby, and I cannot believe they will take you from us, at least until our quest is over and we have returned home and revenged ourselves upon Hjalmvigi. If the Norns have woven you with us, Harðráði *cannot* take you away. Be happy. You are safe from him, and we are one day from success. We are on the cusp, Gunnhild.'

The look she gave him was less than encouraging, and she turned her back. 'I must find the empress. She will have more questions for me, to which she will like none of my answers.'

273

Without a further word, and radiating nervous tension, Gunnhild stalked away along the path, soft boots crunching on the fine gravel. Halfdan watched her go, trying to unpick what was going on with her. It wasn't just Harðráði's pursuit that was troubling her. It was more than that. It was as though she struggled with something inside, something personal, and yet she would not open up to Halfdan with whatever it was, which surprised him after everything they had been through.

With a sigh, he turned and made his own way back through the palace grounds towards the barracks. As he crossed the colonnaded atrium of one of the innumerable churches and passed through a delicately arched marble gateway, he was surprised to discern, amid the murmur of the city and the quiet melody of the palace gardens, the sound of an altercation. He paused for a moment, listening, for it was dangerous in this place to charge headlong into anything before you knew what it could be. There were no screams and no sounds of metal on metal, and so whatever it was, it was not being fought to the death. A little concentration, and he could hear shouts of anger and insults and threats. All in Greek, but several voices carried the telltale inflection of the northerner. There were Varangians involved, but other words were thrown about in the accent of locals.

He tensed as a powerful voice told someone to 'suck Odin's balls' in Greek.

Bjorn. Even if he hadn't recognised the voice, nobody else in the city would say that.

He was running in an instant, heading for that noise. As he passed a small collection of gardeners at work he grabbed a rake and, as he ran, snapped it over his knee and cast away the metal end. Serious repercussions awaited anyone drawing a weapon in the palace without good cause, but a stout cudgel was acceptable.

He rounded a corner, brandishing his club, and paused, taking it all in.

A unit of the excubitores, resplendent in their colourful and ancient uniform, was busy pounding fists, feet and elbows into a small collection of Varangians. More than a dozen Northmen fought back hard, and as well as his friends, Halfdan could see Valgarðr struggling in a martial embrace with a clean-shaven, oily-haired Greek soldier.

Two figures already lay unconscious — or at least, Halfdan *hoped* they were unconscious — but fortunately they both wore the uniform of the excubitores.

Leif was in trouble. He was clutching the side where he'd broken his ribs. They had partly healed now, enough for him to take certain exercise, but clearly he'd suffered further injury. It hadn't stopped him fighting back, though, for even as Halfdan watched, the little Rus stamped so hard on a man's foot that he had to have broken it. The Greek soldier lurched back, howling, lifting his foot and clutching it until Ketil, sensing an opportunity, smacked him hard in the side, unbalancing him on his one leg so that he fell.

Halfdan ploughed into the fracas, snarling, and whacked a soldier around the back of the head with his length of rake-pole. The man gave a strange 'urk' and plunged forward to the ground, clutching his skull as he shuffled this way and that on all fours. The Varangians were outnumbered two to one, but they had already almost evened out the numbers. It was the benefit of a northern origin. These soldiers had trained from early on to fight as an army, but most of the Varangians had fought every day of their life one way or another before joining up, and their natural predisposition to a good punch-up showed.

Someone managed to land a powerful blow to the back of Halfdan's neck, which made him lurch to the side, and hurt a lot. As he turned, club in hand, the attacker was already falling away, Bjorn rubbing his knuckles and cursing. The big man grinned at Halfdan and opened his mouth to say something, only to be hit in the side by a big Greek and barrelled away through the press.

Halfdan turned to find another man and was suddenly knocked down as an excubitor hit him at a run, the two men falling to the gravel, the rough surface painful on the back of Halfdan's scalp. The soldier managed to get both hands around Halfdan's neck and lifted. He couldn't strangle him, of course, for that would be classed as murder, but he would happily smack the Varangian's head against the ground and take his chances with whatever injury that caused.

Halfdan fought back, managed to get his palm under the man's chin and pushed up, hard. The soldier grunted at the pain as his head was forced back. As the two men struggled in a heap, Halfdan's hand came out and he delivered the best blow he could manage from the side with his stick. It was not a strong attack, but the man grunted in pain. Again and again, Halfdan tried to smack the man in the side, as he continued to force the man's head up. He could feel the grip on his neck changing. The man no longer stood much of a chance of smacking Halfdan's head against the gravel, and was actually going for a stranglehold now. Halfdan heaved in a breath and fought against the pain, feeling his lungs struggling to pull in air. He continued to push with one hand, and cast aside the stick now, pounding with his fist urgently, trying to push the man off.

He felt the man pressing back down with his head, trying to push Halfdan's hand down again, and with a grin, Halfdan made his move. At the same moment, he let go of his grip on the man's chin and pushed his head and shoulders to one side as hard as he could. He didn't move far because of the man's grip, but it was enough. The soldier had been pushing his head down and suddenly he was deprived of resistance. His skull ploughed down and met the gravel path a finger-width from Halfdan's own skull. There was an unpleasant sound, and the grip on Halfdan's neck loosened.

The young jarl struggled out from under the soldier, rolling him away and looking at him. The man's forehead was a mess, peppered with pieces of sharp gravel amid a bloody graze. *Still breathing, thank Odin.*

'What is the meaning of this?' bellowed a furious voice.

The fighting broke up slowly, men pulling back from one another, northerners and Greeks alike, the sounds of belligerence giving way to groans and hisses of pain from both sides. As Halfdan rose and staggered over to stand between Valgarðr and Bjorn, the two forces pulled apart and glared at one another. A senior officer in the uniform of the excubitores was watching them from another path, his hands on his hips, his face almost puce with anger.

'Just a tussle,' Valgarðr replied with narrowed eyes.

'Disagreement,' added one of the wounded Greeks, clutching his arm.

The officer threw out an angry finger at his men. 'Get to barracks now. You are all on charges. I'll see you shortly, *before* the physician does.' As the soldiers began to file away, throwing final glares at the Varangians, the officer turned, hand going back to his hip, and looked at them, his eyes finally picking out Valgarðr in the crowd.

'I will get to the bottom of this,' the officer snapped. 'Be certain that your commander will hear about it.'

'Fucking right, he will,' the old Varangian replied with a defiant glare.

For a moment it looked as though the officer was going to argue further, but his authority did not extend to the Guard, and he knew it. With a squint-eyed look of disapproval, the man marched off, leaving the small gaggle of northerners helping one another up and probing bruises and wounds.

'What was that about?' Halfdan said quietly.

'A poorly chosen accusation from our friends over there,' Valgarðr replied, stretching an aching shoulder.

'Of what?'

'You've not heard, then?'

Halfdan shook his head. 'What?'

'There is no gold.'

No gold? Halfdan felt his senses reel at the news. He had been relying on a small share of that prize to put everything right. He stared at Valgarðr.

'What?'

The old Varangian steadied himself again. 'We managed to clear the blockage this morning, and found the cistern under Constantine's house. All it contains is water.'

Halfdan frowned. 'No. The blind uncle wasn't lying. I watched him. He would have sold his family and given up an arm not to be burned in that final moment. It wasn't a lie. When he admitted he stole it, he was telling the truth, I would wager my life on it. He truly thought it was in his cistern.'

Valgarðr nodded, and gestured to Leif. 'Tell your jarl what you told me.' The old man turned back to Halfdan and explained. 'Leif here was one of the first men in when the stones were lifted.'

The small Rus, still gripping his side and wincing, nodded. 'We went in, Halfdan, and the cistern was empty. But it *had* been used recently for more than water.'

'Explain.'

Leif licked his lips. 'It's about water displacement, Halfdan. That cistern is on a minor water pipe, probably long since part-blocked. When we went in, the water level was only waist-deep, and you could see the line much higher up where the water usually reached. There was a small torrent of water coming in from the pipe, refilling the cistern. So you see, if the water level has dropped so far, something big has been removed from the cistern.'

Halfdan tried to make sense of the words. He thought he had an idea what the man meant. 'Like when you lift an eel out of a bucket and the water drops?'

'Exactly. Water displacement. It is my personal belief that the gold has been in that cistern until very recently, but has been removed.'

'When and how, though?'

The Rus chewed his lip. 'As well as the steps into the cistern we cleared, there was an access point near the water source. I presume it's there for maintenance. It's on the far side of the cistern, and leads up to a street behind where we were clearing the house rubble. It sounds brazen, but I tell you, the water level has changed in just the last few days. That access has been opened recently. I think someone, or likely *several* someones, were at work in the street, shifting the gold out of the cistern even while we were digging through the rubble to get to it. Some clever bastard beat us to it and took all the gold before we got there.'

Halfdan stared. That really *was* brazen. 'But it can't have been the blind man's work,' he said. 'He is away in his monastery now, and with no power. I think he is watched still by the empress's spies, just in case. Who else knew about the gold?'

Valgarðr shrugged. 'This is Constantinople. I think you know by now that rumour and gossip flow through the city faster than the water supply. On Harðráði's orders I informed the empress. Within a day it will have been common knowledge throughout the palace. All the garrison troops will know, all the nobles, and probably everyone down to the lowest fisherman. And we made sure to guard the site of the house while we worked, but we had no idea there would be a second access from a street nearby. We did what we could, but *anyone* could have done it.'

Halfdan ground his teeth. *One day*, he'd told Gunnhild, but now all his plans were coming undone. She was right, of course, about needing to get away. She was always right.

'What does that mean for the Guard?'

'We look bad,' Valgarðr replied. 'We will be seen to have failed in our duty. Already word is spreading, as you saw by this little fight. Already the excubitores accuse us of having stolen the empress's gold. We didn't, of course, but its recovery was our responsibility. This will be turned against us in general, and against Harðráði in particular. The new emperor, his lover and her brother already hate Harðráði. We are heading towards more arrests, I fear, and this time we cannot reasonably deny it. Whatever our innocence, we've clearly failed. Monomachos and Skleros will use that to destroy Harðráði and remove all his supporters from the Guard. We'll be working under a new Ari soon, mark my words.'

Halfdan sagged. He'd identified his men's problems, and he'd found a way to overcome them using a share of the gold. Now there was no gold, and so the problems were back, unsolvable. He didn't have sufficient crew to take the *Sea Wolf* away, and could not afford to take anyone on. Worse still, just as Gunnhild had warned, he was bound to Harðráði, and would fall with him. The chances of the new emperor letting them go with the gold still missing were minuscule.

If anything, things had just got worse.

Chapter 21

'I have better things to do with my time than to try and plug your sinking ship with a handful of caulk, Empress of Byzantium,' Gunnhild said, citing the nickname of her former damned husband with no small irony.

'You forget your place, Gunnhild,' Zoe Porphyrogenita replied in dangerous tones.

'No, I do not. You sought me out as an advisor because I would talk to you straight and deliver the wisdom of Freyja, and not fawn around you and tell you what you want to hear like most of your court. Like a certain jarl I know, you claim to rely upon my counsel, and yet when I give it, you blindly ignore it and walk self-destructive paths regardless. I am becoming sick and tired of this whole place that saps my connection to the goddess. I do not believe that even Odin's ravens can see through the fog of self-centred complication that this city creates. I would depart, but I will not leave my friends to their fate here. You do not need my advice, Empress, since you will not follow it anyway.'

The empress glared at her for a short while, then sat back and folded her arms. 'I am resigned to certain things, Gunnhild, but I will make the best of what I have been given.'

'What you gave *yourself*,' corrected Gunnhild, rather more harshly than she'd intended, but even as the empress's eyes narrowed, she continued. 'Without a care for you, your new emperor, whose coronation was far too lavish for his position, brings his mistress into the court? We all know he is building her a palace in the city with money from your treasury. The

Sklerina, who is manipulative and dangerous, is now being honoured as an empress in her own right while you are quietly brushed aside and ignored. And through her, Romanos Skleros now has his hooks into the governance of your lands. He and Monomachos conspire together and rule almost as a pair, while once again you have less authority within your own empire than any clerk. And where you could still have limited the damage, instead you signed a document *permitting* him to do all of this? You Byzantines and your contracts. Now he is quite legitimately allowed to put his mistress above you, as long as you remain empress. You plummet down the slippery slope, Zoe Porphyrogenita, and disaster and obscurity await, for both you and your empire. You have signed away all your power. How can you possibly intend to make the best of this?'

Zoe Porphyrogenita had gradually paled through Gunnhild's tirade, and yet when it finished, she simply sat there, fingertips white as she gripped the arms of her throne, and finally her face fell into a delicate melancholy, and she nodded.

'I made a mistake. I did not listen to you, and I walked into this open-eyed. I admit that. I have put myself in a difficult position. Unfortunately, the Church only allows three marriages and this is my third. I cannot marry again, so I must do with this what I can. Constantine does not come to my bed as I had hoped, Gunnhild, and I am too old to conceive an heir anyway. The issue of import, then, is the future of the empire. No child of Constantine and the Sklerina can take the throne, and so I shall secure a strong future the way my last husband secured a weak one. He had me agree to adopt his nephew Michael. I shall have Constantine agree to adopt a favoured heir. Someone who will be good for the empire, in the hope that we still have one when he is finished with it. I have a number of candidates in mind, and I would seek your advice upon them.'

Gunnhild felt the acidic retorts lining up, yet she held her tongue. Just for once, it seemed as though the empress had thought through her problem and had come up with a sensible solution. The Byzantines were more bound by their contracts and laws than they ever could be by ropes or chains, and so if the empress could secure a succession, it *would* happen, no matter how much Constantine Monomachos tried to avoid it.

'Promise me something, Zoe of Byzantium.'

'What, Gunnhild?'

'Promise me you will select them for their manner, their mind and their heart, and not for how pretty they are.'

The empress gave a sad chuckle. 'That is my sole intention, and that is why I need you so closely involved in my decision-making. I give you my word that your advice in this will be heeded.'

A distant commotion two rooms away arose in the silence as the empress's words fell away. Both women listened intently, and the three attendants who had been hovering at the periphery hurried towards the door. A muffled but clearly angry male voice demanding access. Argument. A crack, and a whimper. The thud of doors opening and footsteps into the antechamber beyond the nearest door.

'Where are my Varangians when I need them?' the empress hissed, gesturing for the three servants to gather protectively in front of her.

'I think you will find that that *is* your Varangians,' Gunnhild said.

The Guard had discreet positions around the Gynaikonitis, where they would not interfere with the empress's complex, but where they could be sure that no one approached the imperial rooms without consent. This could only be the Guard approaching, especially from the heavy booted footsteps. One man alone, but a military one. Moreover, though they had not quite been able to hear the speakers during the altercation, Gunnhild had recognised the manner of the argument well enough.

It came as no surprise when a eunuch burst into the room, throwing open the doors and announcing the commander of the Guard in a virtual torrent of hurried syllables. He'd barely managed to get his words out before Harðráði was in behind him, all purpose, face grave.

'My dear Sigurdsson,' the empress said calmly, arranging herself a little more regally, 'this is an unseemly way to approach your empress. I assure you that had you gone through the appropriate channels, you would have been given an audience immediately.'

Harðráði came to a halt and his gaze slid to Gunnhild. For once, he did not smile, but he did nod his deference to her before turning back to the empress and folding his arms.

'Your Imperial Majesty.'

'My husband continues to plague you, I presume?'

'The emperor seeks little less than my head on a platter, Empress, but that is a matter I intend to pursue directly with him in due course.'

Gunnhild winced. The man's tone suggested violence. She had images of Harðráði and Monomachos involved in holmgang, a legal dispute taken to its ultimate end in a ring, with axes bared and only one survivor. She would not put it past Harðráði to try such a thing, and by northern law, rank was no protection from such a duel, though she could hardly imagine Constantine Monomachos, that weak, avaricious cowpat of a man, accepting such a thing, since the Varangian would carve him to pieces in moments. Still, the commander's blood was up. It was a good job she had taken that pouch of powders from him. There was no telling what the bear might have done with no restrictions upon his will.

'I can only wish you luck with my husband, Sigurdsson,' the empress sighed. 'Had I any influence, I would try to help you, but I am fighting to maintain a hand on the tiller of empire myself. Ask of me anything else, and I will see what I can do.'

The commander nodded, his expression still flat.

'Good, Majesty, because I had no intention of seeking your intervention. I understand your position, for all it grieves me that you have brought yourself to this place. I came to Miklagarðr – to Constantinople – to serve you, as you know. I gave you my oath before any emperor, and yet you continue to provide obstacles for me to overcome merely to stand by your side.'

The empress's face darkened for a moment, but her eyes slid to Gunnhild, who had said something very similar only just before. She sighed. 'I am weak sometimes, Sigurdsson. What can I do for you, then?'

Harðráði straightened, his eyes dipping to one side for only a moment, then back to meet the empress's gaze directly. 'I ask only one thing of you, Empress of Byzantium. Give me Gunnhild.'

The empress sat still and silent for a moment, surprised.

Gunnhild chided herself. She should have seen something like this coming. The fool had been nagging at her for months now, had been hovering outside her door. He had wheedled and pleaded, demanded and asked. She had denied him at every turn, and yet every reason she gave him, thrown into the air, he had shot down with arrows of logic. He was relentless, and he wanted her. And the worst thing was that the longer it went on, the more she was having trouble fighting it. Perhaps it was that the Norns had clearly woven a path for them, and she railed against it, but recently, while her lips spat denials, her heart had fluttered with possibilities. It was becoming difficult. Still, she rallied, and stepped forward, a finger jerking up at the commander.

'Am I some chattel to be bought and sold, Harald Sigurdsson?'

'I mean no insult,' the commander said, turning.

'Then why direct your demand to the empress and not me?'

Harðráði sighed. 'Because directing them at you is like trying to break down a wall with a cabbage. Because, Gunnhild of Hedeby, I can see into your heart better than you think I can, and I fear it is your sense of duty to others that is interfering. Thus I would have the empress relieve you of that duty.'

The empress interrupted now, leaning forward. 'Let me understand this correctly. You have spent months pursuing Gunnhild, and she turns you down repeatedly. And now, because she will not give herself to you, you ask *me* to give her to you?'

'It is not as foolish as it sounds, Empress. I know Gunnhild's heart. I am a good judge of character, and you know that. That is why from the beginning I saw something in you above your husband, and why I bent my knee to you and not to him. Gunnhild argues to hide what she really wants. Her angry words are armour, nothing more.'

Gunnhild felt the anger rising, and yet alongside it, twining like the serpents of Loki, she felt the truth of that, the desire, and the future that awaited.

At the prow of a dragon ship with Harðráði, the spray of the whale road in their faces.

He turned to her then, and the bleakness had gone from his expression, the anger and defensiveness all fled, leaving only the bright and wonderful face of Harald Sigurdsson, displaced Prince of Norway. She felt the pulling of the threads of fate. She could see him, a king of three kingdoms, unmatched in the North, with her by his side, every bit an empress herself.

'Tell me it isn't so,' Harðráði said plainly. 'Look me in the eye and tell me in all honesty that there is no desire in your heart.'

She paused. She felt her blood pounding. She could be lost in his ice-blue eyes alone. The Norns had reasons for all they did. Harðráði needed her for that great future. She needed him to leave this strange half-world where she was neither true völva nor shieldmaiden. Their destiny was paired. That had been at the root of everything that had brought her here. Perhaps it was even what had brought Halfdan to her door more than a year ago...

Halfdan.

The image of the young jarl rose in her mind. She had seen something in him at the very beginning. He'd been so young and innocent, yet driven by blood feud and violence. She had seen how much more he could be, and over their time together in Kiev and Georgia, she had seen it beginning. He was no longer a boy, but a warrior, fierce and proud. A wolf of Odin. But he was still so naïve in so many ways. He still needed her, she knew, for without her he would falter. He would fall. He was already doing so. She had put all her energy into the lost cause of the empress and avoiding Harðráði, while Halfdan had slid from being a rich jarl of a solid crew to being a poor soldier, trapped in a city that would sooner or later kill him.

How could she let that happen?

'Gunnhild?' the empress urged her, her brow creased. Gunnhild realised that she had been standing silent in the space of an expected reply.

She took a deep breath. 'We could have a future, Sigurdsson. And I would truly be a better match than any Rus princess. But I still have work to do. There are people here who need me more than you.'

Harðráði's lip curled. 'And not the empress? She is not the duty that binds you?' He frowned in realisation. 'You mean Halfdan and his friends. Gunnhild, we can take them with us. I like Halfdan. I respect him. He is a good man, and a great jarl in the making. I will *need* good men like him when I have Norway once more in my grasp. I can make him rich and powerful. You need not choose between us.'

'It is not that simple, Sigurdsson,' she said, from between gritted teeth. 'The bear that is you and the wolf that is Halfdan cannot walk the same path, and I have seen as much, plain as day.'

'And where does the boar of Freyja go, then?' the man asked, with more insight than Gunnhild had expected.

'Where I am needed most.'

Harðráði turned back to the empress. 'She is troubled, I know. But I also know she belongs with me, and while she fights it, so does she. Release her to me, Empress. I will not take her against her will, but be certain, Majesty, that whatever she says, her will is that she go with me.'

The empress frowned, then looked across at Gunnhild, who suddenly felt the weight of empires pressing down upon her. Much rested upon her reaction. She tensed, apologised to Freyja and to all the gods in the privacy of her head, and gave the empress the slightest shake.

Zoe Porphyrogenita straightened in her seat. 'Whether it is Gunnhild's wish or not, Harald Sigurdsson, I will not allow you to take her. I brought Gunnhild into my circle because of her wisdom and her uncanny sight. She has been the best advisor to the imperial throne in generations, and I am at a dangerous, even *critical*, juncture in my reign. I need her now more than ever. When the world changes and the succession is secure, perhaps ask me again, then.'

Harðráði threw the empress a new look now, and even Gunnhild was startled at the anger in it.

'I have been your man since the start, Zoe Porphyrogenita, Empress of Byzantium. When soldiers and politicians and every manner of man has worked to usurp and ruin you, I have stood by your side. At risk of my own life I backed you when few others would. And now, even though you can see the truth of what I say – for if *I* can recognise it in Gunnhild's eyes, then a woman of emotion such as yourself would have to be *blind* not to see it – still you deny me? I ask for one thing, and you refuse me after I have given my all?'

Again, the empress looked to Gunnhild. Again, Gunnhild fought the urge to scream, apologised to the Norns, and shook her head.

'You cannot have her, Harðráði. Ask for another boon.'

'There *is* no other boon,' the commander spat in fury. 'I am betrayed by she who I have given my life and soul to protect. Well, Zoe of Macedonia, you are not the only power in Constantinople. Perhaps others can be reasoned with.'

With a curt nod of the head in the direction of deference, Harðráði turned on his heel, risking one last momentary glance at Gunnhild, and marched out of the room. Worried-looking eunuchs closed the door behind him, masking those forceful bootsteps as they marched away. In the silence that descended, the empress held Gunnhild in her gaze. Finally, she leaned back in her chair.

'He was right. You are fighting against your own wishes, Gunnhild.'

'It is more than that. There is more. I cannot explain.'

'You do not have to, Gunnhild. I am a woman who is enslaved to my passions, and that repeatedly leads me into trouble. That you have the strength to fight it comes as no surprise to me. But I have known Harald Sigurdsson a long time now. This will not stop him. This is not the end.'

Gunnhild nodded. 'He goes to try once more. Other powers?' She felt her blood chill. 'Surely he cannot mean…?'

The empress nodded. 'There is only one man in Constantinople who can go above my head. Sigurdsson goes to the emperor to ask for you now.'

'But the emperor is his enemy.'

'Men,' the empress sighed. 'Sometimes the wisest of them is a fool compared with even the most irrational woman.'

'Where is the emperor?' Gunnhild asked urgently.

'Now he will be in the Magnaura, greeting foreign envoys with all the pomp and gold he can muster, draining what is left of the treasury after building the gilded cage for his mistress.'

'Are there other ways into the Magnaura? Other than the main door?'

The empress nodded and gestured to a eunuch. 'Alexander? Take Gunnhild to the balcony we sometimes use. Make sure she is not seen or accosted on the way, but grant her her privacy.'

Gunnhild was moving then, on the heels of the man sent to escort her. What was Harðráði thinking? No good could come from him confronting the emperor. He would earn himself only more trouble. All the way across gardens, along corridors and up staircases, she tried to reason any way she could change this, other than simply agreeing to go with Harðráði, but everything she dreamed up would end in disaster. And she could not go with him. No matter how much she wanted that spray in her face alongside the golden prince of the North, to do so would almost certainly mean the fall of Halfdan, for he was still more cub than grown wolf. How could she risk that?

She climbed the last stair no closer to a solution than she had been when she left the empress, and the eunuch opened a small door with a click, admitting her to a long, narrow, colonnaded balcony. She could hear Monomachos now, all unctuous and oily as he fawned around some ambassador. She crept to the balcony even as the eunuch left, closing the door and leaving her alone. She was very high up above a large room that was appointed as well as any of the other throne rooms and audience chambers in this place.

She was just in time, for a heartbeat later, the great door slammed open and Harðráði marched in, unannounced, one man as imposing as any army.

'What is the meaning of this interruption?' barked the emperor, his voice cracking with strain.

'I need an urgent audience, Majesty,' Harðráði said.

'This is unheard of. *Unseemly.* I am greeting the...'

'It will not take long,' Harðráði said. 'The empress holds tight to her seeress, the woman Maria Gunilla, also known as Gunnhild of Hedeby.'

'What?' The emperor seemed confused. Varangians chosen for their loyalty to Monomachos began to move from the corners of the room, converging on Harðráði.

'The empress's woman,' the commander repeated. 'All I want is her delivered into my care. You can override Zoe, for you do it daily, and I find myself for the first time at odds with her. I offer you this: give me Gunnhild, and I give you my oath. Over the empress. To you and you alone.'

No, Gunnhild whispered from her silent balcony. *Not that.*

The emperor snorted. 'You believe for a moment that I would ever trust you, Sigurdsson? You think you can seek a boon from me? You are poison. You should have been flayed and buried a year since, and I would do it myself, but for the fact that there are those in my court who think you might still find my gold. If it does not turn up soon, I might still have you peeled to see what you know.'

Harðráði snarled. 'One woman for my oath. It is little to ask.'

'It is too much,' Monomachos sighed. 'I tire of your presence. You bore me, Sigurdsson. Go away.'

'You would deny me?'

'I *do* deny you.'

Harðráði was trembling now. Gunnhild watched in horror as the commander pulled out his axe, but then he also pulled out the baton of office, and cast both to the floor before him. Every set of eyes in the room, including the foreign dignitaries, watched the display.

'Then I resign my commission here. I have long since passed the period of required service, and have maintained my position since then by my own wishes. I step down as Akolouthos of the Guard and give you my leave. I request that you release my ships in the harbour and give orders for the chain to be withdrawn so that we can sail in the morning.'

The emperor stared at the pile on the floor, and then a horrible, wicked smile passed across his face. 'While I am more than happy to accept your demotion, Sigurdsson, I do not release you from service. There is still the matter of more than five thousand pounds of missing gold for which I continue to hold you responsible. Until that gold is back in my vaults, you will not leave the city. Nor will you take with you any man from my Guard. Your ships are hereby impounded until I am satisfied that my gold is safe.'

'You play a dangerous game, Monomachos.'

'And *you* forget your manners. *No one* speaks thus to an emperor. Begone from my sight and be grateful that you are not being dragged away in chains. If my gold does not turn up, or it turns up in your purse, I shall be merciless. Now get out of my palace, Sigurdsson.'

Gunnhild watched the commander, still trembling with rage, facing the emperor. If Harðráði defied the emperor, only bloodshed would end this.

The moment that she realised something was wrong, it was too late. She had been so focused on the exchange below that she'd missed the barely audible click as the door behind her opened, and the light pad of soft slippers on marble. A rope was thrown over her with immense skill, already formed into a noose that was pulled tight even as it reached her chest. Her arms were yanked in to her sides viciously, the ropes pinching and burning the flesh at her elbows. She struggled instantly, but with little effect. A second rope was thrown over her and this one pulled tight further down to jam her wrists in against her hips. With the cunning of Loki and the wisdom of Freyja even in the split second of disaster, she lifted her left hand at the last moment and the cord tightened beneath it instead. Before anyone could see, she breathed out and forced the hand partially into the loop, giving the appearance that she was bound. What use it might be she had yet to say, but it had been instinct, and instinct was born of the goddess.

'Who is this?' she spat at the unseen assailants behind her in the dark.

As shadowy figures moved to secure her further, the ropes were hauled upon and she found herself spun round. The last thing she saw as the bag was pulled down over her head was the malicious smile of Maria Sklerina.

Part Five

ᚹᛟᛚᚡᛖᛋ ᛟᚠ ᛟᛞᛁᚾ

Odin's Wolves

Chapter 22

'Gather your things.'

The five men looked up in surprise at the door where Harðráði stood, his face unusually grave, eyes flicking this way and that. Even as they turned to him, they saw three of the commander's older veterans standing in the corridor with their hands on the hilts of their weapons, looking around, ready for trouble.

'What's happened?' Halfdan asked, laying aside his whetstone and slipping his glorious blade back into its sheath.

'The time has come to leave the city,' the commander said. 'The emperor will be sending men to arrest me at any time, and they will have orders to take any man known to be loyal to me, which will most certainly include you. No command was given by the time I left the Magnaura, but I'd bet my right arm that the arrest order followed soon after. We have minutes at best. Leave anything you can't carry.'

'*How* do you intend to leave?' Ketil asked, rising from his seat at the table. 'We were just discussing this ourselves. Every gate is held by the emperor's men, and the chain is strung across the river. Constantinople is sealed against us.'

Halfdan nodded. 'It's been keeping me up at night, trying to plan how to get out.'

'Everything is in hand,' Harðráði said quietly. 'I set things in motion before I went to the empress and the emperor. I have two ships in the harbour being readied – my own vessel, the *Golden Eagle*, and your *Sea Wolf*. Valgarðr is in charge of preparations, and he's thorough.'

'And my crew?'

'They should already be on the way there if the message has reached them.'

'But the chain?' Ulfr put in. 'I know my ships and that thing is well designed. Even if it doesn't sink a ship, it can tangle it and keep it in place while the artillery on the walls do the job.'

'All is in order,' Harðráði said. 'Trust me. But we need to move if we are to get out. The quicker we shift, the more likely we are to slip away, and the longer we leave it, the more the city will be on the alert.'

'We can move fast,' Leif said. 'Most of our gear is already packed. We've been half expecting something like this for a while. Halfdan has us ready.'

'Good,' Harðráði nodded. 'I have a couple of things to attend to before we head for the harbour.'

Halfdan squared his shoulders. 'I cannot run yet.'

'What?' Ketil leapt around the table. 'Halfdan, we have to move while we can.'

'Not without Gunnhild.'

Now, Harðráði's troubled face broke into a smile for the first time. 'Oh, I have no intention of leaving without her. She is one of the couple of things I still have to attend to.'

'How many men do you have with you?'

The commander shrugged. 'These three. Nearly everyone is already in the harbour making ready. Numbers don't matter, my young friend. We're in a palace swamped with the emperor's men, so if this comes down to a fight, we're in trouble anyway.'

'Gunnhild will be in the Gynaikonitis with the empress,' Halfdan said.

Harðráði nodded. 'I saw her there less than an hour ago. The empress won't let her go willingly, though. For the first time in this city, I'm going to have to defy Zoe. That sits badly with me, for I took my oath to her, but some things are more important.'

'Come on, then.'

Leif, still at the window, held up a hand. 'Looks like the fight's coming to us.'

The nine men gathered out in the corridor, around the door that led out into the wide garden. Men from three army units, including Varangians loyal to Monomachos, were pouring out of three different doors and converging. They had their weapons bared, which was unusual enough here to clarify the dire situation.

'We can't fight that lot,' Ketil breathed.

'The back way,' Halfdan said.

Harðráði frowned. 'There's no access from the barracks to the women's palace other than across here.'

'If Halfdan says there is, then there is,' Ketil replied.

'Follow me.' With that, Halfdan hefted his bag and ran deeper into the barrack complex, away from the main door. Behind him, one of Harðráði's men closed and locked the door, blocking the way for the troops converging on them.

As they ran, the commander pushed past the others to reach Halfdan. 'That door won't hold them for long. You realise you're trapping us in the barracks?'

'No. I've done some exploring in my time here. Just follow me.'

Around corners and along functional brick corridors they ran, Halfdan leading the way. Like most of the structures in the Great Palace, the huge barracks of the excubitores, which housed not only that unit but all the palace garrison, was self-contained and compartmentalised, kept separate from the rest of the palace. There had, long ago, been a direct access to the palace walls from the structure, but that had long since been removed by some paranoid emperor who liked to be sure of how his guards could come and go. Indeed, to the casual observer there *was* no back door to the barracks. When he'd first arrived, Halfdan would have agreed, but the past few months had changed that.

He'd spent weeks before the riots wandering the corridors and looking for groups of the *Sea Wolf* crew Ari might have locked away somewhere, and more recently several sleepless nights wandering them again, frustrated as he worked through their problem, trying to find a solution, and failed dismally.

The nine men reached an unassuming door, and Halfdan pulled it open to reveal a staircase leading down into the dark.

That was how he'd come across this place. The Great Palace was centuries old. The building they used today was largely constructed on top of great vaulted corridors far older than their superstructures. Most of these corridors were largely the domain of the nameless and ignored palace servants, and miles of corridors were clearly never even used. Such was the case with this section. The door had been forgotten about for so long that it had taken some work to drag it open. The lamps in their niches on the wall had been filled some time ago, but the oil was still burnable, and so Halfdan had spent the last three nights wandering these corridors, partially simply for somewhere to think, but also with the faint and fantastical hope that he might bump into a pile of some five thousand pounds of stolen gold.

He'd found neither gold, nor a solution.

But he had found this.

As they pounded along the dusty corridor in the near-absolute darkness, led only by Halfdan's vague familiarity with the place, he could hear the surprise of the others as they looked about while they ran. From each side, row after row of dark arches marked similar passages leading off into this subterranean world. Once or twice as they ran, the dim glow of evening light emerged from their left, but Halfdan ignored it and ran on. His sense of direction was good, and he knew it. Straight on led them towards the slope down to the women's palace, and he knew where to make for.

He could feel the sense of anticipation building as they climbed a set of stairs now, and dim golden light could be seen as a faint rectangle around the edges of a door. Reaching it, Halfdan motioned for everyone to stop, and waited for silence. Moments later, he lifted a latch and opened the door a fraction, with the creak of ancient and unused hinges.

He looked about. A plain servants' corridor, lit by evenly spaced lamps. This was as far as he'd come before, for he was only concerned with wandering empty corridors, but he'd been surprised as he looked out to recognise the place he'd emerged. He'd passed through here on occasion going about his duty, and he knew it to be but a short hop from the Gynaikonitis.

Pausing only long enough to confirm by both sight and sound that the area was devoid of life, Halfdan beckoned to the others and slipped from the door. For the first time since the day of the riots, he slid his sword free of its sheath and bared it openly in the palace grounds, and shrugged to adjust the hang of the shield on his back. Behind him, as they emerged, the others similarly gripped their shields and brandished axes and swords. Along the colonnaded hall, Halfdan made for the exit to the peristyle garden of the lions with its lifelike statues, and emerged into the evening light with a touch of relief.

Relief that was short-lived.

The night was quiet and balmy, a world that had spent the day seared by the sun and was sighing its ease as the evening drew in, but above the sounds of the palace gardens near dusk, they could hear the distant shouts of alarm and anger as the various guard units searched the massive complex for them. The Great Palace was enormous, and it would take time to locate them, but some places would surely be searched first, and the women's palace was one of them. They had to move quickly. Worse thoughts came with the realisation that every step they took towards Gunnhild took them further from the ships.

With the others at his back, Halfdan scurried across the gardens. Once again, Harðráði was leading the way with him, a sense of urgency about the man more profound than Halfdan had seen before. It seemed that Gunnhild was of as much importance to the commander as she was to her friends. As they rounded another corner, Halfdan instinctively ducked back, grabbing Harðráði and pulling him in as the others stumbled to a halt. Without a question, the commander joined him in leaning slowly against the corner once more and peering around it.

Two guards stood at the main entrance to the Gynaikonitis, both wearing the bright uniform of the excubitores. Halfdan turned and noted with satisfaction that Ketil, in the rush to leave their barracks, had not forgotten his bow. The weapon was slung across his shoulder and his quiver bounced along at his side. Halfdan tried to mime 'guard' at him and then held up two fingers and pointed at the bow on the man's shoulder. Ketil nodded and removed the weapon, testing the string and then unfastening the cover of his quiver. With just a whisper of sound, he removed two arrows, placing one in position in the bow, the other held just by the end near the flights between the fingers of his left hand. The giant Icelander moved forward to where the two commanders were and looked past them round the corner. He frowned, nodded, and then motioned for them to stand back.

Ketil took three slow, measured breaths, and then stepped out from the corner, drawing back the string as he did so.

Halfdan was impressed, even knowing Ketil as he did, but Harðráði stared wide-eyed as the Icelander took his shots. Without the time to aim, the first one still thudded directly into a guard's windpipe, throwing him back against the wall, dead even as he stared in horror at his killer. The second guard started with shock, his sword coming up, turning this way and that to try and locate the archer. His mouth formed an O as he tried to call an alarm, but his dark maw suddenly sprouted flights as the second arrow slammed through his head.

Halfdan had been watching the guards, and had not seen either shot taken, but the sheer rapidity of the paired shots had to be the gift of Odin, let alone their impressive accuracy. The second guard, dying with the arrow transfixing his head, hit the ground only moments after the first, and now the nine men were running again.

'If you ever tire of your jarl,' Harðráði breathed to Ketil as they ran, 'I will pay you well.'

'They must have been expecting us here,' Leif interrupted, pointing at the pair of dead guards. In moments, they were through the door and accosting a startled servant.

'Where is Gunnhild?' Halfdan demanded.

The servant stared at him blankly.

'Maria Gunilla,' Harðráði explained, using her Byzantine name.

The servant continued to frown. Finally, she shrugged. 'She has not come back.'

'From where?'

Before the servant could answer, the door ahead opened and Anna came scurrying out into the vestibule. Any other day it might have made Halfdan smile how she ignored the two powerful commanders and ran straight into the arms of the small erudite Rus, Leif, but his attention now was focused only on one thing.

'Where is Gunnhild,' he demanded again, this time of Anna.

The maid's eyes were puffy and red from recent tears. 'She has gone.'

'Gone? Gone where?' snapped Harðráði.

'She followed you to the emperor,' Anna said, then turned and called to one of the eunuchs, who bore the red mark of a fresh slap on the side of his face and a terrified expression.

'Tell them.'

The eunuch cleared a nervous throat. 'I admitted her to a secret balcony and left her. When she did not reappear, I finally checked on her, but she had gone.'

'Tell them the rest.'

'I do not know who took her, Masters, but Romanos Skleros and his sister were in the complex with a small armed group.'

Harðráði turned to Halfdan. 'Skleros has taken her. The man is self-important, but not stupid enough to kidnap a courtier from the palace without the emperor's knowledge. That means that wherever Gunnhild is, she will be close to the emperor and Skleros both. Somewhere in the main palace, then. She is valuable to them, sadly, because she is valuable to me.'

Halfdan pursed his lips. 'When this is done there will be decisions to be made, Harðráði. Gunnhild is the heart of the *Sea Wolf.*'

The commander gave him a level look. 'She is her own woman, and it will be her choice, Halfdan. You cannot stop that any more than I can, but I tell you now that her destiny lies with me.'

'Can we just make sure that her destiny doesn't lie with Monomachos,' Leif said, leaning in between the pair.

Harðráði and Halfdan continued to look at one another in silence, but then both nodded.

'Well said.'

'Where do we start?' Halfdan asked.

'There are plenty of places she could be kept,' Harðráði replied, 'but that depends on how dangerous they think she is.'

Halfdan didn't have to think long. '*Very* dangerous. She helped bring down an emperor, she freed you from prison more or less single-handed, she warned against Monomachos, and the Sklerina knows her personally. She, most of all, will be aware of just how dangerous Gunnhild can be.'

'Then she won't be kept in imperial apartments anywhere. It'll be somewhere secure. My guess would be the Lazarus Gate.'

Halfdan frowned. 'Where the emperor took ship? Why there?'

'Because there's a place built into the walls nearby that houses a very specialised unit of the imperial garrison.'

'Specialised?'

'Let's just say the walls are thick and it's a long way from anywhere important, so the screaming won't bother anyone.'

Halfdan felt a pinch of panic then. Torture?

'We need to move fast, then, but what about the empress?'

Harðráði's expression hardened. 'The empress is no longer my concern, nor yours. When she gave all her power to our enemy and then denied me, she nullified any oath I took. Gunnhild is the important one now. Come on.'

As they turned, Leif reached out and cupped Anna's chin with his free hand. 'You must go. You're not safe with me. I love you, woman, but I can't put you in danger.'

'You're more stupid than most Rus if you think I'm leaving you.'

Leif huffed and looked to Halfdan, who nodded with a smile. He turned back to Anna. 'All right, but be sensible. Find your way out of the palace and head for the harbour. Look for the *Sea Wolf*. I'll meet you there.'

Anna looked as though she might argue for a moment, but nodded, hitched up her dress hem and hurried away. With Harðráði leading the way, the nine men burst from the women's palace and charged across the lawns. One of the many smaller walls that cut the palace into manageable pieces crossed the hill before them, and a small group of soldiers was in evidence even from a distance, falling in to defend the building. The nine Varangians stumbled to a halt and ducked behind a small stand of decorative trees.

'They're sealing the place off piece by piece as they search for us,' the commander said.

'We have to deal with them.'

'But when we do, we can't do it silently this time. No matter how quick we are there will be noise, and the warning will go up.'

'Then we must manage to stay a step ahead of them all the time,' Halfdan said. 'It's you they're searching for,' he added.

'Yes, I know.'

'Take your three men. March straight along the path to them at a steady pace. Keep their attention. We'll take them in the flank.'

Harðráði sucked his lip, then nodded. 'Be quick.'

Halfdan gestured to the others and they rounded the trees. 'Quietly and quickly,' the young jarl reminded them, 'like the buzzard hovering above the trees and then swooping for the kill.'

With nods they followed him as he angled out around a delicate marble fountain that gurgled and splashed, and then reached one of the many avenues of cypresses that crossed the imperial gardens. At the far end of the line, the trees came within ten feet of the gate and the soldiers that guarded it. With Leif setting the pace, he having the shortest legs, the five of them ran, keeping the trees between them and the waiting soldiers. It was not long before Harðráði was seen, as they could all tell from the shouting at the gate. An aristocratic Greek voice demanded that the commander halt. They heard Harðráði reply, telling them to stand down and let him through. That he was still the commander of the Varangians.

A sneering voice reminded him that his baton of office lay on the floor in front of the emperor, and Harðráði slipped into an easy tone, soldier-to-soldier. They had slowed as they approached, and Halfdan and his friends were past them now, running ahead, praying to Odin that the commander could keep the men talking and sufficiently distracted that they didn't hear the second group of warriors approaching unseen behind the trees.

The dialogue broke down quickly, even though Halfdan didn't hear the cause as they ran. All he heard now was shouting from the guards, more and more urgent demands that Harðráði stop, while the commander continued to address them in a calm manner, the gravel crunching as he disobeyed them and continued to approach.

Even as they closed, Halfdan slowed, reaching the end of the line of cypresses. The five of them, weapons out, settled behind trees, watching. Each man motioned to identify which of the men he would take on, and Halfdan finally pulled his shield from his back and settled it in his grip, sword in the other hand.

With a nod, he burst from the trees, running at high speed. The two dozen men now gathered at the gate turned in shock at the sudden assault. Unsure what was happening, the officer in charge issued no orders and so, as a unit, each of them turned to face the new threat. This was their undoing, for as they turned away from Harðráði and his three warriors, the Varangians were on them, bellowing, swords and axes swinging. Halfdan and his friends hit the guards a moment later, and the carnage began.

Halfdan's sword lanced out, and the excubitor attempted to throw his large, kite-shaped shield in the way, but the young warrior was too quick for him. The sword grated for a moment along the edge of the shield and then plunged into the shirt of bronze scales. The armour was effective enough, and very decorative, but the shirt had one weakness in that the scales were sewn on at the top, and Halfdan had noted this about a lot of the excubitores' armour. As he struck, he jammed the blade upwards, and the tip slid beneath the metal scales and into the leather onto which they were sewn. He felt the resistance of the leather shirt, but he had not stopped running, and he hit the guard now with all his weight, carrying the man back against the wall. The guard stopped moving as he slammed into the stone, but Halfdan and his sword did not, the tapering point of the blade tearing into the leather and puncturing the man's torso, grinding between ribs. The guard screamed, his own weapon and shield forgotten, but Halfdan was already moving on, well aware that they were outnumbered by more than two to one. Ripping his blade free with a little trouble, he turned just in time to block a sword strike with his shield, though the blow carved a deep chunk from the timber, defacing one of the three painted wolves.

Halfdan reacted, bellowing the names of gods these men thought demons, and his sword came round in a sweep, hacking deep into the guard's arm, just below the elbow. He felt the blade bite bone and pulled it back, freeing it as the man howled with agony. A heartbeat later he ended that agony as he drove the sword into the man's neck, which was protected only with a scarf.

Spinning, he looked for his next target and saw a man running at him, but Bjorn suddenly stepped from nowhere in between then, axe in hand.

'Dance with me, little Greek,' the big albino grinned, and then began to swing his axe back and forth in figure eights, blindingly fast. The man's eyes tried to keep up with the weapon's movement, which was why he completely missed the shield as it was suddenly thrust out and smashed him in the face. The shield came back, revealing a pulped, raw mess around terrified eyes which suddenly turned inward in a squint as Bjorn's axe came out of the last figure eight in a whole new direction and fell in a chop like a butcher's cleaver into the top of his head.

'Fun,' was all the big man commented, with a grin, as the last few were finished off.

Halfdan surveyed the damage with relief, and knew once again that the gods were with them. Ketil had taken another leg wound, but it wasn't bad, and he just cursed as he wiped the blood from it. One of Harðráði's men had fallen, a sword standing proud from his chest, but other than a few cuts and bruises, they had come away from their encounter remarkably well. Given Ketil's speed, the leg wound would be unlikely to hamper him a great deal. It might even slow the giant down to the same pace as everyone else.

'Too much noise,' Harðráði noted, glaring at Bjorn. 'Especially from big idiots who can't fight without shouting obscenities. That'll have drawn the attention of every ear in the palace. We'd best move fast. They'll probably know by now we've been at the Gynaikonitis, and when they work out we've been here, they'll know where we're going.'

With fresh urgency, they finished off the last few rolling, wounded, groaning men and slipped through the gate. Emerging into the open at the far side, Halfdan spotted excessive damage around the archway and, seeing the arcaded pavilion surrounding the polo fields ahead, realised this was where Maniakes had led his mob during the riot that had removed the Caulker from power. He found himself briefly wishing the Byzantine giant was still in the city. With him, perhaps they could have toppled a second emperor.

He shook his head. There were more urgent concerns. Half a hundred heartbeats later and they came to another corner and stumbled to a halt, pulling back into cover.

'I think we just walked into the deepest of shit,' Ulfr noted with feeling, as they looked at the serried ranks of soldiers standing between them and the small, well-protected prison that would almost certainly hold Gunnhild.

Damn it.

Chapter 23

'She has no valuable information?'

Maria Sklerina turned to the officer, her expression unreadable. 'She is not here for the extraction of information, but for safekeeping. She is... she is bait,' the woman said, as a nasty smile crossed her lips.

Romanos Skleros, who had been talking to another officer in the doorway, turned and wagged a finger. 'She is of value yet. She is not to be damaged irreparably. By all means practise your art, but she must remain essentially intact.'

'And there is no sealed order from the emperor?'

'An order from me is as good as one from Monomachos,' Skleros said darkly, hinting at unpleasant things in the officer's future if he continued to argue. He then turned to his sister. 'The place is now well-defended, but I have no intention of being caught up in a fight. Come, Maria.'

As the nobleman strode out of the room, Maria Sklerina turned to Gunnhild.

'When you first arrived in this city, before you came to the attention of that hag of an empress, I came to you. You told me only destruction awaited me, and you refused me. Refused to help me solve a problem with my love and an Alani princess. You should never have denied me, Maria Gunilla. I knew even then that Constantine would wear the crown, and yet you helped the Maniakes bitch while shunning me.'

Gunnhild, standing in the corner, unarmed and alone, shrugged a careless, if difficult shrug. 'Maniakes sought only to undo her own mistakes and to prevent disaster. You sought death and power. Death and power are both things to seek at times, but I could see in you something that I did not wish to nurture. You are poison, Sklerina, as are your brother and your lover. Your lover might wear the crown, but he will be the last of his line to do so.'

'You saw this in your pagan witchery, did you?'

Gunnhild just watched, tight-lipped, as Sklerina huffed and turned. As she left the room, she gestured to the officer. 'No permanent damage, but make her hurt.'

The door closed behind her, and Gunnhild remained in the corner, watching her captors. The men wore blood-red uniforms, a nod to practicality, given their purpose. The officer still did not look sure of himself. Without specific orders from the emperor, the palace torturers could get into a great deal of trouble for overstepping their mark, and everyone in the palace was at least passingly familiar with the Varangian woman who'd become a favourite of the empress. Behind the officer, two more of the red-garbed soldiers stood between her and the door.

She had weighed up her chances the moment they had taken the bag from her head. She had no intention of dying here, when she'd seen her thread running on into a glorious future alongside Harðráði. The Norns had woven a future for her beyond this, and yet there was a nagging doubt deep in her mind. She had fought against that weaving. She had denied Harðráði again and again. Had she broken the thread? If so, perhaps this was what waited instead. But she was a daughter of Freyja, and if the weaving had changed she would meet whatever was now her fate with weapon in hand, screaming defiance.

There had been twelve of them around her when she was first led in here and the bag removed. The soldiers had then gone outside to organise the protection of this place against what sounded suspiciously like a rescue party from her friends. That had left only five. Now the two nobles had gone, there were only three.

Still, it would be of little use killing these three, even if that were possible. She did not know this part of the palace, and she would undoubtedly find her way out of the building straight into the waiting arms of the soldiers Skleros had placed there. She had to find another way.

At least her bonds should not be a problem. She'd had the foresight to nullify their efficacy straight away. As she'd been captured and the cords pulled tight around her, she'd taken that opportunity for a little Loki trickery. The top loop had tightened around her upper arms, but her left hand was free of the second loop. Now, looking about, she was beginning to understand what could be done. The timing would be important, though.

The officer wandered around the far side of the room now, looking at various desks. They had not been expecting business tonight, and so the braziers were cold, but still things with points, hooks and serrated edges gleamed in the lamplight across many tables. With some contemplation, the man finally selected a blade and lifted it, examining it in the golden glow. He turned and walked slowly across the room, coming to a halt some four feet from her.

'I admit, I am at a loss,' the officer said. 'Torture with no purpose is wasteful and troublesome. When extracting information, it is much easier to know how far one can go. When there is nothing to draw from you, it is difficult to know how close we are coming to the limit. So we shall start small, and if this turns out to be some grand mistake and the emperor disapproves, the damage will be minimal.'

'Pray to your nailed god,' Gunnhild said quietly.

The man frowned, slightly disconcerted by her manner. Recovering, he turned and gestured to his men with his free hand. 'Strap her to the table.'

As the man had moved, the hand holding the knife had come up, and she had seen with surprise how the hilt of the blade he gripped had been intricately worked into the shape of a boar's head. Freyja had given her a weapon. As the officer spoke to his men, Gunnhild was already moving. She knew what she must do, and now she knew the gods were still with her, for Freyja had shown her the way.

He was only a few feet away, and as he stepped within reach, his experienced eye probing her for probable weaknesses, he was carelessly confident. Her left hand shot up like the strike of a coiled snake, grabbing at his hand. She'd not quite been able to see how to snatch the knife, restricted as she still was, and so she had gone for what she privately labelled 'the Bjorn approach.' Straight violence.

Her hand closed on his index finger, pulling it out and jerking it until it broke with a calcareous snapping sound. Her questing fingers found the knife in his now surprised, loose grip, and pulled it from his hand. In a single move of which Halfdan would have been proud, the knife was in her palm and swiping up across her front. The second cord fell away, cut, and as the man began to make a strange keening noise, staring in horror at the unnatural angle of his finger, her newly freed arm went around his neck, the blade coming up to his face.

In a heartbeat the man had gone from armed and urging his men forward to finding himself with a broken finger, in the grip of a madwoman holding his own blade up to his face as she breathed on the back of his neck.

'Back off,' she hissed at the two soldiers, who were moving forward and drawing their swords.

'There is nowhere for you to go,' breathed the officer, the sound of pain from his broken finger inflecting his words.

'You have heard of me, I know. The pagan. The witch. I warn you only once. Back off.'

'Take her,' the officer said to his men, brave even in the clutches of death.

Gunnhild shrugged. The boar-knife moved up a few inches and the point rested on the lower arc of the orbit below the man's eye. She felt him flinch, albeit carefully. The two men continued to move. With a sigh, she jerked the knife and punctured the man's eye, blood and colourless liquids slopping down across his cheek. The officer screamed.

Now, the two soldiers stopped in their tracks. Gunnhild's hand moved again, the point now below the other eye. 'I believe we all now know what I am capable of,' she said. 'The goddess is with me, and your God is nowhere to be found. One more step and this man is blind for life, and then I shall choose one of you. Which one will it be?' she mused. She could almost have laughed as the two men glanced nervously at one another.

The officer in her arms had devolved into terrified whimpering now. Finally, in strained tones, he spoke. 'What do you want?'

'We are going for a short walk. Your two men will lay down their swords, open the door for me, and then shut themselves in, staying inside and remaining silent. If they do so, they will go home to their wives tonight intact, and you will retain one good eye. I trust we all understand?'

'Drop your weapons,' the officer said.

The two men hesitated, and Gunnhild put a little pressure on the knife, digging into the eyelid.

'Do it *now*,' the man in her arms yelped, and two swords clattered to the floor a moment later. She nodded at the door, and one of the soldiers crossed to it and pulled it open. She could see a dim, torchlit corridor beyond. Silently she cursed herself for not having had the wherewithal to count the paces and turns on her way here with the bag over her head. Still, she might not want to go back out the same way anyway. A large force of soldiers was out there somewhere.

'Where is my staff?'

'What?'

The blade's pressure increased again.

'I don't know what you're talking about,' the man gasped in a panicked tone. 'I was told nothing about a staff.'

Damn it. That was a blow.

'How do we get out of here without walking through the door I came in by?' she said in the passageway as the door clicked shut behind her. The corridor turned at both ends, and she had no idea what direction was what.

'Where do you want to go?'

Gunnhild stood for a moment, thinking deeply. That was a very good question. She needed to find the others, but they had to be nearby, if the guards were being assembled outside to stop them. She needed to be somewhere her friends could see her. An image of the day they had chased down Ari Karsten leapt to mind suddenly, and she smiled. Freyja truly was walking with her this evening. The north wall of the palace was where Ari had left from, for it was the easiest point and the least likely to be observed. And the wall would make her visible, too.

'There will be stairs up to the sea wall somewhere,' she said.

'Where?'

'Turn left,' the officer said, breathing shallowly, trying not to move too sharply. 'You will let me go?'

'You will live and you will keep your eye, as long as you do what I tell you.'

They were moving now, along the corridor. Two turns, a side passage, three doors leading off, ignored, and finally she reached the bottom of a staircase. It marched off upwards and she could see the indigo glow of evening light leeching in somewhere up there. The man had not played her false. She could not climb the stairs like this, of course, or not without likely putting the other eye out, and she had promised the man. In a swift move, she withdrew the knife from his cheek and smashed the boar-head pommel into his temple, hard. The officer folded up in an instant with a sigh and collapsed to the flagged floor at the bottom of the stairs. Mourning the loss of her staff, but grateful for the goddess's knife and the continued presence of the all-important pouch at her belt, she climbed the stairs two at a time.

The exit at the top, a simple brick arch with no door, led out onto the sea walls that surrounded both palace and city.

Normally, guards would patrol sporadically in times of peace. This part of the palace was rarely in any danger and was far from important, and Halfdan had complained more than once when Ari had assigned him here near the polo fields and the horse manure.

She reached the arch and ducked her head halfway out, looking this way and that. She could see a small group of men, Varangians almost certainly, along the wall some way to the north, but nothing to the south. This area was clear, though the wall was punctuated with regular towers, and so the prospect of men arriving unexpectedly could not be ruled out. Still, she knew what she needed to do.

A few paces back, and she looked down at the small building projecting from the wall's inner face, into which she had been led. Of the Sklerina and her brother she could see no sign, but in excess of a hundred armed and armoured soldiers stood outside in lines, protecting the building. At least Halfdan wasn't dead yet, then.

She closed her eyes, could feel the goddess properly for the first time in weeks. She reached down to the pouch at her belt and undid it, dipping two fingers into the contents and then fastening it once more. With a deep breath, she drew two lines of powder down her face from her hairline to her chin, and then licked her lips, tasting the bittersweet gift of the goddess.

She began to hum gently, under her breath. This was not the time, nor the place, for the song, but she could feel it now, the Seiðr at work. She kept her eyes closed, looking this way and that still, relying upon the eyes of the goddess instead of her own. A slow smile spread across her face as she stopped humming.

She opened her eyes.

There were just a few of them. She could see them lurking among trees beyond the army that awaited, figures gleaming in the shadows. Their armour was glittering gold in the last light of the setting sun, which dropped into the Propontis Sea behind them. She needed their attention. If they charged that army, they would all die.

She dug in the pouches that remained at her belt. The three tips for her staff were still there – the stone, the image of Freyja and the spearhead – as well as some coins and the compound, but nothing she could use to signal her friends. Then a thought struck her.

Lifting the knife in her hand, she looked at it. The blade was perfect and unmarked, albeit covered in unspeakable matter right now, and she wiped it on her dress a few times, and then lifted it once more. Now, it gleamed silver. Holding it at chin height, she kept her eyes on her lurking friends as she slowly changed the angle of the knife until it caught the golden rays of the sinking sun and flashed them back. The dancing speck of light she created flitted about among the hidden figures. She couldn't see in enough detail to notice if one had looked up, but after a dozen heartbeats the men began to move, off to their left, among the trees, away from the waiting force.

The beauty of the Great Palace was that though it contained many open spaces and great gardens, hardly any part of it was not divided up with arcades of columns and arches, low walls, avenues of neatly clipped trees, delicate hedges, or the gleaming windowed walls of the numerous pavilions and minor palace structures. As such, it was remarkably easy for a small party to move about without being easily observed. Gunnhild remained in place, though she hunched close to the wall now, to minimise her chances of being spotted by anyone else.

From time to time she lost track of where her friends were, but she knew where they were going, and so it never took long before she caught sight of them once more. At one point shouting drew her attention, and she looked back to where they had been lurking when she'd first spotted them, only to see another group of the emperor's soldiers there, calling to the men guarding the torturers' barracks. Soon, someone would go inside or those guards would come out, and havoc would ensue.

She saw her friends again, then, already past the torturers' barracks and making for one of the towers in the wall, the next one along. Stepping back and straightening, she waved one arm, and as a figure down there waved back she was surprised to see the golden-haired figure of Harðráði along with her friends.

She was running now, making for the tower. In that moment the world exploded into activity. Someone had discovered she'd gone from the building, and the soldiers gathering were in chaos, groups shouting questions and demands at one another. Those distant figures on the wall were running towards her now. The alarm was going up all over the palace, for Harðráði could not be allowed to flee the emperor's clutches.

Gunnhild reached the next tower and pulled open the door. She was surprised as the doorway revealed the shape of a soldier running up onto the wall, but the man was as stunned as she was when the door was torn from his grip and a woman stood in front of him. Before he could recover or decide what to do, she leapt, stabbing with the boar-blade, ramming it into his neck, the only unprotected flesh she could see. She pulled the blade back out at an angle through the side of his neck and was rewarded with a fountain of rich blood that sprayed from the wound across her arm and knife. As she pushed the horrified soldier aside and ran past, blood spattered all across her, and she had to blink it out of her eyes as she hurtled for the stairs. She could hear the sound of some sort of struggle below, and pounded down the steps. Fortunately the arrival of the others at the bottom of the tower had drawn any other guards that way, and so she emerged onto the ground floor unhindered.

A struggle was taking place in the doorway. The men in the tower were outnumbered by her friends outside, but the single doorway was easy to defend. Gripping her knife tight, she leapt across the room and stabbed the nearest guard in the thigh from behind, just below his metal plated shirt. He screamed and fell to one side as she grabbed the next man and pulled. He fell back with a cry and the two of them staggered across the room together.

The last man at the door lurched away, his head pulped and mangled, blood sheeting down him, and Bjorn, roaring, stepped into the room. As the Wolves finished off the men in the doorway, Harðráði barrelled across the chamber and pulled the man away from Gunnhild, gutting him swiftly and efficiently.

'God in Heaven, but it's good to see you,' the commander said.

Gunnhild simply nodded. As the others came in and slammed the tower door behind them, Halfdan looked at her with a relieved smile. 'It had to be you signalling, Gunnhild. But what now?'

'To the ships,' Harðráði said flatly.

'But how? We're in a palace being searched.'

Gunnhild pointed up the stairs. 'The north wall. It's where Ari went over. It's the best place.'

The commander nodded. 'Good. We'll do that. Come on.'

Gunnhild blinked in surprise as Harðráði's free hand clamped around her wrist and spun her around, dragging her towards the stairs. 'Come on,' he bellowed. 'Time's pressing.'

The commander pulled her onto the stairs and she had to run to keep up. She felt she should be fighting to free herself from his grip, and yet somehow she didn't. He was leading her where she needed to go anyway. The others were close behind, running up the stairs. Through the next floor they ran, and on up more stairs until they saw the purple light in the archway ahead and the body of the bloody guard on the floor inside it. Harðráði threw her a strange look as they burst past the corpse for which only she could be responsible, and then suddenly they were out on the wall.

Gunnhild felt her heart stutter for a moment. Men were flooding along the parapet, and the nearest were already on them. A soldier made to grab her, and she was about to jam the knife in him when she was suddenly pulled away again by the wrist as Harðráði yanked her out of danger. They skittered back along the wall walk, and the soldiers moved after them, but were suddenly battered aside as Bjorn emerged from the doorway, bellowing oaths to Odin and something about 'arses', and smashed his axe into one of the gathered soldiers.

Gunnhild finally pulled her hand free of the commander's grip, but as she turned to go and help the others, she realised immediately how hopeless that was. A growing force of men now stood between the two of them and the rest of the Wolves. Halfdan and the others were cut off, with little chance of making it out onto the wall top. Bjorn was being mobbed by them, and the face of Halfdan appeared briefly.

'Go to the harbour,' Harðráði yelled at the young jarl. 'We'll meet you at the ships.'

And with that the commander was grabbing her wrist again and pulling. She looked at him in shock, then back at her friends, who were being pushed back into the tower doorway, Bjorn nursing wounds even as he fought a fearsome rearguard.

A small group of the guards realised that Harðráði was getting away and turned, running after them and yelling. Gunnhild simply stared. She could see it now. The bear and the boar, two threads marching off into the future, the wolf that was Halfdan hurtling off alone.

No.

The soldiers reached her and she fought blindly alongside Harðráði, her hands clawing, her knife stabbing, even as the commander slashed and hacked, barged and pulled, but it was all automatic, all done without conscious thought, for her mind was reeling. The weaving the Norns had made for her... For her and Harðráði...

He was drawing her away again now, for they were free of guards, and running along the walls in the growing gloom, as the final golden gleam of the sun disappeared beneath the sea. 'Halfdan,' was all she could find to say.

'He is clever, that one. He'll get out, but if we go to help, we'll never get away ourselves. He'll meet us in the harbour, I know it.'

She watched the clamour behind them as they ran. More soldiers were coming their way now, the rest trying to tear open the tower door, which Bjorn had managed to close against them.

Gunnhild and Harðráði fled, both feeling the sore heat of cuts and the ache of wounds from their fight. The commander was limping slightly now, but the light was failing, and it took only moments for them to lose sight of the tower behind them. She couldn't fight it any more. Harðráði had taken her – with the best of intention, but it was what had to be. She allowed herself to be led, to be dragged. She said nothing as the commander pulled her into the shadows of a tower and waited for their pursuers to run past.

They reached a low stretch of wall, with a huge haystack outside, and she wordlessly allowed Harðráði to lift her out and drop her into the soft hay, jumping over after her. They ran then in silence, in darkness, across the acropolis hill. The clamour of the palace with its soldiers and searches faded into the distance behind them, as they pounded down a street towards the harbour and the ships that waited to carry them away to safety.

She had fought the weaving of the Norns, and she had lost. Now the bear and the boar made for the ship, while her beloved Wolves fought for their life in the palace.

Odin preserve them...

Chapter 24

'Close the fucking door,' Ketil bellowed, struggling with a wounded guard even as he clutched his own crimson-drenched thigh with his free hand.

'I am... *trying*... to close the fucking door, you lanky streak of piss,' Bjorn called back as he hauled on the timbers while Halfdan stabbed repeatedly into the gap, cutting away the hands and fingers that clawed at it to keep it open.

'Gunnhild,' was all Halfdan could manage.

It was an image he felt would stay with him, especially if it turned out to be the last. Gunnhild, dragged away into the deepening evening gloom along the parapet, just visible over a dozen excubitores who separated her from him. He'd seen Gunnhild's face through the press, and it had startled him more than anything else this day, for in her expression he had seen only resignation.

Well, he was not done with Gunnhild, even if she was done with him.

'We'll meet you at the ships,' Harðráði had shouted, and somehow, with the golden prince and the goddess-favoured Gunnhild together, Halfdan felt sure the pair would make it. Bjorn had done a magnificent job of keeping most of the soldiers too occupied to race off after the pair, at least, and now Harðráði and Gunnhild were lost to sight somewhere in the indigo evening, only a few guards on their heel.

Halfdan concentrated again. His mind was wandering, which was dangerous in battle. His sword stuck another scrabbling arm in the wrist and that, combined with Bjorn's strength, finally yanked the door into the jamb. As Bjorn held it, the timbers shaking and thumping under the angry hands of the soldiers outside, Halfdan pulled the latch bar into place. It would never hold against an army, but against the bare hands of desperate men, the door would remain closed long enough.

Behind him, Ketil finished off the man he'd been struggling with, an axe blow to the skull, and then tore some of the man's colourful uniform tunic hem off and wrapped it around his thigh three times before tying it off with a grunt.

'Can you run?'

'Watch me,' the Icelander replied, 'but where to?'

Leif, nursing those ribs that seemed destined to never quite heal, looked at them all. 'There must be a way out. Anna and Gunnhild will be at the ships. What about the tunnels you found?'

Halfdan shook his head. 'They go all over the place, but only inside the palace. No one would be stupid enough to overlook a tunnel into the palace from outside.'

'What about the kathisma?' Ulfr rumbled as he rubbed a narrow cut on his forearm.

'It's been sealed tighter than ever since we used it to get into the palace,' Ketil pointed out.

Halfdan shook his head. 'We go out the most open way. Through the Chalke Gate.'

'What?' The others turned to frown at him.

'That's ridiculous,' Ketil snorted.

'Think about it. The gate is designed to keep people out, not in. They can't bar it from the other side. The palace garrisons have been mobilised to look for us, so they're all over the place, but by now they know we've been at the women's palace, the polo fields and the Lazarus Gate. The bulk of them will be coming here, and, if we're honest, we all know that we're the small fish here. They'll take us if they find us, but it's Harðráði they really want, and those men on the other side of the door know he's gone north along the walls now. The Chalke Gate might just be the least defended place in the palace now.'

Ketil nodded slowly. 'You're right.'

'And Bjorn and Ketil, you're both a little recognisable. Most of the excubitores and the other Greek units, and even many of the Varangians won't recognise us. To anyone else here, we'll look like another of the search parties. Bjorn, wear your helmet and a cloak. Cover your colouring. Ketil, all you can do is try to hunch over and not be quite so tall. If we play this casually, we might be able to simply walk past most of them now Gunnhild and Harðráði aren't with us.'

They hurried down the stairs into the large chamber halfway up the tower, Halfdan leading the way, and as he reached the top of the next stair he paused, shushing the others. The sounds of men shouting echoed up from the chamber below, and of boots on the lowest steps. With silent motions, he gestured to the others to move, and they backed through an archway into a dark storeroom. Carefully shuffling into the darkness they waited, still and silent. The thumping of footsteps increased, and a moment later half a dozen men thundered past the archway, making for the next set of steps.

Halfdan braced himself. They couldn't delay. There might still be men down below, but the moment those six soldiers opened the door at the top, the gathered group there would confirm that the fugitives were somewhere in the tower.

'Come on.'

With that he ducked out of the arch, just a quick glance to be certain that there was no sign of the men still on this floor, and then ran into the next stairway down. Taking them two or even three at a time, they pounded down to the ground level and burst out into the room there, weapons out. The chamber was empty, the door to the palace grounds closed. All eyes went to Halfdan, who took another deep breath and then pushed at the door.

It opened and then stopped with a thump. There was a muffled snort. Halfdan ducked around the door and stabbed out with his sword instinctively, before he even saw the man he'd opened the door into. The sword slammed into armour and his victim, already stunned by the door, let out an explosive breath as the blow winded him.

Past the guard now, Halfdan took it all in. Two other men waited outside the door. Other than that, this open grassy space was empty. The same hedge they had used as cover on their first approach lay close by. Bjorn was past him a moment later, his big axe held in both hands, the blade reversed. The poll of the axe head swung out as he leapt into the open and one of the two surprised, waiting guards took the blow full in the face. The projecting steel nose guard of the man's helmet stood no chance, bending agonisingly inwards, smashing his teeth as part of the helmet crumpled under the heavy weight.

The third man recovered his wits, but by the time he drew his sword, he was overcome by Ketil, Ulfr and Leif, three axes smashing at him. He gasped and howled in pain as he went down under a rain of blows, Bjorn finishing off his own man with a blow to the neck.

Halfdan turned to the winded, stunned man by the door. He took in the armour, noted that the man's plated jacket covered to below the groin, complemented by short chain sleeves and a chain veil that came up to his eyes. The man was more thoroughly armoured than most. He was, however, still reeling, which bought Halfdan the time he needed. Angling himself carefully, he jerked his shield up towards the man's face. Reacting automatically, the soldier's arm came up to block, and Halfdan struck the moment the chain sleeve slid back, his sword point slamming into the tunic in the man's armpit. It took every ounce of the young jarl's strength, but the blade slid inside, grating off shoulder blade, scything through organs, muscles and blood vessels. The man screamed, blood pouring from his wound as Halfdan twisted the blade and yanked, pulling it free before the man fell, preventing the sword jamming fast.

Shouts above drew his attention, and as his victim crumpled to the ground he looked up to see soldiers on the wall top pointing down at them with cries of alarm.

He was running, then, the others with him, grateful at least that it appeared there were no archers up there, for they reached the manicured hedge without a single arrow thudding into the turf near them. They would still be visible from the wall, but it would take precious moments for the men to run back down the stairs, or to direct any of the other search parties to their location, by which time they could be out of sight and running.

Hurtling along the line of bushes, Halfdan reached the end and turned south-west.

'What are you doing?' Leif shouted, breathless as they ran. 'The Chalke is over there,' he added, pointing off to the north-west.

'And Harðráði went north. That'll be where they're concentrating. They'll not think we've gone south.'

With that he reached the shadowy lee of a delicate marble arcade that cut between two gardens and then connected with the palace buildings. The sun had fully set now, and the last strains of golden light were fading, giving way to a deep purple evening sky. The shadowed parts of the garden were growing darker by the moment, which increased the advantage of the five fugitives all the time.

Running as quietly as they could, holding their weapons and shields tight to prevent too much clattering, they moved south-west, now out of sight of the sea wall. At one point, Halfdan heard voices and they stopped, hunching down into the shadows as a nobleman with a secretary strode past slowly, dictating as he walked, unaware of the danger lurking nearby. Once the man was safely past, they ran again. Halfdan drew on knowledge amassed over almost a year of patrolling these grounds, walls and corridors, occasionally corrected by Ulfr. They moved along darkened corridors, below walls, across lawns, and gradually angled around, heading north once more, occasionally ducking into shadows as small groups of soldiers ran past, shouting.

As they emerged from a doorway close to the barracks, they could see the impressive Chalke Gate, which stood but a stone's throw from their former accommodation. Only four Varangians stood at the gate, but a dozen men of a palace garrison unit were gathered at the entrance to the barracks. Cursing, Halfdan and the others ducked back into the shadows.

'Let me handle this,' Ulfr muttered. 'The rest of you are all a little recognisable.' With that, he marched purposefully out of the archway and across the open space between churches and palaces towards the barracks. The men at the gate were Varangians, loyal to the emperor, but the men at the barracks were excubitores, and Ulfr shouldered his axe as he strode towards them as though he owned the place. Halfdan found himself wincing, watching the shipwright brazening it out with an axe over his shoulder crimson with gore. It had to be hoped no one saw that or picked up on it.

'You lot, what are you doing lurking here?' he demanded.

'What?' an officer snapped in reply. There was no love lost between excubitores and Varangians at the best of times, and their relationship had broken down further in recent months, but right now, for once, they were all officially on the same side, looking for the emperor's enemy. The man might be irritable, but he would be compliant.

'Harðráði is getting away with the witch. We need to concentrate near the north wall. We've got him trapped but we need more men.'

The officer frowned, weighing up this information. He had probably been given conflicting orders, but this news was important. After a few moments, he nodded and gave the command to his men. The soldiers, acting on the word of this lone Varangian, ran off past the gate, heading north, and as they disappeared, Ulfr flashed a brief glance at Halfdan and the others. As he approached the Varangians at the Chalke Gate, the solid shipwright struck up a casual conversation, keeping them distracted.

In a heartbeat the other four were running. They had crossed half the distance to the gate before the four guardsmen became aware of them. One shouted a warning, and the others turned, but the speaker died even in that moment as Ulfr swung the axe he had been idly wielding. The curved edge could not cut through the links of the man's chain shirt, but the blow was hard and the man's ribs smashed to a pulp, lacerating his heart and lungs inside the protective shell.

The Varangian screamed, but Ulfr was roaring and already turning on the next man, axe whirling.

'Odiiiiiin!'

The shipwright's call was picked up by the others as they pounded into the gateway and Halfdan ploughed into the first man, his battle rage rising. He felt an axe catch him on the shoulder, above his shield, but it was only a glancing blow. He knocked the man aside but before he could use his sword Ketil was there, his axe coming up into the Varangian's jaw, smashing his chin, severing the leather tie so that his helmet fell away, useless, from his ruined head.

Knowing that his friends had the situation under control, Halfdan propped his blood-slicked sword against the wall and reached for the blocking bar of the gate. As he heaved and pushed, lifting the immense beam, Bjorn was suddenly with him, adding his impressive strength to the effort. Between them the two men heaved the bar free and as Halfdan retrieved his sword, Bjorn pulled the gate open.

The square beyond was empty for some way, though a crowd of citizens had gathered at the far side, watching with interest, ignorant of the details but aware that something interesting was going on in the palace from the shouting, the moving torches and the clanging of bells.

'To the harbour,' Halfdan said, pointing with his sword down the slope and past the great monuments of Constantinople. They were across the square in heartbeats, the tantalising proximity of freedom lending their legs fresh speed and power. How Harðráði intended to beat the great chain that stopped ships leaving or entering the Horn Bay he could not imagine, but their small group had managed to get out of the palace against all odds, and on the assumption that Gunnhild and the commander had been equally fortunate, they were closer than they could ever have realistically hoped to escape.

The people of the great city watched with casual interest as the five Northmen pounded down the street, armed with bared, bloodied weapons, armoured for war, wounded and cursing, invoking the names of old gods. Halfdan did not even question the lack of trouble as they reached the gate to the harbour at the bottom of the slope and found the great portal standing open, no guards attending it. Seemingly Harðráði, or perhaps Valgarðr, had dealt with the soldiers here as part of their preparations.

They burst out into the great harbour and came to a halt, looking this way and that. Halfdan's gaze raked the scene before them, searching for the *Sea Wolf*, and for Harðráði's ship. The harbour was a hive of activity, which he'd not expected, especially in the evening. A dozen ships were being made ready to sail, presumably with the morning light, and he was surprised to see that the men loading them and settling their kit ready for a journey aboard the twelve vessels were all Varangians. What was this? Harðráði said there were only *two* ships.

As a Northman with a sack of grain on his shoulder staggered past huffing at them to get out of the way, Halfdan called to the man.

'What's this? Where are you bound?'

The man gave him a look, suggesting he thought Halfdan more half*wit*. 'Italy, man. Support for Maniakes. Doesn't your primikerios tell you anything?'

Halfdan blinked. Twelve ships of Varangians. Maniakes must be involved in some impressive campaign to be sent part of the emperor's elite guard to supplement his own field army. He turned to the others. 'Maybe this is why Harðráði moves now? Just two more ships of Northmen preparing among a fleet. He'd have drawn no special attention.'

'But where are *our* ships,' Leif said, tense, and Halfdan remembered that Gunnhild was not the only woman waiting for them.

'There,' replied Ulfr in a tone laden with anger.

Halfdan followed his pointing digit and felt the Earth crumble beneath him. The *Sea Wolf* had thrown off its ropes and was already out in the water, two ship-lengths from the dock. The larger of the two ships, the great dragon beast of Harðráði, was still tethered to the shore. Without the need for words, the five of them began to run again, thumping along the stonework of the dock, making for that ship. As they neared, and their view cleared, Halfdan peered out across the water at the retreating shape of his own ship. Two figures stood at the stern, and he couldn't decide whether what he felt was relief or dismay at the sight. A mix of the two, he decided in the end.

Harðráði aboard the *Sea Wolf*, sailing away from its rightful crew, was something he hated, and the fact that Gunnhild stood beside the man, looking back across the opening gulf of water at him, only made that worse. Gunnhild's place was aboard that ship, for certain, but with Halfdan, not with the golden-haired Harald Sigurdsson. And yet the anger was dulled just a little by relief at seeing the two of them alive. He'd felt sure they would survive, yet seeing them was still a balm to the soul.

'We need to catch them,' he said. 'Get our ship back, and our crew. We need to use Harðráði's ship, the *Golden Eagle*, to get there.' He looked at Ulfr. 'Whoever currently guides this ship, you take his place. Get us in the water and after the commander.'

Ulfr nodded, though the look on his face as they approached the big ship was not encouraging. Even Halfdan could see why. The *Golden Eagle* was a great and heavy warship with a big crew. It was powerful, but they had learned many things in their journey with Jarl Yngvar. The *Sea Wolf* might be small, but it was a dart of a vessel, moving through the water with more speed and manoeuvrability than any great dragon boat.

As they ran across the stone and leapt over the top strake into the great ship, already its crew were working on the ropes, untying her from the shore, ready to sail off after Harðráði and Gunnhild. There were maybe a dozen empty places at the oars. Halfdan gestured to Ulfr and then pointed at the tiller. The burly shipwright nodded and ran aft already bellowing commands at the surprised skipper gripping the steering oar. Bjorn and Ketil, both big and powerful men, dropped their axes, sank to oar chests and spat on their hands. Halfdan stood on the wallowing deck. He could lend a hand to the oars, but he was more intent on the shape disappearing across the water and, had this been his ship, his place would be near Ulfr, throwing out commands. His gaze played across the crew as they readied themselves to row, the last of the lines being cast off, wishing they were his men, who he could only presume were out there aboard the *Sea Wolf* with Harðráði.

A big, heavy man of advancing years, crossed to Halfdan. 'Take an oar.'

'No. Harðráði has my ship and until I get it back, this one is now mine.'

'I take orders from Sigurdsson,' the man said.

'Now you take orders from me. Get out after him as fast as we can. The tower artillery will be winding up to start taking shots at us the moment the emperor's men realise we made it to the ships.'

He became aware of an argument nearby even as the ship began to move out away from the shore, and he turned to see Bjorn and Ketil slinging words at another Varangian, who was proffering two ropes.

'What's this?' Halfdan said, brow creasing.

'Commander's orders,' the big Varangian replied. 'Every man gets tied to a sack.'

Baffled, Halfdan looked at the nearest rower. Crouching, he followed the rope that had been tied fast around the oarsman's waist down to a heavy-looking canvas bag. Ignoring the protests of the rower, he fiddled with the rope at the bag's mouth and pulled it open a little.

Halfdan stared.

Between the folds of canvas, myriad faces of various Byzantine emperors stared back at him from a small fortune in gold coins. He reeled. There must be nearly sixty oarsmen in the *Golden Eagle*, and each of them was tied to one of these bags. Sixty bags of gold coins. And without doubt, since Valgarðr had been prepping both ships, every oarsman on the *Sea Wolf* would be similarly burdened.

'Gold,' he whispered.

The man standing beside him nodded. 'Harðráði's orders. Every man carries a bag, and it includes a share for him. Incentive to row hard.'

'So much gold,' Halfdan said, ignoring the man. His subconscious attempted a calculation, but failed with the sheer sums involved. He stared down at the bag of coins.

'What is it?' Leif called from where he stood, unable to row with his damaged ribs.

Halfdan looked up at the little Rus, his eyes wide. 'I'd say it's around five thousand pounds of gold.'

Bjorn and Ketil, still fighting off having the bags tied to them, stopped suddenly and turned. 'What did you say?'

'Every bag with every man on both ships is full of coins,' Halfdan said, still reeling with sudden understanding. 'The gold from Constantine's cistern. While the Guard was digging for it, it was Harðráði who was stealing it through the water access. The devious bastard had it all the time.'

Bjorn looked at the man with whom he'd been struggling as a grin spread across his face. He gestured at the man holding the rope. 'What are you waiting for? Tie it on, man, tie it on!'

Halfdan continued to stare as the big, heavy vessel slipped out into the water, each of them, even Leif, now allowing the gold-ropes to be looped around them and knotted tight. His calculations worked this time. Sixty oarsmen in this ship and, if Harðráði had it fully crewed, which surely he did, forty aboard the *Sea Wolf*. That was around a hundred men. Five thousand

330

pounds of gold split between a hundred men meant around fifty pounds of gold in each bag, easy enough for a man to carry, though not for long.

All right, the coins were theoretically Harðráði's, but once a Northman got his hands on a bag of gold it would take a lot to make him let go. And even if he only took maybe a quarter share, and gave the rest to the commander, that would still be twelve pounds of gold.

He tried to imagine what fifty pounds of gold could buy a man. He couldn't wrap his mind around it, but he'd be willing to bet that any one bag from this ship could have bought the *Sea Wolf*. His heart pounding, he realised how close, after all the disasters, they were coming to success. They were almost free. Just the sea chain remained to stop them. They had two ships, Gunnhild had been rescued, and each man here could be wealthy. Certainly, Halfdan and his friends would take everything they could get and offer no tithe to the commander. After everything, they had finally managed to leave the city with the riches they had sought from the beginning.

As the *Golden Eagle* crashed through the waters, picking up speed slowly due to its great weight, Halfdan found himself laughing into the spray. He let a man tie one of the bags of gold to him as he gripped the mast and peered off ahead. The *Sea Wolf* was approaching the chain, and had slowed, changing direction, lining up with the central section.

His heart in his mouth, tantalisingly close to freedom and wealth, ploughing the whale road in the wake of Gunnhild, Halfdan turned and gave the order for Ulfr to follow suit and line up as Harðráði had done. The man had a plan, and Halfdan would follow him to freedom.

The gods were watching, breath held.

Chapter 25

'Ready?' Harðráði bellowed across the ship.

He was answered by a roar from the crew of the *Sea Wolf*, Halfdan's men by and large, and an affirmative shout from his steersman.

'Will this work?' Anna asked nervously, gripping the rail.

'I hope so. I've been watching ships foundering on the chain for years, and I've always had this theory. We'll know any moment.'

'It will work,' Gunnhild said. She knew Harðráði would survive, since all her visions into the future had shown her his golden thread alone with hers. Indeed, she had looked at the two ships as they'd raced into the harbour and her instinct had told her that the *Sea Wolf* was the ship with the best chance of success. Harðráði had argued, tried to drag her aboard his great warship, but she'd been insistent. Harðráði went on from here, and her alongside him, and her wit told her that Halfdan's ship was here for a reason.

'I hope you're right,' Harðráði said quietly, and then to the crew: 'Ship oars and run!'

Gunnhild, despite being sure of their success, found herself gripping the rail near the steering oar and gritting her teeth as the manoeuvre took place. The *Sea Wolf* had been pushed to the greatest possible speed, making directly for the central length of chain, the most exposed part. At the last moment Harðráði had given the call, and now every rower hauled his oar up and in, lifted the heavy bag attached to his waist and leapt from his chest-seat, making for the rear of the ship, staggering with his heavy weight but moving as fast as he could.

It was a spectacular sight, worthy of the deeds of the Allfather himself, for as forty-four bodies leaned as far back as they dared at the stern of the *Sea Wolf*, its prow rose from the water as though with a life of its own, shedding spray to either side, lunging up into the air. Harðráði waited, counting, watching the chain like a hawk as the prow teetered, their momentum still carrying them forward like some waterborne horse, rearing.

The moment the chain was beneath the hull, he gave the second command.

'Forward!'

In an instant every oarsman, still hugging his bag of gold, ran to the prow, leaving only Harðráði and his steersman with Gunnhild and Anna at the stern. The see-saw effect happened instantly, and the prow plunged back down like an axe blow falling. The *Sea Wolf* hit the water on the far side of the chain so hard Gunnhild felt a moment of panic that they might sink. Water came up in a massive wall around the ship and sloshed down into the rows of oar chests.

But it stayed afloat.

The ship rocked back and forth for a time, momentum still carrying it forward, away from the chain over which it had see-sawed, achieving what a thousand years of shipping had failed to do, breaching the defences of Constantinople, albeit from within.

With a cheer and a thanks given to the nailed god for some sort of perceived aid, the crew staggered back to their seats with their gold and retrieved their oars. A few oars had been lost in the manoeuvre, bobbing around on the surface behind them, but most had been saved, and Harðráði had brought a dozen spares aboard against this very possibility. The *Sea Wolf* sailed further out into the Bosphorus, free of the city at last, and laden with gold. They continued to move until they were safely out of artillery reach, for torches were now flaring on the tower tops as word of the commander's escape spread.

Gunnhild ignored the jubilation across the vessel, for she and Anna gripped the rail and watched astern, intent on the sight unfolding there.

The *Golden Eagle* was out in the middle of the channel now and picking up speed. She'd had no vision of what would happen here, for she'd simply had no time for the song and the Seiðr since the moment Harðráði had visited the empress, but she had a sinking feeling regardless. Logic told her that Halfdan faced a much more difficult manoeuvre, for his ship was considerably larger, slower, and weighed twice as much as the *Sea Wolf*. Common sense alone suggested Halfdan stood little chance of success, but Gunnhild was facing more than common sense.

Time and again she had seen it over the past few weeks, every time she dared to look. Her thread and Harðráði's marching away into a bright tapestry of their own making, and Halfdan's veering off alone. More than any logic, what she had seen told her Halfdan would fail, for his fate was not to follow Harðráði.

She watched, trying not to wince, as the *Golden Eagle* bore down on the chain, a massive, seemingly unstoppable behemoth of a vessel. Ulfr, she knew, would be at the helm, and there was no better man for the job, but even he would not be able to do this. She watched the ship close on the chain and at the very last moment Halfdan and Ulfr tried to repeat the audacious escape.

The great warship rose from the surface like the kraken, rearing up and shedding water, the keel coming into sight, rising so high that Gunnhild thought it must turn over altogether.

Beside her Anna watched, eyes wide, for Leif too was aboard that vessel, and Gunnhild knew how the girl felt for the little Rus. They had been inseparable now for months and, unlike Gunnhild and Harðráði, there was no reason to keep them apart.

'They're going to do it,' Anna breathed.

Gunnhild didn't have the nerve to tell her otherwise. She just watched, her heart tearing open, as the *Golden Eagle* crossed the chain, but it was just too big, too heavy to manage what they'd done with the *Sea Wolf*. The great ship smashed down on top of the chain, but instead of managing to tip forward over it, the weight pulled the chain inwards, the wooden booms that held it on the surface at even intervals across the water dragged closer, the chain pulling taut towards the far ends. The *Golden Eagle* foundered then, entangled with the chain, and there came a series of ominous creaking sounds.

'Sweet Lord, no,' Anna breathed next to her.

'Halfdan will survive,' Gunnhild said with confidence, though what she was seeing made that seem increasingly unlikely with every passing moment.

'What about Leif? What has your wyrd vision seen for my Leif?'

Gunnhild said nothing. She would not lie, and had no truth to tell. She had only seen Halfdan.

'Gunnhild!'

She turned to the white-faced, panicked girl. 'Halfdan will survive, and Halfdan will never let his men down.'

It was small consolation, and no promise, but it was the best she could do. She was at the mercy of the Norns, as were all men and women, and even gods. She had felt as though she were betraying Halfdan the moment she directed Harðráði to the *Sea Wolf*, but she was following her path, her destiny. No one could fight the weaving of the Norns, and those völvur who had done so in the past were spoken of in frightened whispers, for to defy fate was to draw disaster upon oneself. It was not something a sane woman would ever consider.

'They're done for,' Harðráði said, his face grave as he walked back over to them.

'There will be survivors,' Gunnhild replied.

'Not for long.'

Her gaze followed the commander's pointing finger in time to see by torchlight the great war machines on the towers of the sea walls turning, ponderously, training their shots on the tangled ship.

'Dear God,' Anna breathed again.

'Halfdan lives,' was all Gunnhild could say.

The *Golden Eagle* was doomed now, though. There would be no chance of untangling her and somehow getting her across the chain entire. They could hear the distant clacking of artillery ratchets pulling back, tightening the torsion. She focused on the ship, squinting. Lanterns on the walls had been lit and, backed with silvered mirror surfaces, their light was directed onto the tangled vessel, illuminating the target to aid the marksmen.

The disaster was lit with an eerie glow, but the light that aided the artillery also made it possible for Gunnhild to pick out figures. Her heart began to pound as she saw Halfdan among the crew. He was arguing with someone, the two of them waving their arms. The other man kept pointing at the *Sea Wolf*, while Halfdan repeatedly gestured to the sea walls and the readying weapons atop them.

'Swim,' was all she said, quietly, to herself, under her breath. 'Swim.'

She blinked in surprise as the distant figure of the young jarl suddenly stopped arguing and turned, looking their way. Across the vast gulf of black water, his eyes met hers.

No one defies the Norns...

'We have to go,' Harðráði said. 'As soon as they sink the *Golden Eagle*, their dromons will come hunting us. We need to gain some distance before they clear the wreck and get their ships out past the chain.'

'Wait.'

'Gunnhild, we *cannot* wait.'

She turned to him and the look in her eyes made him flinch. 'Wait.'

Her gaze turned back to Halfdan. The man had a bundle in his arms now. She stared, then glanced at the crewmen near her, their midriffs roped to bags of gold the weight of a sack of grain. *It's only gold*, she told him in the silence of her own head. *Leave it.*

But as she watched, the young jarl stepped up to the rail of the ship, that other Varangian still yelling at him and waving.

Halfdan jumped.

He missed the chain by several feet, and for a moment Gunnhild wondered how she had missed something as clear as his demise in her castings. Then, against all probability, an arm shot from the water and wrapped itself around the chain, and in a moment that made her heart soar, Halfdan rose from the surface, dragging his bag of gold in the water, holding himself above the rippling black with the chain. Slowly, painstakingly, he began to shuffle along the defence towards the first of the wooden booms.

'He is insane,' Harðráði hissed.

'He is a jarl, a hero.'

'Look,' Anna said in a strangely excited voice, 'it's Leif!'

And it was. The small Rus had plunged from the side of the ship and managed to hit the chain. He grappled with it for a while, occasionally dipping beneath the water, not moving away. 'His ribs. He's in too much pain to do it,' Anna said, her voice laden with panic. 'Why doesn't he throw the gold away?'

'Because he's a Northman,' Gunnhild said with a proud smile, 'a Viking.'

Bjorn was there a moment later, hitting the water like a giant rock and sending spray up everywhere, and then Ketil behind him, the two managing to grasp the chain to either side of the small Rus. With difficulty the two big, powerful men began to help their smaller friend along the chain towards the first wooden boom, where Halfdan had pulled himself from the water, outside the glow of the lanterns now, resting and breathing while he waited for his men.

Gunnhild hadn't realised she was holding her breath until she saw Ulfr take the plunge and swim with surprising skill and ease, given the weight dragging him down. He grasped the chain and Gunnhild let out an explosive breath. All five had left the ship.

A heartbeat later the first shot struck – a massive stone lobbed from the nearest tower, angled expertly by men who had spent

337

their entire career practising for this very moment. They needed no ranging shot, for they knew every inch of this channel and every nail, cord and strut in their weapon. The massive stone struck the *Golden Eagle* amidships with a huge wooden crack that echoed across the straits. The damage was both catastrophic and instant. Two men died, crushed by the falling rock, which continued on through the hull and into the water beneath, dragging their remains with it. Some important rib of the ship had succumbed to the blow, for the entire vessel began to crack and fold, both stern and prow rising.

Death then came in a hail, boulder after boulder from eight towers within reach. A few missed, plunging into deep water, their range at maximum, but the nearer weapons were unerringly accurate, and the ship was pounded again and again by great stones as it folded, splintered, shredded and flew apart, splinters a foot long whispering out into the darkness, deadly missiles themselves. The mast succumbed swiftly, and as it fell it crushed a man against what was left of the deck. Men were ploughing into the water now, knowing their ship doomed, but most were heavily armoured and apparently lacked the foresight to throw themselves at the chain.

Gunnhild squinted, for the five men were outside the glow of the targeting lamps. She couldn't see anything for a while, and nothing could be heard over the din of the broken, sinking ship and its drowning crew. She was holding her breath again.

'There,' Anna said suddenly, a finger thrusting out into the darkness.

Gunnhild followed the gesture and her heart began to pound again. She'd not been able to see them because while she, like everyone else, had been distracted with the sinking of the *Golden Eagle*, the five Wolves had made use of their sudden invisibility and had hauled themselves across the next stretch of chain to a wooden boom closer to the city shoreline.

Gunnhild smiled. They would make it to the shore. What happened then was anyone's guess. They would be back in the city that hunted them. But it was not her concern. She was done with the Wolves of Odin. The Norns had woven her a future with Harðráði in the North, and she had seen it clear.

No one defies the Norns...

Gunnhild only realised how hard she had been biting her lip when she tasted the rich, red blood.

No one...

'Take me ashore, Harald Sigurdsson.'

Harðráði frowned. 'No.'

'I am not asking you, Prince of Norway, I am ordering you. Put me ashore.'

'Your destiny is with me, Gunnhild. You know it as much as I do. I feel it in my bones. It is the will of God, and I think it is the will of your goddess too. We sail north. We are free.'

No one defies the Norns...

She turned, and the boar-head knife was in her hand. He stared in shock as she lifted it, waving the tip at the former Varangian commander. 'Harald Sigurdsson, you will die, for all men die. It is a rule of life. But how that comes about is in your hands right now. Put me ashore and you will die many years from now a powerful and famous man. Deny me, and it will happen less than half a mile upriver, and no one will remember you.'

Harðráði recoiled in surprise. 'You *know* you need to come with me, Gunnhild.'

'Immaterial.'

'Gunnhild, I *cannot* take you ashore, even if I wanted to.'

'Why?'

His finger stabbed through the night at the city walls. 'We'll be sunk long before I reach land. The artillery are watching us. We have to go.'

Her eyes found the five figures on the chain once more, closing on the shoreline below the walls. Only disaster awaited anyone who defied the Norns. And yet Halfdan was there with the others, struggling to make it to the shore of a city that held only death.

'Good luck,' she said to Harðráði.

He blinked.

Taking a deep breath, and with a heartfelt apology to Freyja, Gunnhild threw herself from the rail of the ship. She hit the cold water of the Bosphorus like a knife, plunging into dark depths, the blade still in her hand. She felt the icy pressure of the flow grasping at her, pulling her down, and wondered if this was to be her new fate for discarding the one she'd been given. She pushed and struggled and swam until her muscles burned, for the currents in this water were stronger than she could ever have imagined. Finally, when she thought her lungs would burst and her entire body was afire with the strain, she burst from the surface and heaved in a breath.

'Gunnhild!'

It was Harðráði's voice, and she blinked away water until finally she saw him, leaning over the rail of the *Sea Wolf* and calling to her, arm outstretched.

Two threads, stretching off into a brilliant tapestry...

With a single shake of her head, she turned and swam away.

She never looked back when she heard the second splash, for she knew it was not him. Harðráði remained on the ship, calling, reaching for her. The second splash had been another woman who had tied herself to the crew of the young jarl. Anna swam ashore for Leif.

Gunnhild was ploughing through the water now, moving sleek and fast like their ship, making for the shore. She was more than a little surprised when Anna began to overtake her, but the girl slowed then, keeping pace with Gunnhild as the two women angled for the point where the great chain reached the city. Where the shore rose from the water, silty and empty and just ten feet wide beneath the walls, the chain stretched overhead, disappearing through a wide hole in the tower into the room where the giant capstan which could wind it in sat.

Gunnhild had rarely felt such a tumult of emotion as her feet touched the riverbed and she finally stood, slogging her tired way through the last of the water and up onto land. She was filled with euphoria, for she was moments away from her friends and had managed to survive the cold, fast open water, but she was also filled with a deep existential dread at having turned her back on her defined destiny and challenged the Norns themselves.

Anna's hand found hers, and together the two women pressed themselves against the city wall, keeping as close as possible to the cold stone to stay out of sight of both the parapet and the chain window.

'Gunnhild?'

She turned and her heart soared once more at the sight of Halfdan, bedraggled and shaking, as the young jarl ducked under the chain and closed on her. The huge looming shapes of Bjorn and Ketil loitered, grinning, behind him, clutching bags of gold coins, but Leif had untied his and ran past his friends to gather Anna up in his arms with a squawk of discomfort.

'I thought you'd go with him,' Halfdan said quietly.

'My destiny is elsewhere,' she lied easily with a smile covering her near panic.

She turned, then, to see the *Sea Wolf* was now little more than a distant dot, sailing away up the Bosphorus towards the great Svartahaf and the Dnieper beyond, which would carry Harðráði home to the North.

'Our ship,' the young jarl said with a frustrated sigh.

'What is lost can always be found,' Gunnhild said quietly. 'The *Sea Wolf* is not sunk, she is simply elsewhere for now.'

'You think we'll get her back?'

'I think you will never stop trying.'

Halfdan gave a small laugh. 'It feels like an odd victory, for we've lost our ship and we're still in the city. I can't see how we will leave.'

'Can't you?' she answered. 'Then come with me.'

Head high, she strode past them, and she heard them turn and pad along, squelching and cursing in her wake. Still keeping close to the walls to prevent being spotted from above, hard to see anyway now that night had truly fallen, Gunnhild led them back beneath the chain and along the shore of the Horn Bay. Small Byzantine ships were now converging on what was left of the *Golden Eagle*, preparing to untangle the floating wreckage and to fish out any corpses or survivors, the former for cheap mass burial, the latter undoubtedly for painful interrogation.

The harbour was in chaos. Soldiers hurried this way and that, officers barking orders all over the place. Small ships ploughed out into the waters, searching for survivors and patrolling, while others prepared on the dockside. Lights flared and bells rang. Halfdan caught up with Gunnhild as they moved into the busy port.

'What are we *doing*? The city garrison is looking for us.'

Gunnhild shook her head. 'The garrison is looking out there,' she said, pointing across the water towards the Bosphorus and the chain and wreckage that lay before it. 'They must know by now that *Sea Wolf* made it out into open water, and they know that Harðráði's other ship foundered and broke. They will never know who was on what ship, though perhaps they are still hoping to fish your bloated bodies out of the water. But right now, here in the harbour is the very last place they will look for you.'

Halfdan nodded. 'But we cannot hide forever in Constantinople. Ari tried, and still we found him.'

'We're not going to hide in Constantinople,' Gunnhild said without looking around.

'What?'

She pulled a little ahead once more as they approached a large dromon that wallowed heavy in the water by the dockside. A Varangian leaned against a stack of barrels close by, wiping the sweat from his face.

'What ship is this?' she asked.

The man looked up, brow furrowing. '*Tyche's Arrow*,' he replied.

Something fell into place. That name… the statue and the temple that became her house when she first set foot in the city. The goddess of fortune, patron of the city, an ancient power, fallen but not entirely gone. She had turned her back on the Norns but was Freyja yet watching over her? Surely this could not be coincidence?

'You're missing some crew,' she said.

'Not as far as I know, but we won't be sure until muster at dawn, when we leave.'

'You are missing crew,' she said, this time rather more forcefully. 'We are the replacements.'

The man straightened and his frown deepened, a furrow creasing his brow. 'Wait a minute. You're the witch. The völva from the palace.' His hand went to his belt, fingers dancing on the axe there.

'I am. And this is the ship that will carry the seven of us west.'

'Now wait. The palace guards are searching for you.'

Gunnhild gave him a very unnerving smile. 'What's your name?'

'Sten Arnesson.'

'You're a Svear.'

He nodded, that frown still evident.

'For a thousand generations, your people have owed the völvur and respected us, Sten Arnesson. Are you going to be the man to break a pact of a thousand generations? The man to defy your ancestors in their graves?'

She saw him shiver. His hand went to the cross hanging around his neck and yet, when he looked her in the eye, she knew she had him. He bowed his head. 'I am certain there will be seven seats free,' he said finally.

'Six. Anna will not row.'

The man looked past her at the girl in the arms of the small Rus.

'No, of course not,' he said with a hint of embarrassment.

'See us aboard. We will spend the night here, ready for the morning and departure.'

As the man did so and then hurried off to be anywhere where he wasn't being talked to by Gunnhild, Halfdan gave a light laugh. 'I swear you could do anything you wished if you set your mind to it. You are a dangerous woman, Gunnhild.'

'I am a fool,' was her only reply as she followed him aboard.

Perhaps, though, *just perhaps*, she had not called disaster upon them. *Tyche's Arrow* seemed ready to take them away in the morning. For the first time in weeks, she relaxed a little.

Epilogue

'Will the empress survive?'

Halfdan watched the copper roofs and white and red walls of Constantinople becoming little more than a blur on the horizon as the ship cut west through choppy waters. The sun had risen far enough to illuminate the world, and once the great dromon had managed to manoeuvre out of the city, the oars had been shipped as the vessel made the most of a strong easterly, filling the sails. Saved the effort of rowing for a while, the friends had gathered at Gunnhild's place near the rear of the ship and stood around the rail.

'Her days are short now,' Gunnhild replied. 'Zoe Porphyrogenita's thread grows frayed. I believe she will die peacefully, but I suspect we have seen Byzantium's apex in our time, and a fall begins. This is a good time to be leaving.'

'I imagine Harðráði will be a little irked that he has lost half his gold.'

Bjorn chuckled. 'Not as irked as the pretty little emperor will be that he lost *all* of it, especially since half of it lies at the bottom of the sea so close to his walls.'

Ketil snorted. 'Harðráði escaped with his life. He'll be grateful for that. And even *half* that gold is over two thousand pounds. That's enough to buy and equip an army. Add that to what he's been shipping north for years and I'd say he's got a good shot at taking his throne back.'

'The smarmy bastard will be taking his shot from the *Sea Wolf*,' Ulfr reminded them in an irritated voice, 'while we're stuck lumbering west in a big fat imperial dromon that belongs to someone else.'

'We could buy another ship with all the gold we carry,' Leif smiled, 'and still have plenty spare.'

'Not like the *Sea Wolf*. Months of my best work there.'

'When we get to Italy, I'll buy you the timber to build another,' Bjorn laughed.

'The shit timber down here? And who'll work for me? Your mouth is plugged straight into your arse, Bjorn Bear-torn.'

'And I suspect we might be expected to do a job or two for Maniakes when we get there anyway,' Halfdan murmured. 'There will be a price for this free journey.'

'As the world serpent eats its own tail,' Gunnhild said quietly, silencing them, 'so does the world often move in circles. We have not seen the last of Harald Sigurdsson, and I think we will have our chance to take the ship back before the end.'

'We're building a list of debts to collect,' Bjorn grunted. 'First a blood debt from Hjalmvigi, and now a ship from Harðráði.'

'Heed Gunnhild's words, though,' Halfdan said with a smile. 'I spoke to some of the crew this morning as we prepared, and learned a little of where we're bound. It seems that Maniakes fights to take Italy for his empire, but the men they face there are our brothers from the North. *Normans*, they call them. Our path carries us slowly, but it does seem to take us home. These Normans may hold the key to our return.'

'Do they speak a proper language, then, these Northmen?' Bjorn asked, brightening.

'Torsten over by the tiller says not. He'd only just come back from fighting in Sicily before he was turned around and sent back with us. He says they have their own language, but with some of our words. A weird mix. He can get by in it, though.'

Leif smiled. 'Then I think we need to speak to this Torsten and find out what he knows. I'm sure you all agree that learning Greek has served you well over the last year. Perhaps Torsten can teach us this Norman tongue, since we'll have a month of sailing to get there.'

Halfdan nodded, and leaned on the rail once more. As the others drifted off into conversation, Gunnhild dropped into place next to him.

'Are you regretting your swim?' he asked. His manner was easy, but the question was deep.

Gunnhild took a couple of long breaths. 'I fear the time will come when I do. For now, no. My place is with you and the others.'

There was a long pause.

'You made Harðráði take the *Sea Wolf*, didn't you?'

Gunnhild's eyebrow shot up. 'Oh?'

'Harðráði is a scoundrel and a thief among other things, but he is loyal to his friends. He would never have taken our ship without good reason. You directed him to it. Why?'

She shrugged. 'Sigurdsson has a destiny. I may have messed around with it already, but I couldn't let him fail now. I did what I had to. We will see the ship again.'

Halfdan nodded and turned to look at the waves once more. Above them, two black shapes, high in the air, swooping among the wisps of grey, wheeled and made north. Odin's ravens returned to their master with new tidings, while storm clouds gathered in the west.

Historical Note

In the previous volume of this saga, *Blood Feud*, I combined two sources to create the plot: one a Viking saga, the other a historical timeline. The *Saga of Yngvar the Far-Traveller* was the source of my story, but it had to be tempered using the historical references of contemporary accounts, such as the *Georgian Chronicles*. The character of Halfdan was drawn from a single carving in the Hagia Sophia that says 'Halfdan was here', and was inserted into that story simply because I had stood at the balcony and looked down upon those thousand-year-old runes. Halfdan was here, and so was Simon Turney. And since Halfdan was clearly a Viking from around my era who had been at large in the south-east of Europe, he was a perfect choice for my lead. The moment I started this series, I always knew where I wanted to take it, all the way through a potential six-book cycle, and Book 2 I always wanted to set in Constantinople. As such, I set up the lead-in to this book at the end of the last. The greatest city in the world was always going to be Halfdan's second destination even before I'd started writing *Blood Feud*.

The simple fact is that too much is happening in Constantinople at this time to possibly not explore. Firstly, we know that Halfdan was in the city, as his name remains carved in the balcony of the Hagia Sophia, as well as the name of one 'Ari' nearby. The Varangians are a fascinating unit, the heir in many ways of both the Praetorian Guard and the German Guard of the Roman emperors, and yet manned with Vikings from Russia and Scandinavia. I had already seen vague links between Harald Hardrada and the presumed Viking/Varangian involvement in the Georgian Civil War of Bagrat IV. Moreover, Harald was quite definitely the commander of the Varangians at this time. Everything was falling into place for a plot, and so I threw tantalising hints about Byzantium and Hardrada into the latter stages of the first book. You may have noticed a similar approach towards the end of this volume, which might give you clues as to where Book 3 is bound…

I took the same approach with Book 2 as with Book 1. Once again, I could draw on the glorious Viking past by using Snorri Sturluson's *Saga of Harald*, which was much easier than Book 1, for it was exciting and epic, but was also considerably more believable than that of Yngvar, without monsters and magic, and I only needed a short part of it anyway. I knew what Harald was doing over this year, thanks to Snorri. On the flipside, Byzantium was one of the greatest keepers of records in history, and the period (1041–1042) is well covered by the writers Michael Psellus and John Skylitzes, and to a lesser extent by even more contemporary historians. Byzantium has a rich history, but this particular year happens to be one of the juiciest, with emperors coming and going and that most rare thing – a powerful empress – controlling the city. We had riots and blindings and usurpations. The perfect milieu into which to throw my heroes.

When I first started putting the plot together, I was initially stumped with Gunnhild. There are six heroes in my little band, but one of them was never going to join the Varangian Guard. This was not a world where a woman was going to exist comfortably. I had to have Gunnhild separated from the crew, and so from the very beginning, I planned for this tale to be told from both points of view. Byzantium, like other medieval worlds, is a place where, while Christianity controls men's hearts, there is still always a strange fascination with wyrd, with magic, with astrology, with the unexplained. The scene where the emperor Michael has consulted all his astrologers as to his course of action is true, according to Byzantine sources.

Moreover, Zoe Porphyrogenita is the very epitome of that sort of character. She is said to have been a poisoner, to have been fascinated with perfumes and potions. She pushed society's boundaries with a third marriage, which was so frowned upon that the Patriarch of the Church refused to officiate. It seemed entirely plausible that a woman of Gunnhild's skills would come to the attention of a woman of Zoe's interests. Between her and Halfdan, then, we were going to see the whole of Byzantium during this dangerous year, in the court through Gunnhild's eyes and in the wider city through those of Halfdan.

Harald Hardrada had been in the city some time. We are told that he acquired the nickname Harald the Bulgar Burner in the recent war, and we know he was in the city at the time this story is set, and so his being essentially exiled, shoved out of the way to a foreign war, where he went to Georgia and met Halfdan, seems quite feasible, even though it is not mentioned in our sources.

Hardrada is said to have bowed to the empress when he took his position, and not to the emperor, and the sources do suggest that he cleaved to her side rather than to her string of disastrous husbands and co-rulers during his time. He was unpopular much of the time, that much is clear. We are told of accusations levelled against him, he was jailed, he is said to have amassed an enormous personal fortune during his time there, and the saga tells that rather than simply resign his commission and leave, Hardrada is forced to flee, the emperor and empress refusing to let him go. What, then, was at the root of this trouble? Well, the saga tells us that Harald became enamoured with a woman called Maria, who is said to have been a niece of the empress. This was a rather interesting angle that fitted somewhat neatly into my role for Gunnhild, but it also seemed too paltry to drive such a wedge between the emperor and the commander of his guard.

The answer comes in only one brief mention in one brief source. Skylitzes is our man. He tells us that after Michael and Constantine were blinded, the uncle revealed under torture the location of five thousand pounds of gold he'd purloined from the treasury and buried in the cistern below his house. This gold was recovered by the empress. That is the entire recorded story. It struck me that five thousand pounds of gold was a rather vast amount, and certainly worthy of mention by all sources. I mused on this for some time, and the connection between that gold and the fabulous riches amassed by Hardrada came closer and closer the more I pondered. The plot was born. Like all things Byzantine, this plot is multifaceted and layered, and the gold is only part of it, but it is a large part of it for such a small reference.

I don't want to ruin Hardrada for you. If you've not come across him before, he is most definitely one of the most fabulous characters ever to rise from Viking history. His biography is extraordinary. That his fate might have been different had Gunnhild been by his side is a wonderful question to think upon. Hardrada is known as the last great Viking. And, be assured, you have not seen the last of him. After all... he has Halfdan's ship now!

Valgardr is an attested historical person, though I have given a simple footnote in history considerable flesh and character. Ari is my creation entirely. I knew there was an Ari in the city, in the Varangian Guard, for his name appears close to that of Halfdan, carved in the Hagia Sophia. But I found myself wondering about the Guard. Hardrada is fighting abroad at times, and in jail too. He is the Akolouthos of the Guard, but who commands when he is not around? A jealous underling was born to be one of my little cadre of bad guys.

Michael Kalaphates was an atrocious emperor and, it seems, a despicable human being. In truth, his entire family did little to recommend them to history – more of that towards the end of this note. His uncle may have been proud and heroic as he was blinded, but we shouldn't let ourselves forget that a noble end does not excuse an appalling criminal life. The saga tells us that it was Harald himself who blinded the emperor, while Byzantine sources only tell us that the two men were blinded. No one in the sources seems to be able to explain how the retrieval of the two fugitives from the Studion came about. Psellus tells us flatly that they were dragged out of the church, but the simple fact is that sanctuary is an inviolable thing, and no one, if they were good, God-fearing Byzantines, would have defied the Church so blatantly. That there might be pagans around who didn't care was a possibility that made me smile from ear to ear.

The rescue of Hardrada is taken straight from the saga. I have made it the work of Gunnhild, but without much tweaking of the sources. The saga tells us it was a woman with two servants who lowered a rope to rescue him. The location of this prison is not given, and so I chose to make it the one that had been formed out of the ruins of the baths of Zeuxippus and not, for instance, the dungeon of Anemas, which is on the very edge of the city. The riot I have tried to stay faithful to. There were three pushes against the palace from the gate, the hippodrome and the polo field, there was missile fire from the defenders, and the empress was hurriedly brought back and displayed in an attempt to halt the growing revolution. What I have done (and *mea culpa* for this) is to conflate events that actually took place over two days into a shorter space of time. This is historical fiction, and sometimes it is necessary to tweak non-essential timings to maintain the story's pace.

My reconstruction of eleventh-century Constantinople is taken from a number of sources, including the wonderful Byzantium 1200 project, as well as personal experience of wandering among the ruins. It is very difficult to mentally reconstruct the buildings and their geographical relationship, but I have tried to stay true to the archaeology and sources wherever I can. The subterranean tunnels, the gates, the kathisma, all these things are kept as close to source as possible. As for the culture and the people, I will apologise now to the magnificent Eileen Stephenson whose work on this particular era of Byzantium I read, absorbed, thoroughly enjoyed, and then nicked and fictionalised (!) I'm sorry to have taken your beloved Byzantines, Eileen, and made them convoluted, Machiavellian, often wicked, criminals. The more I read the sources, the more that is how they come off. Also of note in my research is my good friend Kerim Altug in Istanbul, a very knowledgeable historian and archaeologist who constantly puts me right when I make small errors.

And so I come to the end. The climax. The flight from Constantinople. The Icelandic saga tells us plain that two ships fled. One got over the chain the way I have described, while the other floundered and broke. What happened to the crew of the lost ship we are not told, and so I have moved our heroes on, while Hardrada is now on the Dnieper and making for Russia. Parts of the Golden Horn chain remain in museums in Istanbul, and while there is no doubt about its existence and its effectiveness, the details remain hazy. I have dealt with the chain before, over a century later, in my Templar series, set in 1204. Some scholars deny that what is described in the saga could happen, and yet since we don't know the precise nature of the chain, how can that be confirmed? Was the chain in large sections between wooden booms? Was it meant to entangle ships and therefore floating loose, rather than in a tight line? We cannot know. But having started with *Blood Feud*, the moment I knew that two ships were making for the chain and only one made it, it was clear that it was going to be the *Sea Wolf* that escaped, even if our heroes weren't on it. I went to some lengths in Book 1 describing the ship as small and sleek and fast, with a minimal crew. As such, if a ship could possibly tip over the chain, the *Sea Wolf* was clearly the ship to do it. No heavy and great dragon boat or imperial dromon was going to do so.

Before I finish, I would like to take a quick moment to dip into the world of Seiðr and the berserkers. We know so little of the Viking völvur. We have references to the song and we know that Freyja was their patron. There are fragments to be found. A staff in the British Museum purports to be that of a völva. But what they actually did, what they believed, and how they achieved it all still remains a mystery, much like the Celtic druids, no matter what a bunch of twenty-first-century hippies in white robes might tell you. But like many sages and wise folk and witch doctors across countless cultures in history, it seems highly likely that some sort of psychedelic trance was involved. Back when I first started the series, I toyed with making Bjorn one of the 'bear shirts' – the berserkers – but I decided against it, as they belong to a bygone era, when paganism was still the norm. However, it is suggested that somehow the berserkers, before a battle, would do something to get themselves so worked up, they would fight anything that got in their way, friend or foe, with little acknowledgement of pain. That they would bite the edge of their shield in a foaming fury. Some suggest that they drank copious amounts of alcohol, but to my mind this would hinder their physique too much, and so the use of psychedelic drugs seemed much more plausible. Since I was going to be exploring Gunnhild's use of them in this book, it seemed logical to make the two things the same compound, and so I have attempted to explain berserkers and völvur with the same source.

I have enjoyed bringing Gunnhild to the fore in this book, and the same might happen in due course for other characters, but this is still in essence Halfdan's story, and even Gunnhild knew that, defying fate and gods to stick by her jarl. But before I sign off and start planning Italy, I will say that, as we leave Byzantium, you have witnessed its lowest ebb in terms of power and leadership. It will fluctuate between now and 1453 when it falls to the Turks, but this dynasty, despite Zoe's impressive character, is the beginning of the end. In three decades' time, the Byzantines will meet the Turks at the Battle of Manzikert, and their power in Anatolia and the east will be broken forever. From this time on, the empire will only ever shrink.

How blind some emperors can be, eh?

Simon Turney
July 2021

Glossary

Aesir – one of the two groups of Viking gods, including Thor, Odin, Loki and Tyr

Akolouthos – a senior military rank in the Byzantine empire, corresponding to the title of commander of the Varangian Guard

Alfar – a supernatural creature thought by the Vikings to bring disease and misfortune, known later in English as 'elves'

Allagion – a unit in the Byzantine military consisting of perhaps one hundred men

Autokratōr – Greek term applied to the emperor, meaning simply 'sole ruler'

Berserkr (pl. berserkir) – lit. 'bear shirts'. The berserkers of Viking fame who were overtaken by battle madness in the name of Odin

Carceres – the starting gates in a circus or hippodrome

Draugr (pl. draugar) – the zombie-like restless dead, occupying graves and guarding their treasure jealously

Dromon – a Byzantine warship powered by sails or by banks of oars akin to the Roman trireme or Ottoman galley

Excubitores – an elite Byzantine regiment with an origin as imperial bodyguards, by this time part of the garrison of Constantinople

Fólkvangr – a great meadow that is the domain of the goddess Freyja

Freyja – the most powerful goddess of the *Vanir*, whose realm includes magic, fertility, war and the gathering of the slain to her land of Fólkvangr

Gotlander – one of the three peoples of modern Sweden, the Goths occupied the island of Gotland

Gynaikonitis – the women's palace within the Great Palace, the private domain of the Byzantine empress

Hamingja – a spirit of fortune in the Viking world, not dissimilar to a 'guardian angel' in concept

Holmgang – an official, ritual form of duel between two opponents

Jarl – a noble of power (the derivation of the English 'earl') who receives fealty from all free men of a region

Karl – a free man. Neither a noble, nor a slave

Loki – a trickster god, a shape-shifter, who is destined to fight alongside the giants against the other gods at the end of days

Miklagarðr – Viking name for Constantinople, the capital of the Byzantine Empire, now Istanbul

Mjǫllnir – Thor's hammer

Nobelissimus – a senior noble rank in the Byzantine empire, often held by members of the imperial family

Norns – the female entities who control the fates of both men and gods

Noumera – a prison in Constantinople formed from the ruins of the Baths of Zeuxippus and guarded by a specialist unit called the Noumeroi

Odin – most powerful of the Aesir, the chief god and father of Thor, who gave an eye in return for wisdom and who has twin ravens and twin wolves, and an eight-legged horse

Pecheneg – a nomadic Turkic people who occupied the land south of the Rus

Primikerios – a senior military rank in several Byzantine regiments

Ragnarok – the end of the universe, including a great battle between gods, giants, monsters and the slain who have been gathered by Odin and Freyja

Rus – the descendants of the Vikings who settled Kiev and Novgorod and areas of Belarus and Ukraine, from whom the name Russia derives (Rusland)

Sax – a short sword or long knife of Germanic origin, known to the Saxons as the seax

Scythian – a people of the Russian steppe since Roman times, riders akin to the Huns and Turks

Seiðr – a form of magic that flows around men and gods, which can be used and understood by few, the source of divination

Serk – a catch-all term, perhaps derived from the word silk, which is variously applied to all Islamic lands or to the exotic territories south of the Byzantine Empire

Skald – a poet or bard

Strategos – Byzantine military rank synonymous with 'general'

Svarthaf – Viking name for the Black Sea

Svear – one of the three peoples of modern Sweden, the Svears occupied the northern regions of Sweden, around Uppsala

'Tafl – a Viking board game akin to chess or go, where one player has to bring his jarl piece to the edge of the board

Teicheiotai – an archaic unit in the Palace guards of Constantinople

Theotokos – lit. 'Mother of God'. Greek term for Mary, mother of Jesus

Thor – son of Odin, the god of thunder, one of the most powerful of the Aesir

Thrall – a slave with no will beyond that of his master, often a captive of war

Tzykanisterion – sports field in the grounds of the imperial palace where a game akin to modern polo was played

Vanir – one of the two groups of Viking gods, including Freyja and Njord

Vápntreyja – an arming jacket worn beneath armour by Vikings

Varangian – the Byzantine imperial bodyguard, formed of Northmen

Varangoi – Greek term for the Varangian Guard

Völva (pl. völvur) – a wise woman, witch or seeress with the power of prophecy and the ability to understand and manipulate Seiðr